"*Truth B* ~~~~
uses all ~~~~
edgy, fu~~~~
outgues~~~~, and ~~~~
love Ry~~an's books like I do~~ ~~~~ ~~~~ ~~~~,
and if you're picking her up for the first time, you're
starting with a winner."　　　　　**—Linda Fairstein,**
New York Times bestselling author

"Hank Phillippi Ryan weaves a taut web of suspense in
Truth Be Told. Be prepared to lose sleep once you start
reading, because you won't want to stop. I couldn't turn
the pages fast enough."　　　　　　**—Meg Gardiner,**
New York Times bestselling author

"Hank Phillippi Ryan's latest showcases the author's ability to balance humor, gripping drama, romance, and
contemporary issues. Ryan nails them all in this high-
quality reading adventure."　　　　　**—Associated Press**

"Hank Phillippi Ryan proves herself one of the most ad-
ept masters of plot on the planet with her latest, *Truth
Be Told*. Surprises—major surprises—abound, characters live and breathe, and everything comes satisfyingly
together. . . . This one is a must read."

—John Lescroart,
New York Times bestselling author

"In Ryan's adroit hands, with her brisk prose, appealing
protagonists, and well-limned characters, even foreclosures can be sexy."　　　**—*Booklist* (starred review)**

"Ryan's latest in her Jane Ryland series is a gem. Deception and greed lead to murder in this excellent novel that
is enhanced by Ryan's background as an investigative
reporter."　　　　　**—*RT Book Reviews* (Top Pick!)**

"Smart, well-paced . . . Ryan, a Mary Higgins Clark Award
winner, cleverly ties the plot together, offers surprising
but believable plot twists, and skillfully characterizes the
supporting cast."　　　　　　　**—*Publishers Weekly***

FORGE BOOKS BY
HANK PHILLIPPI RYAN

The Other Woman
The Wrong Girl
Truth Be Told

TRUTH
BE TOLD

HANK PHILLIPPI RYAN

A TOM DOHERTY ASSOCIATES BOOK • NEW YORK

This is a work of fiction. All of the characters, organizations, and events portrayed in this novel are either products of the author's imagination or are used fictitiously.

TRUTH BE TOLD

Copyright © 2014 by Hank Phillippi Ryan

A Forge Book
Published by Tom Doherty Associates, LLC
175 Fifth Avenue
New York, NY 10010

www.tor-forge.com

Forge® is a registered trademark of Tom Doherty Associates, LLC.

ISBN 978-0-7653-7494-3

Forge books may be purchased for educational, business, or promotional use. For information on bulk purchases, please contact the Macmillan Corporate and Premium Sales Department at 1-800-221-7945, extension 5442, or write to specialmarkets@macmillan.com.

First Edition: October 2014
First Mass Market Edition: September 2015

Printed in the United States of America

0 9 8 7 6 5 4 3 2 1

Always remembering You Never Know Day
August 18, 1995

Seldom, very seldom, does complete truth belong to any human disclosure; seldom can it happen that something is not a little disguised or a little mistaken.

—JANE AUSTEN

TRUTH
BE TOLD

1

"I know it's legal. But it's terrible." Jane Ryland winced as the Sandovals' wooden bed frame hit the tall grass in the overgrown front yard and shattered into three jagged pieces. "The cops throwing someone's stuff out the window. Might as well be Dickens, you know? Eviction? There's got to be a better way."

Terrible facts. Great pictures. *A perfect newspaper story.* She turned to TJ. "You getting this?"

TJ didn't take his eye from the viewfinder. "Rolling and recording," he said.

A blue-shirted Suffolk County sheriff's deputy—sleeves rolled up, buzz cut—appeared at the open window, took a swig from a plastic bottle. He shaded his eyes with one hand.

"First floor, all clear," he called. Two uniforms comparing paperwork on the gravel driveway gave him a thumbs-up. The Boston cops were detailed in, they'd explained to Jane, in case there were protesters. But no pickets or housing activists had appeared. Not even a curious neighbor. The deputy twisted the cap on the bottle, tossed away the empty with a flip of his gloved hand. The clear plastic bounced on top of a brittle hedge, then disappeared into the browning grass.

"Oops," he said. "I'm headed for the back."

"That's harsh," TJ muttered.

"You got it, though, right?" Jane knew it was a "moment" for her story, revealing the deputy's cavalier behavior while the Sandovals—she looked around, making sure the family hadn't shown up—were off searching for a new place to live. The feds kept reporting the housing crisis was over. Tell that to the now-homeless Sandovals, crammed—temporarily, they hoped—into a relative's spare bedroom. Their modest home in this cookie-cutter neighborhood was now an REO—"real estate owned" by Atlantic & Anchor Bank. The metal sign on the scrabby lawn said FORECLOSED in yellow block letters. Under the provisions of the Massachusetts Housing Court, the deputies were now in charge.

"Hey! Television! You can't shoot here. It's private property."

Jane felt a hand clamp onto her bare arm. She twisted away, annoyed. Of course they could shoot.

"Excuse me?" She eyed the guy's three-piece pinstripe suit, ridiculous on a day like today. He must be melting. Still, being hot didn't give him the right to be wrong. "We're on the public sidewalk. We can shoot whatever we can see and hear."

Jane stashed her notebook into her tote bag, then held out a hand, conciliatory. Maybe he knew something. "And not television. Newspaper. The new online edition. I'm Jane Ryland, from the *Register*."

She paused. Lawyer, banker, bean counter, she predicted. For A&A Bank? Or the Sandovals? The Sandovals had already told her, on camera, how Elliot Sandoval had lost his construction job, and they were struggling on pregnant MaryLou's day care salary. Struggling and failing.

"I don't care who you are." The man crossed his arms over his chest, a chunky watch glinting, tortoiseshell sunglasses hiding his expression. "This is none of your busi-

ness. You don't tell your friend to shut off that camera,
I'm telling the cops to stop you."

You kidding me? "Feel free, Mr.—?" Jane took her
hand away. Felt a trickle of sweat down her back. Boston was baking in the throes of an unexpected May heat
wave. Everyone was cranky. It was almost too hot to argue. "You'll find we're within our rights."

The guy pulled out a phone. All she needed. And stupid,
because the cops were right there. TJ kept shooting, good
for him. Brand new at the Boston *Register,* videographer
TJ Foy was hire number one in the paper's fledgling online video news department. Jane was the first—and so
far, only—reporter assigned.

"It's a chance to show off your years of TV experience," the *Register*'s new city editor had explained. Pretending Jane had a choice. "Make it work."

Pleasing the new boss was never a bad thing, and truth
be told, Jane could use a little employment security. She
still suffered pangs from her unfair firing from Channel
11 last year, but at least it didn't haunt her every day. This
was her new normal, especially now that newspapering
was more like TV. "Multimedia," her new editor called it.

"We're doing a story on the housing crisis." Jane smiled,
trying again. "Remember the teenager who got killed last
week on Springvale Street? Emily-Sue Ordway? Fell
from a window, trying to get back into her parents' foreclosed home? We're trying to show—it's not about the
houses so much as it is the people."

"'The people' should pay their mortgage." The man
pointed to the clapboard two-story with his cell phone.
"Then 'the cops' wouldn't have to 'remove' their possessions."

Okay, so not a lawyer for the Sandovals. But at least
this jerk wasn't dialing.

"Are you with A&A? With the bank?" Might as well
be direct.

"That's not any of—"

"Vitucci! Callum!" The deputy appeared in the open front door, one hand on each side of the doorjamb as if to keep himself upright. He held the screen door open with his foot. His smirk had vanished. The two cops on the driveway alerted, inquiring.

"Huh? What's up?" one asked.

"You getting this?" Jane whispered. She didn't want to ruin TJ's audio with her voice, but something was happening. Something the eviction squad hadn't expected.

"Second floor." The deputy pulled a radio from his belt pouch. Looked at it. Looked back at the cops. His shoulders sagged. "Better get in here."

2

"Why would he confess if he didn't do it?" Detective Jake Brogan peered through the smoky one-way glass at the guy slumped in the folding chair of Boston Police Department's interrogation room E. What Jane would probably call "skeevy"—too-long hair scraggling over one ear, ratty jacket, black T-shirt, tired tan pants. Thin. Late thirties, at least, more like forty. How old would Gordon Thorley have been in 1994, when Carley Marie Schaefer was killed? Late teens, at most. Around the same age as Carley. "This guy Thorley just shows up here at HQ and insists he's guilty? You ever seen that? Heard of that?"

"Let's get some lunch. Ask questions later." DeLuca jammed his empty paper coffee cup into the overflowing metal trash bin in the hall outside the interrogation room. "Sherrey will get all we need, give us his intake notes after. Could be a bird in the hand."

"Not exactly 'in the hand,'" Jake said. "If he's a whack job. There's also that old 'innocent till proven guilty' thing."

Jake flipped through the manila case file, a disorganized jumble of flimsy-paged police records, scrawled judge's orders, and blurry prison logs. Who was this Gordon Thorley, anyway? Seemed like no one—not the cops, not the DA's office—had ever heard of him in connection with Carley Marie Schaefer. In connection with an armed robbery back in the 1990s, sure; in connection with a chunk of prison time, sure. He'd been out on parole almost five years now. Record since then looked clean.

"Mr. Thorley?" Investigator Branford "Bing" Sherrey's voice crackled over the speaker. "Let's do this one more time. Start with Carley Marie Schaefer. What was your relationship with her? Why'd you come forward now? Why not before?"

The man picked up the can of diet ginger ale from the table in front of him. He examined the label, then, from the looks of it, slugged down the whole thing. He paused, swallowing. Then shrugged. "I get why you don't believe me. I know I should have owned up. But I was just a—okay. Again. Carley and me, we met in high school. We . . . had a thing. We kept it secret. I was older. She lived with her parents, out in Attleboro. Then she tried to break it off. I didn't want that. We went to our special place in the . . ."

"Whack job," D said. "Why do you want to hear this again?"

"Maybe it's true," Jake said. "And we'll clear this case. Finally. My grandfather was still on the job when Carley Marie was killed. I was maybe fourteen. Boston went crazy, I still remember it. Girl's body discovered by a family on a picnic. The Lilac Sunday killer." Jake blew out a breath, picturing those thick black headlines in the *Register* and the *Record*. "Grandpa would talk about it, nights. It was a huge deal. Weighed on him. How Carley's family was so distraught. He 'went to his grave,' Grandma Brogan still says, regretting his squad of murder cops never caught the Lilac Sunday killer."

"You think this is him?" D scratched his nose, looked unconvinced.

"Lilac Sunday's only a week away. We could do with a big solve," Jake said. "Even one that falls into our laps."

Behind the window, Thorley was talking with his hands, illustrating the heavy coil of rope he'd stashed in the trunk of his green Celica, the circumference of the tree trunk in Boston's Arnold Arboretum, the tight twist of the knots he'd made to hold Carley Schaefer in place. Thorley jabbed the heel of his palm toward the window. Jake flinched. Carley's neck had been snapped. *Huh.* Thorley seemed like too much of a wimp for that.

"And gimme a break, D," Jake added. "If we're getting this guy's case, we need to hear his story. Sucks that the Supe didn't call us till now. We should have been doing the questioning. Not Bing."

"Won't matter. The guy's prolly a wannabe. A nut." DeLuca shook his head. "It's like, he read some old newspapers or whatever and now he's making himself into a scary killer. He wants a TV movie, who knows. Lifetime presents the Lilac Sunday Killer. *Crap.* We're supposed to spend time on this sucker when Homicide's working on three open cases? New ones?"

Jake stared through the glass. Gordon Thorley—hands now clasped on the pitted metal table, looked straight ahead, eyes not quite focused. Third time through the Carley Marie story, Jake caught the same inflection, the same word choice. Had Thorley practiced? Contemplated his confession so often that it set in stone?

"It's as if he's been told what to say." Jake closed his file, took out his cell phone.

DeLuca rolled his eyes. Pointed to Thorley. "Oh, yeah. Why didn't I think of that? This is why I'm proud to be your partner. Basking in the glory."

"Stuff it, D." Jake tried to talk and dial his cell at the same time. D was a good guy and a solid partner, but like the entire Homicide squad, overworked and under-successful. Boston had too many murders, not enough arrests. Only a fourth-year detective, Jake was low man in seniority, which meant high man on the Supe's dreaded blame list. It didn't help to be grandson of a former police commissioner. Jake's blue-line "legacy" admittedly provided a leg up at entry level, but not job security or acceptance by his colleagues. D, ten years his senior, and in the "from the ranks" club, didn't always feel the pressure to go the extra mile. If D could close a case, faster was better. Jake still thought "right" was better.

He held up a palm, putting his partner on hold so he could hear his phone call. "Hello? This is Jake Brogan, Boston Police. Not an emergency, but I need to talk to Dr. Nathaniel Frasca. He around? Yes, I'll hang on."

"Who's that?" DeLuca narrowed his eyes. "Doctor who?"

"You'll see," Jake said. "And maybe I'll let you bask in the glory."

3

"Go. *Go*. **Get** closer." Jane almost pushed TJ forward, guiding him across the short driveway and toward the postage-stamp front porch. The Boston cops had dashed inside, radios crackling. Suit guy had slammed himself into the front seat of his fancy Lexus, punching buttons on his cell phone the whole way. "You're rolling, right?"

"On it," TJ said. He held the camera steady, targeting the door, but glanced over at her. "And I got this, you know, Ryland? Chill. I'm white-balanced, I got batteries, I'm up on sound. You don't have to keep checking."

"Sorry," she said. "Ignore me."

Would she ever lose her fear of failure? Her mom used to tease her—probably half tease, half worry—each time Jane predicted certain disaster. She'd fail the test, miss the cut, come in second, lose the story. It never happened. Hardly ever. Maybe fear was good. Maybe fear's what kept her in the game.

Now, the game was clearly on. The cops were freaking. Whatever that deputy found inside 42 Waverly Road was more than some broken piece of furniture. No other reporters were here—as far as the TV stations were concerned, this was just another eviction. Probably not even on their daybook radar. Jane was only here because of her story on foreclosures. Now, whatever this was felt like a headline. And an exclusive.

Jane hovered behind TJ's shoulder, on tiptoe in her flats, trying to balance without touching him. She shoved her sunglasses onto the top of her head, stabbed her pen through her almost-long-enough ponytail, wished she could look through his viewfinder.

"Anything?"

"Nope. Jane, listen. I'll tell you. Soon as there's something."

TJ's once-pressed cotton shirt was limp with the heat, his own RayBans perched on his dark hair, the *Register*'s Nextel clipped to a belt loop on his jeans. A talented guy, her age, a couple years of experience. Seemed tight with the new city editor.

It was a pain, Jane knew, for TJ to keep rolling on nothing. But the minute they stopped down, whatever was going to happen would happen.

The front door was open, but the screen door closed. No matter how much she squinted, Jane couldn't see inside. "Can you make out anything? Maybe we can get closer."

"Nope," TJ said. "Screen door's messing with the video, and—"

"Hear that?" *Sirens.* "Somebody's called the cavalry."

"Ambulance. Or more cops." TJ's camera lens stayed on the front door. "You want me to switch to the arrival?"

"Quick shot of whoever shows up, then back to the door," Jane instructed him. The story was inside.

Two car doors slammed. Jane risked a look behind her, saw the ambulance. Two EMTs, navy shirts, black Nikes, ran past her toward the front door. One carried a bright orange box—defibrillator. The other a black medical bag.

"Someone's hurt," she whispered.

"Duh," TJ whispered back.

The screen door opened, then slammed.

"They're in," TJ said. "Rolling. But can't see a damn thing."

"Clock's ticking now," Jane said. "They come out running, we'll know it's bad."

The door stayed closed.

The house had been empty when the deputies arrived, Jane knew that. She and TJ'd gotten shots of the two of them clicking open the padlock on the front door. No one had come out. She'd only seen water bottle guy since.

The deputies' job was to clear out the stuff the Sandovals had to leave behind. With no place to store it—and no money to do so—their leftover possessions were so much trash. This was the third eviction Jane had witnessed in the last three days. At Fawndale Street, one deputy had let her and TJ get some shots inside. She'd watched the blue-shirts—as she mentally called them—sweep through the rooms without a moment's hesitation, scooping clothing from forsaken closets, emptying drawers into plastic bags, dragging furniture across the floors, gouging the wood and bashing the painted walls and then sweeping piles of dust and litter out the door with a huge push broom.

Now she counted her blessings every time she returned to her Brookline condo. She'd tried to explain to Jake— she smiled, remembering their last clandestine meeting at his apartment—how it'd changed her whole appreciation for "home." Her little place, and her little mortgage, and all her stuff, saved and collected from high school and j-school, her Emmys, and Gram's pearls and handed-down Limoges dinner plates, her mother's last quilt, and even the always-hungry Coda, the now-adolescent stray calico who had selected Jane's apartment as her new domain.

That night Jane had sipped her wine, fearing her happiness could evaporate any second. "What would I do if someone tried to take Corey Road from me?" she'd asked.

"You'll never have to worry about that," Jake assured her.

"That's what the Sandovals probably thought, too," Jane said. Jake's snuffly Diva placed a clammy golden retriever nose on her bare arm. "Then the bottom fell out of their lives."

"Yo, Ryland." TJ interrupted her thoughts, pointing to the front door with his chin. "You seeing this?"

4

Lizzie McDivitt typed her name, letter by letter, on her new computer. Trying it out. Elizabeth McDivitt. Elizabeth Halloran McDivitt. Elizabeth H. McDivitt. The admin types needed the wording of the nameplate on her new office door, and she had to choose. First impression and all that.

Would her bank customers be more comfortable with her as the crisp and competent Liz? Or the elegant and experienced Elizabeth? Maybe this was the time to become Beth, the friendly-but-competent Beth. The motherly Bess?

Lizzie stared at the computer screen, the cursor blinking at her. *Decide.*

"Lizzie," at least, that was a definite no. "Lizzie" was fine for her parents, and even for Aaron, but not here at the bank. "Lizzie" sounded like the new kid, eager to please. Semi-true, of course, but not the image she needed. She needed . . . compassionate. Understanding. Her clients would be the needy ones, the out-of-work ones, the down-and-outers who'd once had the assets to get a mortgage from A&A—but now had to scramble for refinancing and loan modifications.

"If you say it, if you portray it, they will believe it," her father'd always told her. Seemed to work for him. His black fountain pen alone could probably take care of the monthly mortgage tab for a few of her clients. Father was always losing his fancy pens, misplacing them, forgetting them, one after the other. He never flinched at purchasing a new one.

She clicked her plastic ball point.

The bank had so much money. Her new customers had so little.

Click. Click.

What would be the bad thing, she wondered, about making it a little more fair?

Click. Click.

Aaron was still out for lunch, she guessed. She thought of him, his curls, and that smile, and what he'd actually said to her that first day back by the old vault. Their "tryst" last night, which ended—way too late—with her finally saying no and cabbing it home. She shook her head, remembering her girlfriends' advice. *You have to stop being so picky or you'll be alone forever.* True, Aaron was more than cute. True, he had a good job. So, okay, *maybe.* Even though he wasn't *exactly* . . .

"Miss McDivitt? You ready for your one-thirty? Mr. and Mrs. Iantosca are here."

Lizzie jumped, startled at the sound of her own name buzzing through her intercom. She'd started behind the cages in the teller pool, then got promoted to a loan officer's desk in the lobby, visible every single moment of every single day, like a zoo animal. She'd tried to offer suggestions, how to make customers happier, how to streamline the process, how to dump a lot of the ridiculously complicated paperwork and incomprehensible bank jargon.

Now, finally, she'd been named the bank's first customer affairs liaison. With her own private office. It was lovely to have a door that closed. And an assistant, Stephanie Weaver, who stayed outside unless invited in.

"Thanks, Stephanie," she said. She punched up the Iantoscas' mortgage loan documents: a series of spreadsheets, tiny-fonted agreements, and the decisive flurry of letters stored on the bank's in-house software. The green numbers that were entered several years ago had gone red last summer, then bold red in the fall, then starting around the holidays, black-bordered bold red. By now, mid-May, Christian and Colleen Iantosca were underwater and in trouble.

So they thought.

Lizzie clicked a few keys on her computer keyboard. Examined the figures she'd typed in. She leaned closer, calculating. Numbers worked for her. Numbers were—obedient. Predictable. Reliable. Plus, she could always change them back.

"I'm set, Stephanie," she told the intercom. Time to meet the Iantoscas.

She took off her black-rimmed glasses, considered, put them on again. Slicked her hair back, tucking a stray wisp into place. She checked her reflection on the computer monitor. Lipstick, fine. Portrait of a happy magna cum laude MBA. Good job, her own apartment, a potential boyfriend—she clasped her hands under her chin, thanking the universe and embracing her karma. Math geek no more. Future so bright, she ought to wear shades.

Liz, she decided. Compassionate, but knowledgeable. Approachable. And, starting today, starting now, Liz McDivitt was in control.

Five more minutes. He'd give them five more minutes.

Aaron Gianelli waited on the front steps of the triple-decker, peeled the last of the waxed paper from his tuna melt wrap, took a final bite. A mayo-soaked glop narrowly missed his new cordovan loafer, landed on the concrete beside him. Too damn hot for a tuna melt, Aaron decided too late, but this "meeting" was his only chance for lunch. He crumpled the paper, aimed, and hit the already brimming Dumpster over by the driveway.

His first score of the day.

If the others didn't show up pretty damn soon, it'd be his only score. That, he could not afford. He wondered how his partner was doing, at *his* meeting. They'd talk later. Compare notes. Not that there were notes.

Standing, Aaron brushed the dust from his ass. Squinted out at Pomander Street. No cars. Nothing. They'd agreed to meet here at 1:30 P.M. He checked his annoyingly silent cell phone. If they were going to be late, they should have called. If they were jerking him around, they'd be sorry. But no biggie. He'd find other customers.

He'd parked his car down the street, left his suit jacket inside, thank God. It was brutal out here. He'd be a sweat machine when he got back to the office, but the AC would take care of that before anyone noticed. And Lizzie would believe whatever he told her. He smiled. He loved Lizzie.

He patted his pockets, still smiling, feeling for the ring of keys. He'd go in without the clients, check it out. House was empty, that was certain. The bank had made sure of that.

Aaron was still smiling. He loved the bank.

5

"Uh-oh," Jane said. TJ's camera lens still trained on the now-open front door. The two EMTs emerged. Not running. "That's not good."

The EMT carrying the defibrillator shouldered his way out, followed by the stocky one lugging the medical bag. Jane couldn't read their faces, both squinting in the glare, the heat radiating from the hot sidewalk and crushed gravel driveway. The ambulance siren was off, but the red light on the hood swirled silently through the sunshine. The ambulance, rear double doors flapped open, was poised for a fast getaway to Mass General. But the two EMTs stopped. Put their bags down. Stood on the porch.

"Whatever happened, it's over," Jane said. "Come on, Teege. Let's get closer. Sorry this is taking so long, your shoulder must be killing you. But look, the guy's radioing now. Can you hear what he's saying?"

Jane followed behind TJ, straining to grasp the EMT's words as he transmitted over the sputtering two-way radio. The bank guy—if that's who he was—stayed in his Lexus. The splintered bed frame, two chairs, and a couple of fringed pillows baked on the parched front lawn.

"Copy, Unit Bravo." The dispatcher's voice on the other end squawked through the static. "We'll notify. Stand by. We'll inform when you are clear to transport."

"Transport," Jane whispered. She'd edged in so close, she could now hear the hum of TJ's camera, hear her own voice buzzing through his earpiece. "Transport who?"

"You gonna answer that?" DeLuca's radio was squawking, but Jake couldn't take his eyes off Thorley, watching him through the interrogation room glass, knowing the guy couldn't see him and DeLuca in the hallway. Thorley didn't know they'd heard what he'd told Detective Bing Sherrey. Didn't know they'd be taking over the case.

There'd been silence for the past few minutes, Thorley staring at his fingernails while Bing scribbled on a yellow pad. Probably a confession he hoped Thorley would sign.

"Now what?" Jake pointed to D's radio.

DeLuca's two-way beeped again from its leather pouch. Dispatch calling.

"We shall see." DeLuca keyed the mic. "DeLuca."

Jake, cell phone to his ear, was still waiting for Dr. Nathaniel Frasca. After blowing open the Memphis copycat sniper case, Frasca had been called to D.C. to be a big-time consultant for the feds. He'd have to rib supposedly retired Frasca about that when they finally connected.

Plus, Frasca still owed Jake a beer from the Stockbridge Street murder. The young woman the state troopers had browbeaten into a false confession was now back home with her family. The real bad guy, thanks to Jake and the veteran Frasca, was in the slammer for a good long stretch.

DeLuca's two-way radio buzzed static again. "Detective DeLuca, do you copy?" dispatch's voice came through. "What's your location?"

"This is DeLuca, like I said. Detective Brogan and I are downtown. Two floors above where you are."

Jake rolled his eyes. DeLuca was always a trip on the radio.

"Yes, ma'am," Jake said into his cell. "Yes, I'll continue to hold. Yes, Brogan. B-R-O-G-A-N. In Boston. Dr. Frasca actually knows who—"

"Copy that, Detective DeLuca," dispatch said. "Stand by for instructions."

"Standing by to stand by. As always." DeLuca clicked off his two-way, pointed it at the one-way glass. "Jake. Check it out. We have company."

The back door to the interrogation room had opened.

"Good afternoon, gentlemen." Peter Hardesty closed the interrogation room door behind him, plunked his leather briefcase on the metal table, held out a hand. He'd already heard the cops were calling this guy the Confessor.

Confessor or not, Gordon Thorley was innocent till proven guilty. And, like so many others Peter had represented, profoundly in need of counsel. In this place? Alone with a detective? A legal minefield.

"Gordon Thorley?"

"Who're you?" Thorley twisted in his folding chair, scooted it as far from Peter as the cinder-block wall would let him, metal scraping against concrete. Thorley's sallow skin stretched over sharp cheekbones, weary eyes too big. Peter could almost hear the guy's brain shift gears. Surprise. Then fear. Then calculation. Thorley flickered a hard look at Peter, jerking a yellowed thumb in his direction. Spoke to the detective. "He a cop, too?"

"Holy sh—How'd you get in here, Hardesty? Who called you? Mr. Thorley here hasn't asked for a lawyer."

Peter recognized the plainclothes detective in the weary brown suit and ugly tie—Detective Branford Sherrey. "Bing" Sherrey. Veteran cop, beloved of the district attorney's office, and a remarkable asshole. Now he looked like he'd been socked in his shirt-straining gut. *Sucks when the system works,* Peter thought. When you have to provide legal advice to a nutcase who's trying get himself a life sentence. Justice. What a concept.

Peter glanced at the obviously one-way glass along one wall, gave a brief salute to whoever was on the other side. He'd find out soon enough. Other cops listening? A witness, maybe? To what? He'd gotten the call from Doreen Thorley—now Doreen Rinker—only half an hour ago. He'd left half a perfectly good turkey on rye on his desk downtown. Here, things were already out of hand.

"Hasn't asked for a lawyer? I'm aware of that, Detective Sherrey. Nevertheless, here I am. At the request of his family. If you've got an open mic in here? Someone listening behind that glass? You need to turn it off. Now." Peter clicked the two silver latches on his briefcase, opened it. Took out a manila folder and turned to his newest client.

"But you can't just—" Sherrey gestured toward the one-way glass. Pushed a button. "I mean, this is an ongoing—"

Peter ignored his whining.

"Mr. Thorley, I'm Peter Hardesty, from Hardesty and Colaneri? Your sister called, asked me to come make sure you weren't saying anything without legal advice. Good thing, because apparently that's what Detective Sherrey here is leading you to do. My first piece of advice? Don't say another word."

"I can't—I don't—she wasn't supposed—I don't want—," Thorley sputtered, looked at the ceiling, then frowned at the floor. "Anyway, Doreen doesn't have the money to—"

"As you hear, Mr. Hardesty." The detective pointed a yellow legal pad at him. "Apparently Mr. Thorley, obviously of sound mind and clear intent, fully appreciates and understands the significance of what he's said. What he's actually already told us on tape. Several times. In the interest of justice, and perhaps his conscience."

Interest of justice? *Right.* Still, this was a new one. Thorley had left his sister a "good-bye" and "I'm sorry" note on the kitchen table of their family home. He was either crazy or—well, Peter would discover that soon enough. But not while the cops were listening.

"Let's get you straightened out here first, sir. That's more important than the money. Your sister, Doreen, got your note, called me, explained the situation. Now, Detective? You'll need to give us some time. Here, or elsewhere. Alone." Peter smiled, gestured toward the inner window. "With no one-way glass, and no other cops listening."

"Not if Mr. Thorley doesn't want you." Sherrey reached into his jacket pocket, pulled out a package of Winston Reds. Tapped the end, held out the pack to Thorley. "Smoke? Another ginger ale?"

Thorley reached two thin fingers toward the Winston. Guy seemed in bad shape, the ribbed collar of his T-shirt twisted and too big, jacket sleeves fraying at the wrists. Like life had dealt him a losing hand, and he'd decided to fold. Peter's job—any good lawyer's job—was to keep him in the game.

"Your hospitality is admirable, Detective," Peter said. "And theoretically, I suppose, you could ask me to leave. But play it out here. You just told me my client has already talked with you on tape—a tape I'm now formally requesting you to produce and provide. Given that circumstance, how can it cause you a problem to leave us alone for a while?"

Sherrey seemed to be considering it. He snapped a red plastic Bic, lit his own cigarette, aimed the smoke at the ceiling.

"Plus," Peter went on. "You charge him with whatever

it is. We go to court. What's the first thing I'm gonna tell the judge? I'm gonna say you tried to keep me away. Poof. Your precious tape is inadmissible. Mr. Thorley goes home. You lose."

Thorley was already stabbing out the cigarette he'd sucked down, grinding it into a metal ashtray on the table. He eyed Sherrey, a hungry dog. But in fact, Thorley needed more than a cigarette. He needed Peter.

Doreen Thorley Rinker had explained her brother's handwritten note said he was confessing to a murder, and begged forgiveness. Said he was "doing it for the family." What family? The victim's? Bizarre. And more bizarre that Thorley didn't want a lawyer. But hey. Everybody hated lawyers. Until they realized they needed one.

"Detective?" Peter pointed to his watch. "Tick, tock. The more you stall, the more the judge'll be convinced you're up to no good. Remember, Mr. Thorley's already on parole. Correct? Why not let his parole officer look after him? Like he has for the past few years? He's clearly not a flight risk, correct? I mean, he's sitting here of his own volition."

"Lawyers." Sherrey stuffed the cigarettes into his jacket pocket.

"Can't live with 'em . . ." Peter didn't finish the sentence.

"Okay." Thorley's voice was a whisper. "I guess I should have a lawyer. But only so the system works fair. That doesn't mean I didn't do—"

"Not another word, Mr. Thorley," Peter said.

Sherrey strode two steps to the door, opened it, then turned to glare at Peter. "This is bull," he said.

"Thanks," Peter said. The door slammed closed. "We'll be in touch."

Peter might have won this round. But the road ahead was not going to be pretty. Not when the client himself didn't want to be saved.

6

"**Somebody's dead. Got** to be." Jane flapped her notebook against her leg, impatient. "If someone's just hurt, the EMTs would've been running like hell."

The screen door stayed closed.

"Yup." TJ aimed his voice at her, kept his eyes on the door. "But listen."

A blue-and-white Boston police cruiser, blue lights whirling, siren screaming, peeled around the corner of Sycamore, flew onto Waverly, skidded to a stop at the end of the driveway.

The cruiser's blue light mixed with the ambulance's red.

"Here we go." Jane squinted against the sunshine, hoping to ID the arriving cops. If they were pals, she might have an inside track to the story. She yanked on her sunglasses to cut the glare. That made it dark. Tried again without them.

The passenger side door opened.

Work boots. Levis. Black T-shirt. Sandy hair. Sunglasses. Jake.

Jane?

Jake slammed his cruiser door, waited a beat for

DeLuca to join him. Shaded his eyes, surveyed the crime scene. Some man in a Lexus, on the phone. Who was he? A neighbor? Two EMTs standing on the porch. Jake pointed at them, then at the house. One gave a thumbs down. Jake nodded. DOA.

And Jane.

Jane raised a palm at him, acknowledging, but stayed where she was, whispering with the guy shooting video. Must be the new on-line gig she'd described. Weird to see her with a camera again, after all the—

"My, my." DeLuca cocked his head toward Jane. "You two lovebirds have got to stop meeting like this."

"Right," Jake said. "Let's get in there. See what they got."

He and DeLuca had a sometimes-silent truce about their private lives—DeLuca knew about Jane, enough at least. Jake knew about DeLuca and Kat McMahan, the medical examiner who'd soon be arriving, if the deputies had their facts right.

Jake knew he and Jane were going to have to make a decision. Soon. In fact, by this weekend. They couldn't keep sneaking. Cop and reporter? Reporter and cop? Right at the edge of ethical. Over the edge, according to police SOP. The newspaper's, too. They'd tried to stay apart, but that was a miserable failure. To stay together, one of them would have to quit. Which was impossible. The whole thing was impossible.

Jake raised a hand back as they passed. Jane's shooter was getting it all on tape.

"Eviction, huh?" Jake pulled out his cell phone, opened a file. Thumbed in his to-dos. He'd have to check the sheriff's paperwork. Get bank stuff. Get registry records, check ownership, track down tenants or whoever once lived here. "Whoever got thrown out, they're not gonna be happy, that's for sure. *There's* a motive."

The EMTs moved aside, let them through as the screen door squeaked open.

Inside, dust motes floated on sunlight streaming through curtainless windows, the living room empty, the hardwood floor bare. A pile of rags teetered, stashed in a charred brick fireplace. Place smelled like fire, and bleach. One flight of bare stairs to a second floor. Two uniforms blocked what was probably the opening to the kitchen. Vitucci and Callum. Good guys. Who did not look happy. They'd been detailed here, off duty. Not expecting to actually do any work. Surprise, surprise.

"Hey, Vitooch. We were at HQ, dispatch just radioed us the call. Got here fast as we could. Thanks for holding the fort," Jake said. "Where's . . . ?"

"Hey, Jake," Vitucci said. "Upstairs. With the sheriff's deputies. It's an eviction, right? Look, uh, Jake? Thing is—"

"Thing?" Jake said. "Thing" meant problem. Glitch. Snafu. "Thing" meant Jake's day was about to get complicated. "There's a 'thing'?"

"Mr. Iantosca? Mrs. Iantosca?" Lizzie—Liz—came around from behind her desk, gestured her customers to the two new visitor chairs. They'd been delivered that very morning; in fact, no one had ever sat in them before. Liz spotted a paper receipt still taped underneath one of them.

"I'm Liz McDivitt," she said. "Thank you for coming. May I offer you some water? Or coffee?"

Colleen Iantosca looked like she hadn't slept in a year, thin as a memory, eyes red-rimmed. Her dark cardigan, buttoned high over a white blouse, had a tiny hole in the left shoulder. She gave Liz a wisp of a smile, shook her head no, then picked at the clasp of the flat black purse she clutched in her lap. Drew a breath with a little gasp.

Her husband reached out a hand, put it on top of hers.

"Honey," he said. "Thank you, Miss McDivitt. No."

"We'll never be able to—," Colleen Iantosca began. Then she stopped, looking at her husband again.

"My wife is right." Christian Iantosca patted his wife's hand, then clamped his palms on his knees.

His suit, a good one, had also seen better days. Liz knew from their records the husband had been a bakery manager before Scones and Co. went bankrupt; the wife still worked in the back of a West End dry cleaner. Reliable, trusting, honest people. Now with one big mortgage and one small salary.

"We understand why you've called us here. We understand the bank has no choice. But I do have some jobs in line, and I guess we'd hoped—well, you see our position."

Liz remained standing, didn't want to put the desk between them. She took a breath, smiled, and broke the law.

"I have some good news for you, Mr. and Mrs. Iantosca," she said.

She paused, thinking it through one last time. She controlled these accounts, the foreclosure paperwork had not yet progressed through unalterable channels. She understood the work-arounds necessary to avoid the transparent and ridiculously vulnerable protocols the bank inserted to catch manually entered overrides. Numbers always did what she wanted them to. She almost felt her father's presence. *Hi, Dad,* she thought. *Guess what.*

"It appears," she said, "there has been an error in your records."

"An error?" Christian Iantosca frowned. "We didn't do anything wr—"

"What kind of an—," his wife began.

The whisper of hope in the woman's eyes almost broke Lizzie's heart.

Yes. Lizzie—*Liz*—was doing the right thing.

She put up both palms. "I'm happy to show you the documentation, at some point, after our auditors have reassessed the financial essentials and fiduciary elements." That was pure drivel, but they'd never know. "However, bottom line, as they say, the balance of your mortgage, with the calculation of the compounding interest and the escrow payments, as well as the federal allowance offered under Title M for first-time homeowners—" She stopped, as if this actually meant something. Sighed, as if clearing her mind.

"Getting to the point. We're stopping the foreclosure."

Colleen Iantosca made a sound, a gasp or a gulp. Her cheeks went pink, and she covered her mouth with two sinewy hands. Her eyes went wide, then welled with tears.

"How could—," Christian Iantosca began. "But what about the—"

"I understand you'll have questions." Liz went behind her desk, sat in her new swivel chair, felt tall. She tapped on her keyboard, bringing up a blank spreadsheet, and turned the monitor so the Iantoscas could see. Not that it would show them anything. "I'll be your direct and only contact on this," she said, pointing to the empty grid. "Okay?"

Both Iantoscas nodded.

"Two things." Liz thought of something. "Oh, first, you didn't have a closing attorney, correct? You and the bank handled this directly."

Both Iantoscas nodded.

Okay, then. "And your house is on the lis pendens list at the registry of deeds, the pre-foreclosure notice, you understand?"

"Yes, they told us that," Christian said. "The bank's real estate person came to see us. The man, Mr. . . . ?" He checked with his wife.

"Gianelli," Colleen Iantosca said. "We had to show him the house, and he told us we might have to be out in eight weeks."

Aaron. Liz couldn't believe how perfectly this was going.

"I'll speak to him," Liz said. "Meanwhile, I'll withdraw the lis pendens. Then I have to reorganize your debit situation in accordance with the overpayments you've been charged in the years past. When I recalculate your payments, I'll inform you, in person, of your obligations."

She stood, fingertips on her lovely big brand-new desk.

"But for now? Go home." Liz smiled. In control. "Don't worry. Find a job, Mr. Iantosca. But your home is your home. And so it shall stay."

7

"'Thing is' what?" Jake said. Vitucci and Callum were fidgeting, the two detail cops getting in each other's way. It obviously wasn't only from the damn heat. The EMTs hovered on the porch. Jane, for sure, would soon be trying to get the scoop. No one seemed in much of a hurry to let Jake and DeLuca get to their crime scene.

"Yeah, well, the vic is on the second floor, rear bedroom, third of three." Vitucci hitched up his pants. "Says the deputy. The two of them are up there now. I guess. But see, the thing is, they—"

"Show us this 'thing.'" DeLuca put a hand on the banister, raised an eyebrow at Jake. "Seems like these two don't want us up there, you think?"

"I hear you, D," Jake said. "Vitooch? You got something to say? Now's the time."

"Okay." Vitucci raked his hands through his hair, like this was the last crime scene he'd ever see. "So thing is, the deputies, you know, were clearing out the—"

"We decided to hang outside, in case rent-a-demonstrators showed up, you know?" Callum said. "And then the deps yelled out the window, but when we got upstairs—"

"Where we are going right now," Jake said. "If one of

you could manage to finish a sentence. Vitucci, that's you."

Vitucci's shoulders sagged. "Seems like they'd gotten rid of everything. The deputies did, you know? Bleach, and disinfectant, all that. Sweeping. Apparently, the vic was in the last room they'd hit. In the closet. Which they didn't open, until too late. Then she, like, slid out of it. That's why she's—like that. Sitting up. Sort of."

"I see." Jake could not believe it. A crime scene ruined by the sheriff's own deputies. This was a new one. Jake and D reached the top of the stairs, took a left toward the back. "So fingerprints, trace evidence, whatever?"

"What I've been trying to tell you," Vitucci said. "It's like, gone. The deputies cleaned all of it, before they found the—"

"Female. Caucasian. Maybe. Mid-thirties," DeLuca interrupted. "Dead since yesterday at most, who knows, just my guess."

DeLuca'd stopped in the doorway, looking past a rusting twin bed frame, and down to the hardwood floor. No curtains, no rugs, no other furniture. Just a dead woman sitting in an empty closet. In a room where all the evidence was gone.

"Shit," Jake said.

"Where are those two morons, anyway?" DeLuca said.

"Down the back stairs?" Vitucci said. "Maybe?"

"Find 'em for me, Vitooch," Jake said. "Go. Take Callum with you. And look, no way you could have prevented this. Right? You did your jobs. You're fine."

"But we should have—," Vitucci began.

"Go. Find me the assholes." Jake pointed toward the street. "And find out who that guy is. The suit with the Lexus. We'll need to chat with him."

At this, Vitucci perked up, all business. "We asked when he showed up, we did that, says he's the real estate guy," he said. "So—"

"Go," Jake said. "Bring back those deputies."

"Look at this." DeLuca scanned the small room as the cops bolted. "There's no purse, no possessions. No nothing."

The deputies had done their stuff all right. Dresser, drawers pulled out, empty. Closet, now open, empty, a few metal hangers. Window open. "Whoever killed her took the purse, maybe," DeLuca continued. "Maybe a robbery? Think she was the owner, maybe? Former owner, I mean."

"Maybe," Jake said. Well-cared-for, short dark hair. A slash of pink lipstick clownish on her pale skin. Bare legs, sandals, a simple dress like Jane always wore, a light navy blazer flapping open. A necklace with a tiny gold horseshoe dangled from a delicate chain around her neck. "But check it out. She's got a diamond-looking ring, a good haircut, that manicure. Gold necklace. Doesn't seem like a foreclosure type. No gunshot wounds visible. You calling the ME? Tell her no bleeding, no sign of—well, wait."

"Yeah," DeLuca said. "I see it."

Jake crouched, keeping his balance on the hardwood floor, as close to the victim as he could without touching. The sun blasted through the eight-paned window, making a shadow latticework on her motionless form. Jake squinted at the tiny gold insignia pinned in the lapel of the blue blazer, shining in a patch of light.

"Whaddaya think?" Jake asked. "'M' or 'W'?"

"I'm trying to get all that right now," Jane said. She'd borrowed TJ's phone so she could brief the city editor and use her own cell to text bullet points to the copy desk at the same time. This was no longer a straightforward foreclosure on Waverly Road. But that's all Jane knew for sure.

She hit SEND, multi-tasking, TJ's phone clamped between her cheek and shoulder. Victoria Marcotte, the new city editor, continued to fire off questions. Jane surveyed the scene as she answered.

"Yes, cops. Nope, no movement. We're on the sidewalk. The EMTs are in the front seat of the ambulance, probably soaking up the AC. Bank guy, or whoever he is, just got into his Lexus," Jane said. "So listen, Victoria, if there's a body inside, we've got it. Exclusive."

TJ had risked setting his camera on the sidewalk and now sat on the curb next to her, feet splayed onto the potholed asphalt of Waverly Road. He looked as dust-coated and sweaty as she felt. But she was relentlessly curious. And patient enough to wait.

"I can send you a cell phone photo, even video, soon as I see anything," Jane told her editor. After three years in TV battling the deadlines and stress and pressure for live video, her admittedly unenthusiastic entry into newspapers had—at least for a while—removed that tension from her work equation. Now, with the *Register*'s online edition, she was back to instant news. Not only getting the info, but often taking the pictures. It was fun, juggling it all. When it worked.

A change in the light. The front door was opening.

"Victoria? Gotta call you back." Jane saw TJ was already rolling, headed toward the house. She had to catch up with him.

Victoria was still talking.

"*But—*," Jane tried to get a word in. "Yes, yes, forty-two Waverly Road. But you can't say it's a 'possible homicide,' because we don't know if—well, sure, I suppose it's a possible homicide until it isn't. But I think we should wait until the police—"

The front door had closed again.

"Fine," Jane said. Marcotte had not let her finish the sentence. "Watch for my e-mail."

She clicked off, caught up with TJ, gave back his phone, and switched hers to photo mode. Snapped off a shot of the exterior, door closed, one of the ambulance, one of Lexus guy, one of Jake's cruiser. Jake, who was still inside. Jake, who had not answered her text. Jake, who, well, that was for later. She punched in Victoria's number again, muttering. Hit SEND. Photos were on the way. *Fine.*

"It's bull," she said as she caught up to TJ. "Marcotte demanded photos, so they can do a breaking news in the online. 'Possible homicide' "—Jane made quote marks in the air—"in Hyde Park."

"We have no idea if it's a homicide." TJ took his eye from the viewfinder, frowned at her.

"Exactly what I told her." Jane kept her eyes on the front door. "She didn't care."

Jane pitched her voice into the imperious Marcotte manner. " 'Are you saying it's *not* a possible homicide?' That's what she actually said to me. She's like, 'I understood that's why you were calling me. Possible means possible. I'm only repeating what you told me, is that not correct? Are you calling me with information that's not correct?' "

Jane stuck out her tongue. TJ's eye was back on the viewfinder, and he couldn't see her probably inappropriate gesture. "I hate that," she said. "She doesn't seem to care what's true."

"It's as good as true, right?" TJ told her. "If it's in the paper? If it turns out it isn't, we correct it. Usually."

"And when we don't, the truth disappears," Jane said. "Exactly what I'm afraid of."

8

If Aaron were any handsomer, Lizzie thought, she literally would not be able to stand it. Stephanie was still at her desk, Lizzie supposed, but as far as the secretary knew, Aaron Gianelli was coming to her office to talk business. Aaron had a way of talking business that made her feel not very businesslike.

"You been outside?" he said. He'd loosened his tie, and leaned against the doorjamb, lounging, both hands stuffed into pockets of his pants. "It's incredibly hot."

Lizzie tried not to stare, but that meant she had to look into his eyes, which was even harder.

"You don't look hot." Lizzie blushed, dying. "I mean—"

"Hey, Lizzie. Now you owe me." He gave her that smile, then unbuttoned one shirt cuff and rolled it up to his elbow. Then the other.

She wondered how the rest of him looked. Her skin, if it were right next to his, would not be as tan. Now she was probably blushing again. She wished her phone would ring. The intercom buzz. Fire alarm. *Anything*.

"I came to check out your new digs. Welcome to the big time." He gestured at her office. "Looks terrific, Lizzie. Nice chairs, nice desk, all the comforts of home."

He walked toward her, before she even had a chance

to say anything. Came around behind her chair, she could feel his presence there, imagined she could smell him, even though she couldn't, felt the back of her neck prickle, felt her brain catch fire.

He leaned closer. She didn't move, couldn't move.

His breath was in her ear.

One arm, so close she could see the freckles dotting his suntan, reached past her, opened a file on her desk. The Iantoscas' file. Labeled with their name in big Sharpie block letters.

Was he going to kiss her? Right now? At *work*?

But Aaron had snatched up the Iantoscas' file and stepped away from her, leaning against the windowsill. Now he was actually paging through the paperwork inside.

"Whatcha working on here?"

He was smiling, but he didn't look happy. She'd never seen that expression on his face before.

This wasn't how this was supposed to go. This was her secret. Her. Secret.

"Five-forty-nine Nordstand Boulevard?" Aaron turned one page, then another. She could hear the swish of paper as he thumbed through the financial disclosures and deeds and legal documents. "Christian Iantosca. This is one of our REOs. From *our* department. Why's it on *your* desk?"

She could actually feel the frown on her face, and struggled to change her expression, wanting to please him, but needing to protect her file. She was the one with the numbers, not him. The numbers were the power. The numbers would always save her.

Change the equation.

"Yes, the Iantoscas." She swiveled her chair to face him. Her new vertical blinds cast slashes on the wall behind him, the afternoon sun coming through as slivers of light. His face was shadow, the manila file a silhouette.

"A happy story. Such a sweet couple. I'm so thrilled it's all turned out for them. Aren't you? That they're current now?"

Okay, he'd missed something, a big something, and Aaron sure as hell could not figure out what. The freaking Iantoscas? No way they were current. No matter what Lizzie said.

He'd flipped through the paperwork trying to figure out what happened while Lizzie kept babbling. He wasn't the numbers guy in this deal, that was kind of Ackerman's department, but crap, there'd be no reason the bank would assign this home if there wasn't a slam dunk foreclosure.

Nordstand Boulevard was set to be a kick-ass property for him. In Allston, right by Boston College and BU. Three bedrooms, big ones, a finished basement. All good. Now Lizzie was telling him the Iantoscas were paid up?

"How'd that happen? Them getting current?" He scanned the numbers. The pre-foreclosure filings were all there, he'd seen those before. Now they had red lines through them. Top copy signed by Elizabeth H. McDivitt. "They win the lottery?"

Lizzie was blushing again. He could make her feel uncomfortable, good to know. Plus, losing this one house wasn't gonna blow the whole deal. Lucky he'd found out. Before it was too late.

"They didn't explain that to me," she was saying. "It's maybe personal? Family? Someone died, something like that." Big smile, as if that would matter to him. "I only fill in the blanks. Make sure the columns add up. I'm the numbers girl."

"Well, you've got mine." Aaron slid the folder back on Lizzie's desk. He'd check with Ack about it. If they'd paid, they'd paid. It happened. The Nordstand Boulevard deal wasn't signed. He could still cancel, and move on. Three o'clock. Ack would know what to do.

"Got your what?" Lizzie was frowning, a lock of her hair dropping into her eyes.

For such a book-smart chick, she sure had a clueless streak. Luckily for him. Cute enough, though. He could handle a "relationship" with her. Who knows what it'd do for his career. Couldn't hurt.

"Number," he said. "You've got my number. So how about dinner? Tonight?"

9

"Maybe Gordon Thorley killed *this* vic, too." DeLuca sniffed, scratching the back of his neck as he looked at the body on the floor. "Maybe we could get him to clear all our cases. It'd be like, a public service."

"Have a little respect, dude." Jake took a final reference shot with his cell phone. Crime Scene would be here on Waverly Road soon, but he kept his own records. Like his grandfather taught him. Jake had been thinking about Thorley, too. But that case had to go on hold. "So. The victim's lapel pin. 'M'? Or 'W'?"

"It's both." The voice came from behind them. "And she's a real estate broker. What do I win?"

The gang's all here, Jake thought. His cell pinged for the second time in two minutes. He knew it was Jane. He also knew he could not answer. They'd relaxed the rules a bit, impossible not to. But he couldn't give her the scoop, especially not in front of DeLuca. And now the medical examiner.

"Hey, Kat," he said. "Perfect timing."

"As always," DeLuca said. "Hot enough for you?"

"You should know, Detective." Dr. Kat McMahon looked at D, a fraction too long. Today her white lab coat was unbuttoned. Underneath, the T-shirt tucked into her blue scrubs read SUMMER IN THE CITY.

Jane always described the ME as one of those curvy Russian dolls in a doll, all red lips and sleek hair. The two women had clashed at a couple of news conferences since Kat came to town last year, Jane demanding information about the latest homicide, Kat refusing to give it. Doing their jobs.

"Real estate broker?" Jake said.

"Yeah. Mornay and Weldon." Kat snapped open her boxy black ME bag, yanked out two lavender latex gloves. "Don't you watch late-night cable? Real estate brokers. That's their logo. It flips upside down in the ad, you know? 'M' or 'W'? They found me my place when I moved here." A glove snapped onto one hand, then the other. "This how you found her? You got photos? I take it you don't know who she is?"

"That's a one phone call, now, thanks to you," Jake said.

A real estate broker. Huh. If that was true, maybe the bad guy was a potential buyer. He tested that idea, his mind spinning out theories. Maybe she'd been here showing the house. The would-be buyer shows up, maybe attacks her? Some kind of robbery? Maybe to get keys? *She struggles, he panics, and* . . . If that was true, so much for his initial focus on the former owner. Or—maybe not. It was okay to speculate at this point in a case. Had to. But kiss of death to make a decision early on. That's how cops made mistakes. "Yeah, this is how we found her. She fell when the deputies opened the closet door. That's why she's like this. Any hope for a cause of death?"

"Ninety degrees outside? The body moved?" Kat crouched in front of the victim. "Could be tough, because— ouch. Strike that. Look at the back of her head."

"What the heck are they doing in there?" Jane's back was soaked; her now-grimy white T-shirt would never be white again. Her black flats were caked with dust, her hair plastered to her head, and if she didn't get water she would die. There was a big bottle of it in the car, but it was too risky to leave their stakeout spot in front of 42 Waverly to go get it.

Had they missed something? "TJ? Maybe the cops went out the back."

TJ pointed to the ambulance. "Chill," he said. "We're fine."

He was right. Her real problem wasn't the fact that Jake and his posse were taking forever, or even the heat. The problem was that her boss was at that very minute, probably, going online with a story that there was a murder victim inside 42 Waverly Road, and Jane simply wasn't sure that was true. What if Marcotte put her byline on it and it was wrong?

"Am I overreacting?" She pointed to herself with one finger. "You know I got fired, right, by the jerks at Channel Eleven? When they lost that lawsuit? When the jury said I was wrong?"

"Yeah, sure," TJ said. "Everyone knows—"

"All I need," Jane interrupted, "all I freaking—excuse me—need, is to have my byline on a story that actually *is* wrong. I could never salvage my career from that. I'd have to leave town and change my name."

"Jane." TJ, camera now on his lap, aimed a puff of air at the lens to get rid of the dust. "The medical examiner is inside. That's a, well, I don't want to say a good sign. But you know what I mean. There's probably a dead person. The story will be correct."

Jane had to give him that. She probably *was* overreacting. Being unfairly fired would do that to you. Having a crazy editor would do that to you.

"And, I hate to say it," TJ added, "but would people really care? If it turned out there wasn't a body?"

"I'd sure as hell care." So would Jake, Jane didn't say.

He'd be pissed if the paper got his case wrong. Victoria Marcotte's zeal for headlines could ruin everything. Jane's career. Jake's. Their relationship. Such as it was. "If the story is wrong, what're they gonna do, run a correction on page twenty-six? Or some tiny online brief? People remember what they read. That's what makes it history. Like I said, there's only one true."

"We're about to hear it," TJ said, hoisting his camera to his shoulder. "Check out the door."

Jake pulled open the wooden front door, saw Jane and her photographer through the closed screen. Lens pointed right at him. No other reporters were on the porch, at least. Score one for Jake.

"Detective Brogan?" Jane said. "Couple of questions?"

They were always formal in public.

Jane had a smudge of what appeared to be dust across one cheek, her hair pulled back in a ponytail. She'd pushed up the sleeves of her white T-shirt, and held a little microphone toward him, its thin cord stretched to the max and attached to the camera.

"I'll tell you as much as I can tell you," Jake said. "Which isn't much. We have a white female, mid-thirties. The medical examiner, at this early juncture, is calling it a 'possible homicide.' That's all we can say at this time."

Jane had a funny look on her face. Wonder why? But Jake went on.

"No cause of death at this time. That's about it."

"Do you have a name of the victim?" Jane asked. "Why she was here?"

"Not at this time, Ms. Ryland," Jake said. "The Crime Scene unit will arrive soon, we'll continue our investigation. Anything else will have to come from PR at HQ."

"Any connection with the former owners?" Jane asked.

"Like I said, Ms. Ryland, any further communication

will have to come via our headquarters' public affairs office." He tried to look stern. "If you have information that you feel might aid us in the investigation, we're eager to hear it."

He paused. Knowing Jane wouldn't—couldn't—tell him anything. Although, of course, she already had. *Former owners.*

"Anything else? No?" he said. "And we're done."

"Thanks, Detective," Jane said. "As always."

He caught a wisp of a smile. He'd see her later. Alone.

"Jake!" a voice came from within the house. DeLuca appeared at the screen door, gesturing him to come closer. "When you have a minute?" he said, voice low. "Got something."

10

"**What's this all** about, Mr. Thorley?" The rye bread on Peter Hardesty's turkey sandwich was turning up at the corners, and by now, four hours after he'd opened the waxed paper, the mayo was risky. He tossed the whole thing into his trash basket, regretting the waste. Thorley, sullen, sat in the visitor chair of Hardesty's law office, running his tongue over his teeth and staring at the framed diplomas on the wall. The interview was not going well.

"Columbia Law, as you see," Peter said. "And then the Northeastern prisoners' rights program. I understand what you might have experienced down at MCI Norfolk. You were inside for—how long? Fifteen years? But you've been doing great on parole. So. I admit, I'm confused."

"Can I go?" Thorley said.

And we're having a wonderful day. Peter took off his suit jacket, draped it over the back of his chair. Stacks of rubber-banded file folders and red-brown accordion files lined the wall under his curving bay windows. Outside, the Boylston Street side of the Boston Common lawn was transformed into a multicolored expanse of college students, maybe staying for the summer, now tossing Frisbees and skateboarding on the Revolutionary War pathways.

"You can go, sure," Peter said. "But how about giving me five minutes? All I want to know—what's going on here, Mr. Thorley? Your sister is confused, upset, as you might imagine. Should we give her a call? Reassure her you're fine? She seems to have a lot of affection for you."

Some lawyers didn't care about the reality, they simply wanted to get their client off. He'd heard them say it to suspects—*don't tell me what happened. I don't want to know.* Peter preferred to work from truth, though clients didn't always tell it. Innocent or guilty. He'd be a zealous advocate, no matter what.

Thorley fidgeted in the upholstered chair, like he was trying to sit without touching it. "You know the drill. I went to the cops, confessed, bang, that's it."

"That's *not* it. I have your file, Mr. Thorley." Pulling teeth. "I can get the Carley Marie Schaefer evidence from the police. I can see if there's anything to tie the case to you. Trust me here. It'll be easier if you tell me the truth."

"It's already easy. I told them everything." Thorley cleared his throat, a sandpaper rasp. Patted his empty shirt pocket, maybe imagining cigarettes. "How many times do I have to—this is crap. Why don't you believe me? Why don't they? Don't they want to catch the guy? I'm the guy."

"They had nothing to hold you, that was why they let you go."

"I *confessed*. What the hell else do they need?"

Peter's phone rang, the bell making Thorley flinch. He let it go to voice mail. "Mr. Thorley? I have all the time in the world. But you? You don't. How about you tell me what's really going on?"

"They let him go?" Jake took a deep breath, considering. Paused at a blinking yellow light, just long enough to be legal. Hit the gas. D had just gotten off the phone with Bing Sherrey. "They let him *go*?"

"Yeah," D said. "That guy we saw in the interrogation room before they cut the mic? He was a lawyer. 'Parently he convinced Bing there wasn't enough to hold him." D shrugged. "I mighta gone the other way."

"Yeah," Jake said. "I remember Grampa—I mean, the commissioner—saying 'it's got to be someone we haven't questioned yet, Jake.' Maybe he was right. He knew this case, start to finish. Wish I could ask him about it."

Jake hit the remote, waited to see if the often-stubborn cop shop garage door would open this time.

"There's no DNA test results," Jake said as they finally drove inside, the door clanking down behind them. He pulled into a space marked HOM SQD. "It was too long ago. Thorley was inside before they pulled samples from every convicted felon like they do now. If there's even anything to compare his sample to. She wasn't sexually assaulted."

"That we know of."

"True. But that's all there is, right? What's in the evidence file?" Jake shook his head as he turned off the ignition. "Wouldn't that be a helluva thing? If we closed Lilac Sunday, after all this time? Especially now."

"You think he did it?" DeLuca opened his door.

"Doesn't matter what I think," Jake said. "Only matters what's true."

Jake punched the button for the ancient elevator. The gears ground into place, the cables whirring.

"You handle the lab," Jake said. "Okay? See what they make of that two-by-four you found in the closet. Good thing the news conference was over by then, right? I can imagine the headline if—well, we lucked out on that one. And check the bank records. See who owned that house."

The elevator door slid open. The inside walls were

plastered with taped-up handwritten posters for a retirement thing at Doyle's—someone had magic-markered
pointy black devil horns on the short-timer's face—a
pitch for supplemental health insurance, and a union
meeting at the post in Southie.

"Never a dull moment," Jake said.

"You wish," D said. "One of these days that retirement
poster's gonna be for me. Then you'll be sorry."

"No doubt," Jake said. He pushed 4. Nothing. He
pushed again, then jabbed the close button. "I'll call on
Mornay and Weldon. See if they're missing an agent. I
don't want to e-mail them a crime scene photo—there's
no shot where she doesn't look dead. It's after five, so
maybe someone hasn't come back to the office who
should have."

Jake's cell trilled from his jacket pocket.

"Brogan." He paused, smiling. "Well, you too, Nate.
Here I thought you'd gone all big-shot doctor on me. Not
calling back. Or maybe you're afraid I'll have a case you
can't—damn it." Jake looked at his phone. The line was
dead. "This freaking elevator."

He hit REDIAL. Nothing. "I'll call when we get upstairs."

"Who is this guy, anyway?" D said. "Nate Frasca?"

The doors opened onto the gray and steel hallway. "In-
stitutional neutral," Jane always called it. A rank of
closed doors. At the end of the hall, an ell of double-tall
windows fronted the Homicide squad offices. Jake could
smell the coffee.

"Nate Frasca? He's gonna tell me if Gordon Thorley
is Lilac Sunday," Jake said.

11

"See, Jane? I told you it would work out. It's all about trust, right? I'd never steer you wrong." Victoria Marcotte took a sip from a sleek white china mug, leaving behind a faint trace of her trademark red lipstick. She wiped away the color with a manicured thumb. "Jane? You have—someone has to tell you—a smudge on your face."

The city editor touched her own sculpted cheek, illustrating where Jane's was dirty. Marcotte was only ten years older than she was, but the editor had developed a kind of destabilization technique. If an employee was uncomfortable, they were vulnerable. Jane tried not to let it get to her.

She wiped at her face with two fingers. "Off?"

"You can fix it later." Marcotte crossed her legs, leaned back in her swivel chair. The screensaver photo of fireworks on her desktop computer monitor clicked to black. "You're not on TV. Anyway, Jane. Sit sit sit. What've you got for me?"

Jane perched on the edge of her boss's nubby navy sofa, sinking so low into the cushions she had to look up at Marcotte. Jane shifted, sat up as straight as she could. Marcotte probably had a low couch on purpose, another technique to make visitors feel small. Small, and with a dirty face.

Jane cleared her throat, regrouping. "'Possible homicide.' Luckily for us."

"Luckily?" Marcotte raised an eyebrow.

Why even try. "Anyway. Cops say they don't have an ID yet. I'll stay on it. Thing is—"

The cell on Marcotte's desk pinged, and she sneaked a look at it. Then back at Jane. "Sorry. You were saying?"

"Thing is," Jane went on, "I called the Sandovals— they're the ones who owned the house before the foreclosure. Remember? They were both out doing errands, they told me, all morning. Weren't at the house, hadn't been at the house. It isn't their house anymore, after all."

Marcotte stood, smoothing her black suit jacket over a narrow black leather skirt. "You could put them in your story, though, Jane. I mean, it's good headline, a murder in their house, it's—" She nodded, seeming to agree with herself. "It's buzzable. It's water cooler. It's multimedia. Did you ask if they knew the victim?"

"Knew the victim?" Jane didn't mean to be an echo, but no, she hadn't. Could the Sandovals know the victim? "Ah, no. I didn't ask."

Jane suddenly felt itchy in her ratty T-shirt and possibly too-short skirt. Her feet were grimy in her flats. Maybe she should have checked on that. But how?

"We don't know the person's name, remember, and—"

"Did they say *anything* quotable?"

"Well, I wrote down a phrase or two. They had no idea, they said, about any of it. The police hadn't called them."

"So we broke the story to the grieving family. Fabulous."

"Grieving?" *Fabulous?*

"Yes. Grieving." Marcotte held up her hands, as if bracketing a headline. "*Register* reporter breaks news of real housing crisis—murder in their own home. Hang on, let me think."

Marcotte sat at her desk, lips clamped shut, eyes narrowing.

"Ah," Jane began. That was outrageous. Not to mention incorrect. "Let me call the police, okay? See if they have anything new? And we can go from there."

"That's old school, Jane," Marcotte said. "We have an online edition. We go with it as we get it. When you get more details later, terrific. We'll use that, too. Figure out something the—what did you say their name was? Samovar?"

"Sando—"

"Figure out *something* they said. Make it work. We only need a paragraph or two. You gave them the news? That's hot."

Jane stood in the doorway, hearing the rumble of the *Register*'s rattletrap elevator down the hall, the clatter of the air-conditioning system struggling to cool off a newsroom of overworked—and over-worried—reporters and editors. The *Register* had laid off more than its share in recent days, staffers fearing more cuts at any moment. Newspapers were endangered. Worse than endangered. Jane privately thought editors like Marcotte were the reason why.

"Suburban—no. Neighborhood Nightmare, we'll call it," Marcotte said. "Go. Write. You have fifteen minutes. Then we're going to press."

"It's early for dinner," Aaron was saying. He'd convinced her—Lizzie still couldn't believe it—to leave the bank early and join him for a stroll across the Public Garden.

She'd actually done it. Told Stephanie she had a meeting, and just—left her linen jacket over her chair back. In her sleeveless dress and little patent heels, she walked through the revolving door and into the May sunshine, out Tremont Street and past the Parker House and the cemetery where Mother Goose was buried.

Free. And off the radar.

Aaron was waiting for her, as he'd promised, by the pushcarts outside the Park Street T stop. He'd handed her a big twisty pretzel, salt crumbling from its warm edges. They'd shared it, walking along the winding paths, the sun gleaming on the gold dome of the State House; the trees, some from hundreds of years ago, in full leaf above them. The last of the tulips, gasping in the heat, spread yellow and crimson across the green.

"Pretty, huh?" she'd said.

"Yes, you are," Aaron had said.

And then, on the lacquered park bench, he'd draped his arm across her shoulders. She felt the starched oxford cloth of his shirt against her bare arm.

Aaron threw a pretzel piece, landed it at the edge of the pond. Two fat mallards lurched out of the water to get it, ruffling their feathers, green heads and purple-slashed wings shiny in the last of the late afternoon sunshine.

"Be great not to have to work, wouldn't it?" Aaron tossed another piece at the ducks. "Sit in the sun and do nothing? Have someone feed you? To be that rich."

"Mmm," Lizzie said. She'd never thought about being "rich." Growing up the way she had, her father and all. "I suppose I'm just as interested in helping other people with their finances."

"Like the Iantoscas?" Aaron said. "Guess they got lucky."

Lizzie's heart flipped, just for a second, wondering. Was Aaron checking on her? Had someone gotten wind of what she was doing? She shook her head, trying to dismiss her silly fear. No way. She'd been careful.

"What?" Aaron said. "Why are you shaking your head?"

"Oh, nothing." She hadn't realized she'd actually done it. "Work."

"So, the Iantoscas? I'm only asking because their house was in my portfolio." He shrugged. "Although it won't be there anymore."

"Less work for you, right?" The last of her pretzel devoured, Lizzie didn't exactly know what to do with her hands. She folded them in her lap, pretended the parade of ducks was fascinating.

"Any other accounts suddenly come into cash, that you know of?" Aaron turned toward her. Taking his arm away.

It felt like the sun had gone behind a cloud. She looked up. It hadn't.

"You know, Aaron, we're not supposed to talk about this."

"You goofball." Aaron poked her in the arm. "We're both bank employees. It's not like you're chitchatting with someone in a bar. Right?"

He was right. She supposed. "Um . . ."

"If I came to your office, made an appointment, sat in one of these fancy new chairs, you could tell me all about it, right?" He raised one eyebrow, challenging. Then shrugged. "Listen, the spreadsheets'll get to me sooner or later. I was hoping it wouldn't be later. But I'll be fine. I can handle it."

He stood, wiping the seat of his pants. He seemed disappointed with her. She could tell.

She didn't want this to be over. Didn't want to overanalyze, like she always did, make too much of it. Besides, he'd seemed interested in her even before all this Iantosca stuff. He hadn't known about it when he approached her by the vault that day. Or when he came to her office this afternoon. He'd come to see *her*. Given her his photo, a strange—but nice—surprise. But now, if he was suspicious of her bookkeeping—he probably wasn't, but *if*—it might be revealing to see where he was going with this. To be safe. To be careful.

"Wait, Aaron?" If he was playing a game, she could do that, too. She could find out what she wanted, and all the while letting him think he was finding what *he* wanted. Aaron clearly wanted something. What?

He stopped, turned to her.

Sometimes people were exactly like numbers. You just had to understand them to control them. With great risk comes great reward. Her father used to tell her that.

She stood, wiping the pretzel salt from her hands. The ducks, startled, plopped back into the pond and paddled furiously away from shore. She smoothed her dress, and smiled. "Aaron? What is it you want to know?"

12

"**I am so** sorry for your loss," Jake said. "Let me assure you, sir, we're focused on finding who killed Shandra. As much as you are." Jake had shown his gold badge and creds to Brian Turiello, the office manager of Mornay and Weldon Realty, at the door of their South Boston office. It had taken Jake about thirty seconds on the M&W website to pick out the postage-stamp-sized business portrait of a much more alive Shandra Newbury. At least Jake didn't have to show the guy the crime scene photos. That was never pleasant. Not that murder was ever pleasant.

They were in Turiello's corner office, the walls patchworked with engraved plaques and awards and photos of Turiello smiling next to other white guys in suits. A gold shovel, attached to the wall by two metal brackets, had the place of honor. A man who knew his place in the world. On the golf course, if Jake read it right. Now his world had been shaken a little. More than a little.

"She was an up-and-comer." Turiello lowered himself into a padded swivel chair, his navy blazer flapping open, elbows on the glass-topped desk. He wore a lapel pin like Shandra's. He looked over Jake's shoulder, narrowing his eyes at the open doorway to his office. Jake had seen it a million times, the victim's acquaintances not really believing the person was dead. Almost expecting them to come through the door. "Such a talented agent. Aggressive. But smart-aggressive. Always out getting new listings. She loves—loved—the business."

Jake nodded, allowing Turiello to process the bad news. The problem with law enforcement, there was no time for grief. Jake's job was about moving fast. Carefully, but fast. Grief took time. It was a balance.

Jake waited. Sometimes you had to wait. The air conditioner kicked on.

"Where did it happen?" Turiello finally asked.

"Forty-two Waverly Road." Did Turiello know the place? Jake could imagine it, this semi-good-looking— Jake checked the man's ring finger—not married, real estate mogul type, meets the up-and-coming wannabe, they tangle, she refuses, he lets her have it. An accident, maybe. It could happen.

Jake waited.

"It was my fault." Turiello looked out the window at a T bus chugging by.

"Fault?" Jake had grabbed a little spiral notebook from his desk at HQ. He often used his cell phone to take notes, but here it seemed disrespectful. Now, while Turiello wasn't looking, he flipped the notebook open, found a blank page. "Fault" was an odd word. This was a big day for confessions. "Sir?"

"I'd put her in charge of our foreclosures. That's why she was there." Turiello talked out the window, shrugging. Turned back to Jake. "Not my *fault*, I suppose. Not really. There was nothing that should have been . . . untoward about that site visit. Standard."

"Anyone go with her?" Jake asked.

"Not that I know of."

"Was she meeting someone?" Jake stood, pointed toward a bullpen of desks and telephones in the front of the office space, empty. He checked his watch. After six.

No employees or colleagues here to give him any answers. "Which was her desk? Does she have a computer?
We'll need to look at that. And sir? Do you recognize the
name Sandoval? Elliot Sandoval?"

Turiello stood, running two fingers down the front of
his elaborate tie, a grid of red houses on a navy background. "She does have a computer, but it's password
protected. Has to be, all that personal information we
gather and process. Financials, mortgage application,
credit referrals. We'll have to get our IT guy get into it."

"Thanks," Jake said. Easy. They'd find her clients, find
who she'd planned to meet this morning, or last night—
and case closed. He could get back to Nate Frasca and
Lilac Sunday. "Her appointment book as well, sir."

Turiello still fidgeted with his tie, opened the collar
button. "Detective? I'm a branch. The big guys at headquarters call the shots." He scratched at his neck, making thin red lines across this throat. "To give you open
season on Shandra's computer data and paper files? I'm
not authorized to do that."

Jake had a few choices. Push, which might be futile. Get
a warrant, which would certainly take a while. Negotiate.
Or a little of all three.

"I understand." Jake waved his notebook at the
phone. "Make your phone call, get the show on the road.
Meanwhile, show me the details on the house at forty-two
Waverly. That, at least, is public. Correct?"

Turiello didn't look happy. But hey. It wasn't a happy
time. It was murder.

Time for the push. "I can get a warrant, of course. And
will." Jake smiled, barely. "But what if I were in the market for a house?"

He could almost see the office manger weighing the
options. Looking out the window. Clearing his throat.
Probably wishing all of this, including Jake, would vanish.

It wouldn't.

"Yeah," Jake said. "I know. So show me. For Shandr. Newbury's sake."

"Bless you," Jane said. She stopped at the opening to her cubicle, watching the woman at the other desk inside yank a tissue out of a flowered box and then sneeze again. "Are you sick?"

If Chrystal Peralta had a cold, Jane was seriously not going to sit down at her own desk. The fabric-walled cubicle they shared was crowded enough without adding cold germs. On a regular day Chrystal took up more than half the space, and it wasn't just her hair. Chrystal's side of the cube was practically a yard sale, a mishmash of promotional loot snagged from various feature stories she'd covered. Coffee mugs with bank logos, mouse pads with inspirational slogans. Access passes from junkets, meetings, and trade shows, each encased in shiny plastic and dangling from a slogan-bearing lanyard, dangled like holiday decorations from her half of the bulletin board. Every pen in her A&A Bank holder probably had someone's company's phone number on it.

Jane's "half" of the bulletin board had a snapshot of a sunset in Nantucket, a souvenir from a political scandal she'd uncovered, and a goofy-toothed school picture of a little boy, now happily adopted, from her investigation on foster care. She'd saved a space for a new picture of a pink-sanded beach. A photo not yet taken.

Chrystal sneezed again.

"Sick? Big time." Chrystal wadded a shredded mass of tissues and tossed them toward the tissue-filled wastebasket. Jane cringed, dodging. "I'm not contagious, though. Probably."

If Chrystal was sick, Jane was bailing. She absolutely could not afford to be sick this weekend. No sneezing, no runny nose, no puffy eyes, no—she smiled at the mental picture—snoring. Jane backed into the hall. "I'll work down in the conference room, okay? I only have fifteen minutes—fewer now, actually—to bang out this story."

"It's probably allergies," Chrystal went on as if Jane hadn't said anything.

"No, really. You stay here. Feel better." *Twelve minutes.* Jane almost ran down the hall, yanked open the heavy glass conference room door, hit the mouse to wake up the computer on the mahogany table. Nothing. Tried it again. Nothing. On the fritz. Again?

Eleven minutes. Damn. She raced back to her own desk, swiveled into her chair, hit her own mouse. "Hey Chrystal, I'm back, gotta do this."

Chrystal sneezed.

Maybe Jane could avoid breathing for the next ten minutes. She pulled up her story page, typed almost without thinking. *Former owners of a now-foreclosed home in Hyde Park were shocked this afternoon when they were told police had discovered the body of a potential homicide victim in a second-floor bedroom.*

The cursor blinked at her, taunting, as she tried to figure out what to say next. Victoria was insisting on a story about the Sandovals' reaction, but they really hadn't reacted. *Two paragraphs,* she told herself. *Everything doesn't have to be Pulitzer material.* She dug into her bag, pulled out her notebook, flipped the pages.

"Damn," she said.

"What?" Chrystal's chair squeaked as she turned to her.

"Marcotte wants quotes, I got nothing."

"Make something up," Chrystal said.

"Right, great idea," Jane said, cocked an eyebrow. "Sure would make life easier." Back to the keyboard.

The Sandovals' eviction was finalized last week, ac cording to Suffolk County Registry of Deeds documents

At least she had those.

Police say they have not identified the victim, nor has the medical examiner determined the cause of death.

The cursor blinked, silently demanding, as Jane struggled. Seconds ticked by. She grabbed her cell phone. Punched in a number. Prayed.

"Mr. Sandoval? This is Jane Ryland at the *Register.*" Thank goodness. He was home. She paused, knowing she had to be polite. She was on deadline, but she was asking about a murder. "Fine, and I'm so sorry to bother you, but I have to write my story about what happened this afternoon at your . . . on Waverly Road. And I wonder—"

Elliot Sandoval interrupted, talking faster than she'd ever heard him.

"What?" Jane said. "When? Then what?"

Sandoval answered, still at top speed.

"Mr. Sandoval? Sir?" Jane tucked the phone between her shoulder and cheek, and turned back to her computer keyboard. Sandoval barely took a breath between words. "Excuse me? Sir? Did they give you a name?"

Five minutes.

Plenty of time.

13

The phone rang just as Peter stepped toward his office door. Five o'clock. Officially, the law firm was closed for the day. But the phone on Nicole's reception desk rang again, insistent. Thorley didn't have that number. This was someone else.

Through his tenth-floor window Peter could see happy people, normal people, a couple feeding the ducks, throwing bread crumbs or something at the mallards gathered in the pond. A sunset swan boat glided by, full of tourists, probably, and people who didn't have to think about cold-case murders of high school girls and the misguided men who were inexplicably confessing to the crimes.

Why would Thorley confess? One easy answer. He was guilty. Fine with Peter—he'd represented worse. Even the guilty ones needed lawyers. Especially the guilty ones.

The phone rang again.

Peter blew out a breath, remembering the lawyer's prayer. This phone call might bring him his case-of-all-cases. Tobacco, or lead paint, or a new Dalkon Shield. Some hideously widespread but provable injustice, or a victim with a stash of incriminating e-mails, finally ready to blow the whistle on some big-bucks government corruption. If Peter ignored the phone, the desperate plaintiff would call someone else, and someone else would get the glory. And the 30 percent.

His assistant, Nicole, was long gone, headed out at close of business to do whatever paralegal slash secretaries did on a Boston spring evening, sail or skateboard or dance or drink a pink cocktail with friends. Defeated, Peter picked up the phone.

"Hardesty and Colaneri," he said. Too late to turn back now. "This is Peter Hardesty."

He paused, listening to the person on the other end.

"Yes," he said. He put down his briefcase. Lowered himself into his desk chair. Grabbed a yellow pad. Clicked open a pen. Still listening. "Yes."

"I'm telling you, Jake, it's a slam dunk." D was still trying to convince him, had not stopped trying for the past few miles, that the person they were about to go visit was Shandra Newbury's killer. Jake stopped at a red light, almost tuning D out. Sure, that would create a certain symmetry about the whole thing. Irony, too, since the suspect was right out of Mornay and Weldon's own real estate listings.

"Do me a favor, D." Jake turned onto Olivet Street, then onto Champlain. "Look for number four-twenty-five. Then try to stay a little objective. Maybe the guy's innocent, that ever cross your mind?"

"Oh, mos' def," D said. "He's innocent, and so is Gordon Thorley. Everybody's innocent. It's a wonder we still have our jobs, with all those innocent people out there."

"It's only one day until your vacation, D." Jake pretended to be sympathetic. "Once you and Kat hit one of those sandy beaches, all your pent-up hostility will vanish. You'll be better when you get back."

"There it is." D pointed. "Tan siding, dead grass. Crappy pickup truck in the driveway. Bad guy inside."

"We'll see." Jake eased the unmarked cruiser to the curb, slid into a just-barely-legal spot north of the fire hydrant. A few random kids sauntered up the sidewalk, baseball caps backward, shapeless T-shirts, skateboards under their arms. Most driveways had cars, nothing fancy. Middle class, lower, seemed like. Struggling strips of gardens, homeowners clearly losing the battle with their yellowing lawns. Someone was grilling out, Jake could smell the charcoal. "He didn't bolt after you called. That's a not-guilty, right there."

"Maybe it's the wife." D opened his door, eased onto the sidewalk.

Just past seven, and it was still as sweltering as it had been this noon on Waverly Road. *Jane*, he thought. He'd see her again in less than two hours, if all went as planned. This time, by themselves. They could talk without using code.

"Doesn't take much to clobber someone with a two-by-four," D was saying. They crossed the narrow empty street, dodged a couple of potholes, headed for the modest ranch house. Curtains hid the small front windows. They couldn't see inside, only that at least one light was on. "I might not have left it there, just saying. But who said killers are smart. We'll know more soon as Crime Scene takes over."

"And the wife's motive would be what?" Jake asked. "Buyer's remorse? Or how about jealousy? Because her husband and Shandra Newbury were—"

"Hey, check out the truck," D interrupted. "There in the back."

Jake took two steps. Saw what D was talking about. A stack of two-by-fours. "We just called him, you know? Ten minutes ago. Not enough time to get rid of them."

They stopped, looked at each other.

"Plain sight," Jake said.

"Am I right, or am I right?" D said.

* * *

Aaron would pay for this dinner, probably in more ways than one. The Ritz Café was a splurge, all white napkins and shiny glass plates. It was the Taj now, whatever. Question was, what would be the return on his investment?

As Lizzie talked nonstop, he watched her lift the circles of red onions from her overpriced hamburger, then ferry them with a fork to her empty bread plate. Then she removed her hamburger from the sesame-seeded bun, and put the bun on the side plate, too. Lizzie sure seemed at home here, handing the waiter her scorned onions and rejected bun. Aaron took a bite of his well-done with cheddar, pretending to listen to whatever she was talking about.

At least she was drinking her wine.

The Iantosca situation churned though his mind as Lizzie continued her life saga. She was into her college business classes now, her "epiphany" from some econ professor about "banking for the people" and how the "balance of the economy" needed to be "reset" and "recalculated" to include customer service. All Aaron could think about was how to make his deal work. He had to find a solution.

"That's cool," he replied. Whatever she'd said. He dunked a seasoned fry into his pool of ketchup, watched Lizzie finally take a bite of burger—with her fork—and pulled out a phrase he'd heard Ack use. "Did your class discuss 'informational silos of customer data'?"

Lizzie's eyes widened. "It *did*, how amazing you know about it, yes, it did, and . . ." And she was off again.

It was shortsighted of him to worry about the Iantoscas. So what if their house was off the foreclosure list? Maybe he could even convince Ackerman to be happy about that info. They rarely talked, of course, and never e-mailed or texted, that was way too risky. But next time they connected, Aaron could easily make it seem like he had the scoop on the incoming properties. The real inside dope.

He nodded, agreeing with himself.

"I'm so happy you agree," Lizzie said, watching him. "Most people don't even think about how banks should work for the customers, not the customers for the banks."

"Hmm," he said. Whatever. And if he *was* getting the scoop, maybe this whole Lizzie thing was even more potentially productive than he'd initially imagined. He could definitely envision the well-connected Lizzie as information pipeline.

Another French fry. It made a gully as he drew it slowly through the ketchup. He did it again, watching the red separate, then move together again, seamless. As if he'd never touched it.

Now she was yapping about her first day at the bank. Interesting, she hadn't mentioned her father at all, which seemed—well, maybe it was too early. He'd have to feel her out on that. A good salesman knew when to push. And when to wait. He was selling tonight, that was for sure.

His client-line cell phone buzzed on the table beside him, vibrating on the white tablecloth.

"You need to get that?" Lizzie asked.

He did need to, damn it, but now was not the time to talk to clients. "Not at all," he lied. He couldn't let this deal progress, and that was certainly what these calls were about, but he couldn't get rid of her long enough to stop it. *Bathroom,* he thought. *If they call again, I'll just excuse myself.*

"I feel bad, going on like this." Lizzie blinked at him, eyed his phone. "When you're obviously needed. By . . . someone."

"No, no, nothing's going to interrupt us tonight."

Aaron had about two swigs of his beer left. He'd need a refill. "This is Lizzie night. Correct?"

She took a sip of her twelve-dollar-a-glass rosé. She could have all she wanted. He wasn't sure exactly what would happen later, but a two-glass-of-wine girl was more likely to be agreeable to whatever it was. Outside, he could see, it was turning dark, headlights and streetlights already on, Boston's date-nighters heading out of the parking garage across the street. Half the people wore Red Sox caps. Still hope for the baseball season. This was only May.

Lizzie pointed to his vibrating cell phone with her fork. "Come on, Aaron. I can handle you taking a phone call." She stood, plopping her crumpled napkin on the table. "I'm going to the ladies' room. And I'll have another glass of wine."

She hadn't taken two steps away when he grabbed his cell and hit answer.

"This is Allen," he said, keeping his voice low. You never knew.

Aaron waited, listening. It always killed him to say his fake name. If he ever screwed up—which a couple times he actually had—he always pretended the other guy had heard him wrong.

"Thanks for calling back," he said. "Listen, the house on Nordstrand Boulevard isn't going to work out. There were some undisclosed problems. It happens. Lucky for you, I've got a perfect replacement. You'll be even happier with it, it exactly suits your needs, and I can show you tomorrow afternoon. You'll be the first."

He paused, as his client interrupted, yammering a whole list of questions, ending with a request. "Morning?" Aaron thought fast, figuring how he could pull this off. "Tomorrow at nine A.M.? Well, sure. Can do. The address is . . ."

Lizzie. Was on her way back.

"Listen," he said, smiling across the room. Lizzie

waved. "I'll text you the address. Yes, furnished. See you tomorrow at nine."

He clicked off as Lizzie arrived. He stood, pulled out her chair.

"Got any plans for the rest of the evening?" he said.

Lizzie looked at him from under her eyelashes. Two spots of red appeared on her cheeks, and she fiddled with a hoop earring. She'd combed her hair, Aaron saw, freshened her lipstick.

Lizzie sat down, took a sip of wine. "What do you mean, plans?"

"How'd you like to go look at a house?" He pulled his chair closer to hers.

"A—?"

"House. House," Aaron said, teasing. "You ever really see the ones in those portfolios of yours? You stay in your office all the time, adding and subtracting and doing amortizations or whatever. People live in *those* houses, all good. But the houses I handle? They're empty, you know? Furnished, but empty."

He raised an eyebrow, smiled at her. "We could have the place all to ourselves."

Lizzie tilted her head, as if she were calculating. "Isn't that . . . ?"

"Isn't that what? I have the keys, sweetheart." Aaron picked up his beer, considering his strategy one last time. No harm in taking her, was there? It might even be worthwhile. "I'm the only one who legally *does* have access. You *ought* to see them, if you're going to be handling mortgages. You know? To you, it's all on paper, all numbers, all theoretical. To me it's—"

Aaron eyed his glass, drained the last of his beer.

"To me it's—*real* estate. Know what I mean? Real."

Lizzie picked up her wine, stared at the pink liquid.

"Finish up," Aaron said. "Then you and I are going to have an adventure. It's Lizzie night, remember?"

14

"The name on the mailbox is 'Michaelidis,' " D said.

"Yup, that's the one. The sister-in-law." Jake punched the black-button doorbell. Three chimes echoed inside. He tried again. Chimes. Dented screen door over gray-painted front door. He cocked his head, listening.

"Someone's coming." He nodded, mentally checking— badge, weapon, radio, plan. "Ready?"

The gray door opened. A beefy guy, late twenties, sandy mustache and hair to match, stood behind the screen. Hard to read his face, shimmering through the small-gauge mesh. Jake assessed the muscles under the man's Red Sox T-shirt, saw one hammy hand clench into a fist at his side. His other hand held an open bottle of IPA.

"Elliot Sandoval?" Jake held his gold badge up against the screen. A radio or TV played in a back room. A left-over dinnertime smell, baked beans maybe, mixed with the fragrance of Sandoval's beer. "I'm Detective—"

"Yeah. I figured. The one who called." Sandoval did not open the screen. "You need to call my lawyer."

"About what?" D took one step forward. "I'm Detective Brogan's partner, Paul DeLuca. We have a couple of quick questions, hoping you can help us out. No pressure. Happy to call your lawyer."

D looked at Jake. Then back at Sandoval. "Of course, sir, that'll make it somewhat more complicated."

"True," Jake said. "Then we'd have to go down to the station, sign you in. It's more—shall we say—formal. We're here to make your life easier. But your call."

Sandoval didn't move. Didn't slam the door. Stood there. Jake could ask anything at this point, he'd be within his rights. Lawyer didn't mean shit if the guy wasn't under arrest. The logical option was go for it.

"Sir?" Jake changed tactics. "We need your help on a very sad case. As we told you, there was possible homicide at forty-two Waverly Road. You're familiar with that address, of course. We know you don't live there anymore, but—"

"Honey?" A smaller figure joined Sandoval at the door, tucked in behind him, only shoulder-length curly hair and pink T-shirt visible. "The lawyer said—"

The door opened, Sandoval moving the woman—his wife? pregnant wife, if that's who she was—out of the way with the palm of his hand. She stopped talking. D and Jake stepped inside, the narrow foyer leading to a living room on one side, one table light on, TV on mute, and on the other side, a hallway. Jake could see to the half-open door at the end of the hall, the glow from a TV showing behind it.

"You told me about that on the phone. The possible homicide." Sandoval didn't offer them a seat. "Look. I got nothing for you. I'd help you if I could, you know? But like I said on the phone, we haven't been at that house for weeks."

Be that as it may. They were inside, *invited* inside, meaning Jake could now proceed on steadier legal ground. "She was killed with a two-by-four, we believe, Mr. Sandoval. Exactly like those you have in the back of your truck, out there in the driveway. That *is* your truck,

I assume." Jake eyed the pregnant woman, who was quickly moving lower on his "possibly guilty" list. "Or is it yours?"

"It's—this is my wife, MaryLou." Sandoval stepped away from them and put his beer onto the glass-topped coffee table, next to an open do-it-yourself magazine and a catalog from some baby store. "As you can see, she's—and you know what? The lawyer's right. I don't have to tell you anything."

"We can easily run the plate and registration. Sir." Jake eased a few steps into the living room, taking up the space Sandoval had vacated. "Police investigation one-oh-one."

"Listen. I'm in construction." Sandoval's wide forehead furrowed, and he looked at Jake, then at D, then back at Jake, as if searching for an ally. "All two-by-fours are exactly alike. The ones in my truck don't prove a thing."

His wife let out a sound, a whimper or a sigh, and sagged to the dark cushion of the low-slung couch, placing one hand on the round of her belly. Cute girl. No makeup. From her frown, obviously worried. As well she should be. A husband who could be on trial for murder and a baby on the way was not an optimum combination.

"Elliot!" MaryLou Sandoval whispered. Jake could see her struggle for composure, her fingers touching the sides of her forehead. "Remember. The lawyer told you—"

"I don't care what the lawyer said. Time the hell *out*." Elliot Sandoval turned to his wife, making the time-out sign with his hands. "If I had hit someone with a two-by-four, which, Mar, I most definitely did *not*—do you think I would have left all the other damn two-by-fours in the truck? In my driveway? Knowing the cops were on the way?"

He turned back to Jake. "You called me. Right? There'd have been plenty of time for me to—"

"Aren't you even interested in the victim's name?" Jake cut off the guy's excuses, exchanged a glance with DeLuca.

Where had Sandoval been, time of the murder? Not that they exactly knew when that was. Was MaryLou his only alibi? Maybe the stay-at-home wife was now putting two and two together, Jake thought. Two by *four*.

"You know, Detective Brogan, it does seem odd." DeLuca spoke to Jake, as if Sandoval wasn't there. "Doesn't it seem odd? I'da thought he'd wanna know."

D turned back to Sandoval, as if begrudgingly acknowledging his presence. "*If* you really were interested in helping, that is."

They hadn't told Sandoval the victim's name, on purpose, to see how he'd react when they sprang it on him. That Sandoval hadn't asked did seem odd. Unlikely. Suspicious. Jake mentally shrugged. Or—not.

"I had nothing to do with it. Why would I ask?" Sandoval took a couple of steps backward, eyed the door. "It's not our house anymore. Why does it matter if I know? Why would I need to know?"

"El, you've gotta be quiet." MaryLou used the edge of the coffee table to pull herself to her feet. She swayed a moment, catching her balance. "This isn't about us, Officers, and I can't understand why my husband is—"

The doorbell rang, the bing-bong chimes now echoing inside the house.

"Thank heaven." MaryLou turned toward the door, tucking her hair behind her ears. "Now maybe you'll finally stop talking."

Sandoval put up a hand, a command. "You sit."

She sat, the couch cushions adjusting to her weight.

The doorbell chimed again.

"You expecting someone?" Jake said.

* * *

It was way too early to pack. Four days until the weekend. *Their* weekend. Finally. Jane smiled as she hoisted her black roller bag from the shelf of the front hall closet. It was kind of delicious, choosing what to wear for such an occasion. She and Jake were going for it. Flying out Friday, after the *Register*'s deadline. They'd each leave from work as usual, in their own cars, meet at the airport.

Silly. But necessary.

The Cape was too risky, too public, they'd decided, everyone from Boston headed south on the weekend. Even this early in the year, from Falmouth to P-town, it'd be crowded. But they'd found a not-too-expensive Boston to Bermuda flight. The tickets were purchased, and the hotel booked. Even at Logan Airport they could pretend they weren't traveling together.

No more stalling. It had been six months, eight? They'd danced around this. Dated others, briefly and unenthusiastically. Jane, at least, always testing the unfortunate candidate against the template of Jake: his brain, his compassion, his sense of humor. And his body. The challenger always lost, so often Jane felt guilty about continuing. This weekend, she and Jake were—Jane smiled again, or maybe she hadn't stopped—going for it. It was too difficult, they'd decided, always living in a created reality. Sneaking around was unpleasant. Distressing. Tiring.

But what could possibly happen to change their situation? Jane couldn't imagine, now, giving up her job at the paper. She was a journalist, after all, finally back on her feet after the horrible lawsuit. Was she supposed to change careers? And Jake—his grandfather had been police commissioner. Even Jake's father—so he'd said—teased Jake about his "blue" blood. Jake's mother was the actual blue blood. It would be pretty fascinating when she and Priscilla Dellacort Brogan finally met.

Jake would never meet Jane's mom. She sighed, feeling that familiar wave of memory.

"Hi, Mom," she said it out loud, as always, looking at the ceiling. "Missing you. You'd like him."

So. It was finally going to happen. Jake and Jane. They'd cross this bridge first. Then, if necessary, cross the next one.

Coda jumped into her open suitcase, curling up in the middle with her tail carefully wrapped, depositing calico cat hair on the lining and using one paw to bat the crinkling tissue paper Jane always used. Coda would be fine over the weekend, with a stash of cat toys and water, and fed twice a day by the super's son, Eli, from upstairs. Jane used to pay Eli in LEGOs, the currency of nine-year-olds. This year, turned a "grown-up" ten in March, he wanted scary chapter books, which Jane was happy to provide.

She extricated Coda from the suitcase, a shred of tissue dangling from one still-extended claw, and closed the top. Jane sat beside it on her bed, and Coda pounced onto her lap.

"Hey, Codarita." She stroked the cat, head to tail. "Bermuda. Don't tell."

The glowing green numbers of the clock on her nightstand clicked ahead. After eight thirty? Jane frowned. Her cell phone was in her yoga pants pocket, silent. Not even a text. Where was Jake?

Coda settled in, purring, nudging Jane with a paw. "I know, cat," she said. "I'd like some attention, too."

She *had* gotten attention for today's story. Victoria Marcotte herself arrived at Jane's cubicle door, giving an elegant thumbs-up to Jane's scoop on the Sandovals' phone call from the police.

Jane stood up so fast Coda hopped to the floor, gave Jane a reproachful sneer, and scuttled under the bed.

At the Sandovals'. That's where Jake probably was.

That'd make for some stimulating beach-blanket discussion.

You suspect Elliot Sandoval of murder? she'd ask.

No comment, he'd say.

But Elliot Sandoval wouldn't—I mean, why would you suspect—did you arrest him? she'd ask.

Jane, he'd say. We agreed. No work talk, no cop shop details, no newsroom stuff, no exchange of information and no speculation. Just two—

—people on a pink sandy beach, she'd say. Pretending to agree.

Because all the while she'd be wondering if she was missing a story.

She opened her suitcase again, reassuring herself. Today was only Monday. Maybe whatever was going to happen would have already happened by Friday, and they could take off into the sunset—well, okay, they'd be flying east, but she knew what she meant. One day at a time.

Maybe by Friday, they'd have all the answers. Jake's case solved, her story written. No need to worry about all that now.

15

"Game freakin' over," DeLuca whispered.

Jake nodded. DeLuca was right. They were both watching Elliot Sandoval confer with the man who'd just arrived.

Rumpled hair, rumpled jacket, briefcase, and big-shot attitude. Smart of the Sandovals to get a lawyer.

Still at the doorway they whispered, heads almost touching, Sandoval pointing to him and D. The lawyer shook his head, slowly, clearly unhappy. The wife sat on the couch, chewing gum, watching.

The new arrival was the same man who'd shown up at the cop shop to see Gordon Thorley. Dispatch had sent Jake and D to Waverly Road, and when they got back to HQ, a snarling Bing Sherrey told them of Thorley's release. By then, Jake was focusing on their current murder, not the twenty-year-old one. But this guy had been in the interrogation room, no question.

Lawyer. Not the best news. But not necessarily game over.

"I'm Peter Hardesty, gentlemen." The man turned to them. "*Detectives,* I should say. Which makes it all the more essential for you to understand that Mr. Sandoval here is my client. Correct, Elliot?"

Sandoval nodded, ruining Jake's day. Even more.

"Fancy meeting you here." DeLuca rolled his eyes, not even attempting to disguise it.

"Fancy?" Hardesty seemed confused. "Here?"

"Nothing," Jake said. He gave D a "shut up" look. Hardesty had no idea they'd been watching and listening, through the one-way glass, during the Thorley interrogation. No need to let this guy in on that bit of intel right now. If they were destined to meet on the Confessor case as well, they could all cross that legal bridge when they came to it.

"However," Jake continued, by-the-book, "your client is not under arrest in the forty-two Waverly Road homicide. Mr. Sandoval, is there a reason you need a lawyer?"

"If you got nothing to hide," DeLuca added, "no reason to shell out big bucks for a high-priced—"

"If I'm not a suspect?" Elliot Sandoval took a step forward, a bluster of red starting at his thick neck, the color creeping up his jaw and blotching his cheeks. Even the scalp under his close-cut hair was turning red. "Why are you here?"

The AC kicked on, a dim mechanical roar. From down the hallway, a voice called out. "Who's here?"

"Nobody, Sis," Sandoval called back. He opened the front door, and the air conditioner rattled again. "You hear me? Because—"

"Mr. Sandoval?" Hardesty was shaking his head in earnest now. "I must advise you not to say anything."

"Honey?" MaryLou Sandoval reached out a hand as if her additional protest could stop her husband's voice. It couldn't.

"I wanna know," her husband persisted. "Why are you here?"

"Good question, sir," Jake said. If they could get this guy talking, maybe they could elicit some information before this interloper lawyer killed the deal. "Let me ask you—"

"We're done here, Detectives," Hardesty said. "You know your way to the door."

"It's so dark inside. Are you sure we should go in?" Lizzie peered through the open front door into the gloom, seeing an entryway, a breakfront maybe, and a kitchen in the distance.

"Where's your sense of adventure?" Aaron closed the door behind her, nudging her out of the way. He touched her, so carefully, so tenderly, it seemed she could feel the outline of his hand on her back, escorting her inside.

Oh-*kay*. She could handle herself perfectly fine, thank you very much, even after two glasses of rosé. Or was it three? She was overthinking again, making too much of it. She turned to him, trying out a brave and *adventurous* smile.

He was tucking a ring of keys into his pocket, its jangling the only sound in the stillness of the empty house on Hardamore Road. She'd never heard of this address, but she only handled the pending foreclosures, not the past ones. It was still furnished, in a haphazardly random way, like someone had to leave in a hurry. Which, she suspected, they did. A shame she couldn't have given the owners another way out. *The Liz treatment.*

"I'm working late, right? That shows how diligent I am, right?" Aaron was saying. "This is my REO, the bank owns it, and I'm only checking whether it's ready for the next step."

"Next step?" It felt like trespassing. But if Aaron had the keys, she supposed he was correct, it was okay. She shook off her dumb unease. Funny kind of date. But this was their profession. Something in common. Something they already shared.

"Property removal," Aaron said. "Maybe a call to the deputies to get rid of this abandoned stuff. Maybe a lock change. But someone's gotta look at it firsthand, right? Take responsibility? Can't let these things just sit here. Ever since that girl got killed, trying to get inside a foreclosed house last week. You hear about that? The press went crazy."

Lizzie remembered that, for sure. She'd crossed her fingers it wasn't an A&A foreclosure. The bank grapevine soon reported some lawyer was already suing the bank, calling the empty house an "attractive nuisance," charging it hadn't been properly secured and had led to that poor girl's death. It was a mess, a potentially expensive mess. But, at least, not A&A's mess.

"Sure, of course I heard." Lizzie stood in the sweltering entryway as Aaron paced off the living room, opening drawers and the glass doors of the breakfront. She realized she'd crossed her bare arms, as if she had a chill. *Silly*. No air conditioning, and the thick air weighed heavy in the half-light. It was after nine, she knew, and even though the electricity was on—Aaron had flipped the lights, and a few fixtures still had bulbs—it was still disturbing. Haunting. The vacant living room, abandoned, half-empty, with only the things people had left behind. Tweed couch, cushions sprung and askew, a scatter of pillows, mismatched armchairs. A discolored rectangle on the hardwood floor—someone had taken the television.

"Kitchen," Aaron said. "Back in one minute."

The place reeked of sadness. And loss, and defeat. She tried to reassure herself, get tough, thinking about what was on her computer. This is why she did what she did. This shouldn't be happening. She would do her best, her little part, to stop it. Not enough to change the whole world, that was impossible, but enough to change *some* people's worlds. She couldn't do too much, she couldn't help everyone; at some point the numbers would not support her. But she could do something.

"Wanna wait for me in the living room?" Aaron said,

reappearing. "I have to go upstairs and check the windows, then look in the basement, make sure no assho—sorry, I mean, jerks—have ripped out the copper pipes." He waved toward the couch. "Have a seat."

"Oh, no thanks, I'm fine standing here," Lizzie said. She was part of this, in a way. Her bank now owned this house. Her bank had taken money every month from whoever once lived here, until the money ran out and they realized that for some reason—a disaster, or a firing, a calamitous health issue, or some horrible miscalculation—they couldn't pay anymore. They'd signed a contract, a legal document. To the bank, it was a binary issue. You could pay, or you couldn't. If not, thank you so much and good-bye.

Too late for her to help whoever had lived here, whatever struggling family had lost at life roulette.

Real estate, Aaron called it. This was the real part she didn't like.

"Suit yourself," Aaron said. "Two seconds."

He grabbed the banisters, one hand on each side, and took the stairs two at a time. Upstairs? She imagined two bedrooms, maybe three, and a bath or two. All the ghosts of whoever lived here seemed to taunt her. All the memories, wisps lurking around every corner. Kids taking first steps, and bringing finger paintings home from school, and birthday parties, and prom snapshots in front of that fireplace.

Family. That was why she'd gone into banking. To please the father who'd never read her homework, never put her drawings on the fridge, never seemed to care if she was happy. She'd inhabited an emotional black hole after her mother died. And now she—well, she'd grown up, despite it all. Future so bright—

"Hey, Lizzie!" Aaron's voice from upstairs. "Come up here!"

Aaron. Two glasses of wine, the heat, the empty house.

This afternoon in her office at the bank, the real life of the regular Lizzie, seemed far away.

Aaron appeared at the top of the stairs, trotted halfway down, held out a hand.

"Lizzie?"

He wasn't wearing his jacket anymore. He'd loosened his tie, rolled up his sleeves.

It *was* hot in here. And, she had to admit, there was no one handsomer than Aaron Gianelli.

"Lizzie," he was saying. He took another stair step down, closer to her. "Come on. Come up here. With me."

16

Finally. **Jane's annoyance** evaporated the instant her cell phone rang. *Blocked,* her caller ID said.

"Hey—" She stopped herself from saying "sweetheart." She was so sure it was Jake, the words almost escaped, but of course, it might not be him. "I mean, this is Jane."

She put the phone on speaker so she could multi-task, getting some pepper jack and a thing of Brie out of the fridge.

"Miss Ryland? This is Elliot Sandoval. Again. Sorry to bother you at home."

"Oh, hey, Mr. Sandoval, no problem." She projected her voice as she grabbed a cheese board and tried to peel the plastic wrap from the gooey ripe Brie. When Jake got here, they could have it with some crackers and wine. And talk about lovely Bermuda. "The story worked fine, thank you. Ah, listen, Mr. Sandoval? I know you told me the officer who called didn't give you a victim's name— that's correct, right?"

"No," the fuzzy voice came from the speaker.

"Okay," she said. Had to make sure. She scrabbled in the utensil drawer for a ceramic-handled cheese knife, leaning toward the phone. "You said the police were coming to your house. Did they? Do you remember their names? They're gone now, right?"

"They did," he said. "And they are. Gone. That's why I'm calling. I'm here with—"

The doorbell. Coda dashed through the kitchen and streaked down the hall, a flash of calico. Silly cat hated the doorbell. It chimed again. *Jake*. Had to be.

"Mr. Sandoval? Can you hang on one second? Someone's at my door. I'm going to put the phone down, forgive me, but don't hang up. I'll be right back."

This would be a juggle. But she'd manage it somehow.

She punched her cell phone off speaker, left it on the counter. Touched her hair as she ran to her front door, stopped, took a breath. Wiggled her shoulders. After all this time, she was still nervous every time he arrived. But he shouldn't know that.

She yanked open the door. "Hey, swee—"

"Hey, you swee." Jake leaned in, gave Jane a brief kiss on the cheek. His black T-shirt was a mass of damp wrinkles, his jeans grimy, he needed a shave, and he was the bearer of bad news. He had to admit he was still damn nervous around her, though he tried not to show it. Did she want him as much as he wanted her? Would that change after he told her? "Sorry I'm late, Jane, but D and I had to—"

"I'm on the phone," she was saying. "In the kitchen. Grab the couch, I'll be back in a sec. Wine glasses are on the coffee table." He took in her black stretch pants, Cubs T-shirt, bare feet. He'd allowed himself to imagine her in a bathing suit. Too bad that reality wasn't gonna happen now. He'd have to tell her. Soon.

He was screwed. Doomed by a guy confessing to murder. Doomed by a probably guilty contractor protected by a hotshot lawyer. And doomed because the woman he loved—yes, he did—was probably, within the next half hour, going to kill him.

He collapsed onto the couch, moving over the spread-out pages of the morning paper and a couple of striped pillows to make room.

Worse, tomorrow the news would be full of the Waverly Road homicide. Everyone clamoring for answers and an arrest, like they were for Lilac Sunday. The public had no idea how difficult it was to close cases, even when you had a semi-suspect. Everyone watched TV, so now they all expected loose ends to disappear after fifty-two minutes. PR had already fielded a raft of questions from reporters, prodding them for "updates" on the dead woman. What if there were no frickin' *updates*? They were doing all they could.

"Jerks," he said.

"Who's a jerk?" Jane stood in the archway to the kitchen, holding a silver tray and an open bottle of wine.

"No one." He stood, smiling. Obviously couldn't tell her the answer was *reporters*.

"Cheese," she said. "And wine. I'm still on the phone. Two seconds, okay?"

And she was gone.

At least it put off the inevitable. D was home, packing. To add to the impending shitstorm, DeLuca would be gone for the next week. His partner, higher seniority, got to take his vacation as planned. Jake picked up the wine bottle, poured a glass, then stabbed a cracker shard into the melting brie, scooping up a chunk and crunching it down.

He toasted the universe, shaking his head. "Happy days," he said.

Jane kept her voice low, needing to hurry, not wanting Jake to hear her. She edged away from the open door. Put her head down and clamped the phone to her ear.

"So it was Detective Brogan at your sister-in-law's?

And his partner. Okay. But you're saying they were only asking questions. Didn't charge you with anything. Correct? So how did they leave it?"

She nodded as she listened, even though Elliot Sandoval couldn't see her. She heard the frustration in his voice, the worry. She'd been right, that's where Jake had been, and that made sense, since the Waverly Road house once belonged to the Sandovals. Now she was intrigued by what Sandoval was asking.

"Your lawyer?" Jane replied. "Well, sure. Happy to chat with him. Her. Tomorrow?"

She wanted to focus on this, but it was a challenge with Jake right in the other room. *Jake.*

"Mr. Sandoval? Did you mention to either of the detectives that you had told *me* they were coming to your sister-in-law's house?" Jane asked. This was getting complicated. *Was getting?* Had gotten. "No? Lets leave it that way, okay? It's best if this is just between us." Jane tucked the phone under her chin, dug in the kitchen junk drawer for a pencil and paper.

"And what's your lawyer's name?" She was incredibly curious—how had the penniless, foreclosed victim Sandoval afforded a lawyer? He hadn't been charged, he'd said. So a public defender couldn't have been appointed.

She had one more thing to tell him. And she hoped she was right.

"Mr. Sandoval?" She paused, considering, then went on. "Don't worry, okay? I'm sure everything will be fine."

She clicked off, wondering if that was true. As a reporter, it didn't matter, really, how Mr. Sandoval felt. It didn't even matter whether he was a murderer. All that mattered was the truth.

17

Aaron watched Lizzie try to re-zip the back of her dress.

"I mean, we shouldn't be doing this," she was saying. "We shouldn't."

The minute he'd come up here, seen the fluffy white comforter, and the puffy pillow, all as if they were just waiting for someone to come back to bed, he'd stood, looking at it, his mind going a hundred miles an hour. Three beers—was it four?—maybe that was it.

He teased her up the stairs, promised a "surprise." Now, after fifteen minutes of whatever, was she pretending to be reluctant?

Lizzie perched on the edge of the bed, sitting up, her hair wild and her cheeks flushed. It was so quiet he could hear the hum of the electricity, hear her trying to catch her breath, hear the zipper release again as he leaned closer, his mouth at her ear.

"Shouldn't? There's no 'shouldn't.' It's our house, Lizzie," he breathed. "We're here, alone, just us. Let go a little. Life isn't all numbers and spreadsheets. . . . Sometimes, it's—" He pulled at her zipper again, pulled down. "Sometimes it's just—sheets."

He waited.

Lizzie burst out laughing. *Laughing?* She'd flopped

back onto the rumpled comforter, then instantly sat up again.

"Sheets? Aaron Gianelli, you have lost your—" She was shaking her head, making fun of him? Not at all the reaction he was going for. "You are too much."

She stood, lifting her arms to zip her dress, and succeeded, laughing the whole time.

He stayed on the bed, frowning at her. Watching her struggle with that dumb gray dress.

"Just trying to inject a little humor," he said.

She was looking right at him now, still kind of laughing. Tossed her hair, as if she was in charge, and then fiddled with the back of her dress, twisting the fabric into place around her hips.

"Oh, you certainly did *that*. For a minute, I was even—" She stopped. Gestured at the room. "I don't know, Aaron, it's crazy, and I was trying to, as you suggested, let myself go for once. But this is—"

Lizzie cleared her throat, trying to get her bearings. She fumbled for the little hook and eye at the top of her zipper, managed to get that fastened again. Found her shoes, wiggled into them, one bare foot at a time. She could not believe, simply could not, that she'd let herself be lured up here by this guy.

Wine or not, messing around with a fellow employee on the abandoned bed of a foreclosed home was not romantic. Or sexy.

Or was it? She looked at him, so handsome, and a funny look on his face, like he was concerned she wouldn't like him.

Maybe she *was* being too picky.

She tried to recalculate, reset the equation. What if this was—an adventure? An exciting adventure. There weren't that many good men left, her girlfriends kept telling her. Aaron had his pluses, as well as his minuses. So did everyone, right? And it wasn't like she had any other offers. She felt her apprehensions about Aaron beginning to dissolve, but even so. This didn't feel like the proper place. That wasn't being "picky." "It's not you. It only— this is someone's home, you know?"

"It isn't 'someone's home.' " Aaron sat on the edge of the bed, hadn't quite buttoned his shirt. "This house belongs to the bank. *I'm* in charge of it. If it's anyone's, its mine. And anyway, Lizzie, this is all your fault."

He smiled at her, that smile she still couldn't ignore. The way he'd looked at her outside the vault that day, and Sunday night, and on the stairs fifteen minutes ago.

"My fault?"

"I couldn't resist you," he murmured. He stood, drawing her closer, his arm sliding around her waist. "It wouldn't have mattered where we were. Can you forgive me for that? Can we start again? Try again?"

She felt the last of her resolve melt away, from the heat of the gathering darkness, and the desire in his voice, from his embrace, and her need for—whatever it was she needed. A partner. A future. Her one plus one.

"Stay," Aaron whispered. "Just a little bit longer. . . ."

Lizzie couldn't help it. She burst out laughing again. Now he was *singing*?

"You. Are. *Kidding* me." Jane tried to process what she was hearing. She took Jake's hand, unwrapped his arm from around her shoulders, stood up from the couch. Counted toward ten, silently, not looking at him. Turned around when she got to about four.

"But you *could* be back in Boston in *plenty* of time." He could, she knew he could. "What if talking with this—what's his name? Only takes a day? Or two?"

"Frasca. Dr. Nathaniel Frasca. I've got to go to D.C.,

that's the only way I can look at the files. They're on paper, originals, even sealed court documents. It could take a while, there's simply no way to predict. Plus, we need to talk in person, and he's about to go out of town, and it's—I'm sorry, honey." Jake stood, too, tried to put his arm back around her.

She didn't want him to. Shook him off, stepped away.

"How long can it take for you guys to discuss false confessions? Why can't you do it on the phone? Or by e-mail? Don't you have to be here this week to handle the Waverly—" She stopped, hearing the whine in her voice. This was Jake's job, he had no choice, he'd gotten a chain-of-command assignment, there was a murder involved, and she'd be doing exactly the same thing if their positions were reversed. It wasn't about her. Sometimes life didn't work out the way you hoped.

"I'm sorry, Jake." Jane quieted her voice and touched the sleeve of his T-shirt, surrendering. "Do whatever you need to do. It's fine. We can always go, right?"

And here she'd predicted this evening's only conflict would be about whether Jake knew she knew that Elliot Sandoval had—*hey.* She rewound to the sentence she'd cut off earlier. "Jake? Seriously. Don't you need to be in town? Working the Waverly Road murder?"

"Supe's assigning that to someone else," Jake said. "I'm out of town, D and Kat are on vacation."

"*They* get to go?" Jane heard the annoyance in her voice. *C'mon, Jane.* "I know it's not your fault, Jake. Really. I'm just disappointed."

And truth be told, Jake being off the case did make her reporting on that story less complicated. Still, she'd rather be complicated and in Bermuda with him.

"I thought you'd kill me," he said.

"Don't tempt me." She reached for her glass of wine, thought about draining it, took a sip instead. "But then

I'd have to get rid of your body somehow. And I like it too much to dump it somewhere."

"I like yours, too," he said. "As you well know. And I'll make it up to you. Somehow."

"Okay, deal. In fact . . ." She faced him, hands on hips. Half teasing. ". . . how about starting right now. You said 'false confessions.' Who confessed? To what? Why do you think it's false?"

Jake was shaking his head. "Uh-uh, sister. I can't tell you that." He sat back on the couch. Patted the spot next to him. "Truce?" he said. "Rain check?"

Jane sank down beside him, slowly. She pressed her arm against his, leaned her leg against his Levi's. He was leaving town, first thing in the morning, and this would be their last time together for however long. "I had a great new bathing suit," she said. "It's very, very, very small. Too bad you won't get to see it."

He kissed her, his lips brushing her hair. "Someday," he whispered.

They sat, silent, watching out the bay window as the streetlights came on along Corey Road, hearing only tinkling music, Scott Joplin, as an ice cream truck trundled its way down her street. Jane thought about juggling and balance and how plans sometimes worked. Sometimes didn't. About whether the whole thing was doomed to failure, because of his job, and hers, and the impossibility of it all. About what had happened to ruin their weekend, and take Jake out of town without her. About how she would have made the same decision, to follow a story and leave Jake at home. About whether this was the universe notifying them they should face reality and call it off.

"Someday," she said.

The music outside faded, then disappeared.

18

"**You'll need to** tell me the truth, that's all there is to it."
Peter Hardesty tried to decide whether he was visiting the
cramped and faintly mildewy studio apartment of a murderer or a liar.

The liar part he could handle, but first he'd have to
get Gordon Thorley to reveal why he was fabricating a
confession. What would cause someone to playact like
that? Maybe his client was a headline seeker, needed the
spotlight, craved the attention. Peter had seen a few of
those types in his legal career. Maybe Thorley was a nut.
Peter had seen even more of those.

The murderer part he could also handle, if it eventually turned out law enforcement could provide sufficient
evidence Gordon Thorley was at the Arboretum on that
Lilac Sunday nineteen years ago. Even if Thorley's sister's
financing ran out, he could probably get appointed to the
case and make sure the guy received a zealous defense.

Innocent, guilty, or crazy. Peter simply had to discover
which legal path to pursue.

But right now, Gordon Thorley seemed most interested
in the large-no-sugar that Peter had provided. A slug of
caffeine was occasionally enough to get guys like this to
talk. Not Thorley. Not today.

"Sir?" Peter tried again.

"Like I said." Thorley hunched over a plastic-topped kitchen table, his white T-shirt barely touching the curved metal back of the lone chair. Peter imagined he'd be able to see the man's bony spine through the shirt's thin cotton.

Peter stood at the entryway to the kitchen area, since Thorley's chair was the only place to sit other than a sorry-looking couch in this . . . rooming house, they used to call them. Probably a more politically correct name now. Kinder words wouldn't erase the smoke-stained paint, the discolored patches on the threadbare carpeting, the matchbook shoved under one metal leg of the kitchen table.

Loser, Peter thought, then corrected himself. *Client.* Innocent till proven guilty.

"Like you said—what?" Peter had not been offered a seat on the couch, not necessarily a bad thing, so he waited, arms crossed, briefcase open on the floor, standing between the front door and the back window, pretending he was comfortable. Two steps would take him to Thorley. There was not enough air for the both of them. Peter had seen worse. He had to get his guy to talk, or this was going nowhere.

"Forget it," Thorley said.

What bugged the hell out of him, it appeared there was more to Thorley than semi-squalor. Along one wall, in black frames and matted in white, a single line of photographs stretched from one corner to the other. Aligned precisely, not one corner tipping higher than any another. Each black-and-white was similar to the next, but different. Branches. Bare tree branches, some unmistakably ancient, gnarled and battered. Others delicately young, thin, fragile. No leaves, no buds, no flowers, only stark slashes of black, backlit against a cloudless sky.

"You take those?" Might as well try to understand the guy. Murderer? Or liar?

"What of it?"

"They're good. You're talented." Peter had a thought. Not a good one. "Where'd you shoot them?" The Arboretum?

"Around," Thorley said.

"The Arboretum?" He had to ask.

"Maybe." Thorley flickered him a look. Then stared again at the table.

So much for conversation.

Peter pulled an accordion folder from his briefcase. This folder was still thin, not yet filled with the research and documentation he'd gather as the case went forward. If it went forward. Peter was used to recalcitrant clients, to combative clients, to those who didn't understand he was the only thing that stood between them and a justice system that would as soon keep them in the slammer forever, tax dollars and the Constitution and actual guilt be damned. Had to admit, though, he wasn't used to having them confess to cold-case murders. That made this interesting. Unusual.

"Like I said." Thorley took another sip of coffee, then coughed, one miserable hack, clapping a wiry hand to his chest. His once-white T-shirt, ribbing around the arms and neck spent and shapeless, said BARDON'S GYM in fading orange lettering. That place had closed ten years ago, Peter knew, maybe longer. "I did it."

"Did what?" Peter flipped though the folder, finding the pale blue onionskin he needed. "According to your parole records here, you have no priors before your armed robbery conviction in 1995. And after you got out in 2010—your second try at parole—you stayed clean. What's the deal now with this sudden confession?"

Thorley drained the last from his paper cup, crumpled it, tossed it in the aluminum sink. He licked his lips, patted his chest, then his jeans pockets.

"You got any—?" he asked.

"Sorry," Peter said. "Gave it up." He felt his phone vibrate in his pocket, the alarm set to remind him of his meeting with Jane Ryland. For which he was now verging on late. Time was also running out, he predicted, for Elliot Sandoval. "Look. Thorley. Your sister called me. I'm here to help. You need to let me help you."

"Carley and me, we met at high school," Thorley said. He looked over Peter's shoulder, so intently Peter turned to see if someone was there.

"We—had a thing," Thorley went on. "We kept it secret. I was older. She lived with her parents, out in Attleboro. Then she tried to break it off. I didn't want that. We went to our special place in the . . ."

"What was she wearing?" Peter interrupted. He'd already heard Thorley tell the "special place" part. They needed to get this show on the road.

"When?" Thorley said.

"When you killed her."

"A dress. With flowers."

"Remarkable." Peter riffled though the sparse paperwork, found the ragged photocopy of the *Register* article he'd been looking for. "That's exactly what the newspaper reported."

" 'Cause it's true, I guess."

"You ever kill anyone else?"

"Nope.

"Just Carley Marie Schaefer."

"Yes."

"Why?"

"Huh?"

"Why? Why'd you kill her?"

Thorley looked at the kitchen sink, as if fearing he'd thrown away the coffee too soon. He splayed his narrow fingers across the yellowed Formica table, stared down at them. Stretched one hand, then the other.

"Why?" he asked. "Why not?"

* * *

"Her jacket is here, Mr. Gianelli, so she must be here."

Aaron hated Stephanie's voice. Almost as much as he hated what she was telling him. The secretary sat behind her damn little desk, wearing that damn little headset, and didn't seem at all concerned that Lizzie, her boss, wasn't in her office. Even at eleven in the morning, way past the time she should be here. As for the jacket, Aaron knew what Stephanie clearly didn't. Lizzie had left that jacket on her chair last night, not this morning. Last night, when Aaron had lured her to the swan boats, and then to that expensive dinner, and then to the second floor of the Hardamore Road house.

The office door behind Stephanie was wide open, showing Lizzie's vacant desk. And that meaningless jacket over the back of her black leather chair.

Ridiculous that their "date," or whatever, ended so absurdly. Him slamming the door as he stormed out. He'd tossed his whole ring of keys at her, so frustrated, even kind of told her to lock up and find her own way home. It was a bush-league beer-fueled mistake, but she'd made him so damn angry, laughing at him, first about the sheets, and then about, seemed like, every freaking thing he said, that he'd pretty much lost it. Now, before the whole thing blew up in his face, he had to get those keys back. Keep Lizzie happy. And make sure he hadn't created a career-ending mess.

"Is she in a meeting?" That would be a reasonable explanation. "Can you check her calendar?"

Stephanie yanked open a drawer, but pulled out a packet of sugar instead of a calendar, dumped it into her mug of coffee, stirred it with a little stick.

"Oh, sorry, we don't do the calendar thing yet. She's new. We're supposed to work that out this week."

This girl was Lizzie's secretary, she ought to know

where Lizzie was. If she didn't, she should be smart enough to wonder.

"Did she call you? Tell you she was gonna be late?" Aaron yanked at his tie to keep it from strangling him, tried to "eavesread" the paperwork on Stephanie's desk to find any clues to Lizzie's whereabouts. He'd put off the meeting with his client, but if he stalled much more, that deal'd fall through.

"Nope." Stephanie took an agonizingly slow sip. "She might be at the doctor, and forgot to tell me. Or she might be upstairs. I was a little late myself."

Upstairs? Shit. Exactly what Aaron feared most.

Had Lizzie told anyone about last night? Did anyone know they were together? She *probably* hadn't, since it could be equally damaging to her as it would to him. Mutually assured destruction. Might keep her quiet.

Might.

"Will you have her call me, soon as she gets here?" He adjusted his tie, made himself into a confident bank employee again. "Nothing urgent. Just—whenever."

He walked toward the elevator, checking behind him one last time. Praying to see the one person who might save his life.

If Lizzie gave the keys to anyone, anyone upstairs especially, he'd be screwed. Beyond screwed.

Okay. It was his fault. But fault didn't matter at this point. *Lizzie* was the problem now, because she had the keys. All the keys.

The elevator door opened. But Aaron didn't budge. He'd just realized what would make this even worse.

What if she didn't have them?

19

"**What the hell** time was your plane, Brogan? Here it's been however many years—and suddenly now you can't live without me?"

Jake slung his briefcase onto the too-luxurious-for-government-issue wing chair in the corner of the office, shook Nate Frasca's outstretched hand. He'd left Boston when it was still dark, arrived at Dulles before eight, grabbed a taxi, and battled the beltway morning traffic to the ordinary-looking brownstone in the three-syllable streets way past Dupont Circle. Ordinary on the outside, at least.

"Yeah, worried you'd blow it in the big time." Jake gestured to the lacquered white office walls, the lofty floor-to-ceiling bookshelves, the wall-to-wall windows with the view of the winding green trails and iconic stone bridges of Rock Creek Park. "Guess I was wrong. Or maybe you're fooling them, too."

Frasca waved Jake to a plush leather chair, gestured to a tray with a shining silver pot, a matching sugar bowl, and tiny pitcher of cream. A lacquer tray presented twisty glazed crullers and three bagels. "I know it's not Dunkin's," Frasca said. "Sorry I can't make you feel at home."

"I'll live," Jake said. He poured a steaming cup, ignored the add-ons. "You doing okay, Nate? Getting some downtime, finally?"

A shrill beep interrupted, followed by a voice over an intercom. "Dr. Frasca? Fifteen." And then silence.

"Welcome to D.C.," Frasca said. "Downtime, my friend, is somewhere in the future. So cutting to the chase, Jake. I hope we get to grab lunch, maybe tomorrow? Sorry you had to come all his way, but it's all classified, archived, no copies. We had no choice. There's some DVDs, too, of the confessions. You can watch them in that laptop on the console. The false confessions are labeled 'F.' "

"That's why you get the big bucks," Jake said. "Thanks."

"I've got a hell of a day, too Washington to describe." Frasca stood, packed his briefcase while he talked. "But while we've got a few minutes—sounds like you've got an interesting thing going on."

Jake painted the Thorley confession with quick strokes. Told Frasca how every year the cops took a beating from the press, taunting the hell out of them for the still-open case. How Carley Marie's parents came back to Boston every year, made a big deal of trying to ensure their daughter wasn't forgotten.

"The legacy of Lilac Sunday," Jake said. "One dead girl, one still-grieving family, a killer on the loose, and a colossal failure for the BPD."

"Your grandfather's case, right?" Frasca took a swig of Diet Coke, put the plastic bottle on a silver coaster. "Potentially significant, that this Thorley'd show up confessing to *that* one with you now on the force. Did he know your grandfather?"

Jake frowned, considering. Did Gordon Thorley know his grandfather? Never crossed his mind. How could they have been connected back then? A punk from the suburbs and the sixty-five-year-old Boston police commissioner? Lots of ways, actually.

"I don't know, Nate." He eyed his dark coffee, swiveled the cup in its delicate saucer, left it there.

"Could be it's you he's after now." Frasca dropped the empty plastic Coke bottle into a blue recycle bin tucked under an antique-looking side table.

"Keep that in mind," he went on. "Sometimes in these confessions there's an element that pushes someone over the edge. Guilt that finally festers, the poison of remorse, or—" He paused, interrupting himself. "It's almost the twentieth anniversary, right? That could be an emotional trigger."

"Trigger? I thought the anniversary made it—" Jake paused. Thorley showing up, right as the anniversary loomed? The Supe's annual push to close the case? "Well, more unlikely."

"The contrary. Anniversaries are frequently significant. They're symbolic, and that makes them powerful. Waco? Ruby Ridge? Oklahoma City? The bad guys can't resist. It's like returning to the scene. They think the history makes the action more potent."

Jake nodded. *History.* The cardboard boxes of case and investigation records his grandfather kept, now stacked on metal shelves in his parents' basement. There'd been some thought of destroying them, but Grandma Brogan wouldn't allow it. It's history, she'd insisted. It's trash, Jake's mother had argued. She'd called them "toxic records of failure and unhappiness."

Gramma Brogan, as always, won. Did those boxes of history contain some answers?

"Lilac Sunday's less than a week from now," Jake said. *Five days.* How well he knew. "Thing is, Nate, I don't see how Gordon Thorley could know I'd be involved. It seems too elaborate. I gotta think this is something else."

"Something else what?" Frasca clicked his briefcase closed.

"That's why I came five hundred miles. To ask you. Who would confess to a murder they didn't commit? Why?" Jake stood as Frasca headed for the door. Were there answers in the stacks of files he was about to open? "Or, hello. Maybe he's guilty. I'm equally satisfied with that. Just tell me how I'm supposed to know."

Jane tried to remember what Professor Kindell taught them in Journalism Law and Ethics 101, or even 201, but that was almost fifteen years ago, and it seemed much more logical back in j-school. Now, faced with real-life journalism law and ethics, the black-and-white textbook pages were almost laughably unhelpful.

Each decision was different, that was journalism reality. The only basic certainty, the unchangeable, was to tell the truth. How you did that, and when, and whether there actually was "truth"—that was the stuff her class never discussed.

Jane tapped on Victoria Marcotte's office door, heard a "come in" from inside. This new city editor was no Murrow, but at least she was someone to talk to. And they had a lot to talk about.

Elliot Sandoval's lawyer had called Marcotte, offering a deal. He'd provide all the inside info on the Sandoval investigation, but only if the paper agreed to hold off running the full story until the case was adjudicated. He'd called it "a front-row seat at a murder case."

Jane couldn't have agreed to such an arrangement with Sandoval's lawyer on her own. "Risk" and "gamble" were not concepts she was comfortable with, nor were "scooped" and "fired," either (or both) of which were unpleasantly looming possibilities if this deal went bad.

"Have a seat, Jane." Victoria Marcotte pointed to the couch. Her chocolaty leather jacket was probably worth

Jane's salary for a month. Two venti paper cups, both with lipstick imprints, stood by her computer.

Jane ignored the couch, grabbed one of the strappy black and chrome chairs from against the wall, scooted it closer to the desk, sat there.

"Legal agrees we're on solid ground," Marcotte said. "If there's an arrest, I'll send another reporter, Chrystal or whoever. You'll eventually do a big takeout—multimedia, goes without saying, that's who we are these days, right?—on the story of an accused murderer. How he felt, how he was treated, how he was nailed, how he was charged—or not—how he was ultimately exonerated. Or not. However it plays out. Use TJ when you need pictures. Got it?"

It was similar, Jane theorized, to how network reporters were embedded in the Gulf wars. Or those long-term projects on *60 Minutes*. It wasn't breaking news, where you went live, telling everything you learned as soon as you learned it. It wasn't "day of" news, which aired the same day you reported it. This was a long-term, long-form investigation. She might have time to make it important. Life-changing. Award-winning. Still, holding back information didn't feel comfortable.

"Are you sure that we're okay with—," Jane began.

Marcotte's phone buzzed.

"He's on the way up," Marcotte said. "Peter Hardesty is the lawyer's name."

Jane wished she had known that earlier so she could check him out. She'd asked Sandoval for the name, but she'd been too distracted by Jake to realize he hadn't told her. She hated going into this meeting playing catch-up, with no research or background.

"What if Sandoval's guilty?" Jane said.

Marcotte patted at her hair, then smiled at Jane, conspiratorial. "Then we have an even better story."

* * *

The first key hadn't worked, neither had the second. Or the third.

Standing on the front porch of a two-story redbrick house in Jamaica Plain, Liz McDivitt glanced around, checking for nosy neighbors or a late-morning mailman. Or, worst of all, someone from the bank.

It had been a snap to pull up Aaron's REO records on her home computer. Her in-house password was essentially all-access when it came to the real estate department, so she knew exactly which homes were in Aaron's portfolio. He'd used this key chain—the one he'd tossed at her, ridiculous—to open the house on Hardamore last night. Made sense keys to other empty houses were on this chain, too. The chain had about a million keys, and big metal "A" dangling from it. Atlantic & Anchor Bank, she assumed. Or Aaron.

Key number four. It slipped into the lock perfectly. She took another reconnoitering look. No cars in neighboring driveways, no kids on bikes, not even any birds in the saplings lining the sidewalks. The last of the red tulips, unhappy in the heat, were giving up their petals, but someone had mowed the grass. Made sense. Part of Aaron's job was to keep the place up, since city inspectors could fine the bank if properties were neglected. Not the best thing for the bank's image, first taking people's homes, then leaving them to rot, ruining the entire neighborhood. She gave the key a twist.

Nothing. Her shoulders slumped. Should she even be doing this?

Clearly not, she had no business. But something was up with Aaron, she'd been awake all night, thinking about it. Replaying it.

Pursing her lips with the memory, she yanked key number

four out of the lock, flipped to key number five. If she predicted correctly, this would be another empty house. Why she wanted to make certain of that, she wasn't sure.

The key slipped in. Turned. Clicked. Worked.

All she had to do was turn it again. The door would open.

What would her father do? What would he think?

Lizzie stopped, fingers on the key, and almost laughed. Well, that, at least, was an easy one. She would never tell him about any of it. Never never never.

She turned the knob. And pushed.

20

This was Peter Hardesty? When Elliot Sandoval said his defense attorney wanted a meeting, Jane had envisioned a wizened professor-looking type, maybe white hair and battered briefcase. The actor who played Clarence Darrow in *Compulsion*. Or maybe a rabbity kid, some newly minted true believer, accepting difficult cases and hoping to grow up to be Atticus Finch.

This guy—khaki suit, hair darker than Jake's, navy-striped tie in place, and an aura of casual confidence—arrived at the open door of Victoria Marcotte's office as if he'd been there a million times. He paused, briefly, then entered the room, hand extended.

"Ms. Marcotte. I'm Peter Hardesty, of Hardesty and Colaneri. Peter." He stepped to her desk, shaking her hand as she half-rose, then turned to Jane, giving her a polite once-over. "You must be Jane Ryland. I've seen your byline, many times. Great job on that big adoption story you wrote. Elliot Sandoval speaks highly of you. My law firm consulted on his foreclosure, that's why he called me. Thank you for hearing our proposal."

He stood between them, the apex of the triangle. Each of them wanted something. Maybe even the same thing. Maybe not.

Hardesty's loafers were shiny, but not too shiny. Cool

wire-rims, but not pretentious. His suit fit, but not perfectly. Thirty-something, she guessed. Her age, a little older. Independent enough to have his own law firm. Okay, she liked him. Snap judgment, but that's how it sometimes worked.

Marcotte yanked off a chunky earring, examined it, clamped it back on. A tendril of artfully streaked hair fell into place over the glisten of gold. *Making him wait.*

"Of course. Have a seat, Mr. Hardesty," she said. "The ball is in your court."

Hardesty eyed the couch, then pulled up a side chair next to Jane. "Okay, bottom line. It's simple. My firm is tired of cases being tried in the media."

The lawyer looked at Marcotte, then at Jane, shrugging almost apologetically. "Mr. Sandoval is innocent until proven guilty. His wife is pregnant. We can't do anything about the TV types—sorry, Jane—and their coverage is shallow at best. But the *Register* is the paper of record in Boston. As I told you on the phone, Ms. Marcotte. You leave him and his family alone, we'll give you an inside look at the case. You can do a quality story for your readers. An exclusive. Afterward."

Jane exchanged glances with Marcotte. *This was a new one.*

"Your client's okay with that, Mr. Hardesty?" Jane said.

"Who wouldn't be? And it's Peter." He looked at Jane. "Right?"

"Sure," she said. "Jane."

"Okay then," Marcotte said, ignoring them. "Off the top of my head? We love new. We adore exclusive. I ran it by legal, of course. So far, so good. We'll let you know if there's a snag."

"Of course," Peter said.

"Nothing signed, nothing on paper, and we pull out whenever we want."

"Fine," Peter said. "At that point we'd be free to give the exclusive to another news outlet."

Jane watched the news negotiation, the two sides volleying their points. Peter had the advantage of preparation—but Marcotte could kill the deal in an instant.

"Fine. We're on board." The editor stood, reaching out a hand. "Deal."

Peter stood, returned the handshake. "Deal."

"We'll take Jane off day-of coverage of the Shandra Newbury homicide," Marcotte said.

"And we'll provide you"—Peter nodded in Jane's direction—"with exclusive access to all of the evidence, the police interviews, as well as . . ."

Jane sat, half-amused, as the editor and the lawyer planned her future. The participants in this drama were certainly rearranging. Jake out of town, probably in D.C. by now. DeLuca and Kat wherever they were going. Jake had told her other detectives would handle the Shandra Newbury–Waverly Road homicide. So instead of Jake and Jane having to dance around reality, hiding the truth from each other, Jane'd finally be able to dig into a case with someone who was *providing* information, not protecting it. This time she didn't need cop sources. She'd get her scoop from the other side.

And, hooray, Peter Hardesty would not have to be aware of her relationship with Jake. Another life problem successfully solved.

"Peter?" Jane managed to wait until this conversation wound down, but there was a key question the editor hadn't asked. "Do you expect Mr. Sandoval to be arrested? When? And why? I'm wondering, frankly, what's the point of this arrangement if you don't?"

* * *

Elliot Sandoval had told him Jane Ryland cut right to the point. Here was proof. Peter was surprised this Victoria Marcotte—the *Wizard of Oz* witch theme hummed in his head, though the stylish and superior Marcotte was not green—had posed every damn question but the critical one.

He'd seen Jane on TV, of course, one, maybe two years ago, before she was fired from Channel 11 in the fallout from that defamation case judgment. She seemed to have come through it unscathed. She looked better in person than on TV—younger, maybe, and thinner. She never smiled on the air, he realized, maybe that made the difference. He'd focused on her boss for this meeting, figured winning over Marcotte was key. But it was Jane who'd asked the big question. Now he had to answer.

"Yes, we're expecting it," he admitted. He pulled out a manila folder, placing it on the edge of Marcotte's glass-topped desk. "The police, two homicide detectives, tried to interview him, you're aware of that."

Jane nodded. She turned toward him in her chair, a thin black sweater tied around her shoulders, wearing some kind of little sleeveless dress, bare legs, flat shoes.

"But they didn't charge him," Jane said. "Why not?"

Peter opened his file, pulled out the stapled paperwork, handed it to Jane. "Good question. This is a cobbled-together transcript of what the police asked my client and his wife prior to my arrival. Before the Sandovals forgot, I questioned them about it, made sure it was documented."

"The Sandovals talked to the police?"

"Cops." Peter shook his head. "They pushed. Hard. Clearly took advantage of the Sandovals. You know the bullsh—sorry, stuff, those detectives always try to pull."

Jane had a funny look on her face. "Yeah."

"Take a look at the transcript, such as it is. It's not admissible, in any way, it's simply their memory of a conversation that I think, frankly, was improper." Peter leaned closer to Jane, wanting to point out a certain paragraph. Got a whiff of some kind of citrusy-floral fragrance, clean and fresh. She'd pulled her hair back in a stubby little ponytail, strands falling out and curling over her cheek. He looked at her left hand. Looked away. Looked again. Bare. Couldn't believe what he was thinking. "We'll fight them on it, if need be. It's arguably a Miranda violation if they suspected Mr. Sandoval. Let me show you, here's where they—"

"Did they?" Jane looked up from the transcript. "Suspect him?"

"Page four," he said. "You know he works construction, freelance. The detectives mention a two-by-four as the murder weapon."

"And then, according to this, Elliot refers to the ones in his truck." Jane turned the pages of the printed transcript. "Which Ja—I mean, the cops—say they'd already noticed. So, yeah, I understand what you mean. Seems like they were on a mission, and not simply fact-finding."

Peter nodded. "Exactly. If they considered him a suspect, and didn't read him his rights, then by law—"

Marcotte's desk phone trilled, a sharp triple tone that cut through what Peter was trying to explain. The editor rolled her eyes, apologizing, then narrowed them as she picked up the receiver and listened.

Peter checked with Jane. She shrugged, smiling.

"Where?" Marcotte trapped the phone between her cheek and her shoulder, pulled a pen from a silver container, began writing on a white legal pad. Peter noticed she glanced at Jane several times as she listened. "Really? When? Do they have an identification yet?"

Jane stood and turned for the door, so Peter did, too. Maybe Marcotte expected privacy.

"No. Wait." The editor pointed to them. "Don't leave. Stand by."

Jane stopped, and Peter almost ran into her. "Sorry," he said.

Marcotte put her hand over the mouthpiece, aimed her words at them. "We're set on the deal, okay? And you two can continue without me. I've got a possible situation here."

"What's up?" Jane said. "Anything I can do?"

"Yes," Marcotte said. "There is. Will you get me Chrystal Peralta? Tell her we've got a body on Moulten Road. Homicide is on the way."

21

"This is Jake Brogan." Jake's cell showed caller ID blocked, so maybe it was Frasca checking in. But there was no one on the other end. "Hello?"

Jake hung up, figuring whoever it was would call back. He'd spent the last three hours pulling rubber-banded manila folders from accordion files, reading the fusty multi-syllabic psych-talk that analyzed the reasons a raft of poor saps confessed to crimes they didn't commit.

Four cups of fancy coffee and two crullers later, plowing through all the professional lingo, Jake felt he'd been reading fiction, stories too bizarre and unbelievable even for the movies. And, he had to admit, law enforcement manipulation so brazen it was embarrassing.

Jake read stomach-churning cases of overzealous detectives and special agents, battering confessions out of the semi-defenseless or totally confused in the pressure cooker of an interrogation room, usually plying them with phony reassurances and false promises.

The case where he and Frasca met—a young Vietnamese woman, in barely marginal English, confessed to killing her child because the cops had guaranteed her if she did, "it would all be over" and she could go home. Instead, she was slammed into the Framingham House of Correction awaiting arraignment for murder. Jake and Frasca had discovered the baby had been sick, doctors' records proved it, and the young woman was completely blameless. Now free but humiliated, she hadn't come out of her home in the last year.

She'd confessed all right. They all had. But none were guilty. Misguided, confused, or impaired or young or stupid or manipulated or coerced. But not guilty. Jake powered through Frasca's case files, absorbed, almost forgetting why he was here. The guy in Sweden trying to impress a girlfriend who thought he was a wimp, a poor dupe in Illinois who'd been kept awake by the cops for forty-seven hours until he finally caved. And forget about recanting. Once a confession was "given," it obliterated any other evidence. Witnesses, alibis, everything, would be ignored—because why would someone confess to a crime they didn't commit?

Jake sighed, leaned back in the soft leather, stared out the plate glass at the gathering gray clouds, thought about Gordon Thorley. No question his confession to Bing Sherrey had been taped. The Massachusetts courts frowned on what had once been the norm, those "we forgot" or "the machine broke" excuses by detectives about why their interrogations weren't recorded. Jurors had actually been ordered to be skeptical of "confessions" where the questioning wasn't on tape—judges instructing jurors they could infer that a lack of audio meant police had behaved inappropriately.

But Bing Sherrey hadn't offered solace or security or release or redemption. He hadn't offered anything. Thorley'd shown up on his own.

All the more reason to be perplexed.

Jake glanced at the stack of DVDs Frasca had left. Might as well watch those. But now, faced with dozens of similar but unique cases of false confessions, he wondered if any of it mattered. What was he expecting to learn, really, from all this? Some kind of key to Thorley? Some kind of psychological explanation for his actions, or scientific proof of guilt?

Or maybe, just maybe, finding nothing was the proof of something else. That Gordon Thorley—not young, not mentally ill, not stupid or manipulated or strong-armed— actually was the Lilac Sunday killer.

Jake stared blankly at the dregs of his coffee and the cruller crumbs, imagining the future.

What if this year's Lilac Sunday, five days from now, was the first without the ghost of Carley Marie Schaefer hanging over it? The first the Schaefer family could hope for some justice? The first without the memory of failure sending Gramma Brogan to face Gerald and Maureen Schaefer at their annual "Remember Carley Marie" news conference, and then to her room for the rest of the day.

Jake, lost in speculation, flinched when his cell phone rang again, dropped his pencil. Was Frasca already done with his meeting? Already close to noon. No wonder he was starving. Was that thunder outside?

"Brogan," he said. He paused, listening, then inserted a DVD into the slot in the machine under the TV monitor. He didn't push play, though, his hand frozen in midair as he listened to Bing Sherrey's terse recitation. "Are you serious? Was it an accident? No? Are you sure?"

Peter's cell phone, set on vibrate for the meeting with Jane and Marcotte, buzzed in his jacket pocket. Peter ignored it, focusing on what Victoria Marcotte was telling Jane.

A homicide? With ninety-three murders a year in Boston alone, it wasn't surprising there'd be one reported while he was at the *Register*. His lawyer brain instantly wondered if the bad guy needed a defense attorney. He had his hands full already, he decided. Someone else could have this one.

Jane had raced off down the hall, holding up one finger in a "be right back" gesture. He stood in the doorway, realized he was watching her jog away. He'd assumed she'd be kind of a pain, tough or bitter or a hardass. Or a diva, full of herself and her career. He'd been wrong about all of that. He was still embarrassed with himself for checking out her ring finger. His phone buzzed again. Someone who had his cell number, so probably Nicole at his office, reminding him of something. Or maybe—had Sandoval been arrested for Waverly Road?

That'd start the wheels in motion with Jane, even sooner than he'd predicted.

"Peter Hardesty," he answered. Marcotte, he could see through the glass, was still on her phone, now clamped between her shoulder and cheek, peering at something on her computer screen.

"This is Detective Branford Sherrey, Mr. Hardesty. We met yesterday? I'm calling about your client, Gordon Thorley."

"What about him?" Bing Sherrey. The blowhard cop who'd tried to keep Thorley in custody. The news he'd just overheard in Marcotte's office. *A homicide.* Was Thorley dead? The victim? Or who?

"We cannot seem to locate your client, Mr. Hardesty," Sherrey said. "He should have checked in with parole this morning. When he didn't, we sent an officer to his LKA. Last known address."

"I understand LKA," Peter said. Down the hall, Jane was walking with a tall salt-and-pepper brunette, both women gesturing toward Marcotte's office. The other woman, older, with wild curls and dark glasses perched on her head, wore a flimsy too-small sundress. He could see the woman's sunburned shoulders and surprising cleavage all the way from here. This was probably Chrystal, the reporter Marcotte mentioned. "My client was not home? So what?"

If Thorley was missing, was he dead? Killed? By whom? Why?

"Nope. No answer to the knock, no sign of him. Your client is gonzo. We went inside—"

"You went inside? You have a warrant to—"

"Landlord let us in, what if he's in trouble, right? Plus, he gave up his Fourth Amendment rights the moment his homey waved a .45 at that liquor store owner back in 1995, Counselor. As I am sure you're aware."

Jerks. "And?"

"And nothing, Mr. Hardesty."

Peter waited.

"That warrant?" Sherrey said. "We do have it. Violation of parole. Not to mention fleeing after an interrogation, suspicion of—"

If there was a homicide, and the cops were looking for Thorley, he wasn't the victim. Was he a suspect?

Peter turned his back on Jane and the other reporter, his forehead touching the wall, focusing on this new development. Sherrey was reportedly not a devotee of the rules. But if he'd deigned to call about Thorley's whereabouts, he apparently decided to toe the legal line. Why? And what he was saying was absurd.

"'Fleeing after an interrogation'? Where'd you come up with that? Suspicion? Of what? Listen, Detective. How do you know Mr. Thorley isn't at the grocery?" Peter got more annoyed by the second. "Or having a real life, visiting his sister, or seeing the doctor, or having his tires rotated? I've seen his records. He's no slacker about his parole reporting. God knows the department doesn't go after every ex-con who's ten minutes late calling in, Detective. You want to tell me what this is really about?"

"Yeah," Sherrey said. Peter could hear the smile in his voice. He remembered he didn't like Sherrey's smile. "I do. Stand by one, okay?"

The connection went muffled, as if Peter were suddenly listening to cotton. This cop had put him on hold?

"Peter?"

He turned, surprised at the brief touch on his back. Jane.

"Oh, sorry." She pointed down the hall. "I'll be at my desk."

"Thanks." He mouthed the word at her, held up two fingers. *Two minutes.*

"Gotcha," she said.

She had a great smile.

The line clicked, the connection opened.

"Detective?" Peter'd let this guy jerk him around long enough. "Suspicion of what?"

"Here's what, Mr. Hardesty. We're actively looking for your client. If you find him first? You'll bring him to the station ASAP. If we find him first, well, he'll get his one phone call. I assume he'll call you. If not, then, we'll see you around campus."

"On suspicion of fricking *what*?" This was harassment, pure and simple.

"Oh, my error." Sherrey's voice had that arrogant smile again. "But you know what? We'll fill you in when we see you. With your client."

22

Something was certainly up.

Jane moved back into Marcotte's reception area, watching Peter on the phone. His body language screamed bad news. Forehead touching the wall, one hand gesturing, whispering into his cell. Maybe Sandoval had been arrested?

If Sandoval was in custody, or about to be, at least that'd take her mind off whatever assignment Marcotte was now apparently giving Chrystal Peralta. Chrystal was a veteran reporter, around for maybe twenty years. Maybe more. Her stories were fine, straightforward, Jane supposed, not much flair, but she apparently made her deadlines and had some good connections. Who wouldn't, after twenty years, if you were worth your salt.

Twenty years from now, when Jane was Chrystal's age, where would she be? Still banging out murders at the *Register*? That was a question she wasn't quite ready to face.

Right now, though, Jane still craved the headlines. A good reporter always does. Maybe someday she'd stop caring. Maybe.

Chrystal opened Marcotte's office door, whooshing back into the reception area with a blast of musky perfume and a hint of cigarette.

"No problem, Victoria," Chrystal was saying over her shoulder. "I'll give you a buzz when—oh, hey, Jane."

Jane smiled, oh so friendly. "Got a good story?"

"Dead girl near the Arboretum." Chrystal stuck her pencil into her curls, left it behind her ear. "A week before Lilac Sunday? And there's another murder around the Arboretum? City's gonna go nuts."

What did Lilac Sunday have to do with anything? "What about Lilac Sunday?"

"Lilac Sunday? The festival at the Arboretum. Every May, around Mother's Day. Picnics, families, you know. And that girl was killed? Like, twenty years ago. They never found the guy."

"Oh, right. I know that," Jane said. "So they think this is connected? Why?"

Chrystal turned to Peter, who'd come up beside her from the hallway. "Can I help you?" she said.

"He's with me. We're working on a story together." Jane answered before Peter could, no need to tell Chrystal about this. "See you later, Chrystal. Good luck with the—"

"Hang on, Jane, sorry." Peter took a step toward Chrystal, holding out a hand. "I couldn't help but overhear."

Chrystal checked with Jane, eyebrows raised. *He okay?*

Jane shrugged. Whatever. *Sure.*

"You said there's a—," Peter went on.

"*Homicide,* I should have said," Chrystal interrupted. "Apologies. Not 'dead girl.' Though the police haven't formally called it a homicide. So far. But yeah, apparently there's a young woman they found, strangled, so says our source. And since you can't strangle yoursel—oh, sorry." Chrystal held up both hands. "Sorry. Been in the business too long."

"It's okay. Peter's a lawyer, and—," Jane began.

"When was she killed?" Peter asked. "Where? Exactly, where?"

Chrystal took a step back, made a skeptical face like, *who is this guy?* "Forgive me, sir. I've got to head out."

Jane watched Chrystal trot away down the corridor, her sturdy black sandals clopping against her bare heels, her curls hardly moving.

"Peter?" He'd come in all confidence and conviction. Now he looked upset, like someone had changed the rules. "Did something happen? Is this about Elliot Sandoval? Was he arrested?"

He didn't answer, and Jane frowned, trying to arrange the puzzle pieces in some logical way. Chrystal had said there was another homicide. "Do police think Sandoval killed someone else?"

That didn't make much sense, but neither did Sandoval killing Shandra Newbury, even though apparently police suspected he had. Who knew what "made sense." Jane had covered enough stories of arbitrary and random disaster to appreciate that "making sense" was not always achievable. Reality was impossible to predict. That's what made it headlines.

"Sando—oh. No. Its not that." Peter shook his head, pulled out his phone. Now he was checking his screen and talking to her at the same time. "Listen, Jane? Could you find out more about this possible homicide? Who the victim is? When it happened?"

"Maybe." Could she? Should she? "You have to give me some reason, though. I can't march into the city editor and—well, what's up, Peter? We're working together on the Sandoval case, but that doesn't mean you have access to everything."

"Jane." Peter stashed the phone in his jacket pocket. "Listen. Can you keep a secret?"

"Are you from the bank?"

Those were the last words Lizzie expected to hear. She

actually didn't expect to hear *any* words, since every document indicated this house would be vacant. She'd checked the listings on Aaron's logs, and this address had been foreclosed on months ago, the deputies had evicted the family soon after, and it had been vacant and for sale ever since. But now a college-looking girl in a white Sam Adams T-shirt, cutoffs, and flip-flops stood in the doorway. Looking worried.

Lizzie wondered how *she* looked. She pulled the keys from the lock.

"The bank?" Lizzie said. Why would this girl think she was from the bank? Why was this girl even here?

"Oh, I get it, not the bank. From the real estate agency, maybe? Sorry, I was in the shower." The girl canted her hips, sticking one hand into a pocket, making the lining stick out past the frayed edges of her little jeans. Her sunburned face spackled with freckles, her wet hair pulled back in a scrunchy, she seemed unaware of Lizzie's bafflement. "It's not about the rent, right? We paid that. I'm sorry for the mess. Long weekend. I'm Maddie Kate Wendell."

Lizzie stood still, staring at a person who should not be there. Music, faint but insistent, came from upstairs, and an entryway side table held a haphazard pile of textbooks. Students? Students in the empty house. The not-empty house. Paying rent.

"Ma'am?" the girl was saying.

Maybe the records weren't up to date. Maybe the place was sold and rented, but the bank's internal paperwork had failed catch up. Certainly its record-keeping systems weren't foolproof. She herself was evidence of that. Lizzie almost nodded, mentally agreeing with this logical explanation.

"Sorry, Miss. Yes, it's about the—" Lizzie paused, considering what it *was* about. It was about her own curiosity. Her compulsion to make things add up. Which now, faced with reality, might not be prudent.

Because reality could create problems.

What if Aaron got wind of her visit? Would he have something on her? Or would she have something on him? The girl, Maddie, was waiting for an answer. Lizzie needed answers, too.

"It's about the rent," Lizzie said. The words tumbled out almost before she realized. "I'm checking, routine, to see if we have the correct address where you're sending the rent check. Can you confirm it?"

Lizzie hoped the girl's definition of "confirm" didn't include Lizzie having to provide something for her to confirm.

Maddie nodded her head. Like she was eager to help. *Good.*

"Oh, no prob. We send it to, like, a post office box in Boston. I don't have the exact-exact place, you know, because Frank, he lives here, too, always pays it, after we pay him. So, um . . ." She brightened. "I could have him call you?"

"Who at the post office box? I mean, can you confirm the name on the P.O. box?" Lizzie was Miss Helpful. Miss Unthreatening.

"I can look," Maddie said. "Want to come in?"

She did, and she didn't. *Decide.*

She did. Lizzie took a step across the threshold as the girl scurried away. Two laptop computers were open on a coffee table, a big-screen TV on mute, showing some music video with singing dogs and what must be hookers on motorcycles. Music continued from upstairs, louder now, thumping through the ceiling. Certainly several people were living here. Why? How? And if the house was sold, why did Aaron still have the keys?

Maybe they hadn't changed the locks. But still, even if

the sales and transfer paperwork was delayed, it shouldn't be *this* delayed. Certainly Aaron would be interested in hearing about that. It wouldn't be Aaron's fault, of course, he didn't handle the sales end of it.

Problem was.

Would those questions domino onto her own . . . "activities"? The housing market was coming back, all the analysts agreed. Not a full recovery, but the outlook was positive. What if they started auditing the foreclosed properties and the transactions connected to them? Would the audit fingers reach into her files? They might. They would. They definitely would.

Best to leave it alone.

If the numbers were taken out of her control, it would ruin her plans. Ruin her families' lives. Because they were *her* families now, and no way near recovered. They needed her, relied on her.

"Might be upstairs." Maddie came back into the foyer, empty-handed. "Two more seconds."

Lizzie blew out a breath as the girl trotted up the stairs. An array of running shoes, laces dangling, lined each step. Maddie kicked a pair out of the way as she came back down.

Lizzie's mind computed risk and reward, curiosity versus consequences. She'd simply *imagined* the place would be empty. She'd overanalyzed, like she always did, and now, bottom line, it put her where she had no business being.

"Sorry, I'm no help at all," Maddie was saying. "But seriously, I can have them call—"

"Never mind," Lizzie said.

23

"So where is he, Sherrey? Yeah, I'll hold." Waiting for Bing to finish whatever he was doing, Jake eyed the array of documents and files he'd spread across Nate Frasca's desk and office, wondered how fast he could put everything back in place, wondered how fast he could change his plane reservation, wondered how life managed to throw a monkey wrench into his plans at every damn turn.

He almost laughed, though humor was the last emotion he felt. A monkey wrench? What his grandfather used to say. Grandpa was on his mind a lot these days, as Lilac Sunday loomed.

Sherrey had told him there was another dead body near the Arboretum. Five days before Lilac Sunday. Boston would go ballistic.

Jake was on the verge of ballistic himself.

There had been not one thing in Frasca's elaborate files that pointed to any established reason Gordon Thorley should be suspected of making a false confession. The more Jake turned pages, the more he'd warily allowed himself to believe that this guy might be the solution to the crime that'd haunted his city—and his family—for twenty years.

Jake had listened to the rumble of D.C. spring thunder

as, page by page, he delved into the documented world of fakers, phonies, liars, and losers. Even the clinical cop-and-doctor speak was unable to disguise the torment—or manipulation—that would drive an innocent person to confess. But there was nothing in all the science, nothing in all the precedent or patterns, that explained Thorley.

He'd come here looking for answers, looking for some magic piece of paper that would slam Thorley into an understandable category, make him another sad but predictable loser.

"Be careful what you wish for," Jake said out loud.

Be careful what you wish for. His grandfather had said that, so many times. He'd explained to teenage Jake, in those mosquito-swatting summer evenings at the Cape cottage, what happened when cops wanted a solution too much.

Grandpa, who wore his badge even with his khaki shorts and boat shoes, also confessed the sorrow, the disappointment, when the cops failed. Telling a family their loved one had been murdered, that was the first hell of it. The only redemption, Grandpa had said, blasting more lighter fluid on the sizzling charcoal or turning the bluefish the two of them had just caught, the only redemption was when they could tell a family—*we got him.*

He'd never gotten to give Carley Marie's family that news. Even at age fourteen, Jake knew his grandfather blamed himself for that. Died blaming himself for that.

A splat of rain hit Frasca's picture window, and then another. This time Jake could see the lightning before he heard the thunder, Sherrey's speaker-amplified voice barely louder.

"Thorley is in the wind." Sherrey sounded full of triumph. "Means that bottom-feeding lawyer used a technicality to make us let the bad guy go. I oughta make fricking Hardesty tell the victim's parents."

"I'm headed to the airport," Jake said. "We're gonna get him."

It had to be connected, another dead girl in the Arboretum, right before Lilac Sunday. Was Thorley crazy? Or determined? Either way, a suspect. *The* suspect. "His sister, his family, his parole officer. Someone knows where he is. We'll find him."

He stopped, remembered another of his grandfather's warnings. *Don't jump to conclusions.* "This is Boston, though. Someone gets killed every week. Even Lilac Sunday week," Jake said. "But yeah. We need to talk with Thorley."

"Count on it," Sherrey said. "Soon as we find the jerk."

The dial tone buzzed over the speaker.

Jake stashed his phone, zipped his briefcase closed, stepped into the reception area.

"Miss Cardenas? Will you tell Dr. Frasca I had to go? A case heated up and—I'll be in touch. Maybe from the airport."

Frasca's secretary took off her headset, raised one eyebrow at the window. Jake could hardly see the park now, the rain now gushing in rivers down the slick glass, muddling the spring day into incomprehensible green and brown. "Good luck with that," she said. "I'll call a cab."

He perched on a side chair, close as he could to the door. He needed to go.

It wasn't the cops' fault that they'd let Thorley loose. Peter Hardesty had barreled in, all law books and legal threats, demanding his innocent client be released. Jake looked forward to confronting this guy. Finding out how he slept, knowing what he'd done.

What he'd done?

Jake listened to the rain, realized what brought them to this turning point in the story. He tried to stop thinking of it, but there was no ignoring it.

If Gordon Thorley killed someone else—strangled her, Bing had said—that innocent victim could be the proof Thorley was the Lilac Sunday killer.

But how did they get that proof? The cops had let Thorley go.

Jake had let him go.

They might catch a murderer. But to do that, the police had allowed someone else to be killed.

"Where were you, Lizzie? I was worrying about you."

Lizzie looked up from her spreadsheet, saw Aaron silhouetted in her office doorway. Where was Stephanie? Weren't people supposed to make appointments? Aaron took up the whole doorway, one hand braced against each side, suit jacket flapping open, blocking her view of the reception area.

"When?" She didn't stand, it was all she could do to stop herself. But this was her territory. As long as she stayed in her desk chair, she was in control.

"This morning. Up till half an hour ago." He didn't move either.

"Why?"

"Because of last night." This time, Aaron took a step closer.

Lizzie could see—what, contrition? On his face.

She had practiced, mentally, for this moment. "What about it?"

"It was your fault."

"*My* fault?"

Aaron took another step into her office. Reached behind him. Put his hand on the doorknob. Pulled.

Lizzie heard the hiss of the door closing over the thick pile carpet, heard the click of the latch.

"Your fault for being irresistible," he said.

Another step. Another. He faced her across her desk, his palms flat on the surface. She saw his blue college ring, his white cuffs under the navy blazer, his yellow tie touching a file on her desk as he leaned toward her.

"Your fault," he said. "Your fault for being fabulous."

She sat back, put her fingertips on the desk. With the toe of one foot, inched her chair away.

"Your fault for being—"

A rear wheel of her chair hit a stack of files on the floor. She couldn't get any farther away from him.

"Your fault for being here. In my life."

He couldn't possibly mean this. He was such a— *could he?*

"Aaron, I—"

"Lizzie, I'm a jerk. I am. Can you give me another chance? Everyone deserves another chance, right?"

She tucked a strand of hair behind her ear, but it didn't stay there.

Another chance? Well, they did, of course. Of course they did. No one was perfect. She certainly wasn't. A real person had faults, and who was she to judge? "Another chance" was what she gave her clients every day. Maybe this would be not only a second chance for Aaron, but a second chance for herself. For her future.

"If you put it that way . . . ," she began.

"I've never met anyone like you." He still leaned on her desk. She could smell the citrus and musk and whatever he wore, masculine and leathery and unfair.

Lizzie tried to figure out what to say. Could he be sincere? How could anyone ever tell? Numbers were easy for her. Words, not so much. People, not at all.

"Can we try again?" Aaron asked. "Tonight?"

"I . . . guess so," she said. She didn't like to guess, wasn't a good guesser, but unlike her precise numbers, sometimes life was unpredictable. It suddenly made her feel, what, free? To think so. Take a risk, she thought. *For once.*

"Tonight?" Aaron was saying. "Lizzie?"

"Sure," she said.

Aaron pulled out his cell phone, seemed to check something. "By the way . . ." His voice trailed off, his eyes on the cell phone screen.

"Yes?"

He clicked off his phone, closed his eyes for a fleeting second. "Lizzie? I'll make it up to you. I will. But do you have my keys?"

The keys. The keys he'd, well, maybe he'd actually dropped them. By mistake. In disappointment.

Maybe.

The keys that had sent her to Maddie Kate the college student. And the not-empty house.

Aaron's phone beeped, a text signal, and he pulled it out again.

The keys. They were in her purse, under her desk, and now felt like they emitted a radioactive glow, some sort of unmistakable signal she was hiding exactly what he wanted.

How was she supposed to react? If she returned the keys, she could please him. That was never bad. His one-liners were pitiful, but was she being picky again? It wasn't like she had other plans.

"Yes," she said. "I do. Have them."

There was something in Aaron's face that let her know she'd done the right thing. But she had one more thing she had to check on—sorry, Aaron, but she did.

"They're at my house," she lied. "I can get them for you later today, but—"

"Tonight then?" Aaron was texting and talking at the same time. Shouldn't he be paying attention to her? She tried not to change her mind, now that she'd said yes. But he wasn't helping. Or was that picky?

"Your place?" Aaron was saying as his thumbs moved across the keys. "We can text about what time."

"Okay." Lizzie drew out the word, knowing when she finished saying it, it was decided. Maybe a lot more than tonight was decided. "Okay."

24

"Keep a secret about what?" Jane tried to predict what Peter was really asking her. He certainly knew she'd lost her Boston TV job by keeping a secret, a heartbreaking lesson about terrible bosses and television's terror of lawsuits. She'd protected a source—as she had promised. Done nothing wrong. After the jury's defamation decision, she'd been fired from Channel 11, right when she was making a name for herself in television. That disaster changed her life, but not her devotion to journalism and the sanctity of secrets. Every story had a secret at its core. "Of course I can keep a secret."

They stood in the *Register*'s postage-stamp "visitor" parking lot, on the way to—somewhere. Peter said he'd explain as they drove. Jane was also struggling to jettison her envy over Chrystal Peralta's plum assignment, and focus on her own work. "You're too competitive," her mother always told her. Was there such a thing?

"Sorry to be so circumspect," Peter was saying. He smiled. "It's a lawyer thing, right? I'm trying to gauge what I can tell you without breaking the privilege. So let's just go, and then—"

"Go from there?" Jane said. *Lawyers*. Sometimes you had to be patient.

"Exactly." He pointed Jane to the passenger side of his

dark red Jeep, then hopped into the driver's seat, tossing his briefcase in the back. Jane saw a sleek tennis racket, two of them, on the backseat, next to a battered canvas Adidas bag. Two yellow tennis balls rolled onto the floor, landing on a pile of grimy Boston *Registers* and a wadded-up towel. "Sorry for the car." Peter waved at the chaos. "You're not allergic to dogs, I hope?"

Jane put her iced coffee in the cup holder, clicked on her seat belt, tucked her tote bag at her feet. "Dogs?"

"Dog. At home, luckily for you." Peter eased the Jeep out of the parking lot, the metal barrier arm creaking up. "Black lab. Named Harley. He'd be trying to sit on your lap if he were here."

"I have a—" Jane always hated to tell people she had a cat. She loved Coda, and had loved Murrow. But did it sound spinsterish? *Single woman with cat*. Still, possibly that was her own issue. "Not allergic," she said.

Peter headed up Dorchester Ave., turned onto the Southeast Expressway, instantly hitting the left lane, passing whenever he could, weaving through the snarl of traffic more aggressively than Jane might have. There was never a moment, even on a Tuesday afternoon, when 93 South wasn't teeming with cars, headed to the South Shore, or the Cape. Boston had gone crazy over the hot weather, celebrating the ending of another gloomy winter, and anywhere there was water became a magnet to hooky players. Jane bet half the cars on the road were workers who'd banged in sick. Who'd return in a day or so suspiciously sunburned, telling stories of "food poisoning."

The speed limit was fifty-five, but as the highway passed the JFK Library, the traffic braked to a crawl. The Jeep's digital speedometer flirted with twenty, and lost. That gave Jane time to find out what the heck was going on.

"Peter? What secret?" She smiled, trying to encourage

him to talk. "Did you lure me into the car under false pretenses? I have a cell phone, you know. Or the way this traffic is going, I could easily hop out and walk back to the *Register.*"

"Sorry, Jane." Peter edged into the left lane again, swerved back into the middle, sneaked between a mini-van and a Subaru with a ponytailed woman texting at the wheel. "I'm trying to decide how much I can tell you. It's tricky."

He punched on the radio, AM 1030, the all-news station. *Traffic on the threes,* it was saying. "Heavy and slow on the Southeast . . ." He changed lanes again, swerving.

"Hey!" Jane grabbed the strap, steadied her coffee. She never liked being the one along for the ride. "The deal is, you tell me everything. This is the way to Sandoval's sister-in-law's house. We weren't going to talk to them again until there was an arrest. So was there an—"

Jane stopped, mid-sentence. Another possibility. Peter had questioned Chrystal about the woman's body found in the Arboretum. They could get *there* this way, too. "Hey. Are we going to the Arboretum? Why?"

Jane turned down the radio. Why was he making her guess? "Peter? You think Elliot Sandoval had something to do with this murder? The new murder?"

Two crazies on motorcycles zoomed past them, weaving flamboyantly though the sluggish traffic.

Peter swore at them, then punched the radio back on. "Listen, I need to see if the cops are—well, let me hear the news, okay? Since you won't get me the details from your editor, I have to hear it somehow."

Jane took the elastic out of her stubby ponytail, shook out her hair, opened the window, letting in a puff of crazy-hot May air. This wasn't how she'd imagined this day. She'd imagined going to the drug store, buying sunscreen. Imagined pink sand and turquoise water and no deadlines. Now she was zero for three.

She waited, twisting her hair back into semi-place, letting Peter hear the newscaster's voice describing a house fire in Brighton, a state legislator forced to resign after some graphic tweets, and then, a body in Jamaica Plain. *A woman, no identification as yet, police say no suspects.* Jane saw Peter's grip change on the steering wheel, saw him flinch, even though he probably didn't realize it.

"What's the deal, Peter?" Jane was done speculating. "You get me out here asking if I can keep a secret, then you don't tell me anything. Now you're listening to the radio as if someone's life depends on it. And I'm wondering—whose?"

"Would you confess to a murder you didn't commit?" Peter asked.

"Confess? To a—?" Jane shifted in her seat, holding on again as Peter accelerated through an obviously too-small gap in the traffic. "Confess?"

This was either a ridiculous coincidence, or a potential disaster. Or both. This is exactly what Jake had mentioned the night before. Jake—*Jake*—had clammed up when she'd pushed him on it.

For a million reasons, she couldn't tell Peter what Jake had told her. Even the non-thing that it was.

"You think someone's offering a false confession?" Might as well go for it. If she was off base, she'd know it instantly.

"Why would you say that?" Peter turned to her, frowning.

"Well, you just asked me if—" Jane fussed with the window, wished she knew what was going on. There'd been a dead woman, Shandra Newbury, killed in a vacant house on Waverly Road. Now another one at the Arboretum, if she had it right. Were they connected? What did Elliot Sandoval have to do with it? Why didn't Peter—who clearly was involved—simply explain what the hell was up?

"Peter, listen. We agreed I won't report what you tell me about Sandoval. So why don't you just tell me?"

"Because it's not about Elliot Sandoval confessing," Peter said.

"Then who?" Jane frowned, trying to make sense of it. "What confession?"

"It'll work, trust me," Aaron said into the phone. "I'll switch the Nordstand Boulevard clients to another property. Same size, same everything."

Though the bank was still open, tonight till five, Aaron's office was deserted, secretary gone and other VPs pleading "off-site meetings." Aaron took advantage of the privacy, knowing no one could overhear. "I'll tell them the old tenants couldn't be out until tonight so we can't let the new ones in until tomorrow. I'll waive the key deposit. They're kids, they won't care."

Ackerman hated when he called, Aaron knew that, but sometimes it was the only way to connect. And so what? There'd be no incriminating record of it, no way to prove exactly what they'd been talking about. If anyone asked, they'd been discussing the bank's foreclosed properties. Exactly what they were supposed to be doing.

He rolled his eyes as Ackerman responded with his typical semi-cryptic half-sentences, meaningless or explainable if anyone happened to overhear. Ackerman had his own issues to juggle, and Aaron knew the pressures on him were relentlessly unpredictable. Which made Ackerman the same way, relentlessly unpredictable. Aaron was used to it. Didn't take Ackerman's arrogant and dismissive behavior personally anymore. It was all part of the deal.

"I'll make the rounds of the other places, let you know the score," Aaron said. "Sound good?"

But there was only silence. Ackerman had hung up.

Par for the course, Aaron thought, as he put down the phone. He checked his calendar and spreadsheets. One property's rent was a few days overdue. He smiled as he grabbed his car keys. College kids. What would he do without them?

25

Lizzie McDivitt stood on the sidewalk, half a block from the house. Just another Jamaica Plain saltbox, white, dandelion-dotted lawn, flagstones up to the screened front door. No cars in the asphalt driveway. Curtains over the front windows, closed, curtains over the second floor windows, closed, too. It *could* be vacant. Like it was supposed to be. Like the bank records said it was.

She fingered the keys in the pouch of her purse. Aaron's keys. Yes, she was meeting him later, and whatever she discovered, she could easily pretend none of it happened. Didn't have to decide that now.

She felt the sidewalk through her flat shoes, felt the humidity frizzing the ends of her hair, barely a breeze fluttered the leafy maple saplings that lined this street. Almost too hot to be outside. Maybe everyone was at a neighborhood swimming pool, or inside, grateful for air conditioning.

Maddie Kate Wendell. Why was she—and apparently a bunch of other college kids—living in that first "empty" house? Lizzie had checked the bank records on the downlow, and there was no denying it. The documentation was spot on, current and official. On paper, Maddie Kate's house was empty.

Would this one be empty, too?

A police car screamed by, sirens wailing, blue lights whirling. Lizzie took a step back, spooked. But the cruiser was soon out of sight, the siren disappearing with it. Showed how jumpy she was, that she'd be unnerved by a cop car. She waited until her heart stopped racing.

She didn't like loose ends. Especially when it came to numbers.

Now she was on the flagstone path, headed to the front door. A mailbox, mounted to the white siding, flapped open, but no mail was visible. No newspapers on the porch, no furniture, no sign anyone especially cared about the place, one way or the other. It did give off that shadowy hollow feeling of a vacant house, so maybe her theory was wrong. That would be a good thing.

She pushed the buzzer. No more trying keys without trying the doorbell first. She'd learned her lesson from Maddie Kate. She listened for sounds of someone inside. Nothing.

Maybe the Maddie Kate house was a mistake, and this whole "investigation" thing was a goose chase. She smiled, thinking about how a goose chase would change her evening with Aaron Gianelli. Maybe she'd buy some white wine, and some little appetizers. She'd be a regular person for once, not a—

"May I help you? Sorry, I didn't hear you over the AC."

The front door had opened. Lizzie, startled, took a hasty step back, almost tripping over her own feet.

Through the screen, Lizzie saw another version of Maddie Kate, this time a lanky redhead in sweatpants and a ponytail, a cell phone sticking up from her denim shirt pocket, one earbud dangling. An air conditioner hummed in the background.

"Ma'am?" the girl said. She blew on her fingernails, then looked again at Lizzie, questioning.

The screen door stayed shut.

"I'm from . . ." Darn. Lizzie should have prepared

something, a ruse or a story, why hadn't she done that? Well, the truth was sometimes good. Right now, the truth was about all she had.

"I'm from the bank." Lizzie used her best customer service smile, and gestured at the door. "From customer relations. We're here checking to see if everything is as expected. May I come in? And to confirm, can you tell me your name? Are you the one on the . . ." Shaky ground here. ". . . on the lease?"

The door opened, the girl hardly hesitating to admit a stranger. College kids.

"Oh, no," the girl said. "I'm Mo. Mo Heedles. They told us we could have four people, and that's really all we have. Really, it is. The other girl is here for the, um, weekend. Really."

Mo waved Lizzie into a living room, strewn with wads of cotton and manicure implements. It smelled like polish remover and cigarette smoke. Not the safest combination. College kids.

"Mo, is it?" Clearly the girl was on the defensive, so Lizzie had some leverage here. Lizzie tried to decide whether being nice was her strategy. Or being tough.

"Maureen," the girl said. She tugged out her other earbud, draped the thin cord around her neck. "Excuse the mess. What can I—what was your name again? And you're from the bank?"

Lizzie would avoid the "name" question. "Yes. And we're checking on your rent payments. Can you confirm you send them to"—it had worked before, why not try it again?—"a post office in South Boston?"

"Uh-huh," Mo said. "Fifteenth of the month. So it's not really due yet, right?"

"Exactly," Lizzie said. "I don't have anything to do with the rent, so no worries. And the term of your lease?"

"Well, we're here for the summer. While BU's out? We

have jobs." She waved a hand, then blew on her finger-nails again.

They were a deep navy, Lizzie saw. With white edging along the tips. "So it was perfect that this place was gonna be sold, you know, like, in the fall," Mo was saying. "Right when we'd be eligible to go back to the dorms."

"I see." This girl wouldn't know what was typical and what wasn't. Lizzie could risk pushing it. "Might I check one clause on your lease? It may be we're charging too much rent, that's why I'm here."

"Awesome!" The girl seemed interested for the first time. "I'm not sure, but it might be in . . ." She yanked open a drawer in a sideboard—the surface littered with unopened mail—then stopped, holding her hands up as if she'd been arrested.

"Ah, bummer. My nails," she said. "I can't look through all this stuff, because . . ." She held her fingers up, show-ing her careful polish job.

"I'm happy to check, if you like," Lizzie said. Should she paw through this girl's drawer? Mo had offered. And there might be the piece of paper that would answer all her questions. "I know what our leases look like, of course. I'll be able to tell you instantly if we owe you money."

"Awesome," Mo said. "Knock yourself out."

Peter's cell phone rang, vibrating across the console of the Jeep, hitting against Jane's huge iced coffee. Whoever was on the other end, he'd find it easier to answer the phone than Jane's insistent questions. He'd regretted the "can you keep a secret" remark the minute he said it—his usual lawyer training thrown spectacularly off course by the disturbing possibility that Gordon Thorley was in-deed the Lilac Sunday killer.

He reached for his phone, feeling for it, keeping his eyes on the increasingly exasperating I-93 traffic. What if it was Thorley? Making his one phone call from the police department?

The screen said *caller ID blocked*. Thorley. Damn. Jane was eyeing him inquisitively. With her in the car, it would be difficult to keep anything confidential.

But Jane was digging into her totebag. She took out her own phone, popped in her earbuds, started punching buttons. "Don't mind me," she was saying. "I'll check my messages."

Peter's phone rang again.

They'd never get to Thorley's place at this rate. Thorley hadn't been at his apartment earlier, Bing Sherrey had made that abundantly clear, so maybe there was no reason to hurry. Unless—unless Thorley returned home, unaware of the tumult that now surrounded him. In that case, Peter better arrive before the cops descended. Thorley'd give himself up, no question.

This'd be precisely what Thorley would hope for, in a crazy way. Even if he wasn't guilty. If Thorley could get himself arrested, it would be what he'd wanted from the start.

Suicide by cop, everyone knew about that these days, headlines describing the trapped rats who'd decided—in some insane last stand—to go down in a gun battle, make the police kill them, in some misguided effort to—

Another ring.

Peter yanked the steering wheel, changing lanes, trying to get ahead of the idiot in the Toyota. Maybe this wasn't suicide by cop. Maybe it was—worse, if that could be imagined.

To convince the cops he was the Lilac Sunday killer, did Thorley kill someone else?

Did Peter's zealous representation of an innocent-until-proven-guilty client push that client to kill another victim?

In which case—Peter was as guilty as Thorley.

If Thorley was guilty.

He hit ANSWER before the next ring ended.

Someone from the bank had already been here? This freckle-faced college girl standing behind the screen door had told Aaron someone was here this morning. About the rent. Aaron processed this new information, trying to decide if he was screwed or confused.

It could only be Ackerman. But why would Ackerman visit this particular house? This place was on *Aaron's* list, no question, and the tenants sent the rent checks, written to "cash," to Aaron's P.O. box in South Boston. This check had not been deposited on time and being in arrears was not tolerated. But there was clearly more to this than an overdue rent bill.

Standing on the front porch, Aaron pretended to check his notes, then pretended to check the house number on the doorjamb, giving himself some time to concoct a plausible explanation. The best defense is a good offense.

"Yes, of course," he said. "Sometimes we duplicate efforts, can't be avoided. What did they say?"

The girl shrugged, yanking down her thin white T-shirt, crossed one flip-flop over the other. Even through the mesh of the screen, he could see her cutoffs were impossibly short. Aaron tried not to look.

"Not much," she said. "Asked for my name, I think. And where we were sending the rent? Something like that."

"Which is what again? Your name?" Aaron asked. Might as well keep track of who he was dealing with.

"Maddie. Kate. Maddie Kate Wendell," she said. "Is something wrong?"

Aaron wrote her name on his clipboarded notepad. People always fell for clipboards, they were so official, a perfect disguise. If a stranger came to his front door? Stood on the porch asking questions? He'd never give his name, or anything else. But when the bank asked, people talked. Luckily for him.

"We definitely paid, I wrote the check myself." The girl, Maddie, was frowning now. She stood on one foot, then the other, then put the sole of one foot against her leg, like a gawky stork. "Maybe it's like, held up at the post office. You all have never been here before. Now, there's like two people in one day. Listen, sir, we paid. Are we still gonna be able to live here when—?"

"And then? The bank person?" Aaron interrupted, needing to get to the bottom of this. Had Ackerman tried to get these tenants to pay *him*? Directly? Why? That'd be a bitch. If Ackerman was trying to screw him? What an asshole. Good thing he'd come to get the scoop. What an *asshole*. "I mean, did you give *him* the check?"

"Him?" the girl said.

"The other bank guy," Aaron said. Was this Maddie an idiot? Or maybe . . . in on it? Somehow skimming off the rent money, or sharing it with Ackerman, in some under-the-table way?

"It wasn't a guy," the girl said. "It was a woman."

26

Peter glanced at Jane as he heard the voice on the other end of his phone call. She was deep into her message retrieval, her hair coming loose from that ponytail, fluttering in the breeze from her opened car window. If she was trying to overhear his conversation, she was doing a good job of hiding it.

"Yes, I remember you," Peter answered, keeping his voice low. "What can I do for—"

He stopped as the detective interrupted him.

"No," Peter replied. "As I told your colleague. No idea."

Pretty interesting, Peter thought as the cop went on, that this was the same detective who'd been at the Sandoval house when Peter arrived. Now he was asking about Thorley. Why was he involved in the Thorley case? As far as Peter knew, the primary was Branford Sherrey.

Huh. He'd suspected something going on between this cop and his sarcastic partner. Some undercurrent of agenda Peter couldn't comprehend. Did they know something about Sandoval they weren't telling? Or about Thorley?

Jane had worked on Sandoval, too, come to think of it. She'd been there when the body was found, according to her story in the paper.

Was there a connection between Thorley and San-doval?

Nothing that Peter knew of. What did this detective know? Or Jane? She'd been pretty interested when he'd talked about a confession.

"No," Peter answered the detective's question. "I haven't heard from him since—" The traffic was mirac-ulously thinning out, and Peter managed to ease the Jeep out from behind a Sam Adams truck. He could use a beer about now. "Well, I haven't heard from him."

He glanced across the seat. Jane still seemed involved with her voice mail.

"And you say his parole officer has no idea?" Peter needed to be firm, but didn't want to raise his voice. He'd tried to use only vague and ambiguous words, but "pa-role" and "officer" certainly weren't ambiguous. Espe-cially not together. "Detective? Is there anything you need to tell me?"

But the detective gave him only the predictable "call us if you find him" and "we'll call you if we find him first" routine, then hung up.

Peter clicked off, trying to plan. What would he tell Jane? And what did she already know?

"Bunch of nothing on my messages." Jane yanked out her earbuds as she saw Peter end his phone call. She'd wanted to give him some privacy, let him know she was trust-worthy, even though she desperately wanted to know what was going on. Was there a connection between the confession Peter was talking about, and the one Jake was talking about? Had to be. She was annoyed, and disap-pointed, that Jake hadn't called from D.C. "So much for that."

With traffic easing a bit, Peter careened the Jeep around a diesel-puffing hulk of a beer truck. She could use a beer about now. Jane thought calming thoughts, pushed her hair out of her face. Might as well be August. And she still didn't know where they were headed. A metaphor for her whole life.

"So, Peter?" she began. "You were about to tell me about the confession. Or—the false confession?"

She mentally crossed her fingers. Maybe she'd get some answers.

Peter kept his eyes on the road.

"Jane?" he finally said.

Yeesh. "Still here," she said.

"Do you know a Detective Jake Brogan?"

Three paper coffee cups, the crumpled waxed paper from a turkey sandwich, and the remnants of a double-sized Snickers wrapper littered the airport floor next to Jake's rocking chair. Jake never wanted to see that chair again. The sky had only gotten darker. The rain had only rained harder. Every baby in Reagan National Airport was crying, and even the gate agents, now snarling as passengers lined up to whine, had abandoned their smiley-face optimism. Just when Jake predicted it was meteorologically impossible for it to rain any longer, another torrent gushed across the tarmac, blasting water at the window from all directions.

He should have stayed at Frasca's.

What's more, his cell phone was down to one bar, but if he moved to a place where there were plugs, he'd have to give up his squatter's rights to the rocking chair, and be relegated to one of those not-made-for-humans molded plastic seats. He turned his phone off-off, figuring that'd save the battery.

That lasted about four seconds. He turned it back on. What if they found Thorley? He had to know, even though he was more than powerless—ha-ha—to do anything about it. Or what if Thorley called him, and his phone was off?

This whole thing sucked, big time. His hot idea to come to Washington. But he'd really figured—hoped—there was something in those files, something in history, that would clue him in to Gordon Thorley's motives.

He'd been wrong.

Jake leaned back in the rocker, contemplating the extent of the disaster. Now he was left with a disappointed girlfriend, no relevant information about his case, and a verging-on-dead phone. At least Diva was at Mother's house, so "hungry golden retriever" was not on his list of woes.

All he could imagine was turquoise water and pink sand and Jane in that "very small" bathing suit she'd described. Three things he was not gonna see.

A bolt of lightning illuminated the sooty sky, followed almost instantly by the crack of thunder. The babies cried harder. Jake's phone rang, the trill barely audible. One bar, Jake saw. Caller unknown.

Jane, maybe? Wouldn't be the first time she'd called just as he was thinking about her. But then, he was often thinking about her.

"This is Jake Bro—," he began.

"Got him, Harvard," the voice said. DeLuca? But he was—"Kat got a call from her lab. The two-by-four from Waverly Road has Sandoval's DNA."

"Where are you?" This wasn't computing.

"Irrelevant and immaterial," DeLuca said. "I'm here with the best medical examiner Boston's ever had—shhh, hang on, I'm telling Jake—and what can I say. Guess it pays to have friends in high places. Friends who can move your DNA screens to the front of the line. Maybe even expedite Lilac Sunday when we get home, right? Though why waste a favor when the guy's confessed? But this one? Slam dunkeroo."

"So it's—"

"Yup. Our steroid-happy carpenter—"

"Steroids?" Jake said.

"Oh, yeah, forgot to mention. The whole report was faxed to HQ."

"Son of a bitch."

"Sorry to miss the big takedown, Harvard," D said. "But I'm, shall we say, otherwise occupied. And vacation is vacation. You, on the other hand, are in line to make the big arrest. Make the headlines, bring the sucker to justice."

"We'll need a warrant." Jake thought out loud, watched the bar on his phone struggle and flicker. Dammit.

"So?" DeLuca said. "Get one. And let me know what happens, okay, dude?"

Jake heard a whimper, then a murmur of comfort. A harried-looking young woman, striped shirt and jeans, hair straggling out of a lopsided barrette, switched a squirmy infant to her other hip, and hoisted an oversized diaper bag to her shoulder.

Jake stood, gesturing to the rocking chair.

Hell with it. He scooped up his trash with one hand, then searched the baseboards, scanning for electricity. He needed a plug. First to call Judge Gallagher for the warrant, then to call Peter Hardesty again. This day was becoming more complicated, but more interesting. Closing a murder case, finding the bad guy, was always a good thing.

And maybe the rain was stopping.

"On it, D," Jake said. "Tell Kat thanks."

"You can count on it," D said. "In fact, I've already started thanking her."

27

"Pro—yikes—fessionally," Jane said, wincing as a buzzy little Fiat convertible cut in front of them. Why was everyone in such a crazy hurry? Being a passenger sucked. "Jake Brogan is a Boston detective. Why?"

Jane frowned, facing resolutely forward. She wanted to watch Peter's expression, gauge where he was going with his "do you know Jake Brogan" question, but she felt bound to watch the chaotic traffic instead. Good-sport Jane had about had it with Hardesty's aggressive driving. What's more, good-sport Jane had also had it with his secrecy. If she couldn't take the wheel, time to at least change the subject to one of *her* choosing.

"Peter? Ah, I hate to be a pain in the ass, but where are we—*hey!*"

Jane grabbed the strap again, closed her eyes, then didn't. Then saw the shape of something in her side mirror, something that shouldn't be there, but—

"Damn it!" Peter yelled, and Jane felt the boxy car try to swerve to the left, out of the way of the blue whatever careening into their blind spot and then shoving them into the left lane. Jane heard the skid, felt the wind in her hair and the force of Peter's hard right turn throwing her against the seat belt, then back again. She closed her eyes, then opened them, then closed them, clenching her teeth

and shoulders, waiting for the crunch and the crash and the sound of glass and metal, and how would they ever—

"Hang on, Jane!" Peter's voice, terse, hard, demanding. The Jeep swerved again, a car in the other lane, too, boxing them in, no one's fault but the idiot Fiat's, and if Peter couldn't—

"*Ow!*" The side of Jane's head slammed into the window as Peter tried to yank the car back onto the highway after they'd jounced across two lanes verging on out of control, Jane could feel it, could hear the wheels and the horns and the honking, and she was bracing herself *this was it,* not a chance in the world they would—

The wheels skidded again, the car jouncing and bouncing over the grassy shoulder, bumping down the wildflower-filled culvert—Jane saw it almost in slow motion, pink and white lace, colors blurring as the Jeep lurched and staggered, wheels catching on whatever, Jane could see through the windshield, they were headed—what, down? She braced her arms against the dashboard, locking her elbows, wondering how it felt to be blasted by an airbag, wondering if she would even feel it, or if she would never feel anything again. One wheel hit, then the other, the car went sideways, almost, then not, and then almost, and if the car flipped over, they'd be—

Stopped. It stopped.

Silence.

Jane took a breath, realized she could take a breath. Every muscle in her body was still clenched.

"Peter?" She whispered the word, almost checking to make sure her voice worked, still looking forward. "Peter?"

Silence.

Lawyers. Jake's phone was up to four bars now, for whatever good that did. Peter Hardesty was not answering.

As a result, he would not know his client was about to be arrested. Jake could stall, certainly, until the judge actually granted the warrant. Sandoval—so adamantly protesting his innocence yesterday—was not much of a flight risk.

"Attention passengers at Gate C-one," a voice came over the intercom. "JetBlue flight four-forty-three to Boston will soon be ready for preboarding. We regret the . . ."

A sliver of twilight moon emerged in the now-clearing sky. The tarmac glistened with a sheen of moisture, but other than that and a terminal filled with cranky passengers, it was as if the storm had never happened.

Jake clicked off the phone. He was under no obligation to leave a message for Peter Hardesty. If the lawyer wasn't answering, he was clearly otherwise occupied.

That call could wait.

And Jane? He punched up her speed dial, glancing at the gate agent. The impatient passengers, the ones who somehow needed to board first, were already queuing near the gate agent's desk, casually crowding, pretending they just happened to be standing there. Jake shook his head. They would all get to Boston at the same time.

He smiled, remembering his idea to surprise Jane, and ended the call before she answered. He couldn't tell her about the Sandoval arrest until it was public. That was one of the tradeoffs they'd have to get used to. He'd not even been gone for a day. And it already felt—wrong. He missed her. Missed their connection.

Flowers, definitely. Wine. And a discussion about their future.

And, tomorrow, a slam dunk arrest.

"Peter?" Jane's shook her head, slowly, carefully, feeling muscles in the back of her neck as she turned. Peter sat, back flat against the driver's seat, hands still clutching the steering wheel, elbows stiff, looking straight out the windshield.

"You okay?" Jane asked again.

"Are you?" Peter said. "That idiot—"

"Really, check yourself out," Jane said, doing the same thing. She lifted her shoulders, touched her face, ran her tongue across her teeth. One of the tennis rackets from the backseat was on the floor in front of her, both tennis balls had rolled onto the floor on Peter's side. Jane's coffee now splatted down one leg of Peter's suit pants, tiny ice cubes scattered on the floor like melting confetti.

The whole front end of the Jeep was tipped, stopped by a wildflower-filled gully down the median of the highway. No windows broken, no airbags exploded. Jane heard a siren off in the distance, but the sound faded, and disappeared.

"Peter?" What if he'd hit his head? She searched for her phone, where was it? "We'll need to get you to a hospital."

"I'm fine," Peter said. "I'm so freaking sorry." She heard him take a deep breath, run his hand through his hair, turn to look at her. He unclicked his seat belt, reached over, touched her bare arm.

"You're shaking," he said.

"I know," she admitted. "It all happened so fast, though. . . ." She was more scared now than when it happened. "It all happened so fast"—how many times had people she'd interviewed said that? Now she knew it was true. Six o'clock, the dashboard indicator said. Then, 6:01. The clock still worked.

Cars zoomed by, ignoring them.

"I am so sorry." Peter opened his car door, slowly. "Some idiot ran us off the road, trying to get in my lane, then that other guy wouldn't move so—shit."

"One of those things." Jane tried to stay calm. *It's over, random, not even Peter's fault.* And even though she'd thought he'd been driving kind of aggressively, he'd actually been amazing, keeping the car in control.

She opened her car door, too, stepped out onto the rangy grass. Peter had a hand on the hood, checked the front end, peered under the bumper, then examined each of the tires.

"Not even a flat," he said. He put his hands on her shoulders, looked at her, intent. "Jane? Are you sure you're . . . ?"

"Yeah. Fine." She didn't move, feeling the weight of his hands, and the tiny breeze through the wildflowers, and the gratitude that this had not turned out a disaster. "Are *you* sure? Should we call the—?"

"I think we can back out," Peter said. He took one hand off her shoulder, then the other. His shirt had come untucked on one side, his pants were coffee soaked, and his shoes were coated with dust. "If you're truly okay. I'll call nine-one-one if—"

"Really and truly," Jane said. She touched the side of her head, feeling a spot where it was tender. "I might have a bruise, but I'll be fine. Sorry about the coffee, though. You're kind of—wet. You honestly think the car's okay?"

"The Jeep's pretty forgiving. The engine's working, so step back. I'll give it a try."

She watched Peter tramp through the weeds, get into the driver's seat, close the door. She felt safe with him, it wasn't his driving that caused this. He hadn't panicked. He'd focused, pulled it off. Didn't try to blame anyone else.

They were lucky. Everything was fine.

Jake, she thought. *What if I'd been killed in a car accident, and we'd left—like that?*

The car's engine rattled, then whirred, and Jane stepped farther back. The car lurched, then caught, and the front wheels rolled up the side of the ditch and back onto flat ground. A patch of crushed Queen Anne's lace and two tire-patterned tread marks were the only signs anything had happened.

Jane opened the passenger door. Inside, Peter was smiling. Even the air conditioner was on. "What's the verdict?"

"Good to go, looks like. Hop in." Peter waited until she strapped herself in, then edged the nose of the car around, aiming it to the highway. "Ah, you've got a little dirt on—right there."

Jane pulled down the visor, flipped open the mirror. A pale face looked back at her, blinking. A curling lock of hair hung over one cheek, her cheeks red and shiny with the heat, a smudge of grime painting her forehead.

"All good," she said. "A little dirt never hurt anyone. Wet pants, though, that's a different story. Yours are never going to be the same."

"Tell you what—let's head to my place," Peter said, gauging the traffic as it sped by.

Their heads moved in unison, watching two cars, then a white Boston cab, top speed, an eighteen-wheeler, then another, then—a break.

Jane pointed. "Now."

Peter gunned it, and with one jounce, they were back in the fast lane.

"Good job," Jane had to say. "You did great."

"Got lucky," he said. "Except for the pants thing. Let me change, and then head out. Make sense?"

As much as anything did. Jane was back at square one. "Peter? Where the—hell—are you taking me?"

28

Atlantic & Anchor Bank was closed, if you were a customer, but inside the executive suites and the managers' offices, as in Lizzie's, a few of the lights were still on. It was Tuesday, the end and beginning of A&A's proprietary fiscal week, the day the bank's systems cranked out their internal reports and fed the computations and calculation data—the C&Cs—to those vetted few who had access. And who bothered to read them. These numbers, separate from the rolling daily audits the bank's elaborate financial ledgers computed on a minute-by-minute basis, allowed insiders to gauge business, and inflow, and even receivables, if anyone decided to examine them.

Lizzie watched the spreadsheet unfurl, mentally calculating along with the output, knowing exactly what she was looking for. She had tested her system—a shrug, "system" was good a word as any—with the Iantoscas, the Gantrys, and the Detwylers.

This C&C run was a bellwether. If today's calc picked up her changes, she'd still have time before the formal Friday wrap to make good and erase her mathematical tracks. She was still new, after all. And who was going to argue with her? She allowed herself a smile, thinking of her connection with the fifth floor.

Daddy's little girl, indeed. She'd always wanted to be.

And who'd have thought it would add up this way? She watched a column of black and red scroll by—so far, so good. *Okay.* The Iantosca portfolio wasn't flagged, so all was well there. If she made it through this, it would prove the intricate go-around she devised had defeated the internal oversight controls. Two more "customers" to go.

By the time the computation ended, if it all went as she hoped, she'd have time to race to Whole Foods, get some snacks, maybe cheese? What did people do? Then make it home in time for Aaron at nine-ish, the way they'd planned.

She clicked her computer mouse, pausing the progression of the numbers on her screen. The bank corridors were silent, and she'd left her door open, preferring her privacy, but needing to monitor if anyone—*Aaron*—came by. Snooping. Asking questions she didn't want to answer. Especially since she had a big fat list of questions she wanted to *ask*.

The damn—darn—lease was burning a hole in her briefcase. She told that girl Mo she'd bring it back tomorrow. "After the main office checked the final numbers." She'd made up the perfectly believable lie instantly. Mo had been more than happy to relinquish the paperwork, hoping for a break on the rent in return.

Lizzie clicked RUN again. She couldn't afford to miss anything, and if she saw it in real time, all the better in case she needed to reevaluate and recalculate. The sooner that happened, the easier to cover her tracks. But she hoped she wouldn't have to.

There. The Gantry portfolio. Loan number, dates, origination, sale one, sale two, modification—the snag would be next if it was going to show up. But no. No red numbers. No arrearage. No arrears notification, no lis pendens, nothing that would show anything but a happy family happily making mortgage payments with happy 5 percent interest on their happy home in—wherever it was. Framingham.

That the Gantrys were deep into mortgage debt might be the truth, but thanks to Lizzie, it sure wasn't showing up in the paperwork.

Two down. One to go.

And then, Aaron.

It was a woman? A *woman*? Aaron Gianelli draped his arms over the wheel of his white Fiero, rested his head on his wrists. Paralyzed in the bank parking lot, terrified to go inside.

No matter how he played out the possibilities, the bottom line pointed to only one answer. Lizzie McDivitt had taken his keys and visited his clients. Why? What would possess her to snoop into his business? Actually go to his homes? Homes he was in charge of? Who the hell made her the grand inquisitor?

If she told anyone, anyone upstairs—well, Ackerman was going to be so pissed off, no one on the planet could be so pissed off.

There would be music to face, at some point, whatever the hell music there was. But one false move, one falling domino, and this whole enterprise would blow up in his face. And no way Ackerman and his compadres would step up and share any of the repercussions.

Aaron let the movie of the disaster unreel in his mind: the police, and the prosecutors, whoever they'd be, federal, maybe even, since it was banking? Or, hell, he didn't know. He *should* know. He'd either have to rat out Ackerman and the whole thing, what he knew of it at least, or take the fall on his own.

That was a no-brainer. He was not gonna take the fall.

Question was, was there a way to stop it, right now, prevent any of it from getting out?

What would that be? Aaron lifted his head from his arms, stared into the parking lot. The bank president's place was still occupied, that navy blue Lexus that cost Aaron's entire annual salary, probably more. Ackerman's space was also filled. And so was Lizzie's. She was here at the bank, not at home.

He sat back in his seat, chewing the inside of his cheek. Imagining her journey. Her office. The parking lot. Her apartment.

Where did she park at home? Did she have to walk from there to her front door? Or did she use a back door?

So many things about Miss Lizzie he didn't know.

Still, he knew how to find out.

"Here we are." Peter pulled into his driveway, clicked open the garage door, but didn't drive in. The porch light was on, even though it wasn't quite dark. He hadn't reset the timer for the later-lasting summer light. Harley already had his two front paws on the front bay window, and Peter could see he was barking. He smiled, remembering. Dianna used to say Harley would run to the front window before *she* had any idea he was coming home.

He still missed Di. But life would go on. His, at least.

"Let me run in and change my—listen. If you don't mind the dog and a lot of newspapers on the couch, come on in and wait in the air conditioning. Unless you prefer to—"

"Thanks. I'll hit the bathroom, if you don't mind," Jane said. "Nice house, by the way. I love this part of Milton. You lived here long?"

He watched her gather up her stuff, thinking again how lucky they were that he'd been able to handle the Jeep. Random, ridiculous drivers. Another lesson in how quickly one's life could change.

"A few years," he said. He opened the door, keyed the

alarm system, defended himself against his overjoyed Lab. "Yes, I'm home, yes, you can go out, yes, this is Jane, try to behave."

Peter waved Jane inside, grabbing Har's thick red collar in a futile effort to restrain the four-legged goofball now attempting to wag his entire body. "He's enthusiastic."

"So I see," Jane said. "You sure you're okay?"

"Yeah." Peter waggled his shoulders, rolled his neck. "Creaky, though, I guess. You?"

"Me, too," she said. She flexed her arms, shook them out.

"We're lucky," he said. He saw her looking around the living room, at the photos over the fireplace, and the silver frames on the piano.

"You play?" she asked.

He knew it. Okay, then, the short version.

"My wife did. She died. Several years ago." He waved at the pictures. "That's her. Dianna Nesbitt. She was terrific."

"I'm so sorry," Jane said.

"Thanks." Peter shook his head. Enough explanation. "Listen. Do you mind if I take a quick shower? You can use the downstairs head, I'll go up. I'm sort of—"

"Sure," Jane said. "I'm fine."

Harley yanked away from him, sniffled up to Jane.

"Harley," he said. Exasperated. "Get back here. Jane, I'm sorry, Har's just happy to—"

"We're fine," Jane plopped onto the couch, Harley nudging her leg. "Go shower."

"He can go outside, into the backyard." Peter pointed. "Just open the kitchen door back there, okay? And you can have some peace."

"Will do," Jane said. "We're fine."

29

"Where the hell did you go? A little rain scare you off?"

Jake figured he had only a few minutes to answer Nate Frasca's call before the flight attendant's preflight swoop-through ensured no passenger was using a deadly electronic device in deadly out-of-airplane mode.

"Nope, *you* scared me off," Jake said. "All that bullshit jargon in your files, God help anyone trying to make heads or tails. I'm boarding now, so—"

"You get anything?" Frasca said.

"Maybe," Jake said. "Thing is, it all points to his potential guilt. Excuse me, ma'am." Jake found seat 6A, slid past the woman with the e-reader in 6B. She'd stuck a full paper cup of coffee in the elastic seat pocket in front of her, and the cup was clearly on the verge of collapse. Exploding coffee, just what he needed. "Anyway. Turns out we've got a different case coming to a head back home. Suspect and all. So I've got to—"

"Ladies and gentlemen, from the flight deck, this is Lois, your front cabin attendant," squawked a voice over the PA. "In preparation for takeoff, please make sure all of your cell phones are—"

"Listen, Nate? Gotta go. They're—"

"You said the Lilac Sunday guy's name was Gordon Thorley, right?" Frasca interrupted. "Common spelling?"

"Yeah. At least, that's the one who *says* he—well, yeah." Jake held the phone between his shoulder and cheek, felt for the seat belt while trying to avoid poking his seatmate in the ass, clicked it on. "Ring a bell?"

"Maybe," Frasca said. "Age?"

"Like, late thirties? Early forties," Jake said. "What bell?"

"Maybe nothing," Frasca said. "But—"

"Sir?" A disapproving flight attendant leaned across e-reader woman, eyeing Jake's phone. "We cannot take off until all cell phones—"

"Gotta go." Jake clicked off, showed the woman his black screen.

"Airplane mode, sir," she said.

Just get me to Boston, Jake thought.

Why were numbers so easy and people so difficult?

Lizzie's client handiwork had passed the C&C test with flying colors. She should be happy. For now, at least, no one would notice that the mortgage payments for certain families did not exactly match actual money in the actual bank. According to the records, those customers were stellar, reliable, and double-A risks.

One hundred percent untrue, of course. But Lizzie was sick of banks, marble palaces to greed and acquisition, raking in all the profit at the expense of those they ostensibly served.

Not exactly objective, of course, but when the pendulum swung so far the wrong way, it was immensely pleasurable to be able to push it back. Even just her little bit. Seeing the relief and delight on the Iantoscas' faces, for instance, made it all worthwhile.

Lizzie tilted back in her office chair, leaning into the cushion, stared at the nubby white ceiling. Technically, *technically,* she was robbing the bank. From the inside.

She clicked her seat back into place. Still. The bank would never miss the money, people got to stay in their homes, and she got to do a good thing. A total win-win. Well, not exactly total-total. The powers-that-were up on the fifth floor would certainly not be thrilled. Nor, Lizzie had to admit, would the federal bank examiners or FDIC or the comptroller of the currency. Or the cops. But it was a win for the good guys. And she was a good guy.

When the families were back on their feet, she would undo it. Tell them their payments had to start again, lucky that their new job, new life, inheritance, or lottery win—whatever—had come at exactly the right time. Then she'd back the numbers out, and all would be well.

Question was—what was Aaron doing?

She took out the lease for the millionth time, tried again to find some clue. It was so standard, the header actually said "Standard Lease Form." She smoothed out the two creases in the legal-sized document, read the boilerplate language, customary lease stuff, tenant at will, blah-blah, address, rent payment of $2,950 per month, payable on the blah-blah.

The lessee signature line had a scrawly felt-tip name, which Lizzie decided was the Frank Something guy Mo Heedles had mentioned. The ridiculous illegible squiggle above the typed-out "for the lessor" hardly had any decipherable letters, let alone a name. It was only a line with a loop on the end. Someone writing fast.

Or writing to deceive.

Someone who figured no one else would ever look at the lease, and if someone did, the signature was 100 percent deniable.

Why did her analysis always seem to go in circles?

Because—wait. There was one possibility. One explanation that meant maybe Aaron thought he was doing a good thing, too.

Maybe they just had different ways of going about it.

And if that were true—speaking of circular—then maybe the best option was to leave it alone.

She picked up her ball-point pen, clicked the end of it, up and down, and up and down.

Leave it alone. It's what she'd want him to do if he ever found out about her—not that he ever could.

Click, click.

Leave well enough alone, her father always said that. Well, what if this was "well enough"?

Click, click.

Lizzie put the pen back into the leather container. She folded the lease once, twice, and smoothed the wrinkles.

She'd decided.

She'd take the lease back to that house tomorrow. Stick it in the mailbox, with a note saying "All is correct and current, sorry for the confusion."

Type it, so there'd be no handwriting.

Lizzie tapped her fingers on her desk, weighing the pros and cons. The girl in the house was an airhead. No one could easily connect Lizzie to any of it.

Now she could meet Aaron, as planned. She was late, but still acceptably late. She'd had to work later than she'd expected. Right? He'd understand.

Maybe tonight she could find out what he was doing. Confirm what she suspected.

She popped her computer screen to black, grabbed her linen jacket, and her briefcase, clicked off the lights, locked her office door.

She punched the elevator button P for parking. If she had it right, what was Aaron's motivation?

By the end of tonight, she'd know.

At least she hadn't had to answer Peter's impossibly complicated "do you know Jake Brogan" question. Jane opened the kitchen door for Harley, and the Lab bounded

into the lilac-filled backyard, headed to a patch of manicured shrubs across the lawn. White impatiens blossomed
in ceramic pots, two hunter green Adirondack chairs and
a charcoal grill were arranged comfortably on a modest
wooden deck. Someone loved this yard. Anyway, by now
maybe Peter had forgotten his question. But Jane hadn't
forgotten *her* question.

She watched the dog snuffle around, quiet for a moment in the twilight of the May evening. Jane couldn't
see into the neighbors' yards on any side, fences and
greenery blocked the way. She took a breath, drawing in
the fragrance of the lilacs, trying to erase the car accident
and the fear. Replacing it with beauty. Boston could be
gorgeous this time of year, she thought. Well, this was a
suburb, but same difference. She rarely missed the Mid-
west, where her father and sister still lived. *Lissa.* She
shook her head. Lissa's wedding in June. Looming. She'd
think about that later. The lilacs were here and now, and
so was she, and all of today's bad stuff was over.

Harley was occupied, and she guessed she could leave
him outside. Jane went back in, closing the kitchen door,
which clicked shut behind her. She could hear the upstairs
shower.

She found the downstairs bathroom—clean, a couple
of framed museum prints, Kandinsky, on the walls. No
toothbrushes. She fussed with her hair—*hopeless, why'd
she leave her purse in the living room?*—resisted the urge
to open the mirrored medicine cabinet, and headed back
to the living room couch.

She blinked, not quite understanding.

"Ah, hello," she said.

Did someone else live here? Peter hadn't mentioned a
roommate, but how else would this guy have gotten in?
Maybe this was the person who loved the garden. Seemed
pleasant enough, older, thin, ill-fitting jean jacket. Scrag-
glier than Peter. Not really what she'd have predicted as

his roommate type. But then, who knew. The shower water continued.

"Who're you?" the man said. He must have just come in the door, and stood facing her at the edge of the entryway. She hadn't heard a car.

"I'm so sorry," Jane said. "I'm—"

"Are you a lawyer, too?" the man asked. He shifted, one foot to the other.

Maybe he was embarrassed to see her here. Maybe since Peter's wife had died, there hadn't been any other—well, whatever.

"Oh. No." Jane smiled. "I'm a colleague of his. He's upstairs, taking a shower." She paused, realizing how that might sound. Shook her head. "Long story. No, we're—"

She didn't need to explain herself, Peter's roommate was simply startled to see anyone. She would be, too, if she walked into her own home and saw a strange woman.

"Peter and I are working on a—project. Together."

"Are you?" the man said.

Jane didn't quite like the tone of his voice, but then she wouldn't have to be around him long. She wished Peter would hurry. There was no protocol for this. Or maybe the guy was socially awkward, and she should be more friendly. Make conversation.

"Are you Peter's roommate?" she asked.

"Nope," the man said.

Jane could hear Harley, barking, in the backyard. Barking, and barking. She turned, ready to go let the dog in. She'd feel better with Harley here, for some reason she couldn't quite put her finger on.

"Nope, you don't want to do that," the man said. "Stay right here, miss."

"What?" He hadn't threatened her, exactly. But it felt—off. She wished for Peter, she wished for Harley, she wished for the cell phone in her faraway tote bag, for whatever good that would do. "I'm sorry, who are you again?"

"Shouldn't you know? You're a reporter, right?" The man almost smiled. "You're Jane Ryland."

Jane took a step back, toward the stairs. Closer to where she hoped Peter would soon be. *Wait a minute.* The front door had been open. The garage door had been open. The alarm was off—she'd watched Peter disarm it. Harley was in the backyard. But she was used to being recognized from TV, so maybe he was a fan. "Yes, that's—so you know who I am?"

"I also know your address, and your Amex number, and that you used to have fifty-two dollars in cash in your fancy wallet."

Jane took one more step back. The man took one step closer to her. This was no fan.

"You shouldn't leave your purse around," he said.

"Peter!" she yelled. But all she heard was water.

30

Jake reached up, punched the orange call button. The woman in 6B was on her second Sudoku. The ones in Jake's in-flight magazine had already been done, half-done, badly done, by some previous passenger. Rain pelted the Plexiglas porthole windows. The 737 had moved away from the gate, then stopped. Hadn't budged an inch on the tarmac since then.

"Yes?" The attendant appeared, all smiles.

"Can we at least use our phones? While we wait?" Jake asked.

Six-B looked up. "How long is it going to be, do you know?"

The flight attendant peered from under her eyelashes, squinting at the new torrent against the window, the multicolored lights of passing equipment glaring red and yellow on the drops, then fading to black. A crack of thunder rumbled, then a flash of lightning. Jake could see the Reagan terminal building, the multi-story panes of glass, the passengers inside peering out at the planes. They were grounded. He was grounded. Everyone was grounded.

"I'm so sorry," she said, waving in the general direction of outside. "We thought the rain was ending. Still, they're requesting us to stay on standby, not pulling us back to the gate. That means they're optimistic."

"The phones?" Jake repeated, holding his up.

"Yes, you may," the attendant said. "I'll let you know as soon as we're back in the rotation."

Jake wasn't listening. He'd clicked the cell on before she'd finished, punched in Jane's number, watched out the window as her phone rang, five hundred miles away. She was probably—well, who knew where she was, but he pictured her on that leather couch of hers, stretched out, her long legs across his lap maybe, in one of those little tank tops she wore, her hair down. That damn cat was probably draped over the back of the couch cushion, as always.

Ring two.

Jake focused his reverie on Jane, her hair splayed across that striped pillow, her toes kneading into his thighs. It was raining there, too, he bet. At least *there* it was—cozy. One of Jane's words.

Ring three.

Maybe she wasn't home, if she wasn't answering. Maybe she was in a meeting, or on a story. But this time of night?

What if Sandoval had been arrested? By another detective? If someone had found him, say, and gotten orders to grab him. Maybe Jane was covering that. That'd be tease fodder for God knows how long—the irony of him being trapped on a plane while she was getting photos of what should have been his big arrest.

Ring four. Weird.

On the other hand, equally annoying, Sandoval might have headed for whatever hills he could. With the cop shop short staffed, and DeLuca out of pocket, maybe they'd pulled back on the Sandoval arrest, and as a result of budget cuts and Mother Nature, the bad guy was getting away.

A click on the line, a change in the sound. Finally.

"Hey, Jane, it's—"

"This is Jane Ryland. I'm sorry I can't come to the phone right . . ."

Voice mail.

"Shit."

Six-B raised an eyebrow.

"Sorry," he said. Well, that was too bad. He'd call her when he got back. Or maybe stop by and surprise her. If he ever got back.

"See? They're looking for me." Jane pointed to her tote bag, her phone chiming from deep inside. "If I don't answer that, all hell is gonna break loose. They know I'm here," she lied. Whoever "they" was supposed to be. "You'd better let me answer it."

She took a step toward the phone. It brought her closer to whoever this was, but it might be her only option.

The man put up a palm, narrowed his eyes at her. "I'll have to risk that." Reached into his back pocket. "I don't believe you anyway, *Jane*."

And then she saw the glint of a knife.

This was ridiculous. The intruder was so puny, so scrawny, she could probably belt him with a—she scouted the living room for a weapon. Nothing.

Enough.

Jane put her hands on her hips, hoping she appeared tougher than she felt. "Look. I don't know who you are, but you are clearly breaking and entering. Trespassing. You've now pulled a knife, that's assault, and you've admitted to petty theft, threatened credit card fraud, and there's a lawyer about to come downstairs. So why don't you—" She waved at the front door. "Go. Now. I won't call the cops, I won't tell anyone. You just—"

"Stop right there."

The voice came from behind her. Peter.

He'd heard voices downstairs—had Jane turned on the television? But there was not a TV quality to the voice. Maybe the phone. But then—was that her phone ringing? She was still talking while it was ringing? Someone else was there. He grabbed a towel, wrapped it around his waist as securely as he could, and peered over the banister. Saw Jane's back.

And the face of Gordon Thorley.

What was he doing here?

Then he saw the knife.

On tiptoe back to his bedroom. The .38 in the drawer. Ammo in, all set. *Nine-one-one.* Shit. Phone cradle empty. He'd left the handset somewhere, again. A land line was in the kitchen, and his cell still on the damn console of the Jeep.

How'd Thorley get inside? Peter'd left his own front door open. And the frigging garage. He'd only planned to be inside a minute or two. Shit.

Peter was barefoot. Wrapped in a towel. But there was no time to do anything about that. He took one quick but careful step, then another, then another, heading toward the top of the stairs. Plastered his back against the wall, took a quieting breath. Listened.

There was conversation from below him, Jane talking, quietly; he couldn't make out the words. No screaming. Okay, she was handling it.

But Thorley had a knife. Thorley was a convicted felon, an accomplice in an armed robbery. He'd confessed to murder. And now—if what Detective Brogan said was true—another woman was dead.

If Thorley was already a murderer, he already faced a

life sentence. Killing Jane might not make a difference. To him.

Peter whirled to face downstairs, gripping the gun in both hands, with a fleeting thought for the towel. If it fell off . . .

"Stop right there, Thorley," he said.

His weapon was pointed square at the man. He was a good shot, a confident shot. But Jane was in the way.

Jane took a step back.

"My best idea, Mr. Thorley, is for you to sit on that couch," Peter said. He cocked his head, unwilling to take his aim off the target. "Jane, you get behind me. Upstairs."

Jane darted, got there in three quick steps. Eyes on Thorley, he felt Jane go past him, but she didn't run away, stayed close by. "Where's your phone?" she whispered.

"I give," Thorley said. "Don't call the cops."

"Why the hell not, Thorley?" He'd only used his gun in practice, not like this, but Dianna'd always insisted they might need it. They hadn't, not while she was alive. Maybe she was still watching over him. "I'm the good guy, remember? Put the knife down. Slide it toward me. Now."

"Peter, your phone," Jane whispered again. "Bedroom?"

"Kitchen," Peter said.

"Kitchen?" Jane was so close she could smell Peter's soap and shampoo, see the outline of the muscles in his back, still glistening with the damp of his shower. He wore only a white towel, tucked around his waist. "Peter, we've got to call the cops."

But that man—whoever he was—stood between her and the kitchen.

"Sit down, Thorley," Peter said. "I mean—*now*."

Jane saw the gun move, barely a fraction.

The man coughed, one disgusting hack, looked like he was about to pass out. He lowered himself to the couch, inch by inch, clamping one hand onto the curve of the arm, the creases in his face deepening, his skin almost yellow. He sank into the cushions, then sidearmed the knife across the carpet. It stuck in the loops of the pile, a foot from the bottom of the stairs.

"Got it," Jane said.

She took the steps two at a time. Grabbed the knife, held it in one fist, then looked at it, as if it were going to attack her on its own. It was heavier than she'd predicted, the blade straight and shiny and hideous. She wouldn't throw up. She wouldn't. This was over.

Peter was down the stairs, closer to Thorley, as Jane headed to the kitchen.

"Hang on, Jane," Peter said. "Don't call yet."

"You kidding me?" she asked.

"Trust me," Peter said. "We'll call. When we need to. If we need to. Mr. Thorley?"

Jane edged farther away. She didn't care what Peter said—there was a guy with a knife. Well, he didn't have the knife anymore, actually, she did. She held it at her side, the handle still warm, the curve of the plastic fitting her fingers. She put her other hand on her chest, feeling it rise and fall, trying to be as calm as Peter seemed to be. How could he be this cool? She was on the verge of losing it.

Peter still pointed the gun at the man—Thorley? Something like that? They knew each other, for some reason. Obviously they weren't pals.

"Peter, what the hell—" She didn't want to hold the disgusting knife anymore, but she was afraid what might happen if she put it down. Peter and the guy couldn't be in this together, could they? Whatever *this* was. Peter hadn't been planning to come home, they were only in

Milton because of the crash. This Thorley could not have known Peter'd be here.

"Thorley?" Peter said again.

"What?" the man said. "I'm done, you win, whatever."

Jane took another step closer to the kitchen. If Peter *wasn't* on Thorley's side, then the tide seemed to have turned, and whatever danger she'd been in was somehow over. Still, she'd be much happier if the police arrived to make the odds even better.

"What the hell are you doing here?" Peter was saying. "I'm on your side, you know that."

Jane's brain was going to explode. They *were* on the same side?

31

"Well, fancy meeting you here."

Lizzie turned at Aaron's voice. He stood under the spotlight glow of the halogens illuminating her space in the bank's parking lot. Pale blue shirtsleeves rolled to his elbows. Loafers, with no socks. Khaki pants. Out of his banker's clothes.

"Hi, Aaron," she said. "I guess we're both running late."

"Indeed." He smiled slowly, raked a hand through his hair. Kept staring at her.

It was just the two of them. She heard the thundery rumble of the elevator going back up, the static buzz of the lights. A multicolored maze of interlinked pipes twisted across the ceiling. The parking lot, a grid of mostly empty lined spaces, hosted only the familiar dark Lexus in the president's spot, and cars from a few other Tuesday night stragglers. And the two of them.

Her car key clicker was in her hand. Aaron's keys were in her briefcase.

Lizzie set the briefcase on the pavement, not quite sure what to do. She planned to get those appetizers and meet Aaron at her apartment, maybe even have a second to change into something more—casual. He'd never seen her in anything but banker's clothes, and she had a silk camisole that—

"Maybe we should change our plans," Aaron interrupted her thoughts.

A pang of disappointment. Was he canceling? She wasn't *that* late.

"I picked up your keys," she said.

"Did you get my keys?" he said at exactly the same time.

Aaron laughed, the sound echoing from the parking lot's dingy concrete walls. A reassuring, happy, relieved-sounding laugh.

"Jinx," Aaron said.

Good.

"Jinx," Lizzie said back. She and her father used to say jinx, back when she was little.

"You have them? Here?" He watched her nod. "Terrific."

She felt his arm go across her shoulders, felt him take her hand, point her clicker at her car door, locking it.

"Ka-ching," he said. "Leave your car here. I'll drive. Let's go celebrate."

The beep of the lock ricocheted through the empty lot. Her car was locked. With her on the outside.

"Celebrate?" She bent down, picked up her briefcase. Nothing was how she'd planned it anymore.

"Big time," Aaron said. "Your chariot awaits, milady."

Lizzie felt her cheeks flush as she slid into the front seat of his sleek white car. He was driving, she was the "date." It was silly, and maybe she should be skeptical, but . . . it had been such a long time.

"All set?" He adjusted the rearview mirror, then reached over and placed one hand, briefly, on her shoulder. "Look in the backseat. I brought champagne. And some apps."

"You—?" She wasn't being very articulate, which was

annoying, but she almost couldn't keep up with this. He could be so charming. She twisted around to look in the backseat, saw a bottle of Moët in clear cellophane, and a glossy white box from Cinzano's Trattoria.

"I'm going to make it up to you," he said. "Let's pretend last night never happened. Okay? I'll stay away from beer this time. And you're going to love tonight."

Jake's eyes opened as the wheels rumbled across the tarmac, the reverse thrust of the jet engines pushing him forward against the seat belt. He blinked, assessing, remembering. He'd fallen asleep, his feet holding the briefcase under the seat in front of him.

"Welcome to Boston, ladies and gentlemen, please remain seated until . . ."

Jake yawned, shook his head to clear it, then found his cell, checked for messages. Nothing. Little did Elliot Sandoval know how events had lined up to give him one more night off the hook. Tomorrow, Jake would get that show on the road. Get the results of those lab tests, and assess what D had meant about the steroids. But all in all, soon he'd have some progress to report to Shandra Newbury's family. And to her colleague at the real estate office, that Brian Turiello. Telling the people who cared that you'd nabbed the bad guy, that was what made it all worth it. Like his grandfather always told him.

Jane's silence—not necessarily good. He wondered if she was more upset about canceling the vacation then she had let on.

Six-B finally got organized, let him into the aisle. By the time he reached his car, carrying cellophane-wrapped purple and white lilacs from the airport's "Bring Me Something" stand—he'd realized the irony of lilacs, but Jane would never know—he'd gotten Jane's voice mail again. Ten at night. No answer from Jane. Strange.

Or maybe not. If she was unhappy with him.

So now what? He threw his overnight bag in the backseat, placed the lilacs on the seat beside him, and headed for the exit, trying to decide. Home? And call Jane in the morning?

Or to Jane's now? And surprise her? This time of night, he could hop on Storrow Drive, get off at Kenmore, and be at her condo in fifteen.

She'd love the fragrant lilacs. Maybe he wouldn't go home at all.

Yes. To Jane's. And the trip to D.C. hadn't been a total bust. Frasca had said the name "rang a bell." What bell?

"You have thirty seconds to tell me what the hell you're doing," Peter said. "I'm going to put this gun down, okay?"

Peter slowly lowered the .38, setting it on the breakfront beside him. Still in that damn towel, there was nowhere to stick it and keep the thing around him. Someday this would be funny. He hoped. At least—because of lawyer-client privilege—no law enforcement types would have to hear about this, and he could keep it away from a potential jury. He hoped.

There was still poor Jane to deal with. He watched her, with that bizarre knife in her hand, clearly baffled by his not wanting to call the cops. At least she wasn't yelling. Or flipping out. Had to give her credit.

He kept the weapon within reach. Kept his eyes on Thorley, still slumped on the couch. Shoulders sagging, chest sagging, eyes downcast. All the fight gone out of him. What the hell was he doing here in the first place?

"And listen," he went on. "Because you pulled a knife on Jane here, you've waived attorney-client privilege." Total mumbo jumbo, but Thorley'd never understand that. "Whatever we say, Jane's going to hear it. But one false move, Thorley, and it's the gun and nine-one-one. We clear?"

"Whatever," Thorley said.

Peter saw Thorley's running shoes were caked with dust, the bottoms of his jeans also edged with brown. Where had he been?

"Jane, my client and I need to discuss a situation. Right now. And at some point, it might be a story for you. I could ask you to go upstairs or something, but since we have a deal about the other matter, I'm hoping we can continue it with this case. Agreed?"

Jane rolled her eyes, clearly dubious. Her T-shirt had come untucked, her hair out of its rubber band, one leg smeared with caking brown dirt.

"Curiouser and curiouser." She shrugged, waving the knife—then apparently realized what she was doing. "And curiouser. Okay if I put this thing down? Your 'client' going to threaten me with something else?"

"Jane?" Peter had to admit their situation was through the looking glass but the clock was ticking, and he had to decide what to do about Thorley. Peter couldn't be harboring a fugitive. He'd have to advise Thorley to turn himself in, make a deal with the cops. But not with a newspaper reporter hanging around, unless she'd play ball. "Agreed? We don't have much time to—"

"Agreed," Jane said. "I hardly have a choice."

"So, Mr. Thorley," Peter said. "What the hell are you doing?"

At least she was going to hear the explanation. Jane leaned against the kitchen doorjamb, regrouping. Failing. Her knees weren't feeling quite right, nor was her brain, and it had crossed her mind, out of the blue, that if something happened to her—whatever "something" would be—no one had any idea where she was. She flashed on the body of Shandra Newbury. The cops had found her simply by chance. Today Jane had gone off, without a second thought, with this Peter Hardesty—a man she didn't have a chance to research because she hadn't known he was coming to her office—and now she sat in his house while he held a gun on a "client." A client who'd held her at knife point. And now this Peter Hardesty, supposed to be a good guy, was asking her not to call the police.

Not how she'd envisioned this evening.

"Sorry about your friend," Thorley was saying. "Didn't expect anyone else to be here. I guess I freaked out. I mean, who knew what the hell she was doing here? Getting rid of the dog? Maybe she broke in, right? I could hear the shower, and figured maybe you didn't know that she was here. I was trying to protect your stuff."

Jane rolled her eyes. Engaged with Peter, Thorley seemed to have forgotten she was there.

"Bull," Peter said. "I'm waiting."

"You know the thing," Thorley said. "We talked about."

"I'm waiting," Peter said.

"And you know there was another . . ." This time Thorley glanced at Jane, just a flicker, as if he were trying to decide.

After ten at night. A knife and a gun. Two crazy strangers making no sense. Just another night in Jane world.

"Thing," Thorley continued.

Peter took a step toward him, one hand still on the stupid towel, wary. It was hard to take him seriously in a towel, but this did seem serious. He had to be a good guy, right?

"Yeah," Peter said. "And?"

Code talking. The two of them were having an entire conversation without using any specific words. Oh, sure, she was hearing them talk, but it didn't matter one bit.

She had no idea what they were discussing so intently. And cryptically. But from the look on Peter's face, it was not good news.

"Well," Thorley said. "I did it. And like I tried to tell you, the other one, too."

Tell you? Did it? The other one? Was this code for the Arboretum murder?

"Now do you believe me?" Thorley said.

"Thanks, Jane. There was no other way to do this," Peter said. He'd told her to stand watch at the door of his Jeep, guarding a now-disarmed and seemingly indifferent Thorley who sat slumped and seat-belted into the passenger side, while Peter ran back inside and threw on his pants. Finally. Couldn't go to the police station without pants.

"Thorley's not going to make any more trouble," Peter continued. He waved Jane to the back seat. "And you might need to talk to the cops."

The dashboard clock's green numbers flashed to 10:37 P.M. Peter'd been told Branford Sherrey's shift started at ten. He got in, closed his door. Thorley's rattletrap sedan would have to stay in the driveway until they figured out how to handle it. *Thorley.* The Lilac Sunday killer? How would Thorley's sister, Doreen Rinker, and her family handle that? "Guess you'll get more story than we bargained for."

"Someday." Jane dragged her seat belt across her chest. "A story's the last thing on my mind right now, I've gotta say. I'm not dead. And I have my wallet back. Thank you so much for a lovely evening."

"I know, I'm so—there's no way I could have—again. I'm sorry," Peter understood her sarcasm. Didn't blame her.

Now to the police station. He couldn't begin to predict

what would happen there, or after that. Was this latest victim dead because Peter had engineered Thorley's release? People—even people who confessed—were innocent until proven guilty. It was his job, he reminded himself, to make sure that right was protected. Still, could he have prevented this murder? Could he have predicted—*no*, he decided.

Peter buzzed down his window and cranked the ignition. The law wasn't about predictions. It was about rules. His sworn responsibility was to play by them.

Jane, though. She must be incredibly confused, and he wouldn't blame her for being terrified, but she'd come through two harrowing incidents without tears or panic. Now she was sitting in the backseat of a Jeep with a nutcase and his lawyer in the front, like it was merely another night on the job. *Tough woman*, he thought. Like Dianna.

He backed out of the driveway into the spring night, streetlights illuminating the empty neighborhood, so quiet he could hear the hiss of his tires along the asphalt. He even smelled Dianna's pink peonies, in full first bloom, as he rounded the corner and headed for downtown.

Once again it was his job to do the best he could for Thorley. A confessed double murderer. Who in the eyes of the law was still innocent.

32

"He what? Confessed? Again?" Jake was right, he knew he'd be right. It simply would have been better if he'd been right sooner. Now this Thorley—hell, the Lilac Sunday killer!—had apparently killed someone else to prove his guilt. Why else would he murder another woman?

The phone call from Sherrey had come as Jake was heading for the exit. He swerved his BPD-issue cruiser off Storrow Drive—*sorry Jane, so much for the lilacs*—and toward police HQ.

"Be there in ten," Jake said. "Don't let him say a word until I'm in the room. Not that his lawyer—Hardesty?—would let him, until we get some kind of a deal. Should we get the parole officer to confirm he didn't report in? You're calling the DA, right? She'll love this. Big headlines."

Big as headlines could be. Thorley was on his way to the cop shop, turning himself in. That closed the new Arboretum case, closed the old Lilac Sunday case, and made Jake's day.

Still.

He stopped at a red light and let the entirety of the situation sink in. Someone had been killed, some innocent person, because he—sure, and the other cops—hadn't trusted Thorley's initial confession, hadn't possessed the evidence to prove his involvement. If they had—and if that Peter Hardesty hadn't reminded them of their shaky legal standing—they'd have kept him in custody. And the newest victim would still be alive.

The light turned green. *One step at a time*. Jake couldn't control the universe. He could only make sure those who broke the law were brought to justice. That, at least, was definitely going to happen.

Jake took a deep breath, letting his fears evaporate and steeling his will. "A cop doesn't need easy," Grandpa Brogan always told him. This one sure hadn't been easy. Justice for Carley Marie Schaefer had taken almost twenty years—starting with the killing at the Arboretum and ending with tonight's murder on Moulten Road, just a block from the initial crime scene. Now it was all approaching the grand finale. He wished his grandfather could be here to share what was about to happen.

"No, no. Turn left!" Had she said "right" when she meant "left"? Lizzie'd been giving Aaron directions to her apartment, and she knew she'd said left, but he was turning right.

"I'm so sorry, Aaron, did I say right? I meant, um, the other right." Lizzie noticed how his tanned hands rested on the steering wheel, how his face came in and out of the lights as they passed the neighborhood street lamps. Full moon, she saw.

"Nope, got to make one stop first." Aaron was smiling, thank goodness, but wasn't looking at her. "Okay with you? Two seconds. You don't mind, do you, Miss Lizzie?"

He'd started calling her that, "Miss Lizzie," all through their small talk on the way from the bank. He'd asked about her family, and her job, and her college. Again, even though she knew she'd already told him the same stuff at dinner the other night. Maybe he was trying to forget that whole episode. Like she was.

Was he taking her to *his* place? Was that a good thing? What would she do? She clasped her hands in her lap, and tried to look nonchalant. Like a successful person, on an actual date.

Even this time of night, the BU students were outside. Lounging on porches, smoking whatever, savoring the last of the spring evening, a few mismatched dogs teasing each other on one front lawn. People were happy, appreciating their lives, knowing how to be loved. Maybe she could start that soon. If she wasn't too *picky*.

She sneaked another glance at Aaron, driving so confidently, back straight and his hair a tiny bit too long over his starched collar. A cool guy—"preppy," she'd have called him when she was in college. He'd have called her a nerd.

Here they were. Together.

"Here we are," Aaron said. He pulled into a driveway, then made the turn into a parking lot behind a faded beige brick apartment building, a concrete plot bordered on two sides by craggy maples and newly piled mulch. Most of the yellow-lined spaces were filled, which made sense. Brookline cops were draconian about on-street parking, their enforcement relentless, and that upped the value of the properties with off-street spots like these.

"Is this where you live?"

"Nope." Aaron pulled into space 303—she noticed because it was a numerical palindrome—turned off the ignition, and unclicked his door. "I've got to pick up something in one of our REOs."

Lizzie felt her chest clench, a quick dark gathering of suspicion and panic and inevitability. But she was being silly, right? This was a date, on a soft spring night, and they were bank employees.

If she was right, bank employees with secrets. But she couldn't be sure.

He touched her arm, his eyes—well, they were actually

twinkling. Like in books. "I know. Silly coincidence, right? But like I said, two seconds. And no pressure. So, Miss Lizzie. Want to come in with me?"

"They're definitely going to throw me out of here," Jane said. "They know I'm a reporter. Cops hate when reporters show up at headquarters."

In the car, she'd heard Peter's terse phone call to some detective—not Jake, since he was in D.C.—relating the "situation" with Thorley. They were also madly code-talking, incredibly annoying, but she could infer this was a continuation of some ongoing discussion. Peter had promised to tell her, so all she had to do was wait. It was not yet midnight, so plenty of time to make deadline. If there was a story she was allowed to write.

What did Thorley do? Why were they here at the cop shop? It was clearly more than what happened at Peter's house. But what?

At least Jake wasn't here to make things even more complicated.

In the fluorescent glare of the Boston Police headquarters lobby, they'd checked in with the night-shift desk sergeant and were awaiting the call to go upstairs. He'd asked Jane for ID, the first step toward Jane's inevitable ejection from the interview, but when she simply offered a driver's license, the desk guy carefully printed it on the intake log without comment. Jane had no doubt the "comment" would come soon, probably followed by her being tossed out on her ass.

Right now, though, the sergeant was ignoring them.

"You may be a reporter, but you're also a victim, remember?" Peter kept his voice low, tapping his fingers like he was playing invisible piano on the black laminate of the reception desk, the starched and buzz-cut officer perched on a stool behind it. Still actively ignoring them.

With a cadet stationed beside him, Thorley sat in a row of molded plastic visitor chairs, legs crossed and gnawing a thumbnail. Ignoring them.

To get upstairs, they'd go through a turnstile and a metal detector, then take the elevator to the interrogation floor. Press were usually relegated to a bleakly uncomfortable room on the civilian side of the lobby, a windowless pen with unforgiving benches and no electrical outlets, clearly designed to make reporters give up and go home.

"This isn't just about what happened at your house, is it?" Jane matched his tone, protecting their conversation. She was playing some role in all of this, but she still had no idea what it was. Journalists had rules, but how could she follow them if she didn't know where they were in the game? Should she call Marcotte? "But d'you you think the police will want to interview me about that?"

"Probably." Peter's voice was barely audible.

Jane fingered her cell phone, considering. She might regret calling, but it might be worse if she didn't. Sometimes a decision like this was better left to a higher pay grade.

"I need to call my editor." Jane turned away from the desk, not wanting anyone—not Peter, not Thorley, not desk guy—to hear the conversation she was about to have.

A door opened behind the reception desk, a uniformed young woman approached Peter. "Sir? I'm Cadet McClelland. Jean McClelland."

Jane was sure this cop's elaborate makeup was not in the BPD official manual, and she'd certainly had her sleek blue uniform blouse subtly altered from the boxy standard issue. Jane denounced her own snap judgment. *Unworthy.* Being a knockout didn't make someone a bad cop. Probably Jane had low blood sugar. She decided to be nice. Nicer.

"You're . . ." The woman consulted a silver clipboard. "Attorney Hardesty? Mr. Thorley? And you're—"

Cadet McClelland frowned.

Jane tried to look innocent as well as nice. She stashed her cell in her tote bag. Not good to be on the phone with the newspaper while Peter was trying to convince this cadet she was legitimately here on non-news business.

"Are you the same Jane Ry—," the cadet began.

"She's a victim," Peter interrupted. "She's not here as a reporter."

"Nevertheless." The cadet flipped her clipboard at Jane, pointed with it toward the dreaded media room. "You'll have to wait over there."

"Come on," Jane said. *So much for nice.* "If I was bleeding, or shot, would you make me sit in the press room?"

"Hold it." Peter stepped forward, shaking his head. "Detective Sherrey knows the situation. He's aware she's involved."

"If you'd like to talk with the detective, he may be authorized to arrange it. But press is press, nothing I can do to modify that, sir," the cadet said.

Ridiculous. Sit in that stupid press room? Miss out on all of it, and be forced to wait for Peter to tell her—

One of the revolving front doors whooshed, the rubber sweeps hissing against the once-shiny floor. The glare from the entryway lights put the new arrival in silhouette, but Jane knew the shape. The shoulders, the hair, the determined stride, even the tilt of his head.

She was glad Peter was blocking her from view. She peered around him, trying to watch the door. Trying to make sense of it. Failing.

Jake had told her he was going out of town. Would be gone for days. He told her he had to cancel their getaway because he was on assignment. He'd be gone. But he wasn't gone.

What was Jake doing here?

33

What was Jane doing here?

Jake had about three seconds before the revolving door deposited him in the lobby, though he was tempted to push around one more time to give himself time to figure out what the hell was going on. Jane? At headquarters? This time of night?

What's more, that was Peter Hardesty, the lawyer for the Confessor. And there was the Confessor himself—the Lilac Sunday killer, if Jake was correct. Exactly where he'd always wanted him. It was almost too good to be true—but what was Jane doing with those two? *Hardesty had better not have told her about Thorley.*

Jake pushed the aluminum bar on the glass door more slowly than he ordinarily would, stalling. Going on the offense was the best ploy. They were in his territory. They needed as much from him as he needed from them. If Thorley and Hardesty were here to make a deal, Jake—and Bing Sherrey, he guessed—would be their conduit to the DA's office. So they'd better play nice.

Would it be a conflict for Hardesty to represent Thorley as well as the about-to-be-nabbed Sandoval? They'd cross that bridge when they came to it. If they came to it.

But why was Jane here?

The glass door deposited him on the black rubber

doormat, into the hum of the air conditioning and the crackle of the aging fluorescents. No turning back now. The dispatch radio squawked, pulling him into reality. The desk sergeant, by-the-book Lockerbie, looked up, inquiring. Jane and Hardesty watched him, standing side by side. Thorley, feet splayed and oozing attitude, didn't even glance up. Cadet McSomething hovered with her clipboard.

Jake acknowledged the cadet, pointing to his own chest, then toward the visitors. *I'll handle.* She nodded, taking a step back. Relinquishing command.

"Peter Hardesty, correct?" Jake didn't hold out a hand, but Hardesty did, which Jake accepted. Thorley got to his feet, his guard rising to block him. Jane just stood there—was there mud on her leg?—silent. She had a funny look on her face, but so did he, probably.

"This is Jane Ryland," Hardesty was saying. "She's—"

"She's a—" The cadet pointed to her clipboard.

"A reporter." Jake interrupted. "Thanks, Cadet. Miss Ryland, I'm afraid you'll have to—"

Oh, crap. That's why she'd had the funny look. Jane thought he was in D.C.

Jake started over.

"Let me say, first, ah, I was just *unexpectedly* called back from Washington, D.C." Jake telegraphed a look at Jane he hoped would clarify that he wasn't a jerk or a liar.

"Unexpectedly," he repeated. That was about all the time he had for personal communications. "But, Mr. Hardesty, under no circumstances can a reporter—"

"She's not here as a reporter," Hardesty said. "She's a victim."

"A victim?" *Jane?* He looked her up and down, almost reached out to her. *Victim?* The mud. And her hair was kind of—was she hurt? *Victim?* "Of what? What happened?"

"I'm okay. Really." Jane took a step forward, held out both palms, as if to prove she was fine.

How could she be "okay"? Whatever happened had brought them all to the police station at eleven at night. No way that was okay. He never wanted to hear "Jane" and "victim" in the same sentence, let alone in reality.

"Of what? Victim of what?" Jake's throat tightened, he could hear what it did to his voice. Hardesty was looking at him, then Jane, then him again, obviously detecting some sort of subtext. So what. Let the guy look.

"I'm okay," Jane said again. "Really."

"That's why we're here, Detective," Hardesty was saying. "About what happened this evening."

"The Moulten Road incident," Jake said. "Correct?"

He saw Jane narrow her eyes, give that look she got whenever she'd done the mental math and gotten a curious result. "What Moulten Road incident?" she asked.

Jake winced. *Damn.* Said nothing, trying to regroup.

"What Moulten Road incident?" Jane looked at Hardesty, looked at Thorley, then back at him. "Detective? What Moulten Road incident?"

Damn. He'd assumed Jane would be up-to-date on Moulten Road, somehow, same way she'd been on Waverly Road with Shandra Newbury's murder. Maybe gotten a tip. Apparently he was wrong. She seemed to be unaware the police had found a woman strangled on Moulten Road, a block from the Arboretum. Now he'd said too much.

"Moulten Road? That's out by the—" Jane stopped. Tilted her head slowly to one side, then back the other way. Jake could almost see the click-click-click as the slot machine sevens lined up in her brain. "Out by the Arboretum?"

Why had Jane said that? Picked up on the Arboretum connection?

If Hardesty had told her, there'd be another homicide in the works. Jake himself would kill the guy.

Did she want to go inside with Aaron? The last time he'd taken her to such a place . . . Lizzie sighed, looked out the windshield of Aaron's car at the apartment building, feeling her hopes evaporate. Maybe tonight hadn't been a good idea after all.

"No, thanks." Lizzie fussed with her seat belt, running a thumb up and down between the black webbing and the front of her navy bank blazer. Aaron had parked in a dark patch, out of the glow of the orange security lights. She was grateful he couldn't see the indecision and disappointment on her face. "If you'll only be gone a minute or two? It's okay. I'll wait in the car."

She wasn't handling this well, whatever this was. She needed to be clever and winning, feminine and desirable. She had to be the confident one. This wasn't high school.

"I'll babysit the lovely champagne until you come out." She tried to toss her hair, but then stopped, mid-gesture, embarrassed. *Trying too hard.* "And the Cinzano's box. Do what you need to do inside. I'll be fine." Big smile.

Aaron now stood outside the open car window, both palms on the roof, leaning in over the driver's seat. She could see down the front of his unbuttoned shirt. He didn't wear an undershirt, she saw, and then tried not to look anymore.

"Ah, Lizzie, Miss Lizzie," Aaron said. "You kill me."

He paused, staring at her so intently she fidgeted in the seat, wondering how anyone ever was comfortable with another person, wondering why she was so attracted to him, although that wasn't difficult to explain, he was so handsome, and could be so sweet, even though some of his activities weren't the most . . . whatever. And some of his lines were laughable. But it wasn't like she was going to *marry* him, right? It was just tonight. One random Tuesday in May. No one else but them even knew.

She realized, in a tumbling wisp of a thought, no one knew where she was.

"Okay. My bad." Aaron slapped both palms on the roof, from the sound of it, and got back into the car, slid behind the wheel, yanked his seat belt across his chest—then stopped, holding the buckle in front of him. "I confess. I just—I could use your advice."

"Advice?" She tried to read the look on his face. Tried to keep her own face composed. Tried to predict—advice about what? Could he know she'd talked to Maddie Kate Wendell and Mo Heedles? If so, what would he make of that? What would she tell him?

"I know you understand the bank, like I do," Aaron was saying. "It's in your blood, in a way, right?"

She supposed it was. With her dad and all. But where was this going? "Sure, yes, I—why?"

"So I was wondering if you might be able to help me. With a kind of project I'm working on. It's secret, though, so you'd have to promise it's just between us for now." He let the seat belt go, and it snapped back into place. He turned to her, touching her shoulder again for the briefest of seconds. She felt the exact place, even through her jacket, even after he took his hand away.

"Kind of—a surprise for you," he said.

Sitting in a car, in an empty parking lot, in the middle of the—well, not exactly the middle of the night. She wanted him to like her, she admitted, she did, but her brain was full and confused and—what did he mean by "surprise"?

"And thing is"—Aaron was still talking—"I had hoped . . . you'd come upstairs and come see it. You'll be the first, you know? Because I trust your judgment, and I trust your skills. You're my soul mate, Miss Lizzie. I feel it—" He touched his chest. "Right here."

Despite her misgivings, she could feel herself melting. Soul mate? No one had ever—*ever*—said that to her before. Maybe it was bull. One of his lines. But what if it wasn't?

"So, okay?" he said.

"I admit you have me curious," she said.

"As long as I have you." Aaron smiled at her, that smile. She heard the whir as her seat belt retracted, watched Aaron reach into the back seat for the champagne and Cinzano's box, felt the car shift as he opened the door and got out, waiting for her in the quiet parking lot. A soft breeze rustled the leaves of a big maple above them, the lowest branches tangling against her hair as she got out of the car.

Taking the champagne inside? Why not. She was trying a new life now, her new life, and the lovely wine would seal the deal.

34

"Gotta say. That's the first guy I've ever seen who's happy to take that walk," Jake said. He and Peter Hardesty watched Gordon Thorley, escorted by a gloating Bing Sherrey, head off to lockup. No one should be thrilled to be confined by three walls of gray concrete and one wall of bars, but Jake could've sworn Thorley smiled.

"Who knows what he's thinking." Hardesty shrugged. "Or what he's smiling about."

Jake understood the lawyer was only doing his job with Thorley. But his deal with Jane? *That* Jake did not understand. At Hardesty's apartment? That time of night? Taking a shower? *In a towel?* Hardesty, separated from his client, had related the whole story before they sent Jane home in a cab. Jane hadn't even seemed embarrassed. What the hell?

He and Hardesty had just finished two additional hours of question and answer, bracketed by confessions, including Thorley's recitation of the events of that Lilac Sunday long ago and his acknowledgment that he'd bagged his parole check-in call. He'd refused to discuss exactly what had happened on Moulten Road.

Even so, Thorley knew the victim's name, Treesa Caramona, rehab-needy and a longtime parolee, now a person well-known to Southie's notorious Harvest House Shelter, a seedy brick almost-tenement that was hardly home and barely shelter to ex-cons and transients. Thorley knew she'd been strangled from behind with an electrical cord. Told them where they'd find her backpack. Exactly where they already found it. None of that had been made public.

"Did you know her?" Jake had asked.

"Yeah, sure, all us parolees know each other," Thorley said. "Everyone else thinks we're invisible."

"How'd you get her to Moulten Road?"

"Bus."

"How'd you get in?"

"Front window. Easy."

"Why'd you kill her?"

"Why does anyone do anything?" Thorley said. "She pissed me off."

"And you just happened to have an electrical cord?"

"Found it in the trash," Thorley said. "Where she belonged, too. No one will miss her."

Jake paused, staring at the guy. The Lilac Sunday killer.

"Now do you believe me?" Thorley had said. "You should have stopped me when you could."

Jake knew that was correct, incredibly correct, tragically correct. As he'd feared, it seemed the legal system—supposedly protecting the rights of the accused—had produced a second Lilac Sunday victim. Too late, and too disturbing, to think about that now. The handcuffs clicked on. And Thorley and Bing were gone.

He'd have to be satisfied with tomorrow's arraignment. The judge, any judge, would certainly keep Thorley in jail awaiting trial—a trial Jake had no doubt would send the guy downstate to Cedar Junction for life. There might even be video of him and Caramona on that bus to Moulten Road, if the onboard surveillance camera was rolling.

Because of the death of Treesa Caramona, a Brogan might put the Lilac Sunday killer behind bars. Carley Marie Schaefer's family might finally get their closure.

Gramma, too.

Jake wished his grandfather could know that.

He also wished he could've beat the hell out of Thorley for pulling a knife on Jane. So much for parole as rehabilitation. Crock of shit, some of the time, only you could never predict which times. Murderers weren't like most people. Jake could catch them, but it didn't mean he understood them. Thorley would get his just punishment soon enough.

"So. See you in court tomorrow," Hardesty interrupted his thoughts. He hoisted a canvas briefcase over one shoulder as they walked toward the elevators.

Hardesty had argued to keep Thorley out of custody, but it was a losing battle with a client like that. Now a plea agreement—if one should happen—was in the district attorney's hands.

"I'll expect your call," Hardesty went on. "The instant you hear from the DA."

"Yeah. Sure." But Jake had one more question. A personal one. Why was Jane at Hardesty's house anyway, ten at night, or whenever? The moment he went out of town, she'd gone off with Peter freaking Hardesty. Peter Hardesty and a freaking *towel*. That's why she hadn't answered his phone call.

He turned to Hardesty, keeping his voice professional. "So. The Jane Ryland 'episode.'"

"What about it?" Hardesty kept walking. Almost to the elevators.

"We're supposed to forget all that?" Jake went on. "As if it never happened?"

"Misunderstanding." Hardesty jabbed the lighted arrow on the down button. "She seems pretty cool, huh? She said you guys knew each other. Professionally."

They'd talked about him? Why? *High school,* he thought, but Jake had to ask.

"Why was Ms. Ryland with you in the first place?" He couldn't let Hardesty know why he really cared. Or, he realized, how much he cared. *A towel?*

The elevator doors opened.

"You'll have to ask Jane," Hardesty said. "We done here?"

"Do I want—more?" Lizzie said.

She opened her eyes at Aaron's question, felt his touch on her bare arm. A glow filtered in through the lace curtains of the unfamiliar bedroom—what time was it?—a pale glimmer from the streetlights licking shadows on the white walls. But he was holding a slim crystal glass. Of course, he meant champagne, did she want more champagne.

"Mmmm . . ." Her brain was not finding words. Her body was floating, or weightless, or something it had never been before, *strange,* the incredible pillows and the scent of Aaron, *Aaron,* next to her.

"Advice on what?" she had asked, still timid as she got out of the car, but Aaron had merely smiled, held out a hand, led her inside apartment 303. The REO—he'd explained it was one of the bank's—was still partly furnished. "Just came to us," he said. And after about, oh, who knows how many glasses, he confessed to her what he was doing.

Or maybe she had asked him? It was all kind of a jumble.

Exactly as she suspected, he'd been renting empty foreclosed homes to students—I know when they'll be available, he said, *he'd unbuttoned his shirt, she barely knew where to look,* and real estate brokers can show them no matter who's there, right? He was proud of himself, she could tell.

"Are you afraid you'll get caught?" she dared to ask, couldn't resist. She'd quickly calculated how much money he could make—with say, three thousand dollars per house, per month, and even with a few dozen houses? With the bank paying utilities and maintenance? It was potentially incredibly lucrative. Not to mention tax free.

"We're not Bank of America," he'd said, dismissing her "concerns." "A bank like ours? When you're a big fish in a little pond, you can do anything you want."

Which she knew. All too well. But still . . .

It was wrong, it was illegal, it was—her first reaction, and her second, was to tell him to stop. He could go to jail for fraud, and embezzlement, and theft, and a million other criminal charges. If her father ever found out . . . She paused, smiling, imagining her father being surprised.

She took another sip, then another, attempting to understand Aaron's logic. Could you say Aaron was helping people? Same as she was? *Kind of*. Helping students who needed homes. Protecting the housing stock and the economy. Leveraging resources the bank would never miss. Same as she was. Kind of.

He was making money from it, of course, and she wasn't. But still. Kind of.

And then, in a rush and a flurry of words, she told him everything she'd discovered, everything, about Mo Heedles and Maddie Kate, and the leases now in her top desk drawer. Why was her memory so fuzzy?

"You're so smart, Miss Lizzie," he'd said, drawing one finger up her bare arm, into the hollow of her collar bone, giving her goose bumps and who knows what else. "That's why I trust you so much."

She'd been on the verge, the very verge, of telling him about her system, but at the last moment, something in his face, or something in her heart, stopped her. She needed to keep some things to herself. She'd been alone, essentially, for most of her life. It was probably time to let someone else in. But not yet. Not here.

He'd almost carried her upstairs, not quite, and here they were now, together, and he was offering her even more champagne. The blue ribbon from the splayed open Cinzano's box was tied around one of her wrists, he'd tied it there like a silken bracelet, and he'd fed her the creamy chocolate chip pastry from inside it, holding the confection with the rustling waxed paper, morsel by morsel, sitting on the edge of the duvet cover, making her lick his fingers to get every bit of the custard.

"Don't you want one?" she'd asked, and he'd said, "I'm hungry, but right now, only hungry for you." So the other pastry remained untouched. *Touched*, she thought, thinking of his hands.

Aaron had slid away from her. She patted the warm spot where he'd been. He was using the downstairs bathroom, he explained, the one up here was—whatever it was. And wouldn't her father be surprised? Wouldn't everyone be surprised?

Lizzie closed her eyes for a moment. She yawned, wide and reckless, feeling every cell in her body expand, feeling the downy pillow; her skirt and top were rumpled and wrinkled, but who cared, her suit jacket and watch and purse and everything in a crazy pile where Aaron had placed it. Keeping it safe.

Just like their secret. He'd made her promise not to tell.

She settled into the pillows. Aaron would be back soon, then . . . then . . . she floated for a moment, trying to think.

This is what real people did, people who had a life outside of work. And now she did, too, and she could still love her work but would never look at the world the same way again.

She was . . . happy? Was this happy?

Where was Aaron? Her brain felt fuzzy, happy-fuzzy,

and the bed was so soft, and the chocolate chip pastries were so delicious, maybe she could tuck one in her purse. As a reminder of this delicious night.

"I can't freaking believe it." Aaron started talking before Ack even had the front door closed. "She knows the whole freaking thing. At those houses today? It *was* her. She actually freaking went to the freaking houses."

Ackerman arrived at the condo as they'd planned, and now Aaron had to watch him pace through the sparsely furnished living room, muttering and critical, as Lizzie lay clueless in the upstairs bedroom.

Aaron was so not going to take the fall for this. And the only way to make sure of it was to spread the responsibility. Make sure all involved were equally entangled as he was. "Ball's in your court now, bro," Aaron said.

Lizzie was certainly—he hoped—out cold now, all that champagne followed by all the crumbled pills he'd added to the gooey filling. She'd have no idea they were down here discussing her future.

Ackerman and his nasty questions worried him.

Yes, he told Lizzie the deal, Aaron admitted, but only after it was clear she was already on to it, as they'd suspected. No, he had no other choices, only whether to deny the whole thing, or spill enough to shut her up while he knocked her out. How much of a choice was that? When she had access to all the bank records? And she'd already . . . *damn* it.

Ackerman came around the stubby coffee table for the third time. Now his conversation consisted of mostly "asshole" and "ridiculous." As far as Aaron was concerned, Ackerman was the ridiculous asshole. The rental thing had all been his idea. Aaron had just gone along with it. Happily, sure, and psyched to be included in it—bankrolling his new wheels and a whole lot more. But now, suddenly, it was Aaron's responsibility? Not a chance. Aaron was not the asshole. Even more important, not the fall guy.

"Listen, I'm out there, every day," Aaron whispered. He glanced upstairs, verging on nervous Lizzie'd show up at the top step, half-dressed and questioning. But that was impossible—that chocolate chip thing had enough stuff in it to keep her quiet until they decided what to do.

"*I* talk to the tenants." Aaron pointed to his own chest, his shirt still open. At least his khakis were back on. The rest of his clothes, including his shoes, were upstairs. For now. He pointed again. "*I* arrange the site visits, *I* talk to the brokers, *I* arrange the showings. Front man, you called it. But *you* guys, you're back in your offices, counting your damn money. And stop pacing. You're driving me nuts."

Ackerman stopped, shoved his hands in the pockets of his pants. Boat shoes with no socks, like he'd just gotten off the boat from the Vineyard. Glared at Aaron, in a smirky way Aaron did not appreciate.

"Tell me again how the bank president's daughter got the keys to your REOs?" Ackerman's voice was almost too loud to be safe.

"Shut up," Aaron said. Of course this was looming disaster, but he sure as hell wasn't going to let Ackerman shove the blame on him. Even though in a kind of way, because of the dumbass key thing, he deserved it. But that was the past. "I get it, hell, it's my bad, whatever. Let's go from here. Move on. Let's take care of this."

"By 'take care' you mean like on Waverly Road?"

Aaron still didn't like the look on Ackerman's face. What happened to his big "it's a sure thing" and "we're all in it together, that's what makes it so lucrative"? Ack had also promised "no one gets hurt," but that was obviously way out the window.

If word got out about their project, Aaron knew, like almost happened with Waverly, not only would the whole scheme collapse, so would all their careers. Aaron knew properties from other banks were involved, too. They'd be reading headlines about the bank crisis from their cells at Sing Sing. Theft, conversion, fraud. Bank robbery, essentially. So far, their secret had been contained. But now Lizzie McDivitt, genius daughter of the president of the damn bank, had discovered it.

From moment one, Aaron had known she could never be allowed to tell. But that was Ackerman's department.

"So hey. I did my part," Aaron said. "Got her here, got her upstairs. Et. Cetera. Now back to you in the studio, Walter."

Ackerman was pacing again, his back to Aaron as he headed toward the dinky fireplace, then around the lumpy couch and past the sagging wing chair, its armrests so faded and threadbare they were a different brown than the seat. He didn't answer. *Ass*hole.

"Ack? Hel-lo. I'm serious. What is—?" He remembered to keep his voice down. Started over, quieter. "What. Is. The *plan*? Or are you gonna stall until Lizzie McDivitt comes down those stairs and joins the conversation?"

He was gratified that Ackerman flinched, checked the stairs. Not so gratified when he rolled his eyes again. Jerk. Weren't they in this together?

"So let me get a few things straight," Ackerman said. He stopped by the chair, now leaning against the back of it, his body hidden behind the stripes. "You brought her here from the bank parking lot, and left her car there?"

"Yeah."

"And what, pray, was going through your mind when you made that decision?"

Incredible jerk. "Well, there's only one parking space here, you know? I had to get her to leave her car to get her here."

Ackerman nodded, agreeing. "I see. You wouldn't want her car to be towed from here for violating Brookline's overnight parking laws. Leave a record that she'd been here."

"Exactly." Aaron had thought it all out. Get her here, get her inside and out of sight, see what she knew. If nothing, fine, game over. If something, not so fine, bring out the cupcake or whatever. Call Ack, and assess what to do next.

"And what was your thought," Ackerman said, his voice still at almost a whisper, "about the security cameras in the bank parking lot? The ones that certainly captured the bank president's daughter getting into your car with you? And driving away with you?"

"The—?" *Crap.*

"Exactly," Ackerman said. "So, my young Lothario, back upstairs with you. And good luck. We'll all see young Lizzie McDivitt at her desk tomorrow morning. Won't we?"

Aaron looked up the stairway, at the slightly open bedroom door. Behind it, his future lay zonked in a stranger's bed.

"Crap."

"Exactly," Ackerman said again. He came out from behind the chair, and headed for the front door.

"At least tomorrow morning, she'll remember only what I remind her to remember," Aaron said.

"Possibly." Ackerman turned, one hand on the front doorknob. "If you're lucky."

"But after tomorrow morning," Aaron continued, "after she's back at her damn desk and it's all back to normal—"

"Not your department," Ackerman said. He opened the door, peered into the hallway, then looked at Aaron over one shoulder. "And Gianelli? We'll handle her from here."

35

"No, Jane. Absolutely not. Not one word."

"No, Jane. Absolutely not. Not one word."

"But I think we should—" Jane was not happy with the direction of this morning's meeting in Marcotte's office. "I mean, I could write a terrific—"

"You certainly grasp the logic here, don't you, Jane?" Marcotte, interrupting, ripped the top page from a yellow legal pad, crumpled it, tossed it into a leather-covered wastebasket. "If this"—she consulted another legal pad—"Gordon Thorley? Is indeed a suspect in the Moulten Road killing? Lucky you weren't killed."

"Well—" True, certainly. "But I *wasn't*—"

"I pitched having you write a first-person about the whole incident, of course, it's fabulous reporter involvement. Talk about buzzable," Marcotte continued. "But legal says no. So it's no. Understood?"

"But—" Jane wasn't making any headway in this conversation. Peter had called her from police station Siberia about four in the morning, giving her the outline of what happened with Thorley, and telling her, "Detective Brogan says thank you so much, and he'll be in contact if he needs you."

So far, no call. Not a word from Jake. Did that mean he didn't "need" her? She thought about that suitcase, still packed in her bedroom, like the last memory of a fading dream. Had Jake backed out of their trip for some reason he wasn't saying? The assignment in Washington had suddenly appeared—then disappeared. What was that all about? Why didn't he trust her with the truth?

Last night, she'd been too tired to think about it clearly.

She'd ripped open a can of evil-smelling lamb-and-rice for the complaining Coda, grabbed three hours of sleep after Peter's call, hit the shower, slugged down two coffees, and dragged herself into Marcotte's office, banishing all thoughts of Jake, fueled by the prospect of a big story. She was expecting a pat on the back, since she'd scored the big Thorley-as-Moulten-Road-Killer scoop, such a headliner she could bang it out no matter how tired she felt. She'd planned to leave out what took place in Hardesty's living room. Since it was all a "misunderstanding," according to Peter, there'd be no police report, no record of it, as if it never happened. She could still be objective.

Now Marcotte was saying no.

"But, Victoria? Legal's got to understand the episode with Thorley wasn't reported, formally, so it doesn't count. Doesn't affect my objectivity. In fact, you only know about it because I told you. If I hadn't—"

"If you hadn't what?" Marcotte, interrupting, seemed to look straight at Jane for the first time that morning. "If you hadn't, we'd be having quite a different conversation, I expect. You don't think I wouldn't find out, do you?"

Backpedal time. "Well, of course, and I did tell you," Jane said.

"And so it goes," Marcotte said.

This conversation wasn't the only thing derailed in Jane's life. Maybe she should go home, get some sleep, and start the day again, not exhausted and not bummed out.

She could work on Sandoval, and also the foreclosure crisis story that started this whole thing. A memorial service for Emily-Sue Ordway, the girl who'd fallen from the window, the teenage victim who'd started Jane's interest in foreclosure families, was in the works, and might be a good peg.

"However," Marcotte was saying. "Even though legal's yanked you off the Thorley story, all is not lost. I have a favor to ask, and I know you can handle the assignment. We need to front-burner it for the Sunday editions. Get it in—by Friday? Two days from now. Use TJ for video."

A favor? An assignment? Okay, that was the challenge of reporting. You never knew what was around the next corner. Usually that was the exciting part, but right now, it was the confusing part. Still, she could do it, whatever. It was also a convenient way to get back into Marcotte's good graces, if such a place existed.

"Sure," Jane said. She'd hear what Marcotte had in mind, get more coffee, be a team player.

"Chrystal Peralta is out sick," Marcotte said. "Flu. She's been working on a consumer story about banks and their evolving customer service departments. How they used to give toasters and the like for opening a new account? Now they're all about personal service."

"A consumer story?" Jane didn't really enjoy doing those puffy little pieces. Valuable info, she supposed, readable, and good for the paper. Just not her style. "Banks?"

"You're already working on that foreclosure piece, so it's right up your alley." Marcotte opened her top desk drawer, pulled out a reporter's spiral notebook and a manila file, offered it to Jane. "This is her notebook, it has all her contacts and info, and there's even a printout of her first draft of the story. We only need twelve column inches, we'll run it online and in print, and use a quick video sound bite as sidebar, maybe two, from whoever you interview, office, customers, your call. Have it in by Friday. Plenty of time."

Jane accepted the notebook and file, feeling a looming cloud of cranky that she didn't try very hard to dismiss. "I feel odd, taking another reporter's story. And what if Elliot Sandoval is arrested? And are we just ignoring the Moulten Road body?"

"I've got a nightsider on that. It'll be nothing, I predict." Marcotte waved at her open office door. "So, better get on it, right? As for Sandoval, I don't know how it works in television, but in newspapers, we can handle more than one assignment at a time. Any questions— shoot me an e-mail. The rest of it, you don't need to worry about. We clear, Jane?"

Marcotte paused. Jane could have sworn she saw a hint of a smile.

"I tapped you for this because I know I can trust you," Marcotte said. "We're short-staffed, as you know, and trying to make do. You and TJ did a great job on Waverly, and I know you'll get the rest of the story. I know you won't let me down."

Well. Imagine. A compliment.

Jane's phone, clicked to mute for the meeting, buzzed in her tote bag. This wasn't the time to put Marcotte on hold.

"No problem." She raised Chrystal's notebook, saluting authority and teamwork. And employment. "Happy to help."

Felt strange to have Bing Sherrey beside him instead of DeLuca. They tramped up the front walkway to Elliot Sandoval's place with a warrant for his arrest for the murder of Shandra Newbury. If all went as planned, Jake and Bing would soon be walking back to their cruiser, and putting a handcuffed murder suspect in the backseat.

D would be pissed to miss out, but he'd be in on the rest of it. Lilac Sunday was only days from now, and the confessed killer was in custody. Things were going Jake's way. The way of "case closed."

"You all set, Sherrey?" Jake raised a fist to knock on the metal jamb of the screen door, then decided to press the doorbell instead. Sandoval's white pickup sat in the driveway, two-by-fours stacked in the flatbed. With the impound squad on the way, the truck wouldn't be there much longer. Jake had called Peter Hardesty, professional courtesy, to warn him of the impending tow and the Sandoval takedown, but so far, no lawyer. Jake felt semi-guilty about proceeding without him, but Hardesty'd been warned. All still by the book.

"Ready or not, here we come," Sherrey said. He opened the lid of the metal mailbox mounted on the vinyl siding, peered inside, closed it. Smoothed the rumpled tie he'd yanked over his head in the car, pulled at the now-open collar of his shirt. "Most people, if they're ticked off at a real estate agent, they just fire 'em, you know? They don't kill 'em."

Jake heard the bing-bong of the doorbell echoing inside, squinted his eyes, listened hard for movement inside the house. Kids' voices, laughing, floated in from some backyard, not this one. The street-sweeping truck whooshed by, kicking up dust and brushing away nothing. A window air conditioner hummed, drops of water splatting on some kind of lush green plants below. The rest of the foliage was in bad shape, heat-baked and struggling. The month of May could be a killer in Boston. He pushed the white button again. Heard the bell, and the echo, then nothing.

Pregnant wife, Jake remembered. Living with relatives. Going to be tough for them. "Not that it helped *her*, you know? But Shandra Newbury was smart, she'd kept some angry letters Sandoval sent her. All in that real estate transaction file we finally got from Turiello. Instant motive." He rang the doorbell again. "Not to mention the fingerprints. Pretty much got him dead to rights. Damn it. Where the hell are they? If Hardesty—"

A car door slammed behind them. Jake turned. Sherrey did, too.

"Gang's all here," Sherrey muttered. "And party's over."

Peter Hardesty strode up the flagstone walk, canvas briefcase slung over one shoulder, his Jeep's engine ticking in the heat. He lifted a palm in greeting, then pointed to the doorbell.

"Don't bother, gentlemen," Hardesty said. "My client is here, and well aware *you're* here. But I instructed them not to answer until I arrived, assuming you wouldn't wait. Apparently I assumed correctly. The old constitutional rights thing must have slipped your minds."

"Sor—," Jake began. Then stopped. There was no damn time for sorry.

36

"We're here to see—" Jane checked Chrystal's spiral notebook again. Peralta used both sides of every page, with no recognizable organization, incomprehensible shorthand, and lots of globby purple ink. Maybe the notes helped *her*, but they were driving Jane crazy. "Elizabeth McDivitt? I think she's on three? I'm Jane Ryland from the *Register*, and this is TJ Foy."

Jane and TJ had wandered past the zigzag rope line until a blue-suited greeter approached and pointed them to the "welcome" desk in front of a bank of elevators. Cardboard advertisements bracketed the guard's desk, smiling faces in aluminum frames headlining low interest and free checking. A row of security video monitors blinked in fuzzy black-and-white. Jane resisted the temptation to wave and make a face, see if anyone noticed. She'd dumped her almost-finished coffee in the trash can by the ATM—not the most confident image, appearing for an interview clutching a cup of caffeine.

According to the lavender scrawls in Chrystal's notebook, Elizabeth McDivitt was eager to help with the story, and seemed chatty about her new duties as bank customer service rep. But Chrystal's barebones first draft needed a lot of work and, annoyingly, there was no way to do it without a follow-up. With sketchy notes like these, Jane had to wonder how Chrystal managed to write her stories. Happily, when Jane called to arrange the interview, a secretary recognized Chrystal's name, said Miss McDivitt was expected "shortly," and told Jane to come right over.

So. All good. And yes, Victoria, she could handle more than one story at a time. Unless Elliot Sandoval was arrested today, in which case her brain would explode and deadlines along with it. But so far, no call from Peter. She frowned. That call in Marcotte's office. She needed to check her messages. As soon as she—

"Ma'am? Picture identification?" The guard's demand interrupted her thoughts.

"Oh, right, sure." She showed her laminated news ID to the security guy, gestured to TJ to do the same. A sinewy ninja-wannabe in starched polyester and a shiny badge, the guard perched on a high stool behind the sleek marble desk. He scrutinized their IDs, Jane's, then TJ's, then Jane's again, as if the two of them were trying to pull a fast one.

TJ kept his camera at his side, his non-intimidating stance.

"No cameras," the guard said.

Arguing with security. Always a pleasure.

Maybe she could charm the guy, make it seem like a personal request. "Sir? Could you make a call for me?"

She read the ornate brass and marble nameplate on his desk. William John Leaver, III.

"Sir? Mr. Leaver? William? Bill? Like I said, I'm Jane Ryland, from the newspaper? Ms. McDivitt is expecting us."

"It's Bill. But no can do." The guard one-finger-typed their names into a computer, one agonizing letter at a time, waited for a machine to print out individual passes. Handed them back their identification, and offered each a slick white nametag on a peel-and-stick backing. "Third floor only. You can go up, he can go up, cameras cannot go up."

Jane checked her watch. She'd told Elizabeth Mc-Divitt's assistant they'd be here at ten, and it was ten. Jane had neglected to specifically mention the camera, but who would do an interview without a camera? She slapped the name badge on her black T-shirt, knowing it would leave an indelible gummy mark.

"I'd explained it was an interview." Jane had to give it at least one more try. She needed shots of McDivitt in her office, show her working the phone, illustrate how the bank had a whole department allocated to customer service.

"No one approved cameras, Ma'am." Bill pointed at a red light blinking from a black box mounted on one wall. "We have enough of our own. As you can see. Ma'am."

Jane puffed out a breath. Technically this wasn't her story, she was beyond tired, and at this point she'd be happy to give up—and yet, she had to get it done. Somehow. She looked at TJ, trying not to roll her eyes. The guy was only doing his job. Too well.

"Teege? I'll go by myself. I'll get McDivitt to arrange for the camera, and—"

"Good luck with that," Bill interrupted.

"—then call your cell," Jane went on.

"No prob," TJ said. "I'll get exteriors."

"No cameras," Bill said.

"Don't disappear," Jane said. "I'll make it work."

"Don't say a word, Elliot." Peter clamped a hand on his client's arm, holding him back physically as well as emotionally. The outcome of this living room face-off was inevitable, but Peter would insist the cops go by the book.

Any One-L student knows the first rule after being arrested is "don't say anything." The second and third rules, too. Peter had already argued his client was hardly a flight risk, given his wife was about to give birth to their child. Jake Brogan seemed to be accepting that. Good thing, since it was true.

Brogan—who must be exhausted after last night, just as Peter was—and the guy Sherrey, whom Peter didn't trust any farther than that bad tie he wore, stood right inside the closed front door. Brogan took the lead position, Sherrey slouched behind him. They had a warrant, so legally didn't need to be invited in. Nevertheless, they'd barely entered the Sandovals' territory.

"Guess Mr. Sandoval doesn't want to defend himself." Sherrey directed his words to Brogan. A cheap shot. Legal, but cheap, and clearly intended to harass his client into some angry and incriminating retort.

"You—" Elliot's face was going red, even with the AC blasting. He'd dressed in a suit, as Peter had suggested, in case they could arrange for an arraignment and bail hearing this afternoon. Might as well show the judge Sandoval was a respectable businessman, underscore the image of an innocent good guy who was in the wrong place at the wrong time with a few bits of arguably circumstantial evidence against him. If the arraignment were postponed to tomorrow, Sandoval'd be the best dressed defendant in the Boston PD lockup. Sans belt, of course. And shoelaces.

"Not a word, Elliot," Peter said again. This was shaky ground in some ways. Brogan had the class to call Peter and warn of the arrest. He'd also told Peter there were fingerprints in the Waverly Road house (though of course there would be, Elliot had lived there) and that Shandra Newbury had been the Sandovals' real estate agent, arranged their mortgage, and promised them the bank would understand if they got behind. All well-documented, apparently, in real estate records the cops seized from her office at Mornay and Weldon Realty. Records, including some nasty letters Sandoval wrote, the cops were required by law to turn over to the defense.

Could be a big deal. Could be meaningless. No way for Peter to characterize it at this point, but clearly enough probable cause for some judge to issue a warrant. What else they had, Peter and his client would have to find out in court.

"Elliot, please." MaryLou Sandoval, tears welling, didn't seem to be able to let go of her husband. She had one arm tucked through his, leaning into him, the other protecting her belly. "Peter will have you home again soon." She looked at Peter, pleading. "Won't you?"

"I'll do my best," he said. He wished he could say yes, but that wouldn't be fair. Or honest.

"Elliot Sandoval, we have a warrant for your arrest, for the murder of Shandra Newbury, on or about . . ."

Peter listened to the arrest litany he'd heard in so many living rooms, so many street corners, so many offices. Often, he knew the defendant was guilty, the police not the bozos they were often portrayed to be, but there was still the one in—ten? twenty? times that his client really didn't do it. Not simply that Peter could get him acquitted because the Commonwealth couldn't prove its case or the jury didn't want to convict, but because the guy was actually, literally, not guilty.

Those were the tough ones. Those were the ones that clenched your stomach and kept you awake at night, when you had an innocent person's future in your hands. Was this one of those times?

"You have the right to remain silent." Brogan was now reciting the Miranda, signaling the end of this stage of the game and the beginning of the next. No matter what happened, Elliot Sandoval and his poor wife and family were about to enter the rat maze of the legal system. Even with Peter guiding them the best he could, no one emerged the same way they went in, innocent or not.

MaryLou Sandoval had started crying at the words "warrant for your arrest," and her tears only increased since then, leaving wet blotches on her husband's khaki suit. Soon she'd have to say good-bye. Peter had no way to predict for how long. Overnight, maybe. Or forever.

"Sir?" Bing Sherrey reached under his sport coat, the handcuffs clinking as he gestured them toward Sandoval.

Peter closed his eyes for a brief second, then shot Brogan a look. "Any way we can skip this?"

"Sorry." Brogan looked like he might be telling the truth. "We could have picked him up middle of the night, you know. Not let them say good-bye."

"Not let him change into that snazzy suit." Sherrey took a step forward with the cuffs, motioned to Elliot, *turn around.* "Shouldn'ta bashed Miz Newbury with a two-by-four," he said. "Shouldn'ta left all those prints in the house."

"Sherrey." Brogan raised a palm.

MaryLou wailed, one long, miserable note, then stumbled, backward, catching herself on the arm of the couch. Watching as the handcuffs clicked over her husband's wrists. "He's a construction worker! Just a—she showed us that house," MaryLou said. "We only knew her because—"

"MaryLou." Peter had to step in here. If she got hysterical, started making statements, the cops could try to use that information. Even though it would legally be hearsay, anything the wife said could lead to trouble in the emerging case against her husband.

"I'll be okay," Sandoval said. "I will. This'll all be over before you—"

Sandoval stopped, and suddenly the room was still. Probably everyone thinking the same thing Peter was, he figured. Unless Peter could prevail, Elliot Sandoval would be behind bars when his first child was born.

"You're taking him to the police station? Booking him there?" Peter broke the silence. It was better to keep it cold and legal, no emotion, move this thing along the track, get it over with the best way possible.

"We'll see you in court," Brogan said.

"Elliot." Peter needed to have the last word. "Listen to me."

The cops were at the front door, Brogan's hand on the knob. Elliot turned to him, his face hardened, suddenly ten years older, the cords in his neck threatening to pop as he sealed in his anger.

"Too late now," Elliot's voice rasped, harsh and final.

"Elliot!" MaryLou ran to him, but Sherrey stepped between them, a barrier. "In custody" as reality. She stopped, arms at her side, the picture of defeat. This was never easy, but Peter always tried to see it as the first step on the path to justice. These two would be smiling again. He was sure of it. Almost.

"Listen. Elliot. Not a word. Not a word to anyone, not to these gentlemen, not to anyone you see in the police department lockup, not to anyone who seems friendly or helpful or solicitous. Nothing. Zero. Not a word. Got me?"

Elliot nodded.

"Brogan? You, too," Peter went on. This had to be on the record. No telling what those two would try to pull once they had Elliot alone. "Do not to talk to my client unless I'm present. Not a word."

Brogan nodded, Sherrey not so much. But they'd been warned.

"Good." Peter turned to his client. "This'll be behind us soon. I'll see you in court."

Brogan pulled the front door open, waved Elliot through, Sherrey right behind him. MaryLou whirled, hands clamped over her face, and sank into the couch. A woman appeared at the entrance to the hallway. The sister? There was nothing Peter could do for MaryLou. No comfort, no reassurance, no solace. "Don't worry"? "It'll be okay"? "He'll be fine"? Whatever he told her—he couldn't be certain it was true.

Peter watched as the three walked away into the May morning, one tall, one stocky, one in handcuffs, seeing the blast of sunshine through the open door, the tiny patch of browning lawn, some dumb bird twittering away as if nothing had happened. In a flash, the cops and their suspect were inside the unmarked cruiser, door slamming, taking his client away from freedom. Jane hadn't returned his call, surprising, but just as well she wasn't part of this.

MaryLou was sobbing in the woman's arms.

"See you in court," Peter muttered. Court was Elliot Sandoval's only chance.

37

Where was Elizabeth McDivitt?

"Not here yet," the secretary had just told Jane.

"Have you heard from her? No?" Odd. This Stephanie was the one who'd made the appointment. Jane couldn't write the story until she confirmed her quotes and got a few leads on customers. So here she'd stay, long as it took. "I'll wait."

The elevator bell pinged, then the doors rumbled open behind her. Jane saw Stephanie check her watch, raise an eyebrow, then erase the judgmental expression from her face.

"There she is," the receptionist said, pointing. She cleared her throat. "Finally."

Jane turned to see a young woman coming toward them, attractive enough, slim-ish, hip eyeglasses, wavy dark hair twisted into a messy bun. This was a bank executive? Her navy linen suit was off, somehow, the hem askew and the jacket rumpled, the white silk tee underneath clearly having seen better days. Bare legs with little black heels. Even carrying that obviously expensive briefcase, she looked like she'd just come from the gym, hadn't had time to pull herself together.

"I'm Lizzie—Liz, I mean—McDivitt." The woman approached, holding out a hand to Jane. She looked at

Stephanie, tilted her head. "Do I . . . is she a . . . did we have an—?"

"She's with the *Register*," Stephanie said. "A colleague of that Chrystal Peralta, who's doing the story? She wants to—"

"Follow up a bit," Jane said. Someone had to finish a whole sentence around here. "Do you have a moment?"

The elevator doors swished again, opening. Jane followed McDivitt's eyes as she turned to follow the sound, just in time to see a dark-haired man, suit and striped tie, raise a hand in greeting, then disappear as the doors closed and elevator went up. McDivitt had waved back, kept her hand poised even after the elevator had gone.

"Ms. McDivitt?" Jane said.

"Oh, sorry, sure." The woman shook her head, two little shakes, as if transporting herself back to the present. She gestured toward the closed office door. "Come on in."

"May I speak to Richard Arsenault, please? Yes, I'll hold."

Jake stirred another sugar into yet another cup of coffee, propping his forehead in one hand as he waited for the answer in the open-air squad room. *We got no secrets,* the Supe had recently proclaimed. Not after one of their veteran beat cops went down for accepting kickbacks from a crime scene cleanup company. Supe gutted the old warren of high-walled offices, replacing confidentiality with waist-high barriers and putting all communications in full earshot of everyone in the room.

Jake fidgeted at his new desk, banging one knee into the too-close fabric divider. Best for a cop to be out on the street, his grandfather always told him. Now Jake's cruiser was bigger than his cube. And more private. Sandoval was in lockup, awaiting arraignment, so at least that case was progressing.

Still on hold.

Parole officer Richard Arsenault, the guy who'd reported Gordon Thorley's missed call, hadn't returned any of the messages Jake left. Jake needed Thorley's complete file, all the way back to the armed robbery days nineteen years ago, not only this latest episode. No surprise. The parole department was notoriously understaffed, overegoed, and a general morass of incompetence.

Jake shook his head, clearing the gunk and extraneous thoughts, trying to power though this. At least Diva was at his mom's. Mom had pretended to complain, *just like I took care of your pets when you were a little boy, honey,* but by now she understood Jake's work. Accepted it, at least.

She and his dad had tried their best—even before Jake went to the Academy—to deter Jake from his detective ambitions. Now, finally, after four years and some headlines, they'd adjusted, sometimes even embraced, his decision. Jake's own father had rebelled from Grandpa Brogan's "blue blood" legacy by becoming a big-shot financier and married an actual blue blood, a Dellacort. The family loyalties had battled over him all the way through Harvard, but in the end, Jake was more cop than Brahmin, and both sides had relented. Some days, though, the lure of law school offered a certain temptation. At least he'd have wound up with an office where his legs fit under the desk. And a door he could close.

"Yo." A voice came over the phone. "What can I do you for?"

"Richard? Arsenault?" *Great.* Tucking the phone between cheek and shoulder as he gathered his stuff, Jake explained what he needed. If Arsenault had the records at his house or office, or wherever, Jake could pick them up and save everyone a lot of admin hassle.

"Calling about Gordon Thorley," Jake said.

"Poor guy," Arsenault said.

* * *

Within fifteen minutes, Jane and "Liz," as she insisted on being called, were on the road to BFFhood, even though Jane sat in a tweedy visitor chair and Liz in ergonomic black leather behind her new-looking desk. A silver pen holder, full; a silver business card holder stacked with cards and a pile of glossy bank brochures were aligned with the front edge of the desk. A silver computer keyboard sat behind a sleek black monitor. A couple of black lacquer picture frames faced Liz, so all Jane could see was their maroon-velvet backing. Personal photos, Jane theorized, not power portraits set out to impress guests.

"So, Liz? According to Chrystal—" Jane tried to get the news train back on track as Liz prattled on about her new position at A&A bank, her customer service department, her jargon-riddled ideas for streamlining the banking process and making it "numbers-friendly," whatever that meant. It seemed the woman's mother—"she died a few years ago"—would have loved that she'd gone into banking.

Liz's cell phone pinged, the third time. Apologizing, she texted an answer with a few quick stokes. "Chrystal seemed nice," Liz said, stashing her cell in the desk drawer. "Sorry about the texts. I'm surprised she's not here."

"Flu," Jane said, wrinkling her nose. "I'm backing her up. Confirming her story."

"Got it," Liz said. "I'm a numbers girl, so I know how important it is to be accurate."

"Right." Jane smiled, opened Chrystal's notebook again. "So, trying to read Chrystal's notes here, she has you quoted as saying, 'The first step in finding the best mortgage is to check rates online, then visit local banks to discuss their services with mortgage experts.' Sound right?"

Liz blinked, scratched her cheek with a forefinger. "Yeah." She drew out the word, seeming to consider. "I suppose so. True enough. I don't really remember talking about mortgages, but sure."

Jane peered at the notebook, deciphering. Maybe she'd read it wrong. "It's difficult to read her notes, frankly, so tell me, what *would* you say about that?"

"Well," Liz said, "I suppose it would be—"

"Hang on." Jane found a blank page, then patted her pockets for a pen. Lizzie stood, anticipating.

"Need a pen? Here," she said. "Courtesy of the bank." She pulled a red ball point from the container, the A&A logo emblazoned in white. She leaned across the wide desk as Jane stood to accept it.

Both picture frames fell forward onto the desk, clattering, facedown. "Oh, sorry." Jane stepped back. "Moved too fast. Hope they're okay."

Liz righted the frames, set them back into place. A wisp of a smile flickered across her face. "No problem."

"Family photos?" Jane asked. They were BFFs, after all.

Liz picked up one of the frames, turned it to face Jane for an instant, then set it back into place. "Boyfriend," she said.

Tasting the syllables, Jane noticed, almost as if the word was new.

"Ah," Jane said.

"New," Lizzie said. "He just gave it to me. Recently."

As Jane predicted. Maybe that explained the uncooperative hair and untidy hemline. Ah-*ha*. "Nice."

"Yeah." Liz tucked a curly strand behind one ear, where it stayed only briefly. Jane could tell her mind was elsewhere. Maybe the new boyfriend had texted her, that's why she'd answered so quickly. Nothing like the first tingly throes of new love. *Jake,* Jane thought.

Liz picked up the picture frame, now turned it toward

Jane, full face. "He handles the bank's foreclosed properties."

"Oh. Nice." The reporter-subject relationship was always a tightrope. Reporters had to be genuinely interested—*were* genuinely interested, at least for as long as it took to do the story—in what their interview subjects had to say. From time to time, though, an interviewee would decide their interest and focus meant they wanted to be friends, and the sharing would go a little too far.

Jane took in the smile, the mop of curls, the rep tie just so in what was clearly a corporate head shot. *The dark-haired guy on the elevator,* Jane realized. The one Liz had smiled at this morning when she arrived. Ah-*HA*.

"You also want more names of happy customers, you said?" Liz gave the photo one last look, then replaced it on her desk.

"I do, yes. The ones here are difficult to read." Jane flipped to a new page in Chrystal's notebook, relieved the boyfriend discussion seemed closed. The short list of customers had been scribbled in Chrystal-glyphics, so Jane needed to get her own names. Ones she could read. She'd find them, call them, interview two or three, bang out the story, and then be free to fight her own battles.

Jane clicked open the bank pen. She'd give it back, of course, when they finished. "Ready."

38

"You look terrible."

"Thanks, Mom. Always a treat to see you, too." Jake leaned in and gave his mother a quick kiss as she let him into the foyer of their Back Bay brownstone. Two-forty-three Marlborough Street, circa 1860, where Jake grew up, was an elegant sliver of history fronted by an ancient dogwood and a tiny emerald patch of front lawn. He heard a woof from somewhere in the back of the house, Diva probably so comfortable on the elaborate dog bed Mom kept in the mud room that the pooch decided it wasn't necessary to get up. Jake had half an hour before he was due at Arsenault's house in Southie. Just enough time to check in on Diva—and on Grandpa's files in the basement.

"Coffee?" she said. "Did you have breakfast? I can get Mrs. Bailey to make—"

"I'm great, Mom." Diva finally deigned to greet him, her plumy tail signaling her affection. A great dog, but how the hell had he figured he could take care of her with his unpredictable schedule? Diva turned her attention to his mother, snuffling at the pockets of her turquoise linen tunic.

"Are you giving her treats?" Jake asked. Diva had clearly worked some kind of magic on his usually fastidious mother. A few years ago at the animal shelter, the golden pup used the same tactics on him.

"It's our house," his mother said. Diva chomped, devouring some sort of dog treat in two retriever bites, then turned to Jake, luminous eyes begging for more. "I can do what I want for our guests. And Diva can stay as long as she likes. Now. To what do I owe this visit, kiddo?"

"Business. Grandpa's files, downstairs." Jake scratched Diva behind her ears. "Stay here, pooch."

"What files?" His mother followed him to the basement door, Diva right behind.

"Lilac Sunday," Jake said. He put his hand on the light switch at the top of the stairs. "If I can find them."

His mother frowned. "Sweetheart, is that really necessary? You know how your grandfather—"

"It's a cop thing, Mom." He leaned in, kissed her on the cheek. *And a Brogan thing.* "Don't worry."

Jake flipped on the light and closed the door behind him, down the splintery wooden stairs, smelling the dank earth and cool brick walls. Even when the day was blazing hot, the basement was always like another world. Jake had taken books and flashlights down here as a kid, hidden in his special dark corner reading Justice League of America comics, or pretended to be tracking down clues to the escaped bad guys, who were often found—after Jake's superpower detective skills were unleashed—hiding behind the washing machine.

Now the basement served as a cedar closet for Jake's mother's out-of-season clothing, one rack of clear-boxed shoes lining a side wall. Skis, golf clubs, and tennis rackets were stacked along another, but the back corner stayed pristine, reserved for a pair of battered black file cabinets, full of folders Jake's grandfather brought from the old police station on Clarendon Street. That building was now a chic hotel, housing a hip restaurant called Verdict.

While he was alive, Grandpa kept the file cabinet locked. Years after his funeral, newly-minted cop Jake decided he could look inside. He'd taken the oath, after all, so there could be no more secrets. Although Jake never articulated it to anyone, looking at the files, just looking at them, seemed a way to connect with his grandfather. The commissioner never got to see Jake awarded his badge or receive his ticket to the Homicide squad. Jake always regretted that.

Jake pulled out the rickety file drawers once again, this time with a purpose. He heard the faintest of squeaks, felt a tug of hesitation from the seldom-disturbed metal. Grandpa's rows of manila file folders appeared, the paper now softened by the damp, edges fluting. The labels on each one, handwritten in fountain pen, had blurred with the passage of time, faded into the otherworldliness of forgotten paperwork. These were Grandpa's personal case notes and newspaper clippings, the equivalent of a scrapbook, Jake realized.

Jake kept notes, too, on his BlackBerry. His clippings existed only in the newspaper's online archive, where Jake could click on them if he wanted to, though he never had. If Jake's own son, someday, were to wonder what his father thought, or did, or how he solved his cases—there'd be no basement files to visit.

He drew in a breath, the fragrance of old paper, onionskin, and carbon copies. He recognized his grandfather's handwriting. *Damn.* The files had case numbers or some kind of numerical designation, not the names of defendants or victims.

Jake stared at the rows of numbers, fighting impatience. The system had to be decipherable, maybe even easily so. Case numbers, he knew, began with dates.

The Lilac Sunday killing was in 1994. Jake looked for a label number beginning with "94," but there were none. So they weren't filed by the official police case designation.

Grandpa retired soon after, so maybe the case file would be near the front. One of the more recent ones.

"Or maybe all the way at the back," Jake said out loud.

Jake sighed, smiling, as if he could feel his grandfather challenging him to solve a personal mystery. If worse came to worst, he could pull out each file, one at a time. A pain, but eventually he would succeed. He looked at his watch—*no time right now, Gramps. Gotta go see a guy about a guy.*

Jake closed the file drawers, the slam echoing off the brick walls and the mechanism clicking back into place. He'd come back tonight. He wasn't even certain there'd be anything revealed in the files. But a good detective doesn't need to be certain at the beginning. He just needs to be certain at the end.

Jane Ryland seemed nice enough, Lizzie decided, watching the woman take careful notes in a spiral notebook, checking and rechecking the spellings of the names Lizzie gave her. Iantosca, Rutherford, Detwyler. Of course her "customers" would talk only about the personal service they were getting at A&A, never about the "problems" at the bank, or the "mistakes" in their mortgages. Liz had warned them on day one never to discuss the particulars of their mortgage situations. Hadn't she? Maybe not, not specifically, now that she thought of it. Watching Jane and gauging the reporter's intent, warning them again began to seem prudent.

"Jane? Before you contact these people, I'll need to notify them," Lizzie said. "Reassure them the bank isn't giving out personal information. I know you're exclusively interviewing them about customer service—" She paused. She wasn't used to dealing with reporters, but had so enjoyed her time with Chrystal, maybe she'd forgotten to be wary. Of course the bank PR guy had approved the interview. Colin Ackerman was always out to get good press for A&A, but he'd warned her not to divulge confidential information. Were the names themselves confidential? Maybe she should check.

"Please don't ask them about their personal financial situations, Jane. I'm trusting you here, right?"

"Sure," Jane said.

The reporter smiled, again, she seemed agreeable, but then Lizzie had heard about reporters, and how a good reporter could also be a good liar. That's how they got stories, her father had warned her as a kid. *Half the time they make stuff up.* She could almost hear him say it. "Never trust a reporter."

"I understand about the privacy thing," Jane was saying, turned a page in her notebook, continued to write. "Iantosca. O-S-C-A? Correct? But no problem. I get the parameters."

Lizzie felt a little creep of regret march up her spine, hand in hand with suspicions about Jane and her reporter ilk. She'd already given names to Chrystal, so she couldn't *un*give them, and now she'd confirmed them with Jane, but she had a growing uncomfortable feeling. What if they told her more than they should?

"Jane? Sorry to do this to you, but let's hold off."

"Off?" Jane stopped writing, the red ball point poised over her notebook.

"Yeah. Off." Lizzie stood, fingertips on her desk, then sat down again. In her haste to make the bank look good, and honestly, in her desire to make a name for herself and prove her "customer service" position was valuable and necessary, she might have crossed a line that could get her in trouble. Her in trouble, and the bank in trouble, in ways her father would never believe. Or understand.

Now she had to make this go away. She wished life had an "undo" button, like her spreadsheets did.

"Under section four-oh-one point two of the in-house procedures section of the state-chartered banking regulations, I cannot give you access to bank customers without their direct and written permission," Lizzie lied. There was no such regulation, but Jane would never know.

"The what?" Jane said.

"Yeah," Lizzie said. "I forgot about that. Sorry. So how about this? If you'll hold off until I give you a call tomorrow, I'll—"

"Maybe you could do an on-camera interview instead?" Jane's face changed, her initial obvious annoyance vanishing as she made the request. "Today? I hoped to follow up with the customers and all, but if you could see your way to an on-camera interview, maybe I wouldn't have to call them at all."

Did she trust Jane? "I'd have to get permission for that," Lizzie said. This whole thing might be so out of control it couldn't be reversed. And it was Lizzie's fault.

This had all been designed to engender good publicity for the bank. It was part of her job to reach out to the public, so she had to reach. When Ackerman called her to set up the Chrystal interview, how could she say no? How had it gone so wrong so quickly? That was an easy one. Because Lizzie had a secret. Or two.

Aaron had already texted her, three times, just saying "lata," the signal they'd agreed on last night to confirm they'd see each other later. Maybe tonight she should talk to him about this. Maybe not. She'd have to decide.

"Like I said . . ." Lizzie sat down, trying to use her body language to illustrate the decision was final. Decided it would look more final if she stood. "Please hold off on calling any of those customers until I give permission. As for the on-camera interview, I'll let you know."

"But—" Jane was standing now, too. She didn't look happy, or as personable as she did before.

Lizzie leaned to her intercom, buzzed for Stephanie. What were secretaries for, after all, but to get rid of people you didn't want to talk to? "Stephanie? Can you show Miss Ryland to the elevator?"

39

Peter Hardesty leaned against his parked Jeep, staring past the loops of yellow crime scene tape sealing the front door and the one boarded-up window of 2002 Moulten Road. According to the unenthusiastic beat cop assigned the low-rung job of guarding the place and now pacing the front walk, that smashed window was how his client Gordon Thorley and Thorley's supposed victim, Treesa Caramona, had gotten into the vacant house, a seedy and deserted white vinyl ranch on a melancholy cul-de-sac.

Wrong side of the tracks, Peter thought. The desirable homes are on the other side of the Arboretum. This one, a remnant from the GI Bill, felt left behind and forgotten. Two city blocks from here, under the cool verdant branches of the Arboretum woods where diligent gardeners cultivated and pruned and families picnicked away their afternoons, Carley Marie Schaffer had been killed.

Here on Moulten Road, not a tree had survived the years or the heat or the housing crash. The city had apparently given up the fight. Peter felt the hot sidewalk through the soles of his shoes. The sun, relentless, baked the red paint on his Jeep. At the Arboretum, he knew, there were already lilacs, with Lilac Sunday a few days away. No lilacs here.

This case. There was more to it. Or maybe less to it.

The whole thing was a crock of shit. "Crock of shit," Peter said out loud.

"Sir?" the cop said.

"Nothing," he said. He'd left messages for Brogan and Sherrey, hoping to meet them here this morning. He'd come on his own, before he heard back from them, planning to get the lay of the land before the two detectives or their cohorts tried to fast-talk him out of coming. "You hear back from HQ? About when I can go in? They going to send someone?"

She pointed to the cigarette-pack radio velcroed to her right epaulet. "Negative, sir," she said. "Sorry."

Peter wiped the sweat from his forehead, lifted the limp oxford cloth shirt away from his chest, peeled his pants from the toasting Jeep. Standing out here in the heat was a waste of time. Thorley was in lockup, awaiting "further investigation" as the cops put it. Sandoval was in lockup, awaiting arraignment, which still could come this afternoon. Would the judge grant bail for his client? Often they'd allow defendants to post a bond, but the Sandovals had already lost their home to foreclosure. Could the couple ask relatives to put up their houses to get him released? A tough call for all involved.

Might Elliot Sandoval have to stay in jail because he had no home to offer as collateral? The whole thing stunk.

Peter snapped some photos of the exterior of this crime scene with this cell phone, just in case. He dug out a business card, handed it to the cop.

"I'm headed to another appointment," he said. "If Brogan or Sherrey contact you, can you tell them to call me? No matter when?"

"Will do," the cop said. He saw her put his card into the pocket of her uniform pants, wondered if it'd see the light of day again.

What stunk even more, Peter thought as he opened his

car door, the heat inside blasting him, Gordon Thorley simply didn't feel guilty to him.

If a client said he was guilty, confessed he was guilty, wanted the justice system to agree he was guilty, what were Peter's responsibilities?

Peter cranked the ignition, felt the welcome blast of AC. If Thorley was simply a good liar, for whatever reason, then someone else killed Carley Marie twenty years ago. And in that case, someone else, the same person, or maybe someone totally else, killed Treesa Caramona early this morning. Maybe.

Some lawyers, he figured, would do nothing. Take the fee, accept a plea, get the best deal they could, be done with it.

Peter pulled his car away from the curb, and edged into the potholed asphalt of Moulten Road, considering. What if Thorley was—crazy? Or coerced?

Or lying on purpose? Why would someone do that?

There was a legal responsibility, Peter knew, not to perpetuate a fraud on the court. Rule 3.3 in the code of professional conduct: "A lawyer shall not knowingly offer evidence that the lawyer knows to be false. A lawyer may refuse to offer evidence the lawyer believes is false."

He had a duty to discourage his client from testifying falsely.

He had to take "reasonable remedial measures" if a client lied.

He had to dump Thorley as a client if he persisted in lying.

If Thorley was lying.

Peter flipped on his left-turn blinker, signaling his direction. Wished it were that easy for the other parts of his life—pick a direction, go there. He had one client who insisted he was guilty. The other insisted he was innocent. Who was telling the truth?

He honked at some nut who tried to cut him off, then

touched the brake, letting a Volvo get ahead of him. He'd had enough with asshole drivers. He wondered how Jane was, but decided he would call her *after* this next interview. She didn't need to be there for this one—that wasn't part of their deal.

Traffic increased as he hit Highway 93 South. Two hours for this trip, he figured. He'd be there by three. Should he call ahead? Next time he saw a Dunkins', he'd get iced coffee, make a phone call, and cross his fingers.

Who was telling the truth?

The police didn't care. Far as they were concerned, they'd caught their bad guys. The press didn't care—well, maybe Jane did. But guilty or innocent, she could write her story either way.

Right now, finding the truth was up to Peter. And two people's lives—actually, more than two—depended on it.

Jake hit the Bluetooth as he drove up Melnea Cass Boulevard, a crosstown shortcut to parole officer Richard Arsenault's house. He'd told his mother he'd be back for the files, given Diva a good-bye pat, and headed for Southie. The news he just heard wasn't the best for Elliot Sandoval, but that's sometimes the way the cookie crumbled. The guy shouldn't have killed Shandra Newbury if he wanted to stay out of lockup. The phone rang once, then again, then he heard the buzz and click that meant Peter Hardesty was not going to pick up. But then a live voice interrupted.

"Hello? Hello? This is Peter Hardesty. Sorry, can you hear me? I'm in the car."

"Jake Brogan," Jake said. He stopped at a light, watching cars make illegal left turns onto Mass Ave. Lucky he was on the phone or he'd have nailed them. "You called about getting into Moulten Road? Not gonna happen any time soon."

Jake could have been nicer about this, but right now he wasn't a big fan of Towel Man.

"Crime Scene's still in there," Jake went on. "And the Sandoval arraignment? That's on for tomorrow. Courts are closed today, there's some sort of judge's meeting."

He paused, waiting out the unhappy reaction. Didn't blame the guy, they were keeping him away from Moulten Road, and now he was hearing his client would stay in lockup, overnight, because judges had their little meeting. Win some, lose some, Towel Man. Life was full of disappointments.

"Nothing you can do?" Peter's voice cracked over the speaker. "I mean, that's bullshit, the system of justice grinds to a halt because—"

"Yeah, I hear you." Jake hit the gas, turned right at the high school, and toward the intersection. "But Sandoval is first on the calendar, after the call. Best we could do, according to my guy. So. See you in court."

Jake clicked off before Peter could answer. He didn't need to get beat up on the phone by a disappointed defense lawyer. The tox screen showed Sandoval with elevated steroid levels, so that'd explain the guy's anger. His fingerprints had been all over. He'd lived there, of course, so that was arguably problematic. According to Brian Turiello, the real estate broker, Shandra Newbury had not only shown the Sandovals their home, she'd also hooked them up with her connection in the mortgage department at their bank. A connection who apparently ignored their income-to-mortgage ratio.

The Sandovals wound up over their head, mortgage-wise. And bottom line, Shandra Newbury had arranged it. They'd lost their house. As a result, Shandra'd lost her life.

Losing your house as a motive for murder.

Any jury would believe that. A Sandoval guilty verdict was probably a slam dunk.

Jake checked house numbers, slowing as he hit a narrow cul-de-sac lined by tired triple-deckers with gasping lawns and hanging plants on their last legs.

Fifty-three was the last on the left, Arsenault had told him.

The plastic-coated living room inside doubled as Arsenault's parole office, a bank of walkie-talkies and an electronic monitoring board taking up much of the space on a makeshift set of cobbled-together veneer shelving. A display screen with a line of green lights glowed like a neon sign in the lower left. Looking more closely, Jake saw each had a name on a color-coded label affixed beside it, printed in shaky felt-tip handwriting, apparently Arsenault's jerry-built system for keeping track of his parolees. All lights green, all accounted for, Arsenault had explained. At the bottom, one light was red. G. THORLEY, the peeling label said. Red. *Gone.*

Jake pointed to the red light. "Well, now at least, we know where he is."

"Reported it as soon as he missed his slot." Arsenault took a slug of tea, ice cubes clattering. "Can't understand it. Before that? He'd been clockwork, you know?"

An ancient air conditioner struggled, wheezing, in the front window. His wife, Margy Mary—Jake had confirmed the name, twice, thinking he'd heard it wrong—brought cookies on a flowered plate, and sweetened iced tea, the icy brown liquid sweating a glass pitcher she carried on a clear plastic tray. "I know you boys have a lot to talk about," she said. "But you've got to eat."

"Thanks, doll," Arsenault said, dismissing her with a wave. Margy Mary bustled out of the room. Jake imagined he'd smell something baking soon. Betty Crocker meets Tommy Lee Jones.

"So Arsenault, about Gordon Thorley."

"Like I said, clockwork."

"Right." Jake shifted on the couch, plastic crinkling

underneath him. Who were they saving the couch for, he wondered? Who would be important enough to sit on actual fabric? "But you interviewed him, right, every week? He ever indicate any problems, or anger, anything going on in his life? He ever mention a Treesa Caramona?"

"Nope, zip," Arsenault said.

"Carley Marie Schaefer?"

"The Lilac Sunday girl?" Arsenault's eyes widened. A phone rang at his mission control setup, a light flashed red, then green, then steady green. "My two-thirtys are gonna start calling," Arsenault explained. "Long as we hear five calls, we're fine. It's hooked up to a machine, they'll click in, they'll be recorded. Anyway, Carley Marie Schaefer? How come?"

"Not at liberty to tell you exactly why, right now," Jake said. "You know the drill, right? Under investigation? Trying to get your take on it. He ever mention her? Anything about that?"

"Nope," Arsenault said. "You got me interested, though. You think he's the—" Arsenault stopped, seemed to be calculating. "Ah. Caramona's the one in West Rox. By the Arboretum. And I'm thinkin' that you're thinkin'— okay. Huh. Okay, then."

He nodded, conspiratorial, pretending to zip his lips.

"Thanks," Jake said. "So Thorley's file, his history, you got that?" He held up a palm, heading off what he knew would come next. Arsenault had already opened his mouth in preparation to say no. "Yeah, I could get it from HQ, but you know how long that'd take?"

Arsenault's incoming rang again, the lights flashing, then again, with a different ring.

"Two more to go," Arsenault said, "then the city's safe until four P.M., far as I'm concerned. Anyway. The files." He pressed his lips together, drummed his fingers against the side of his nubby green glass, now filled only with melting ice. With a clink, the ice settled.

"Yeah, the files," Jake said. "And listen. When we talked earlier, and I mentioned Gordon Thorley, you said—'poor guy.' Why was that?"

"I said poor guy?"

"Yup."

Arsenault cleared his throat, swirled the ice cubes. "Well, he missed his parole call, right?"

"Yeah."

"That means he could go back into the slammer, right?"

"Yeah."

Arsenault nodded, agreeing with himself. "So, 'poor guy.' Right? Or 'stupid guy,' if you look at it that way."

"I suppose," Jake said. "So—the files?"

The phone rang. The final green light flickered, then stayed on.

"Life is good," Arsenault said. "You can see the files. Sure."

"Great," Jake said. "So—"

"At headquarters," Arsenault said. "*You* know the drill, right? They'd kill me if I gave 'em to you, or even told you anything that was in 'em. It's all personal and confidential, even to you, Detective. Want some more tea?"

40

"So much for that." Jane poked the elevator button for emphasis, having been summarily dismissed from Liz McDivitt's office right when things were going so nicely. What had stopped the woman, so abruptly? The texts she'd received? Jane shook her head, frowning at the thin gray pile of the bank's carpeting. Jabbed the down button again. No question, this story completely stunk, stunk from moment one.

The elevator doors swished open, and Jane stepped forward, trying to plan her next move. "Oof." She backed up, surprised by a near collision with a suit.

"Jane Ryland?" he said.

Was she supposed to know him? She didn't, she was pretty sure. Pinstripe suit, tie, shiny shoes. At least he didn't have a knife.

"I'm Colin Ackerman. I handle PR for the A&A." He gestured Jane out of the elevator and back into the hall. "Liz McDivitt just called me."

Disaster. Or lucky break? Here was someone Jane might negotiate with, someone who could make decisions, someone with the access to get what she needed. Or someone who could get her ejected from the building.

"Terrific," Jane said, choosing the optimist's view. She didn't want to get Liz in trouble, so she'd couch her request carefully, not mentioning customer names quite yet. "Liz and I were talking about the bank's customer service department. As I'm sure she told you, the *Register* is doing a little consumer story on it. I was hoping—"

Ackerman raised an eyebrow, interrupting her request. "A 'little consumer story'?" he said.

"Yes, we're—"

"Not what you usually do, if I remember correctly, Jane."

Ackerman still looked pleasant enough, his muted plaid jacket open, his yellow tie appropriate for relating to the public. "Right? I mean, you're usually on the trail of some nefariousness. Corruption? Malfeasance? You certainly understand why that'd be pinging my news radar."

"True." Jane did understand. She'd been guilty in the past, like any good reporter, of journalism "downplay," soft-pedaling a story to get in the door. If this guy was suspicious because she usually did investigative stuff, it was ironic that this time she was actually telling the truth. Funny to be caught in her own trap for a consumer puff piece.

"The other reporter, Chrystal Peralta? Has the flu. I'm here as designated hitter while she's on the injured list." This day was a teetering house of cards. The story probably wouldn't matter that much, but always better to succeed, no matter what the assignment. "The story has to run Sunday, so the deadline is . . ." Jane paused. He didn't need to know the real deadline. "Today."

Wait. Idea. "Hey," she said. She glanced at Stephanie, caught her brazenly listening. Suddenly Stephanie had to flip through some very important papers on her desk. She was probably passing along everything they said to her boss, maybe even had the intercom open. If so, it was an opportune moment for Jane to let Liz know she was trustworthy. "I'd asked Liz to do a quick on-camera interview with us about customer service, but she was reluctant. Maybe because that's your bailiwick?"

Jane tried adding an encouraging smile. This might be the perfect solution, or at least a solution. "My photog is downstairs right now. How about if we bring him to your office? I can ask you a few quick questions about—"

"Not about specific customers," Ackerman said.

"Nope, nope, no specific customers, that's exactly what Liz said, too." Jane raised her voice, just a little, in case Liz was listening. "Customer service, that's all. Really. Five minutes, ten, and we're gone."

Ackerman nodded, seemed to be considering. He checked his iPhone, typed in something.

Jane crossed her fingers. *Come on.*

"Sure," he said. He smoothed his tie with one hand, clicked off his phone with the other. "Can you meet me on the fifth floor? My assistant will point you to the conference room. You may have to wait a bit, I need to make a few phone calls first. And Miss Ryland? You promised ten minutes. That's all you get."

"That's all I need," she said.

"We always hoped things would change for him, but they never did."

Peter had listened for half an hour, listened with the patience he'd learned to rely on in his years as a lawyer. People would tell you everything, if you let them. Sometimes they didn't even realize they were doing it. Gordon Thorley's sister—a brittle forty-something with fuchsia-painted fingernails and ill-fitting jeans—sat across from him at her kitchen table in the village of Sagamore, her home a cookie-cutter two-story just off Williston Road. A row of fluttering lace-curtained windows let in the late-afternoon sun and the sight of a couple of sea gulls dive-bombing toward the Cape Cod canal, a blue sliver in the distance. Crazy hot for May, but here the breeze kept tempers down and early-bird Cape tourists happy on the beach.

Doreen Thorley Rinker was not a tourist. And right now, she was not happy.

Peter had to tell her about the Treesa Caramona murder, explaining it was in the early stages, her brother innocent till proven guilty, trying to be reassuring. There were rules about dealing with defendants, all carefully spelled out in the canons. Dealing with families was different. Their agendas, their prejudices, and even their birth order, dictated how a lawyer would most effectively present the facts, as well as the possibilities. Doreen was Gordon Thorley's big sister, maybe ten years older. Now she was still taking care of him, either from devotion or from duty.

"When he left the note, we just didn't know what to do." She looked at him, ran her fingers through both sides of her not-completely-gray hair, fluffed it back into place. "He was confessing for the family? Did he mean—Carley Marie Schaffer's family? Why would he care about *them*?"

"Did he know her? Carley Marie? Or her family?"

"God knows," Doreen said. She stared at her coffee mug as if searching for answers in the fading flowers on the china pattern, then looked at him again, frowning. "I'm not trying to be evasive. I really don't know."

"Maybe he meant—for *your* family," Peter said. "Could that be?"

"My family? The family is me and this house and my kids—they're out at the beach now since they both work nights—and a cousin or two, who knows where. Our parents bought this house, some years ago, and left it half to me and my husband, half to Gordon, when they passed. Then my husband passed, too. So much for the dream house on the Cape. A lot of the time, Gordon was—well."

"In prison." Might as well lay the cards on the table.

She nodded, maybe not wanting to say the word. "Not that he was ever here much. He was what, nineteen? And I was twenty-nine. Nothing in common, you know, at those ages. I was always told he got in with the wrong crowd. But we were willing—happy—to bring him home after all that time. We were so relieved he was paroled. I mean, he'd just been duped into that robbery, had no idea that—anyway, like I said, we were willing to help him start over. He'd actually been a pretty good kid in high school. Played baseball, the whole bit. But he wanted his own place. Insisted he wanted to start over on his own."

She shrugged one shoulder, a thin strap showing under her sleeveless blouse. "Who were we to say? Who knows what he even *does*. That's why this is so upsetting, you know? What if he—"

She took a deep breath. "Maybe it was better he wasn't living here. You think? Hard to believe he could kill any—"

"I saw his apartment." Peter saw she was spiraling herself into fear and panic, worrying about imaginary terrors. "He's a talented photographer."

"Really?" Doreen seemed surprised. She settled her shoulders. "Anyway. That note he left. I mean—the Lilac Sunday killer? *Gordon?* The Lilac Sunday killer? And was going to confess? I just saw my whole life, everything I always believed—I don't know. Crumbling. Like everything I ever thought suddenly wasn't true anymore."

She looked at Peter, as if he could provide some explanation.

"My little brother. Maybe I never really knew him? But family is family. We don't have much, as you can see. And the house payments are—well. We may not be able to keep the place. Who knows? The bank knows, I guess. We'll survive. Anyway, least I could do was hire my brother a lawyer. Who else would do it? I found you on-line, under criminal defense. Now you've gotten more than you bargained for."

She examined her coffee cup again. "I have, too. I'm sorry you came all the way out here. We can't afford you."

Peter'd heard every sob story in the book, he figured, the down-and-outers, the misfits, the misunderstood. The people who had made wrong decisions, or had wrong decisions made for them. How did people wind up where they were? Could they ever change? He couldn't help but be fascinated by it, even knowing the slices of life he heard in his cases were, by dint of his profession, going to be the oddities, the outliers, and the mistakes. A criminal defense attorney hardly ever heard a story of joy or success or redemption. Well, sometimes redemption.

"Mrs. Rinker? Let's talk about the money some other time, okay? I'm involved now, and we'll see where it goes. So confirming what you told me—you never heard Gordon speak of Carley Marie Schaefer. Or Treesa Caramona."

Doreen nodded. "Yes. I mean—no. He never said those names. To me."

"To anyone? Anyone you know?" Sometimes specificity was a good thing. Other times it sounded like evasion.

"No, not to anyone I know."

"The note was a surprise to you."

Doreen nodded again. "On the kitchen table." She pointed with one finger. "Right there."

"How'd Gordon get in to leave it?"

Doreen smiled, just barely, and seemed to look over his shoulder and out into the past. "There's been a key in the third pansy pot from the end of the front walk ever since we were kids. At our old house. I did the same thing here. Guess he remembered."

"I'll need to see the note, of course. Things are not always what they seem on the surface. It may hold some clue or meaning we didn't understand initially. Even a fingerprint, you know? Could be someone else's. Happy to make a copy, certainly, and you'll get the original back as soon as we find out what's really going on here."

Doreen blinked at him, looked at the ceiling.

"I burned it," she said.

Maybe Jane *was* trustworthy. Lizzie's back complained from the ten minutes she'd spent leaning into the intercom speaker, getting her ear as close as she could. She'd told Stephanie to leave the switch open. And, listening, she learned Jane hadn't divulged that Liz had given her any customer names.

What did it mean? Lizzie leaned back in her chair, crossed her arms over her chest, considering. Maybe you could trust reporters after all. Jane Ryland, at least. If Ackerman would do the interview she'd heard Jane request, Lizzie'd be off the hook and she could go back to her real life.

A life which was getting more complicated by the second.

She'd be seeing Aaron "lata." He hadn't called yet to give her specifics. What might he want to do? What might he be thinking?

She plucked at her navy blazer, imagined she saw a crumb or two of sugar from that chocolate chip pastry. He had completely knocked her out.

That's what worried her.

She popped her research back to full screen on her computer monitor. That chocolate pastry. She'd been woozy. Had trouble remembering what happened, exactly. Sort of. She'd attributed it to—well, lust. But thinking about it later, in a clinical moment at the bathroom mirror, she admitted it didn't add up. It didn't.

She'd searched "date rape drugs." And checked off the symptoms, yes, yes, yes, one by one. She still had the headache. Could he possibly have drugged her? Why?

But he'd told her about the rentals. Why?

Well, easy one. Because she already knew. And he was trying to find out how much.

Her office suddenly seemed perfectly silent. As if the world had stopped, and time had stopped, and her brain was the only thing working.

She pulled the metal handle of her desk's top drawer, hearing the whisk of the metal runners, the click as the drawer opened all the way. She pulled out those leases he'd created, one, then the next, on the triple folded white paper. Saw those college kids, paying *Aaron* to living illicitly in the *bank's* houses. Saw the words in black and white. Saw Aaron's double-dealing and downright theft.

What he was doing was wrong. There was no way around that. It was bank robbery.

He didn't care about her. How could she ever have thought he did?

He was using her. To get access to bank records. Her files. Her connections.

Rohypnol, her monitor said. A colorless, tasteless . . .

The intercom buzzed.

"They're gone," Stephanie's voice crackled though the metal mesh. "You heard?"

"I did," Lizzie said. "Great job on the speaker thing."

"And your appointment is here, early," Stephanie said. "The Gantrys."

Cole and Donna. Deep in debt, after Cole's once-thriving company'd lost a government contract, but about to enjoy a financial surprise. Their mortgage numbers had gotten the Liz treatment. The bank's "mistake." They would keep their home.

Elbows on her desk, Liz clasped her hands in front of her mouth, fingers intertwined. Aaron *was* using her. Of course. She was an incredible dupe.

"Give me a moment," Liz said into the intercom.

And what about her own system? Doing the wrong thing for the right reason still made her a liar. Grateful customers or not. What she was doing was just as— immoral—as what Aaron was doing.

Well, no. Not really. Aaron was benefiting from his deals. Taking the money. *Stealing* the money. Not doing it for the renters. Doing it for himself.

She was getting nothing from her system. Nothing. Except the justice of it.

It was doing good. But it was still wrong.

She stuffed the leases back into the drawer, closed it, locked it.

Maybe just this once more. Then she would stop. There was still time to change everything, anyway. She could help her clients in other ways.

Which left the Aaron problem.

He expected to see her tonight. She should simply call it off. Leave it alone. Problem was, Aaron knew that she knew. He would never go away.

She closed her page of research, erased the history.

She blinked at the blank screen.

Erased the history.

She had an idea. About tonight, and about the Aaron situation. It was a little risky, maybe a lot risky, but this time she had all the cards. She'd have time to think it through before this evening.

"Okay, ready," Liz said into the speaker. She straightened the pencils on her desk, saluted the photo of Aaron, and flapped it facedown on her desk. She was ready. Ready for more than the soon-to-be surprised Gantrys. "Send them in."

She loved her job. The realization washed over her with the glow of sunshine from her third-floor window. And she loved her life.

Things all worked out. Eventually. Even growing up with her father, and his criticism, and his focus on his precious bank. She wouldn't be here, now, without that difficult journey of the past. She wouldn't trade it. Her father being who he was had put her in the position to help people. Really help them. She'd had a difficult childhood, well, so what, so did lots of people. It had made her who she was today. And that was worth it.

All worth it.

41

"Just look at me, Mr. Ackerman, not at the camera, okay? I know you've done this before. TJ will make sure it looks good." TJ's portable minicam allowed them to bang out quick sound bites without white-balancing or searching for electrical outlets for the lights. "Now, tell me your name and title."

Colin Ackerman's assistant, all navy blazer and prep school attitude, had tapped a pass card on a black-box locking device, ushering Jane and TJ through massive double-paneled doors into the conference room, an homage to sleek mahogany and cordovan leather. *No wonder you needed a special escort to get to the executive floor.* Customers might not be pleased to discover their fees and service charges were spent on fancy chairs and lavish conference tables. Ackerman had kept them waiting for an hour, a pitiful power play, but whatever. She needed the interview.

TJ finally placed Ackerman in front of the bank's ubiquitous anchor logo, this one in gold, wall-mounted on a navy blue suede background. *Suede and mahogany.* Jane remembered the shabby vinyl of the empty house on Waverly Road.

"You set, TJ?" The recitation of the name and title wasn't only for Jane's reference, but to allow TJ to check audio levels and camera angles. "Great. Mr. Ackerman? Tell me about the bank's focus on customer service," Jane said.

"Certainly, Jane. As a mortgage customer of the bank yourself, you know Atlantic and Anchor's primary concern is for . . ."

The "concern" part was bull, but was Ackerman trying to telegraph that he knew her mortgage information? Creepy, and totally inappropriate, if he'd looked her up. Jane rolled her eyes, mentally at least. *Public relations guys.*

Ackerman continued with canned PR prattle about customers and personal relationships, using her name in every sentence. In a usual taped interview, she'd let him say whatever he wanted, get that over with, then ask the tough questions she actually cared about. But in this case, all she needed was a perfunctory twenty or so seconds for an online sidebar. She'd gotten the video, and that would please multimedia Marcotte, and if Victoria was happy, Jane was happy. And soon she could go home and take a nap.

Sleep. Her thoughts half-wandered as Ackerman continued his boilerplate. *Bed.* Which reminded her of Jake. Who was in Boston, not D.C. Who hadn't called.

She'd phone Marcotte, give her the good news about this interview, and say she'd bang out the story tomorrow, plenty of time. What she wouldn't say was—she was not about to let cleaning up Chrystal's journalism leftovers distract her from the potential headlines she was pursuing on her own. Sandoval. Peter Hardesty. Her foreclosure story. And, perhaps, even Gordon Thorley.

A nap would have to wait. A good story trumped sleep.

"Vierra? It's Jake Brogan. Listen, can you run an address for me at the Registry of Deeds? I need to know the owner of the house." Jake could have run the Moulten Road address through the Registry of Deeds himself, but not while he was driving. Officer Vierra in Records had offered to help. Jake still felt weird to be on the job without DeLuca, and the empty passenger seat changed the whole atmosphere of the cruiser, making Jake feel as though he'd forgotten something. Still, he preferred working alone to warding off the nonstop rancor and "in the old days" complaining that spewed from Bing Sherrey.

Sherrey was assigned as primary on Moulten Road, with Jake as backup. So far, Sherrey seemed to be content with watching Crime Scene do its thing rather than initiate any investigation of his own. But that was not Jake's problem. Until it was.

"Yeah," Jake told Vierra. "It's two-zero-zero-two Moulten Road. Let me know ASAP, okay? And one more thing—call the MBTA flak, make him give us the video from the buses that took the Moulten Street route—you know? Between say, five P.M. and ten P.M. Tuesday night. Got it?"

He paused, heard Vierra sneeze. "Bless you," Jake said. "Got it?"

"Got it," she said.

Jake had a thought. Probably'd go nowhere, but running an investigation of a cold case meant looking up everything, relevant or no. You couldn't know until you found it, or didn't. "One more thing," he said. "Look up the name Gordon Thorley." He spelled it. "Find out if a Gordon Thorley, he'd be around forty years old, owns any property. Start with Massachusetts, see if there's anything."

"Got it," Vierra said. "Back to you soonest."

Jake clicked off the Bluetooth, cranked the AC, grabbed the second half of the roast beef on a bulkie roll he'd gotten at Kelly's. At least no one was there to criticize the cole slaw dripping on the upholstery.

Driving one-handed, he made the right turn onto the expressway, figuring it would be fastest, going against the already-in-progress rush hour. Somehow the five-thirty exodus from Boston now started at four thirty. With weekend inflation, three thirty on Fridays.

His phone rang mid-bite. Jake steered with one elbow as he punched on the speaker.

"Brogan," he said. Hoping it sounded intelligible.

"Jake?"

Jake swallowed. "Yeah."

"You don't sound like yourself," the voice said.

"Who's this?" Jake felt for a paper napkin, wiped mayo from his mouth.

"Nate Frasca," the voice said. "Listen, remember I said—"

"Yeah," Jake said. He put the sandwich on the waxed paper he'd spread out on DeLuca's seat. He'd been wondering about Frasca. "You said the name Thorley rang a bell. You think of the bell?"

"I did. Remember the Willie Horton case, years ago, convict who got paroled and then murdered someone? Pretty much killed the governor's career?"

"Yeah," Jake said. "Hard to get votes when people are convinced you set a killer free. As if anyone would do that on purpose. So?"

"Thorley's parole was like that, controversial. I knew there was something. I tried to look it up in the online newspaper archives, but they don't go back that far. The head of the parole board was replaced after he sprung Thorley. There was a new governor, so that might have had something to do with it. But after Thorley, with the new parole board chairman, paroles pretty much stopped. You can find the details, I'm sure."

"So you think—" Jake turned on to Huntington, could see the lofty high-rise glass of the Prudential Tower ahead, and the flashing weather lights on the stubby old Hancock building next to it. *Flashing blue, clouds due.*

"I don't think anything," Frasca said. "I just said the name Thorley rang a bell. That's the bell."

"Thanks, Nate." So there was something. Or nothing. But at least an idea worth a follow-up. If Thorley's parole was controversial, maybe someone knew something about him that was suspicious—like maybe he really was a bad guy.

Why hadn't Richard Arsenault, Thorley's parole officer, mentioned that?

"You burned it?" Peter tried to grasp the finality of it. He'd been hoping—a slim hope, but nonetheless a hope—that something about the note would exonerate Thorley. It was someone else's handwriting, maybe, or revealed a fingerprint, or a mark, or was written on a unique kind of stationery. So many possibilities, so many opportunities for reasonable doubt. But now . . . none.

Peter couldn't even prove the note ever existed.

He tamped down his disappointment, tried to hide his anger. This was denial. And fear. Maybe panic. People weren't lawyers, and didn't always make the right decisions. Not that lawyers always did.

"I understand. You probably wanted the whole thing to go away," Peter said.

"Well, I thought maybe—" Doreen Rinker's fingers smoothed the plastic tabletop, as if she were trying to wipe away her mistake. "Thought maybe the note would get him *more* in trouble."

"I see," Peter said. The wrong decision for the right reason. So often a signpost on the road to a guilty verdict.

"Okay, then. Moving on." No reason to make her miserable over it. More miserable than she already was. He would assume there really had been a note, since after all, that's what started the whole thing. "Tell me again, exactly what did it say? Try to picture it, Ms. Rinker. Sometimes that helps."

Doreen leaned against the spindly ladder back of the kitchen chair, tilted her head toward the ceiling, closed her eyes. The skin of her neck was mottled and sun-spotted. "Cape Cod skin," they called it, unfortunate by-product of a life on the beach.

He saw her chest rise and fall as she took a breath, let it out. "White paper, like from a copier," she said. "'Do-reen,' it said. And then . . ."

Peter waited, silent.

"It said: 'I'm sorry.' It said: 'I'm doing it for the family. Lilac Sunday was my fault, and I need to take responsi-bility.'" Doreen opened her eyes, blinked as if she'd just awakened from hypnosis, crossed her arms in front of her, and scratched her upper arms with those stubby fin-gernails. "And then it said 'I'm sorry' again."

"Was it signed?"

"No." Doreen drew out the word, remembering. He could see her picturing the note, her eyes moving up and right, retrieving the memory. "Well, no and yes. It was signed 'G.' But that's what the family called him, 'G.'" She smiled, almost. "He hated the name Gordon."

"So it was signed, in effect. Because no one else would have known about G, correct? And it was in his hand-writing? Would you recognize it?"

He was grasping at straws here, he knew. Thorley him-self had accepted authorship of the note. But no harm in pursuing every angle. Even if the angle was now ashes.

"Well." Doreen blinked, then pressed her fingertips over her eyes. "I never considered—well, I don't know. I guess I don't know his handwriting."

"Did anyone else know where that key was?" More

straw grasping. Thorley had admitted writing the damn note, as clear and incriminating a confession as he'd ever seen. A jury would buy into "guilty" without a second thought. But this case would never get to a jury, Peter realized. Thorley insisted he was guilty.

Peter didn't have to prove his client innocent, of course. Likely he actually *was* the Lilac Sunday killer. But it was his job, his responsibility, his constitutional obligation, to make the Commonwealth prove his client guilty. If they couldn't, Thorley should be set free, even if he didn't want to be.

But seemed Doreen Rinker was a dead end.

Peter should head back to Boston, get the latest on the Moulten Road crime scene, see if the cops could produce any real evidence linking that to Thorley. And he needed to check on Sandoval. Poor guy. Now in custody, overnight at best, and maybe longer. He might call MaryLou Sandoval, just to touch base.

Doreen hadn't answered him.

"Doreen? Did anyone else know where the key was?"

"Not that I know of." Doreen tilted her head, the creases in her forehead deepening into furrows. "You think someone else might have—"

Peter shook his head. "Not really," he admitted. "But I need to explore all—hang on. My phone."

His phone buzzed in his jacket pocket, vibrating against his thigh. He took it out, looked at the caller ID. Jane.

"Go ahead and take it," Doreen said. She gestured toward the hallway. "I'll just run to the little girls' room."

"This is Peter Hardesty." Peter watched Doreen walk away, her flip-flops flapping against the hardwood floor.

"Are you kidding me?" the voice on the other end said.

Jane. An unhappy Jane, from the sound of it. He almost smiled, listening to her indignation. He'd be angry, too, if he was—

"Jane? Jane?" He tried to interrupt, no point having

her go on about it. "I'm sorry, really, I am, I called you though, and you never called me back."

She didn't stop.

". . . and now, according to some police source who just called one of our reporters, Elliot Sandoval has been arrested! You didn't even leave a specific message that—"

"I didn't," he admitted, interrupting. "It was kind of a crazy time."

"Crazy?" Jane's voice went up an octave. "Crazy? Critical, I'd call it. And what's more, that was a specific event you'd promised to share with me, exclusively, if *we* promised not to run a story. Remember that? I lived up to my side of the—"

"Yeah, I know." Peter had to interrupt again. "But what could I do? You didn't answer the phone, and my primary concern was with my client, who at the moment was about to be arrested for murder."

"Duh," Jane said. "My point exactly."

"But all is not lost." Peter tried to advance the conversation, distract her from her sarcasm. She was so intent on this, she probably wasn't even listening. Peter could picture her face, her frown, a pencil behind her ear, her hair coming out of that ponytail. It was—charming, how devoted she was. He was glad they were on the same side in this one. Even though she wasn't acting like that now. "The arraignment is slated for ten A.M. tomorrow, so how about if we go from there?"

Silence.

"The detectives would never have let you in, anyway." Peter kept trying. Somehow, it was important that she not be angry with him, that she trusted him. He'd made a battlefield decision, under pressure, and his client had to come first. Deal or not. And of course, Jane could renege on her end of it, too. She and that imperious editor could decide to make the Sandovals' life miserable while they awaited the disposition of his case.

"Jane?"

Silence. He heard a toilet flushing somewhere down the hall. He didn't have long for this conversation to stay private. "Jane? Are you still there?"

Jane leaned back in her office chair, phone in hand, stretching out as far as she could, balancing with practiced precariousness on the two back legs. She'd figured on writing the bank piece, then heading home for an early dinner and falling asleep in front of *Masterpiece*. But then, a colleague had e-mailed her the scoop from the cops. She'd read it fifteen or sixteen times, incredulous, before it actually sank into her brain.

Of all the ridiculous and double-dealing . . . She'd sat in Marcotte's office with Hardesty, and against her better judgment agreed to keep things under wraps in order to get the exclusive. So much for *that* brilliant idea. She was surprised Victoria Marcotte hadn't swooped in on her broom to cackle over Jane's defeat. Although Marcotte herself agreed to the collaboration.

Jane was just—she clunked her chair wheels back onto the floor. A peon.

"Yes, I'm still here. I'm trying to keep my language appropriate." Jane sighed, puffing out a breath of defeat. It was one local story, not Watergate. "Can you bring me up to date, then? If you tell me what happened, who said what, all that, I suppose we can go from there."

She jammed the phone between her shoulder and cheek, clicked open a blank Word file on her computer. The e-mail had warned the Sandoval arrest was on the down-low, cops weren't making it public, so the paper couldn't run it anyway. Did Jake know? Had he made the arrest? She hadn't heard from him, either. *Jake*. What was up with him? Jane poised her fingers over her keyboard. "Peter? I can take the info right now."

She heard sounds on Peter's end of the call, someone talking. "Peter? Are you there?"

"Yes, sorry, Jane," he said. "I'm at a consultation actually, and I can't—"

Silence. Had they lost the connection? She could feel Peter thinking, though, in the empty space on the other end. And certainly there was a clattering, like dishes. A consultation? Maybe in a restaurant? Or maybe she just thought so because she was hungry. She hadn't eaten since—she couldn't remember.

"Peter?" she said again. It was pushing five P.M., and she was on her last reserves of adrenaline. There was still the bank story to write, accompanied by Colin Ackerman's canned video bites. He'd actually offered her another ball-point pen—"For being such a good customer," he'd said. She declined. The paper's rules said you could accept gifts if they weren't valued over twenty-five dollars, but Jane went by her own rules. An honest reporter never takes anything free.

"Yeah," Peter said. "Like I was saying, I can't now. But how about tonight? Over dinner?"

Jane took the phone away from her ear, looked at it as if she could see him through the little holes in the receiver. She put it back to her ear, realizing she was smiling.

"Dinner?"

"Low-key," he said. "I'm tired after last night, and I'm sure you are, too. But we've got to eat. We'll go early, Legal's or someplace, and I'll give you the whole story."

Jane took a long shot. "You didn't happen to take photos of the arrest, did you?"

She heard his quiet laugh. "No photos, Jane. Do you ever stop? But I do have some interesting info about the case. I'm out on the Cape, though, so how about seven thirty? Grilled shrimp, white wine, and the scoop."

Jane assessed her jeans, she was wearing good ones at least, her black T-shirt, and linen jacket, acceptably wrinkled. Black flats. She could go into the ladies', fluff her hair, wash her face, be presentable. Not that it mattered, she reminded herself. It was a work dinner, not a date. Better to be on good terms with this guy than be angry. Nothing was ever gained from holding a grudge.

"We'll split the bill," she said. "You're very persuasive."

"Just ask my juries," Peter said.

42

"**Richard Arsenault, with** A-U-L-T," Jake said into the phone. Slowing down, he scanned Marlborough Street for an available parking place near 243, as if such a thing would be possible at six in the evening in the heart of Back Bay. If Mother was out at some event, he could use her deeded parking place in the narrow alley behind the building. Otherwise, he'd be tempted to use his police department leverage to park in the no-standing zone. It was official business, after all.

"Arsenault's who I talked to, Nate," he continued. "He never said a word about a controversial parole. Do you know him?"

Jake spotted a space—*miracle*—near enough to the front of 243, and edged in between a high-end Bimmer and a Volvo convertible. Ignored the resident-parking-only sign. He was a resident, technically. Just not right now.

"Arsenault?" Frasca paused, his staticky silence continuing as Jake shifted into park. "Ah, no. That name is not familiar. Thorley's parole officer was—wait. Hang on."

Jake checked his face in the rearview. He needed a shave, his jacket had seen better days, and he hadn't been home since yesterday. Mother would make some sort of comment, he was sure. He'd finally decided her attitude came from affection, not criticism. He was still her little boy, weapon-toting badge-carrying police detective or not.

"Smith," Frasca said. "Gary Lee Smith. That's the name on these records I have. That's who he was assigned to, back four, five years ago. When he was first paroled."

"But now he has Arsenault? What happened to Gary Lee Smith? And why?"

"Why? You're asking me, *Detective*?" Frasca's laugh came through the speaker, accompanied by the rush of a motorcycle outside Jake's window and some rat-sized dogs, tangled in their leashes, yapping around the frazzled-looking teenager convoying them on the sidewalk.

"Good point," Jake said. The machinations of the parole department were legendary. Jake would have to investigate whether the PO reassignment was anything but by-the-book. Those guys were legal system nomads, like correction guards and court officers, always shopping for a better gig or cush assignment. At a certain age, though, they were all about the pension. Unless they got caught in some scam or scheme or misguided palace intrigue, in which case they were out on their ass. "Thanks, Nate. Keep me posted."

"I already have," Frasca said. "Now it's your turn. *Adiós.*"

My turn to what? Jake thought, as he stashed the phone, clicked the remote lock on his cruiser, avoided dog shit on the sidewalk, and headed for 243.

He rang the doorbell, so his mother wouldn't be alarmed when he opened the door with his key, and wiped his loafers on the bristling doormat, even though his shoes were clean. It was their home, had been since Jake could remember. What if something happened to 243? He remembered Jane, on the couch that night, worrying about her condo. He missed her.

"Hi, Mom," he said, as she opened the door.

"Why didn't you use your key?" she said. Diva lumbered up from behind her, sticking her nose in Jake's leg, then hiding behind Mom's long black skirt. She'd changed clothes, Jake saw, and added Grandmother's sapphires. After years of "I'm fine on my own" versus "You don't need such a big house all by yourself" battles, Gramma Brogan finally moved "into town" from Hyde Park. Now, compromising, she and her apricot poodle named Lily lived in a little concierge apartment on Beacon Street, a block or so away.

"Fine, how are you?" Jake smiled, ignoring his mother's question, kissing her quickly as he stepped inside. "Are you off to some event? I'm headed to the basement again."

"Sweetheart." His mother fiddled with a bright blue stone at her neck, looked at the hardwood floor of the entryway. She touched the petals of a crimson rose, a bouquet on the sideboard. "Seriously. What're you looking for down there? It's just old papers. Lilac Sunday was a long time ago. There's nothing—"

"There might be," he said. "I'll know when I find it. Don't worry. Have fun."

Diva nudged and snuffled him, following him down the basement stairs, wanting to play, but soon gave up, defeated by Jake's attention to the file cabinets. Eventually, with the dog snoring beside him, Jake realized he'd spent more than an hour pulling individual files, one by one, opening them, and returning each to exactly the same place.

It felt as if Grampa were watching.

Again and again, Jake pulled out a file and flapped it open, scanning for the key words "Arboretum" and "ligature" and "Lilac" and "Schaefer"; found nothing; put it back. The search took on a rhythm of its own. Pull, search, return. Pull, search, return. Bank robberies and kidnappings, child abductions and armored car heists. Newspaper clippings cut from periodicals that no longer existed, the *Record American* and the *Banner,* the *Southie News.* Some old *Registers,* back when the typeface and margins were different. A history of true crime on crumbling newsprint, filed away as a record of—something. Why had Grandpa kept all this? For himself? Or for someone else to unearth, someone digging up the archeology of lawbreakers and miscreants?

A history of law enforcement, too. The record of his grandfather's career. Starting when there was no DNA testing, and no tox screens, no GPS or fax machines, no computer databases or surveillance cameras on every corner. Every file was Grandpa's notes, his intuition or suspicions, handwritten in fountain pen or banged out on a crummy typewriter. Jake smiled, remembering when he'd asked to use it as a kid. The e's were funny. And there they were, a smudge and a twist where every e was typed.

He shoved another folder back into place, assessing the number of them remaining in the drawer. He could use a beer, and some food, and a real shower, not to mention sleep. Gordon Thorley himself, the subject of Jake's subterranean paper search, was in a cell, waiting for the system to put him away for life. Jake would be happy to oblige him—if only some concrete evidence could nail the case closed. The note Thorley had written would help. Bing Sherrey was supposed to be getting it from the sister.

"Two more, then I'm done," Jake said out loud. He still had to prepare for tomorrow's arraignment of Sandoval. He knew the DA would be going for no bail. As well she should. Sandoval was guilty was hell.

He pulled out another file, flapped it open. The police report, dated 1994, described a raid on a Charlestown apartment, cops seizing a stash of "Rihipnil," according to the file. "Rohypnol," Jake muttered. It was probably new, back then, they had no idea how date rape drugs would soon change the law enforcement picture. But this file was no help.

"Two more." Jake smiled at his own pronouncement, knowing he would keep saying "two more" until he found the Lilac Sunday file. He checked his watch. He should call Jane, maybe. Find out what—if anything—this Peter Hardesty meant to her. But that would be a complicated conversation, and might be better in person. Maybe when he finished here? That would give him incentive to hurry.

He leaned against the file cabinet, pondered the wisdom of searching for a needle in a—well, a file in a pile of files. He still had that stuff from the *Register* archives to check, too. He opened the next folder. And there it was.

Jane struggled to keep her eyes open, the words on the computer screen in front of her blurring, verging on mental defeat. Peter had called again, told her Cape radio was warning that traffic back to Boston was hellish, and that he might be late, but would pick her up at the *Register* as soon as he could. It was pushing nine, now, so much for the early dinner. But he'd promised new info on Sandoval, and the lure of that insight made her agree to the delay.

It seemed like a wise decision at the time.

She rubbed her hands across her face, then yawned with every part of her body. Two hours ago she'd spruced up as best she could, but by now her lipstick was certainly gone, and she probably had more mascara under her eyes than on her lashes. She'd passed the time, trying to be efficient, by starting on the bank story. Almost halfway through her column inches, the names of the customers Lizzie had given her taunted her from her notebook.

Jane jiggled one foot, considering. What would it hurt

to look up their phone numbers? Pros, she'd have real people in her story, always good to keep it personal and emotional. Otherwise, it'd essentially be a commercial for banks and their customer service, boring as hell, and the last thing Jane was interested in writing.

Cons, it might get Liz McDivitt in trouble. But Jane had only been using Chrystal's notes, exactly the way she'd been instructed. Still . . .

"Why is this such a big deal? It is such a dumb story," Jane said, the sound of her own voice surprising her in the almost-deserted newsroom. From what she could see over the shoulder-high walls of her cubicle it was only her and the water cooler, now that the bulldog edition deadline had passed. Victoria Marcotte's office was dark. The night shift people were all out on stories, probably, writing on the fly, and production was on another floor. Daysiders were home. Where she should be.

Without realizing she'd made the decision, Jane clicked onto an online phone number search Web site, chose the most unusual name from Chrystal's notes, and typed it into the search engine.

Christian, she typed, *Iantosca.* The screen paused, blinked, and came up with one match, Christian D. and Colleen Iantosca, on Hemenway Street. Near Fenway Park, Jane knew. Probably a brownstone-turned-condo. She copied the number into her notebook. Decided to try just one more. She smiled at her own rulemaking. "Just one more." She knew she would do them all.

She didn't need her whole brain to look up phone numbers, so she could get something accomplished without much effort. She wouldn't actually make any calls tonight of course, it was way too late, she'd never call anyone past eight, unless it was an emergency.

She searched for another uncommon name. Cole Gantry. There might be several Gantrys, but Cole was unusual enough. And there it was, only one listing. Warrick

Road in Allston. She copied the number, and started a new search.

Her stomach grumbled. No wonder she was sleepy. Should she hit the vending machine? Have a little blood-sugar and caffeine boost of Twizzlers and Diet Coke? At this rate, she and Peter would be closing down the kitchen somewhere. She touched her hair again, thinking about a mirror, then took her hand away. It wasn't a date, it was business. At his rate, it would be over breakfast.

Maybe if she put her head down for a few minutes, she could sneak a tiny nap, and wake up when Peter called. No one would see her.

She yawned again, scooted back the keyboard, and crossed her arms on the desk. Trying to get comfortable, she rested her forehead on one arm, and thought about pillows. Bed. *Jake.* She felt a little welling of sadness, a loss. Why hadn't he called?

43

The police report, dated May 14, 1994, indicated two officers had responded to a West Roxbury location, Tollefson Street, and then in parentheses "arboretum."

Basement fluorescents buzzing overhead, Diva still snoring on the raffia rug, Jake couldn't read it all fast enough, but he didn't want to miss anything, either. He shook out one leg and forced his brain to shift into a lower gear, paying attention. Next page. In some cop's misspelled printing, the stilted and mistake-ridden narrative of the story unfolded, the discovery of the "body of Carol Mary Schafer, WF, approx. 17–19 years of age . . ."

The medical examiner's report, signed with an almost-illegible slash of ball-point pen by a guy who'd left town years ago, ruled the cause of death "strangulation by ligature" and "asphyxia."

The damn Lilac Sunday case was lore. The Grail. The white whale in the Boston PD, their commonality, the case they wrestled with over beers and coffee and during stakeouts when talk of current cases and police gossip ran out. A reward, big big bucks, sat waiting for whoever gave information leading to the killer. Every commissioner since Grandpa stamped it top priority. Jake read on, intent. Hunting.

All the newspaper clippings, snipped with pinking

shears and mostly from the *Register* and the *American,* ran the same photo of Carley Marie, a painting that hung over her parents' mantel, her dark hair parted in the middle, a girl with a tentative smile and a string of pearls. Pages from Carley Marie's Attleboro High school yearbook. The DA—now dead—called it "a heinous and brutal crime," and warned he already "had his eye" on some suspects, "some more than others." Jake's grandfather, Boston Police Commissioner Ewan MacIlhenny Brogan, was not quoted. So far.

Jake continued through the musty paperwork, looking for anything—anything—that would lead him to Gordon Thorley. Or to be fair, to anyone else. The DA had said there were "suspects," plural. Where the hell was the info on that? He turned a few more pages. If there were suspects, there'd be some sort of—if not a list, then at least—*huh.*

The back of his neck prickled as Jake ran a finger down the typewritten list of names, trying to read the whole thing at once, looking for the shape of the name "Gordon Thorley." Some names had checkmarks next to them, some were crossed out, some circled, in different inks, the page possibly handled by more than one person. Today they'd euphemistically call these individuals "persons of interest," but this coffee-stained document had no heading. Jake figured they wouldn't have wanted some smart defense attorney to demand it—and then trumpet to a jury that since cops had targeted a whole list of people, wasn't that reasonable doubt? With an untitled list like this, there would be a semblance of deniability. Interesting that Grandpa kept it.

As his finger moved down the list, name after name, Jake felt his disappointment growing.

He was almost to the end, *no Thorley,* and his mind was already rationalizing why it didn't matter. Of course that name wasn't there. No one had heard of Gordon

Thorley, that was the whole dilemma from day one of his "confession." If they had—*wait*.

The name Gary Lee Smith was on the list.

Crossed out.

Jake sank into a wicker chair, its uneven legs wobbling, the woven seat so creaky he worried for a moment that it wouldn't hold his weight. Diva, startled at the sound, raised her head with a halfhearted woof, then went back to sleep.

Gary Lee Smith, according to Nate Frasca, had been Gordon Thorley's first parole officer. Maybe this wasn't a list of suspects? But a list of parole officers? Why? If they were POs, they'd have been on the job almost twenty years ago, so it was possible some of them were still working. Or at least, alive. A long-ish shot, but possible.

Why did Grandpa keep this list? Cops were required to review notes in open cases every ten days. But when a case went cold, so did attention to it. Had Grandpa taken this from the police file? Or made a copy and added it to his own separate set of records?

Jake leaned back in the chair, staring at the list. He turned it over, looking for something, anything, a date, a notation, a mark from a copier.

Why was Gary Lee Smith's name in a file that no one had opened for years?

The armed robbery Thorley'd be nailed for didn't happen until the year *after* the Carley Marie killing. Thorley was a free man—teenager?—when Carley Marie was killed. Had Gordon Thorley known Gary Lee Smith *before* Lilac Sunday?

Jake pulled out his phone, did a quick Internet search. There was a Gary Lee Smith who was an ex-con in Oklahoma and one who was a realtor. There was a dead Marine, and a minor-league baseball player. Nothing about a Massachusetts parole officer.

Nothing that fit.

* * *

Jane grabbed her throat, startled by the sound. She sat up, blinking, trying to figure out where she—oh, right. The newsroom. She'd put her head on her desk only for a moment.

Her phone was ringing. *Finally.* Her desk phone, not her cell.

She checked the time on her computer. Could this be Peter? Where was he? She grabbed the phone before the end of the second ring.

The caller ID showed an in-house extension. Had someone seen her sleeping?

"This is Jane Ryland," she said, trying to sound awake.

"Hey, you at your desk? I thought I saw the light. It's Nick LaGarza, over at the copy desk?"

Jane shook her head, clearing it. Stood up, looking over the shoulder-high walls of the cubicles. A lanky guy in a blue shirt stood popped up like a prairie dog, waving, phone clamped to one ear.

"I see you." She sat down again, preparing her defenses. *It's never a good thing when the copy desk calls.* She hoped Nick needed some advice, or a phone number, and was not thinking of sending her on some story. She was off the clock, technically, dammit. No way, this time of night, she was going to—

She paused, regrouping, finding her team player voice. No need to be upset about an imaginary assignment. "Yeah, I'm here. What's up?"

"We've got a possible homicide," Nick said. "Over on Kenilworth? You know? Over by where the Southeast Expressway comes into Albany? Half a mile from here."

Jane pictured it, the highway ramp with its craggy overpass, graffiti-emblazoned with indecipherable gang tags and farfetched cartoon faces, the entryway to the iffy neighborhood on the outskirts of Boston. Peter had just been driving on the Southeast Expressway. Must have been.

Could he have—stopped somewhere? On the way here? That's why he was late? And now, what if Peter was—she swallowed, reconnoitering. She glanced at her cell. No messages. If the phone had rung, she'd have awakened before now. Where was Peter? *Possible homicide? Peter?*

"Any details?" She was almost afraid of the answer. But whatever happened had already happened. "Do we know anything?"

"That's why we're sending you." Nick's tone allowed no room to argue. "Right now. TJ will meet you there. Let us know, soon as you can. We're holding the front page."

44

Footsteps on the basement stairs. *Footsteps?* Fourth step from the top always creaked. *There it was.*

Jake stopped, tucked the file under one arm, listened. His mother was still out, so who—? He hovered his right hand over his weapon. Diva came to all fours, woofed.

"Oh hush, dog." Gramma Brogan's voice floated down the stairs, followed by chunky black shoes, then black yoga pants, then an oversized white shirt and a cropped bob of silver hair. One of Grandpa's shirts, Jake knew. She still wore them, at least on her casual days. "Jake, are you still down there, dear?"

Jake took his hand away from the Glock. *Shooting Gramma Brogan.* All he needed.

"Yes, Gramma. I'm here." Jake watched her take the last of the steps, hand on the banister, a suddenly dutiful Diva trotting over to prove she was on the case. Jake gave his grandmother a quick hug, a careful hug, felt like she was getting smaller every time he put his arms around her. She still smelled sweetly powdery, same as she had as long as Jake could remember. What was she doing here? This late?

"I didn't know you were—," Jake began.

"Your mother called." She scratched Diva behind the ears. "Good dog. Now shoo."

"Mother called you at this time of night?"

"She knows I don't sleep, dear. It's only nine thirty. I'll be home in time for *CSI*. But she told me, in no uncertain terms, I was to derail your 'obsession' with Ewan's files."

Jake shook his head as Gramma went on, pointing and gesturing in a perfect imitation of her daughter-in-law.

"'Get him away from Lilac Sunday,' your mother said to me. 'It's haunted this family long enough.'" Gramma stood on tiptoe, holding on to Jake's arm, pecked him on the cheek.

The Carley Marie case file was under his other arm, plain sight. There was no hiding from Gramma: Jake first learned that during the cigarette episode of 1992. And then the beer thing. He'd have to come clean and hope she wasn't upset.

"I'm happy to see you, Gram," Jake started again. "But—"

"But what, dear? I never told your mother I would stop you. In fact, I came to help, if I can." She waved a hand, dismissive. "As if she could make Lilac Sunday go away by *ignoring* it."

She took a deep breath, fingered the white collar of her shirt. "That's why Ewan kept these files, you know? For someone exactly like you. Your grandfather told me, again and again, there was something he must have missed. Some truth that escaped him. That's why I insisted we keep them, even after he . . . well, he never got over it."

She stopped, her expression softening as she gestured toward the basement stairs. "Sometimes, before he got sick? He'd sit on that bottom step for hours, right there, turning and turning the pages in some file. Broke my heart."

She paused, looked up at Jake. "And his."

"I know, Gram."

The air conditioner kicked on, a low hum cutting through the silence. Diva growled, then went back to sleep.

Gramma poked at the file under his arm. "So, *Detective*. The Brogans are on the case again."

"Both of us now, I guess." Jake held out the paperwork. "Is this the same file?"

Gramma took it, wrapped both arms around it, held it to her chest. Closed her eyes, briefly. Jake watched the manila rise, then fall. She wore her gold wedding band, still, on her left hand. Grandpa's matching ring hung from a thin gold chain around her neck. Jake saw it first at his funeral, back in 2000. Since then, in sweats or in sapphires, Gramma wore that necklace.

"It's Lilac Sunday, coming up, less than a week. Seeing the poor girl's parents again. It's so—so very sad." She handed the file back. "Yes, this is it. Did you find something?"

"Possibly, Gram," Jake said. "I hope so. Listen—the name Gary Lee Smith? Does it ring a bell?" He risked it. "Or Gordon Thorley?"

Gramma thought, fingers to her chin, then shook her head. "I'm sorry, honey. It doesn't. I don't really know anything, except that you need to keep looking. For Carley Marie's family, of course. And for your grandfather. He'd be so proud of—"

Her voice caught, and she pressed her lips together. "Sorry," she whispered. "I love you, Jakey. He did, too."

"I love you, too, Gram," Jake said. He hugged her again, remembering, with the clarity of a photograph, the two of them together, his steely-haired grandfather in that uniform, his white-gloved wife standing beside him. Grampa had let Jake try on his—way too big—navy blue police hat. "Now, go home. You've done your duty, right? I'll tell Mom you tried to convince me. And you'll be the first to know if we find something. I promise."

"She means well, you know," Gramma said, patting his arm. "She just wants you to have a life. Outside of the BPD."

"I do have a life," Jake said. Would Jane ever meet Gramma? How could that happen? "Right now, though, she's—it's somewhat complicated."

Gramma put a hand on the banister, took the first step up. Turned to him. "Don't 'complicate' your life away, Jakey," she said. "Grampa would want you to be happy. With whoever 'she' is."

Jake shook his head. Complicated was an understatement. "Bye, Grams."

He heard the fourth step creak, then the footsteps stopped. He looked up to see Gramma's face peering over the wooden railing, a silhouette edged with the dim light of the stairwell.

"Don't you give up," she said. "It's never too late for the truth."

Jane saw the blue lights glaring off the houses and parked cars, making spidery shadow patterns with the darkened branches of the trees along Kenilworth Street. Heard the sirens screaming, even before she saw the cop cars careen around the corner and onto the narrow one-lane street. Two black-and-whites had landed with their front wheels up and onto the sidewalk, apparently the first on the scene. A uniformed officer hopped out of one cruiser, siren still wailing, posted herself at the open front door of 16 Kenilworth. Three more cops went though the open door, weapons pointed ahead.

"Police!" one called. No answer. They disappeared from view.

As Jane ran closer, she saw lights flip on inside, moving, somehow. Flashlights, maybe. Silhouettes flickered through sheer curtains covering the front windows. No cars in the paved driveway, no furniture on the porch. No ambulance.

"Hey, TJ," she said. He must have just gotten here, too. She waved at the house. "Anything? You get that? The cops all rushing in?"

"Nada." TJ let out a sigh. "Sorry, Jane. I got here fast as I could, but missed that. Can't win 'em all."

"No worries," she said. Her TV instinct craved the action video of police arriving, but it didn't matter in her new life. A newspaper story—even multimedia—still relied on words.

TJ's denim work shirt, unbuttoned, was open in the front, Red Sox T-shirt showing, tossed over jeans and his running shoes. Baseball cap backward, his little camera on his shoulder. "I'll roll off some shots of the house, exteriors, then come back, see what we can piece together."

He stepped toward the yellow police tape, then turned back to Jane, gesturing down the sidewalk. One after the other, front doors were opening, people coming outside. They trotted down their front walks, and clustered at the curb, gawking. Speculating. Whispering to each other. "Unless you wanna do a man-on-the-street?"

Bystanders were out in force, Jane saw. A perfect selection of men on the street. MOS, they called it. And not just men. It was a sidewalk full of the curious, answering the siren song of the sirens, dressed in whatever they'd been wearing at nine thirty on a May night, teenagers in T-shirts and flip-flops, one guy in a suit, a woman with a trench coat belted over the lacy hem of an obvious nightgown.

Maybe one of them knew what'd happened. Knew who lived there, or—or something. Anything.

She looked back at the house. The front door was closed now. No gunfire, no more yelling. Sirens off. Whatever happened was over.

Jane had called Peter's cell from the car on her way

here, but no answer. The disembodied voice mail freaked her out a little, her imagination so out-of-control disconcerting she almost clicked it off before she left a message.

"Checking in," she'd said, keeping her voice calm. No use to panic. It was just as likely he'd stopped for gas, or even pulled over for coffee and then fallen asleep. She'd done that, after all. There was utterly no reason to believe this victim was Peter, except for her own too-vivid imagination.

"Hoping everything is okay," she allowed herself to say, because anyone would. "Call me, okay? I got sent on a story. I'm on my cell."

She shook her head as she hung up, her concern spiraling as the time ticked by. Why hadn't Peter called? She was incredibly worried, exhausted, and discombobulated—and now she had to cover a story.

"Yeah, let's do that," Jane said to TJ. "MOS, good idea."

She scanned for faces that looked interested, or engaged. She wanted someone who actually knew something, not just some blowhard showoff trying to get their name in the paper. She chose the thirty-something man wearing a Nantucket cap and what looked like hospital scrubs. He'd made eye contact with her, and hadn't grimaced at the camera. And his cap was bill forward, so he wasn't a kid.

"Sir? I'm Jane Ryland from the *Register*," she began as she and TJ approached. "Do you know who lives over there? Any idea what happened?"

The man frowned. "I'd prefer not to give my name."

"Great, fine," Jane said. It didn't matter, for this interview, who he was, and it was often better to ask for names afterward, anyway, after the subject understood her questions were benign. "So, sir? Any idea who lives in that house?"

She cocked her head toward it, although there was

clearly only one house anyone cared about. The one with the yellow tape and the cops in the front.

"Now, you mean?" the man said.

"Now?" Jane was tired, she knew that, but now as opposed to when? Of course now. "Uh, yeah. Now."

"No one," the man said.

"DeLuca's still off, Sherrey's out of pocket somewhere, everyone else would be double time." Superintendent Rivera himself on the phone, calling Jake, was cop shorthand for *don't even think about complaining.* "That puts you in the driver's seat," Rivera had told him.

Which was precisely where Jake was now—Grandpa's files in the console of his cruiser—speeding to primary a DOA on Kenilworth. Not where you'd expect to find a murder victim, Jake thought, careening around the corner onto Huntington. He'd take the shortcut over the T tracks by Diva's old digs, the MSPCA, and then get to the little collection of narrow streets behind the VA hospital. Not much ever hit the cops' radar in that peaceful neighborhood, maybe an occasional wintertime battle when a visitor, clueless to local rules, usurped a shoveled-out parking place. This time of year the disputes sputtered over loose dogs, or kids playing Frisbee in the street. The occasional package swiped from a front porch, or a student whose parents panicked when little Jimmy didn't show up at school. Usually they discovered the lure of a spring day had been too irresistible, and little Jimmy was found someplace like the Arboretum, or hanging out at the CVS, pilfering candy bars.

Jake blasted lights and sirens, just in case, but if anyone had died, it'd be natural causes, he predicted. Some of the houses there had been owned by the same folks for years. Other homes had turned over, like everywhere, old-timers dying and being replaced by yuppies and boomers, or sometimes losing their homes in the foreclosure blight that had fingered every part of the city.

He snapped off the siren, turned onto Kenilworth. Realized with dismay he wasn't even close to the first to arrive. Place was crawling with cop cars. Why was the Supe so hot on him being there, too? Maybe the left hand didn't know what the right hand was doing. Wouldn't be the first time.

Someone had unspooled crime scene tape across the yard of number 16, one uniform, a woman, stationed at the edge of the wood-railed porch. He hoped someone was canvassing door to door. Crime Scene was here, too, but no ME vehicle, and no ambulance. Not exactly by the book.

On the sidewalk, another surprise. A clutch of onlookers in various stages of dress—or not—and right in the middle, under that street lamp, the unmistakable silhouette of Jane Ryland. How'd she get here before he did?

He clenched his fingers around the steering wheel, stalling, even though there was no way to stall and no way to avoid any of what was ahead. Slamming the car door harder than was probably warranted, he kept his head down and headed toward the house and the uniform who could give him the lowdown on the scene.

He'd deal with Jane later.

Jane looked up at the sound of a car door slamming. She'd heard the siren, figured more cops were on the way, wondered who'd show up. The instant she saw the silhouette, she knew.

Jake.

She tried to focus on what the man she was interviewing had just said. Tried to ignore the continuing worry about Jake. And that she hadn't heard from Peter. This wasn't a car accident, so that fear was unfounded. There'd be no reason for Peter to be in some random house in this random neighborhood. Would there?

"Ah, excuse me, you said 'no one' lives there? I mean— I'm talking about sixteen Kenilworth? Where they apparently found—"

"Yup, nope, no one," the man said. He adjusted his cap, put the bill in the back, then back to the front. "That's why we're all out here, you know?"

"Did anyone ever live—?" Jane began.

"Evicted," the man said.

TJ lowered his camera, then quickly put it back up. "Evicted?" he said. "Whoa."

"Evicted?" Jane tried to process this. If the eviction was by Atlantic & Anchor Bank, that'd be interesting. "Do you know what bank? I mean, where the people had their mortgage?"

"Colonial," the man said. "Colonial Bank. I know because we have ours there, too. And the Gerritys, they lived there, used to complain about what hardasses they were about paying." He shrugged. "What are you gonna do, though, right?"

"Right," Jane said, just to keep the guy happy and talking. She looked at TJ, raising her eyebrows. "So, Mr.—?"

"Doctor. Dr. Alvin Wander."

"Dr. Wander. So they moved out—"

"Not happily," Wander said.

"Got you," Jane said. "When was that?"

"Month ago, I'd say."

"And—"

"And there've been, I don't know, people, hanging around since then, time to time. Suits. And some women, too. Don't get me wrong—real estate, bank types, I figured. Wanting to sell it." He frowned. "Going to create a serious property value situation now, isn't it? If someone's dead inside?"

45

"And you are?" Jake said.

The young officer saluted, looking him square in the eye. "Rosie Canfield," she said. "I mean, Officer Roslynne—"

"No need to salute, Officer Canfield," Jake said. It hadn't been that long since he was the new kid. He pulled out his BlackBerry, opened a new file to take notes. "So what've we got here?"

"At approximately nine twenty-seven P.M., dispatch received a nine-one-one call for an open front door at this address, sixteen Kenilworth," Canfield said. She kept her hands at her sides, fists clenched. A strand of brown hair escaped from under her billed cap, and she puffed it away out of one side of her mouth as she continued her recitation. "Two units responded to the scene, and upon entering through the open door, discovered a—"

"Detective Brogan? This is dispatch," Jake's radio squawked from his jacket pocket.

"Excuse me, Officer," Jake said. He stashed his Black-Berry, pushed the talk button. "This is Brogan."

"Are you ten-twenty-three, sir?" Dispatch's voice, measured and careful.

What the hell? Jake bit back a curt response. Why were they checking on him?

"Superintendent Rivera is inquiring," dispatch said,

her voice telegraphing *it wasn't my idea, but I'm follow-ing orders.*

"Gotcha," Jake replied. He rolled his eyes at the young officer, bringing Rosie onto his team, *can you believe the big shots?* "Yes, Dispatch, I'm at the address."

"Superintendent said please report on the situation ASAP."

"Will do in five," Jake said.

"Copy that, thank you, Detective."

A siren wailed in the distance, the high-pitched howl of Boston Medical Center's go team. About time. Al-though since whoever was inside was apparently DOA, it wouldn't matter when they arrived. To the victim, at least.

In this case, Jake thought as he pulled out his phone, the bad guy couldn't have been Elliot Sandoval or Gordon Thorley. Both of them were in custody. "Okay, then," Jake said. "You heard the dispatcher, Officer Canfield. The Supe himself is standing by to hear the latest. What've we got?"

The house was empty? Foreclosed? Maybe Jane had cho-sen the perfect person to interview, proving man-on-the-street sound bites could be more than filler.

"Thanks, Dr. Wander," Jane said. She gestured to TJ, drew a fast finger across her throat. *Cut.* Was this guy making stuff up to get his name and face in the paper? Didn't seem like it. It was all easy enough to confirm, and if true—pretty darn interesting. "Give me a wave if you hear anything more, okay?"

Jane sneaked a look at the now-closed front door of the house. Jake stood, right under the porch light, the screen of his BlackBerry catching the glow. Typing notes, as always, in his usual black T-shirt and those jeans, talk-ing to the uniform stationed near the door.

That was the frustrating part. How she knew the Jake thing would have to change. Any other crime scene, any other detective, Jane'd be right up there on the front lines, not pushing, but persistent, probing, making her presence known, asking questions and trying to get the story. Nothing on the record came from inquiries like that, cops and reporters tacitly—well, openly—agreeing that attributable stuff came only from the PR flak. But a little judicial pointing-in-the-right-direction was the currency of those relationships.

Cops would give reporters a bit of juicy takeaway, something exclusive, and reporters would make sure the cop shop looked good, if they could. Mutual trust bred mutual benefit.

But with Jake, there was baggage. He had to be careful not to treat her any differently, she knew that, and as a result, he treated her completely differently. No scoops, no exclusives, no insider info. Good for him, bad for Jane. And she knew she often might do the same with him—holding back, being one level less insistent. Also good for him, bad for Jane.

Their whole existence was out of balance. And even more now, she realized, that Jake's going-to-Washington story cast a shadow of mistrust between them. He had been called to D.C. "unexpectedly." Then came home "unexpectedly." What was "unexpectedly," except an excuse to do whatever he wanted?

"Now what?" TJ asked. "Siren."

The wail got closer, screaming onto Kenilworth, the crowd, as one, stepping away from the street, as if the high-speed arrival of the ambulance might mean the driver would skid out of control. The swirling red lights slid across each bystander's face, glowing each one red for a fraction of a second. Soon as the ambulance stopped, the crowd inched forward again, closer to the action. The streetlights made amber pools on the sidewalks; the red ambulance lights, silent now, continued to spiral; the stars were full out in the expanse of velvet night sky. The neighborhood light show, Jane thought, all illuminating tragedy.

"Let's see what's going on." Jane pointed to the jump-suited EMTs emerging from the red and white van. The phone in her jeans pocket had stayed silent. Where the hell was Peter? If he was in this house—but, she silently repeated her mantra as she and TJ headed across the street. *Whatever happened, happened.* Nothing she could do about it now but wait and see. And ask questions.

She was a reporter, no matter what detective was in charge at the crime scene. She'd do her job. She'd ask the professional questions now. The personal ones later.

Jane. A few steps away, down the front walk, behind the crime scene tape. In the shadows from the streetlights, Jake couldn't read her face.

"Hey, Jane," he said. Sure, they usually used their full names on the job, elaborately careful, but at ten at night at a crime scene, he figured he could ditch the formality. Who were they trying to fool, anyway?

"Detective Brogan." She gave half a wave. "You remember TJ Foy."

Jake nodded. He hadn't finished talking to the officer at the door, and until he did, he had nothing for Jane. He'd give her the lowdown, he figured, then make her call the cop's PR flak to confirm before she went with the story. He'd do the same for any reliable reporter, he reassured himself, so why not for her?

Although they each sought the same information, right now, the balance was on Jake's end. He had access, she didn't. He could go inside, she couldn't. The flimsy yellow crime scene tape was the inviolable barrier, the delineation of the information battle lines. She'd have to wait for him. This time. She recognized it, too. She'd called him "detective."

"Give me five minutes, Jane," he said, holding up a palm, five fingers. He pointed to himself, then to her, pantomiming, *then I'll talk.*

He saw her agree, nodding, then whisper to her photographer. The crowd across the street stood three deep now. Where had all these people come from, giving up their TV shows and their families and their sleep to get a close-up look at someone else's disaster? He'd never understand that. As a detective, his job wasn't to prevent crime—by the time he was called in, the bad thing already happened. That was his whole life, now that he thought of it, dealing with one bad thing after another. Was he drawn to that, same way the bystanders were?

No, he decided. *I solve crimes. I don't watch.*

"Officer Canfield?" he said. "What have we got here?"

"White female," Canfield pulled out a pocket-sized spiral notebook, already open, the pages dog-eared and wrinkled. She smoothed out the top page with one finger, then squinted at her handwriting. "According to the identification, it's one Elizabeth McDivitt, age thirty-three."

"Mc—" Jake typed the name into his own notes.

"Divitt." Canfield spelled it out. "It was on a Mass driver's license, and on her work ID. Officer Vitucci's inside."

"She live here?" Jake asked, listening and typing at the same time.

"No, sir," Canfield said. "The license gives an address in Brighton. This house is empty."

Jake kept typing. "Empty as in—no one else was there?"

"No, sir," Canfield said. "Empty as in—there's nothing in it."

Jake looked up, thumbs poised, stopped typing. "Huh?"

"Like, no furniture, you know? Nothing."

Jake turned, his eyes locking briefly with Jane's. He saw her take a step forward, gesturing to TJ, expectant, but he held up two fingers. Two minutes, he mouthed.

"Is there a car?" Jake frowned, surveying the driveway, the curb, the neighborhood. "I don't see a car. How'd she get here?"

Canfield shook her head. Jake saw the trace of a smile. "That's why you get the big bucks. Sir. Ready to go inside?"

46

Reporters don't cry, not ever, not in public at least, that was a sacrosanct tenet of objective journalism. Jane had never felt so close to breaking the rules.

"Are you sure?" was all she could come up with. She'd felt the blood drain from her face as Jake related the details, the row of onlookers across the narrow street now a sea of colors blurred by her welling tears. The crickets had started, a raggedy underscore of chirping, accompanied by the low buzz of the crowd and the hum of the idling ambulance. Jake hadn't been inside yet, but too impatient to wait any longer, Jane had come to the porch, pressing for details. Now she almost wished she didn't know. "Elizabeth McDivitt? Is—was—her name?"

"You know her?"

Jake was frowning at her. She didn't blame him. This whole thing was suddenly even more out of control than it had been five minutes before, when she secretly was convinced it was Peter Hardesty inside.

"Jane? I said Elizabeth McDivitt. Might have worked at A&A Bank?"

"Yeah." Jane stared at the house, almost unseeing, trying to make heads or tails or anything that made sense. She'd been with Liz McDivitt this morning. Liz McDivitt. A conservatively blue-suited bank executive, fast-tracked, office and secretary, a job she seemed to enjoy. A person with some scruples—she'd tried to keep her customers' names private. A person with a heart. She'd shown Jane that picture of her boyfriend. Jane let out a sigh. Now someone would have to tell him what happened, too. Whatever that was. But what was Liz McDivitt doing in a—the neighbor guy had said the house was vacant.

"Who lived here?" Jane said. TJ was still at her side, camera on his shoulder. "Do you know the"—how would she say this if the victim was a stranger?—"cause of death?"

"You didn't answer me, Jane. Did you know her? Pretty intriguing that you'd show up at the scene of a—of someone you know. And turn off that camera. You can't go with that name. Understand? Like I said. We're still checking next of kin."

Jake's face had gone hard. She could tell he was deciding how to deal with her. She knew him well enough. How his chin came up when he was thinking, how his eyes narrowed, even how he took a step away from her. This wasn't Jake and Jane. This was cop and reporter.

"Yes," she said. "Well, 'knew,' maybe that's not exactly the word."

She signaled TJ with one finger again, *cut the camera*, adding a shrug and an eye roll to signal "it's okay." She knew TJ would never stop simply because a cop told him to, quite the opposite. Only Jane could give that order. But now it was more important to get information than to try to get Jake on camera. According to protocol, he wasn't supposed to be talking to her, anyway. Possibly she shouldn't be talking to him, either. They'd stepped up to the line so many times it was becoming harder and harder to gauge what was acceptable.

"I interviewed her," Jane continued. "Met her for the first time, this morning. I was asking—"

"What? About what?" Jake was in full investigative mode, thumbing in notes on his BlackBerry. "Did she seem—worried? Did she say where she was going this evening? Did she say she was—"

"Sir?" A young cop tapped Jake on the arm, ripped a page from her little spiral notebook, handed it to him. "Um. NOK information, sir. I thought you'd want to—"

Next of kin, Jane knew. *Liz's family.*

Jake took the paper, and Jane watched his expression change as he read whatever was there. "You sure?" Jake said. "This info is direct from the Supe?"

He steered the officer away from Jane, turning their backs, the two of them, heads together, conferring. Jane gave eavesdropping a valiant try, but failed.

Her phone buzzed in her back pocket, and she reached to grab it. Damn. Probably the city desk asking for updates. Which she should have already called in. *Poor Liz McDivitt.* What the hell was Liz doing here in the first place?

"We have company," TJ said, pointing. Jane looked across the street as the Channel 3 news van pulled in.

"Damn," Jane said. She hadn't called the desk, and now their exclusive was about to disappear. She ignored the incoming call, figuring she'd pretend to be calling them first. She punched in the speed dial for the city desk, and all business, fed them the rundown in bullet points. Possible homicide, name, location. No ambulance or EMTs had emerged from the house yet, pretty clear indication someone was dead. Investigation underway.

"They haven't notified her next of kin yet, so we can't go with that name," Jane told the desk guy. *Ha.* She'd done her job, called before they could call her. Another employment obstacle successfully avoided. "We can say—well, you know what to say. Channel 3 just showed up, more's the pity, so if you want to post what we can on our breaking news site, that'd be good. More to come. 'Kay?"

She clicked off, watched some notebook-toting reporter she didn't recognize lead her lumbering photographer to scout the bystanders. Jane would've worn flats to a scene like this, but that girl would learn. She didn't miss TV. *Not at all.* Jane watched the blonde at work, almost unseeing, as she tried to sort out all she knew, tried to separate her sorrow and surprise from the rest of the story. Tried to stay objective. Tried to see the big picture.

Liz McDivitt. Bank employee, found in an empty house. Shandra Newbury, real estate broker, found dead in an empty house. Did the two victims know each other? Elliot Sandoval was under arrest for killing Shandra Newbury— but he sure as hell had an alibi for Liz McDivitt.

Did that matter? Did it mean the two were not connected? Did it prove—somehow—that Elliot Sandoval was innocent?

Jane grabbed her phone, punched in the website for the county registry of deeds, looked up the records for the house where Liz was found. And there it was—proof the neighbor she'd interviewed had it right. Sixteen Kenilworth was sold in foreclosure. Just like the house on Waverly Road. It was impossible to read the entire series of ownership transfer documents on her phone. Blurred images of already blurred copies partially displayed on a tiny cell phone screen were making her eyes cross—but she'd make a printout as soon as she got back to the *Register*.

If it mattered. Lots of houses were in foreclosure. But in the past week, police found murder victims inside two of them.

Different banks, though. Did that matter? Maybe it had nothing to do with foreclosure. Maybe they were simply empty houses. After all, what better place to kill someone?

Jane stood on the flagstone path, staring at the vacant home. A trio of moths fluttered around the glass panels of the brass porch lamp, frantic, unable to resist the lure of the light. Their tiny shadows danced on the white vinyl siding.

She tried to lose herself in the story, envision what might have happened, make a mental movie of it, watch it unfold. Liz walking up the path to the porch. Arriving at the door, the porch light—had it been on then? Translucent curtains cover the window. Liz can't see inside, even hours earlier in daylight. Was someone already there, waiting? For her? The door opens.

Why would Liz have gone in? Was she meeting someone? Who? Who had the key? Liz? Or the "someone"? Liz was in love, that was clear at the interview. But murders weren't about love. They were about hate. Or fear. Or power.

Did someone hate Liz McDivitt? Or fear her? Or need to control her? Or was she in simply the wrong place at the wrong time?

The front door of the house opened, Jake came back onto the porch. The young officer, arms folded in front of her chest, appeared a shoulder width behind him. Jane signaled TJ, *finally,* twirled a finger in the "roll tape" sign.

But Jake went back inside. What the hell was going on? Jane shrugged, waved TJ off. The TV blonde was still working the crowd, hadn't even approached the porch to check with the cops. Poor thing. The eleven o'clock news was looming. Jane felt that deadline, after all these years, without even checking her watch.

But for Jane, this night was about Liz McDivitt.

Jane sighed, trapped where she was until Jake emerged again. It wasn't her job to solve this crime, of course, but she couldn't resist. This was more than a news story. Liz McDivitt was someone she knew. It felt almost like her *responsibility.*

More frustrating, if she told Victoria Marcotte about the connection, would she be yanked from this story, too? But Liz had been Chrystal Peralta's source.

Maybe Liz hadn't been killed here. Maybe that happened somewhere else, and the bad guy stashed her in this empty house, figuring no one would ever go inside. How would they know that? Who would have a key? Maybe no one had a key. Maybe, realizing the house was vacant, they'd broken in. Broken in? She nodded, envisioning how that could have worked, and all the evidence it would've left behind. Jake would know. And he could tell her.

Jane flipped through her notebook, checking for anything, *anything,* from Liz she might have missed.

Then she saw them.

The names of McDivitt's clients, the names Liz had tried so diligently to protect, the names that Jane had already matched to phone numbers. And addresses. She ran a finger down the list, wondering if—no. None of them matched Kenilworth. Or Waverly. So much for that idea.

Still. Maybe the list was not worthless. If she were doing a story on Liz McDivitt, these names now provided instant interview prospects. Too late to call them now, but tomorrow she'd have a head start on everyone.

The door opened again. She watched Jake survey the street in front of him, one hand shading his eyes. He batted something away, probably one of the moths, its mothy plans disturbed by the lights and the people and the intrusion.

"I'm with you, moth," Jane muttered. Not how she'd envisioned this evening, either.

Jake's eyes locked on hers. He raised a palm, beckoned her toward him.

Finally. Now she'd get some answers.

47

What the hell was Jane's phone number? Peter could instantly recite the number from his childhood home in Ithaca, which his mom insisted on calling Melrose 6-5175, and the number from his first apartment at Stanford, (312) 551-0104. Dianna's, he'd never forget. Sometimes he still thought about calling her. But cell phones made it unnecessary to remember current numbers. There was no reason to remember, because they all were stored in the handy dandy phone. He hardly remembered his own.

As the green highway signs flashed by, VISIT HISTORIC PLYMOUTH, then NEXT EXIT PEMBROKE, he could picture his cell phone, right now, on Doreen Rinker's scarred kitchen table. Where he—*idiot*—had left it more than an hour ago. He hadn't even thought about the damn phone, had decided to zone out to NPR and give his brain a break on the way back to Boston. Eventually, mired in the as-promised hellish traffic, he realized he'd be amazingly late. Even later than he'd already warned Jane when he talked to her from Rinker's house. He reached for his phone, in full denial as he patted every one of his pockets, anger growing as he kept the Jeep in the center lane by steering with one elbow, then, finally, accepting his

loss. Jane'd be fuming. Or worried. Or both. There was
no way to contact her.

Okay, not quite true. He could stop at a Burger King,
or whatever joint was off the closest exit, and use the pay
phone—did they still have those? He'd call 411—did
they still have *that*?—get the number for the *Register,* and
call her there. But that would make the whole ordeal take
even longer, half an hour, no matter how efficiently it all
happened. Maybe he should just try to get to Boston
faster. He hit the accelerator and froggered into the fast
lane, inciting a symphony of angry honking.

"Sorry, sorry," he muttered, apologizing to the universe
in general. Thing was, he needed the damn phone. Not
only was Jane's number stored in it, but Thorley's, and
the police lockup, and Sandoval's, and Jake Brogan's.
Technology. He reconsidered. The technology worked
okay, he had to admit. It was his brain that was failing.

The traffic parted, because the universe runs on irony,
and the concrete barriers strobed by, highway signs taunting him with the geographical reality. *Boston, thirty
miles*. That meant now it would take about as long to
get to Boston as it would to get back to the Cape. Point
of no return.

He could turn around, go back, get the phone, and
then call Jane. Maybe cancel the whole thing, since it'd
be far too late for dinner—or anything—by the time he
went back across the bridge to Sagamore and retrieved
the phone—if Doreen Rinker was even home!—and
drove back to Boston.

He was an idiot. Jane would never forgive him. Well,
she would, of course, to her it was only dinner. The real
source of his frustration, he admitted, he'd hoped this
dinner might lead to more than business. So much for
that idea. He needed the damn phone.

Decided, then. Peter swerved off the highway, veered

right onto the off-ramp, made the loop past the deserted BK, where a forlorn sign promised Two-fer Tuesdays, decided against the seedy gas station Dunkins', and headed back toward Sagamore. He needed his phone. No faster way to get it than to retrieve it himself.

The glowing numerals on the dashboard clock clicked forward, underscoring his defeat. Gordon Thorley was in custody. Elliot Sandoval was in custody. The only good thing that had happened to Peter in years was about to be disappointed in him.

What else could go wrong?

"I've got nothing more for you." Jake needed to go back inside the Kenilworth house, get his own eyes on the situation. What Canfield had described was the definition of a frigging can of worms, but he was trapped on the porch. Like some kind of news target, with him the center mass.

Jane had commandeered the top step of the porch, manning the front lines, stationed against the spindly wrought-iron railing. TJ, whose shouldered camera might as well be his weapon, hovered behind her on the closest flagstone, and that new reporter from Channel 3, Kimberly something, led the charge of the new arrivals. The picture of high-heeled determination, microphone in hand, camera guy keeping up, hot to score whatever news tidbit Jake could be convinced to offer. If it'd been just Jane on the story, he might be able to slip her something— how could he not? But two reporters, that changed the equation. What he told one, he'd have to tell the other. And the answer to that, now, was absolute zero.

"Nothing," he repeated. Jane would never accept this, but protocol was protocol. Especially since they were not alone. "You'll have to call headquarters."

"Jake, are you kidding me? Nothing?" Jane clamped

her hands to her hips, giving him that look. She paused, and for a moment, her voice softened. "Did I—are we—is there something—?"

"For *either* of you," Jake cut her off, pointing to the other reporter. She had to understand this wasn't personal, even though she apparently—wisely—suspected he was annoyed over Peter. But this was only business. "See what I mean? Looks like you've got some competition. Two reporters makes a news conference. News conferences are handled by HQ."

"Listen. Jake." Jane's voice was low, and she took one step toward him, grabbed his arm, just for an instant. The TV crew was almost upon them. "Listen. I get what you're doing, and okay. It's business. But you know this must be connected to Waverly Road, right? Two empty houses? Doesn't it have to be? You know?"

"That's one conclusion." Jake shook his head. What Officer Canfield had told him about Elizabeth McDivitt's death was a disaster in the making, if you asked him, and no way he could tell Jane about it. Besides the other reporter would potentially hear everything he said. "I'm not sure I'd draw the same one, but I'm sure you know best."

He paused, making sure both reporters were paying attention. Two camera lenses aimed at him, but he could see the red tally lights were off. For now, they were all playing by the rules.

"Ladies and gentlemen, we're done here," Jake announced. "You know the phone number for downtown."

Jake put his hand on the wooden doorknob. The questioning beams of Crime Scene's flashlights crisscrossed the empty room inside, scanning for whatever secrets might be left behind. Maybe Liz McDivitt could give him some answers.

* * *

If Jake was going to be such a pill, Jane thought, she'd have to handle this another way. She understood he was constrained by the rules, especially since yet another TV crew had pulled in, onlookers shifting and elbowing and whispering, the local-celebrity news crews just as fascinating as the story they'd arrived to cover.

Spindly masts of the two microwave vans extended skyward, section by section, poking up through the sidewalk trees, snowing crabapple blossoms to the pavement. Both stations would be broadcasting live at eleven, and at that journalism Rubicon, so much for the *Register*'s exclusive. After eleven, anything Jane wrote for the paper was instantly outdated and stale. All she had in her arsenal, the only thing that could make headlines, was to dig up something exclusive. Something the electronic media didn't know. Something like that list of names. And the knowledge that Liz had a boyfriend. It was a start.

Her phone buzzed again, reminding her she'd ignored the last call. But that was from the desk, so there was no message. It had to be Peter, who, of course, was not dead but simply late. When she had a brain cell available, she'd have to examine that episode. She'd escalated her panic about Peter to the point she truly envisioned him dead, murdered, in this house on Kenilworth Street. When, truth be told, nothing was more unlikely. Where had all that anxiety come from? And why?

The caller ID said *private*. She hit ANSWER, smiling. Ready to hear what Peter—not dead—had to say for himself.

"Jane Ryland."

"Jane. Nick at the desk."

Calls from the *Register* were ID blocked, in case reporters wanted to surprise whoever was on the other end. Which served, sometimes, to surprise the reporters as well.

"Hey, Nick at the desk," Jane said. Okay, not Peter. Where the heck was he? "Listen, I got nothing more, so far. The cops are—"

"Jane? You listen. You said the vic's name is Elizabeth McDivitt? And you said she was with A&A Bank?"

"Yeah. Like I said we can't use that yet, because—"

"You know who she is? Was?" Nick interrupted.

Jane frowned, confused. "I *told* you who she was," Jane said. "What d'you mean, 'who'?"

"We think she's the bank president's daughter," Nick said. "We were looking for her photo and title on the bank website, and did a search, you know? She's not on it, for some reason. But Hardin McDivitt? Is the bank president. Didn't you interview her? Marcotte just told me you interviewed her. How come you didn't know that?"

Marcotte was in the newsroom. Overseeing. Lovely.

"I would have found out at some point," Jane began. "I mean, no, she didn't tell me who her father was. I didn't know she was going to be—" Jane stopped, lowering her voice, her shoulders dropping. "Killed."

"So here's the scoop," Nick said, stepping on her words. "We'll put together whatever story we can from here. Marcotte says you should head to Hardin McDivitt's house. It's in Newton, by the reservoir. I'll send you the deets. Stake it out, see if you can get a statement."

Fifty thousand reasons why this was a terrible idea battled to the forefront. "It's after ten at night." Jane began with the most obvious and least whiny, but the other reasons insisted on being included. "They have no idea their daughter has just been—it's such an invasion of—they'll never agree to an interview, and we'll look like—I mean, can't we just call and ask for a statement? What's the point of sending me and TJ to show up at the house of a—"

Nick cleared his throat, waiting as Jane's rant wound

down. Vulture patrol was part of the reporter deal. She might as well not even argue.

"We're on it," she said. A job was a job. Victoria Marcotte was there, in charge. No doubt monitoring Jane's every move. *Mortgage, health insurance, food.*

She waved at TJ, gesturing him to follow her, gave him the quick explanation. She'd ride with him, they'd pick up her car after.

"Vulture patrol," he said. "Sucks."

"Yeah," Jane said. "It's why people hate reporters."

"But they still read the paper, right? Watch TV?" TJ opened the hatchback of his van, stashed his camera in its molded plastic holder. "If they hate it, why do they watch it?"

"To reassure themselves it's not them, I guess," Jane said, making sure her car was locked. When she was focused on chasing a story, sometimes she forgot. "That bad things happen to someone else."

She tried to look at the bright side. If she were still on TV, they'd have wanted a live shot during the eleven. With her standing in front of the McDivitt home. Morbid. Invasive. Not to mention meaningless. As a newspaper reporter, she'd probably still get a door slammed in her face tonight, but at least it wouldn't be on TV. And she wouldn't be raking through someone's private grief with klieg lights and a microwave mast.

It never got any easier. Jane hoped it never would. She was rattled, she had to admit, because Liz McDivitt was someone she knew. But every victim was someone's acquaintance or friend, or lover, or loved one. Jane's job, any reporter's job, was to tell the story of what happened, as clearly and purely and objectively as possible. To care, because a storyteller has to care. To tell it, whether the public cared to hear it or not. Every news story becomes the fabric of history, the record of motives and failures and outcomes and successes. Jane would be careful with her contribution.

TJ cranked the ignition, pressed the clutch, and shifted into reverse. Jane tried to change the direction of her own weary-brained over-analysis. This was only a news story, she decided. In the paper one day—and what did her father always say? Fish wrap the next.

Another car turned the corner onto the side street, probably a resident, strafing Jane with blue-bright headlights. In the glare, Jane punched McDivitt's address into TJ's GPS, and they pulled out into the night, toward the front door of a grieving family. If she was writing history, she had a million questions.

Why was Jake keeping secrets? Where was Peter Hardesty? And why was the bank president's daughter—Lizzie McDivitt—in a stranger's vacant house?

The traffic lights turned green as they headed east, for the first time in her memory every one of them blinking "go" when they arrived at an intersection, as if the universe wanted her to get to the McDivitts' home as quickly as possible. Exactly what she didn't want. One eye on the GPS, they wound their way through the impossibly random streets of Jamaica Plain, around the treacherous Pond Street rotary, and onto the Jamaicaway, the winding too-narrow boulevard that lined the deserted and no-longer-safe jogging paths of Jamaica Pond, dark shapelets of stubby mallards and long-necked geese drifting in the tentative moonlight.

48

Nothing. Nothing. Not a bar, not a flicker, not a glimmer of power as Peter clicked the flat white button on his cell. Once. Twice. Not only had he left his phone at Doreen Rinker's house, he'd left it *on*. As he'd blithely powered up to Boston, the phone had powered down into a useless brick. Still, at least he had it. He could charge up again in the car.

Peter'd arrived at the Rinker home for the second time that day—night—relieved the porch light was on, and the blue glow of a big screen TV visible through the lacy living room curtains. The front door was open, the screen closed, the porch guarded by a dark green Adirondack chair. At least he hadn't had to bang on the front door of a house with a sleeping family, sheepishly admitting he'd been so eager to get to Boston—and Jane—that he'd forgotten his lifeline to the world.

And then he discovered it was dead.

He'd used Doreen's landline to call the *Register*, got Jane's cell number from some cooperative guy at the news desk, and now after all that, Jane wasn't answering.

He shook his head, smiling, signaling no as Doreen held up a glass carafe of coffee. Listened to the phone ringing. And then, the click and the pause. Right to voice mail. Jane was probably—he looked at his watch, grimacing—ignoring him. Now that it was ten fifty. He couldn't blame her. *Leave a message after the beep.*

He wouldn't be back in Boston until just after one. If he was lucky.

"Jane, it's Peter Hardesty," he said. "Tonight did not go as plan—huh?"

Doreen Rinker was back, this time holding up a piece of paper, showing him something.

"Sorry, Jane, ah, I'll call you. Or you call me. Whenever. Traffic was ridiculous, and, sorry to be such a—" He held up a finger to Doreen. *One second.* "Anyway, again, sorry. I'll make it up to you."

He clicked off, distracted, half-annoyed and half-confused. What was Doreen trying to show him?

She'd pulled her graying hair back in a pink plastic clip, and added a pale blue sweatshirt over her jeans. Its faded lettering promised Fun in the Sun 2001.

"You have a second? Now that you're here? I felt bad about the note." She pulled out a kitchen chair, waved him to the other one. Back where they'd started. "I was just—frightened, I guess. And so—well, this."

Doreen handed the piece of paper across the table, a copy of a newspaper article, Peter saw, skewed on the page, half blurred. From the *Register*. The date—April 2010—written in tiny red ball point printing across the upper left.

"So I was looking around, in desk drawers you know, just—I don't know," Doreen said. Her shoulders lifted, then fell, and she pushed the too-long sweatshirt sleeves up over her elbows. "Seeing if there was anything I could find to help you. Since you were nice enough to—you know. Even though we can't pay you. Right?"

"Mrs. Rinker? No worries, okay?" He'd never get back to Boston. The fates were lining up to make him miserable and tired, not to mention being saddled with two possibly guilty murder defendants and an understandably pissed-off reporter he couldn't wait to see again. Times like these, no use in fighting it. "What did you find?"

"We saved this newspaper story, at least. From 2010, when Gordon was paroled."

Peter saw the headline: "Armed Rob Accomplice Freed." He skimmed, basically what he already knew, Gordon Thorley, age nineteen when he'd been arrested in 1995 as the getaway driver—of the orange Dodge Charger, shown below—in the armed robbery of Holsko's Package Store. Freed on parole. Parole Board chairman Edward H. Walsh under political fire for the move, the state's "liberal" governor taking a hit in the polls for his soft-on-crime stance. A quote from Walsh: "The goal of incarceration is rehabilitation as well as punishment. It's up to us, as a civilized nation, to accept when a person has paid their penance and is ready to be given a second chance to join those who enjoy their freedom. We all deserve second chances."

Walsh himself, Peter remembered, hadn't been given a second chance. A former county sheriff, up-and-coming political big shot, he'd been ousted not long after the controversial Thorley decision. Some said scapegoat, others said good riddance. Where was he now? Probably happy to have washed his hands of the forgiveness end of the justice business. Nobody'd forgiven him, even after Thorley had a clean record for the last four years, until he—

Peter stopped, realizing. What if Walsh had made the biggest mistake of his life, unwittingly letting the Lilac Sunday killer go free?

"Anything here you think is relevant?" Peter said.

"I hoped *you* might find something," Doreen said.

He looked at the article again, hoping to discern some hidden clue. But it was just a newspaper story. "I mean, thanks so much for pulling this out. You never know what's going to be useful, so I appreciate . . ."

"What?" Rinker said.

Peter blinked, staring at the article, thinking back, trying to remember. He looked at the name again. Had to be, he thought.

"Nothing," he lied. "May I take this with me?"

Aaron Gianelli had stopped a block or two from Kenilworth Street, parked his car in a municipal lot, clamped a baseball hat over his forehead, and pretended to yawn all the way to the sidewalk. Figuring that would cover his face. Stupid, probably, but who knew what surveillance cameras were out there.

Talk about stupid. She had his picture on her frigging desk. He'd actually given it her!

And now she was dead. And now the cops would come find him, and question him, and he'd have to lie the hell out of everything he said. Or at least be incredibly frigging careful. *He* hadn't killed Lizzie McDivitt, of course. Not technically.

He should have just let the phone ring. Ignored it.

Dumb. If he hadn't picked up? He'd have had one more night's sleep, he guessed, but eventually he'd have to answer to reality. And there would be Ackerman's voice, giving him the news. "Keep your head down, kid," Ack had instructed, after the bottom line. "I don't know how it happened."

"And I'm the king of freaking Spain," he muttered to himself.

Head down, fists jammed in the pockets of his jeans, Aaron walked as fast as he could toward the house, calculating.

He was in this up to his ass. No doubt about that. But now he had to see. He had to. He hadn't done anything, nothing at all, really, so there was no reason for him to stay away. No one in this measly suburb would know who he was. Which, he reassured himself, was nobody. He was nobody. And he had to see.

Ackerman had killed her, somehow, no freaking doubt about that, he was such a freaking creep, and also no doubt about why. Because he—Aaron the moron—had been incredibly reckless enough to tell her about his—their—rental system. He'd thought it was a brilliant and strategic move, after the whole key debacle, to bring Lizzie into it. She already knew, anyway.

She'd discovered Maddie Kate Wendell and Mo Heedles, and it was merely a hop, skip, and a jump to the bank records to find out what those two houses had in common. She knew. So hey, why not make her part of the—he paused, jabbing the button for the crosswalk, wouldn't want to jaywalk, right? Get stopped by the cops?

He almost laughed. Almost. Around the corner, the silent blue lights, flashing on the white siding. A crowd looking on. Ambulance, parked. Cop cars. So much for making her part of his—their—operation.

He'd agreed with Ackerman. Made the decision. Knew the score. It was him, or her. Ack put it to him, simple as yes or no. You or her. Aaron had made a mistake, and he was sorry. But her snooping and prying and interfering had put Lizzie in over her head. Right where Aaron was. It was her, or him. He knew that.

A block to go. TV antenna things stuck up through the trees, those trucks they used for going live. So, reporters. The whole freaky deaky nine yards. Well, the murder—or whatever—of a bank president's daughter would be big news.

Freaking Ackerman. This was actually all his fault. Big-shot bank guy. Big talker. Telling everyone what to say and do. Where was he, anyway? Not here, this was sure as hell the last place he'd show his face. Had anyone seen him? Before?

Aaron felt the pull of the murder scene, almost magnetic, heard an undercurrent of activity as he walked closer. Late this afternoon, he'd summoned his courage and gone to Lizzie's office, full of the plan, but she'd been "out," Stephanie told him. Would he like to leave a message? No frigging way. No messages.

He'd ridden the elevator up to five, then down to the lobby, then up again, stalling. Should he forget the whole thing? But finally he'd called her cell and told Lizzie where to meet him. The front door would be open, he told her. And then he'd arrive, get her advice on the place, and then, together, they'd go someplace fabulous. He promised. If she'd take a cab, he'd drive, and she wouldn't have to leave her car.

It had taken all he could to get the words out. But she agreed instantly, even putting him on speaker so she could write down the address. She was so trusting, and that puppy-dog face she had. How she always looked at him, all needy. He'd marshaled his courage—if you could call it that—remembering, with the clarity of inevitability, that it was him or her. What was he supposed to do?

Aaron insinuated himself into the pack of onlookers, back row, peering out over the heads of the curious. Baseball caps, like his, one woman in curler things. The cops were all over Kenilworth Street—where had Ackerman come up with this place, anyway? It sure wasn't on his REO list. But made sense Ack wouldn't choose one of their own props to . . . do this.

They would stay out of it, if all went as planned. If it didn't—well, it wasn't Aaron's fault. If he had to choose "him or me" again? Again, he'd choose himself. That was his backup plan. He had all the dirt on this deal. He would tell, if need be.

He adjusted his baseball cap, pulling it lower, as two EMTs opened the back doors of the idling ambulance. Two girl TV reporters, side by side but ignoring each other, stood in front of the house, big lights blasting them. He could see their lipsticked mouths moving, but couldn't hear a word they were saying.

He didn't need to hear. He knew exactly what happened.

49

Peter heard sounds from Doreen Rinker's living room, familiar, then realized it was the almost-muted techno-frantic theme of the TV news. Already eleven?

He could almost feel the copy of the newspaper article tucked into his pocket. The article written by Chrystal Peralta, the veteran reporter he'd met at the *Register*. She'd covered the Thorley parole. Interviewed the past board chairman, Sheriff Walsh. Maybe she knew something about the case, something to prove Thorley was innocent. He'd grasped at thinner straws.

Doreen Rinker led him toward the front door, apologizing again for burning the note, offering him more coffee.

"Maybe in a paper cup?"

Which actually sounded like a good idea. He was zonked, and could have a two-hour drive back to Boston. "Sure, thanks."

"Be right back," she said. "Have a seat. Watch the news."

Peter didn't want to get comfortable, didn't want to risk dozing off, so he stood by the door, half-interested in the flickering image on the big screen. He tried to remember. Had Chrystal Peralta mentioned Gordon Thorley when they'd talked at the *Register*? She hadn't, he was sure of it. But she *had* talked about Lilac Sunday, explained it to Jane.

The lights on the TV screen shifted. Peter's peripheral vision was caught by a swirling graphic, BREAKING NEWS. *Huh.* Jake Brogan and a uniformed cop. On the front porch of some house.

The sound was too low to understand, but a printed crawl unspooled across the lower third of the screen. *Police investigating . . . possible homicide in Boston . . . Jamaica Plain . . . woman found in empty house . . . no identification of victim . . .*

Peter watched the video scenes, reading the no-details outline of Boston's latest murder.

In an empty house. Just like the one on Moulten Street, the one Gordon Thorley confessed to, the death of Treesa Caramona. Peter smiled, a reasonably compelling motion-for-dismissal taking shape in his head. Since this woman—whoever it was—had apparently been murdered while Thorley was in custody, who was to say the bad guy in *this* case hadn't killed Treesa Caramona, too?

And that might mean, based on—well, he'd come up with something—they'd have to let Thorley out, at least while awaiting trial. Possible.

Should he tell Doreen Rinker? False hopes were the scourge of the profession; the worst thing you could do to a frantic family was dangle the possibility their loved one might be freed. In reality, the legal system was such a minefield nothing could be absolute. That's why jury decisions were based on reasonable doubt. Nothing was ever certain. Nothing predictable.

Lilac Sunday was the complication. There was no proof Thorley was innocent of . . .

Wait. Innocent.

Gordon Thorley wasn't the only one who might benefit—yes, *benefit*—from this latest murder.

* * *

The three loveliest words Jane had ever heard.

New York City.

The door to the McDivitts' faux-Georgian semi-mansion had opened almost before the last bong of the doorbell. Jane had told TJ to wait in the van—she'd try to get a comment, that was her job, but no way was she going to barge up to the door with a camera. The whole encounter was invasive enough without pointing a lens at a devastated parent. Liz had told her—Jane shook her head, remembering. Her mother was dead, another thing they'd shared. A trim young woman in a navy blazer and linen slacks opened the door. Housekeeper? Assistant? New wife?

Jane introduced herself, saw a flicker of recognition. Asked for Hardin McDivitt.

No, the woman told Jane, Mr. McDivitt is not in at the moment. A dog barked, somewhere down a corridor. Might she take a message?

Jane could barely keep from thanking her. Not the new wife, if there even was one. This woman was all business.

Did the woman know when he'd return? Jane had crossed her fingers the answer would be "never."

He's in New York City, the woman said. She'd asked Jane for a card.

"They'd like some privacy," the woman had finally said. "If there's a comment, they'll be in touch." Then she'd closed the door.

It was all Jane could do not to run back to the van. Score one, at least.

"No one home," Jane said. "A housekeeper or something. Says they're out of town. Great, huh? The police must have called. She didn't look upset, but they're asking for 'privacy.' We know what that means."

"Yeah. Your phone is beeping," TJ said as she opened

the car door. "And the desk called. Marcotte sent an overnight crew to Kenilworth Street. So we're clear. Day is
done."

"Another disaster successfully averted. Let's go get my
car," Jane said. "Geez. I hate this stuff."

She sighed, pulling on her seat belt as TJ eased his van
around the wide asphalt driveway, past a stand of lofty
poplars and banks of pale hydrangeas subtly spotlighted
by hidden fixtures. The Liz situation haunted her. Cop
or not, she would call Jake tomorrow. This had to be connected to the death of Shandra Newbury. Jake must
know it, too.

From inside the depths of her tote bag, her phone
beeped.

"Like I said." TJ pointed. "Someone wants you."

Two messages, according to the little green 2. Jane
looked at the phone number of the first one, not a Boston area code, not a number she recognized. She punched
the message. Hit play.

"Jane, it's Peter Hardesty," he said. "Tonight did not
go as plan—huh?"

Jane listened to the rest of the message, Peter explaining about the Cape and obviously talking to someone
else at the same time. Okay, then. At least he was fine.

She hit the second message, from a different number,
this one a Boston area code.

"It's Peter," the voice buzzed, and this time Jane could
hear honking in the background. "It's uh, late, long story,
I just left the Cape and—hang on."

Jane laughed, envisioning it. He was driving? Still on
the Cape? At this hour? She could stop worrying, about
that at least, and this ridiculous night was almost over.

"What's funny?" TJ said. "You laughed."

"Did I?" Jane held up a palm, putting TJ on hold as
she listened to the rest of Peter's message.

"I got your message, thanks, looks like both of us have

had unexpectedly complicated nights. Anyway. I'm in traffic again," Peter was saying. "I'll explain tomorrow, okay? And just to prove I'm—well, the Sandoval arraignment is tomorrow at ten. Suffolk Superior."

Peter's voice paused again, and Jane stared out the windshield into the glare of the streetlights and the dark storefronts along Route 9. *Poor Liz McDivitt.*

"And I owe you dinner, Jane, okay?" Peter said. "On me."

A buzz and a click. The message was over.

Jane stashed the phone in her bag and watched the streetlights and shadows play over TJ's face. It was easy to forget, in the hustle and the deadlines and the competition, that news stories were about real people. She half-smiled, hearing the voices of every j-school teacher and news director repeating the same thing. The truth was not always easy, and not always pleasant, and not always fair, but it was her job to tell it, no matter what. No matter whose life had intersected with hers—Liz McDivitt's, or Peter Hardesty's, or Elliot Sandoval's.

Even Jake's. Nothing mattered except what was true.

Jake stared at the streaked hardwood floor of the empty living room, the last to leave 16 Kenilworth, imagining it.

Elizabeth McDivitt, the bank president's daughter. Jake tried to put together the pieces of what happened, and decide what his own next moves might be. Liz McDivitt was gone, the ambulance was gone, and the press was gone, thankfully, without bugging him any further. The rest of the cops had packed up their crime scene stuff and headed out. The Supe had set a strategy session for the investigating officers—him, and Sherrey, Roslynne Canfield as backup, and someone from the bank to give them an all-access pass—to begin at 0900.

The Sandoval arraignment was still set for ten, Suffolk Superior Court, newbie judge Mavis Rockland presiding over what had now become quite the legal balancing act. The Supe was conferring with the DA right now, Jake had been told, and they were all on standby until given the plans.

He walked toward his cruiser, through the now-silent neighborhood, past darkened windows and drawn curtains, not even the bark of a restless dog, as if nothing had happened, the glimmer of red alarm lights in parked cars and the occasional glow from a television screen the only indication anyone even lived here.

Television. Jane.

He stopped, closed his eyes for a fraction of a second, imagining their next encounter. What would he say about the Peter thing? She had a perfect right to see whoever she wanted, he was simply surprised it happened so fast. *Don't complicate your life away,* Gram had said. Too late.

Six hours till the Supe's meeting. He slid behind the wheel of his cruiser. A few triangles of white paper stuck out from inside the center console, Grandpa's Lilac Sunday file from the basement of 243. Because of Lilac Sunday, he had to make one quick stop in the morning before that shit show began. It would all work. Had to.

50

Too early to call. Wasn't eight in the morning too early to call?

Jane hadn't been able to sleep, restless half-dreams crowded with images of Liz McDivitt, and Gordon Thorley's knife, and Elliot Sandoval in jail, and that teenager, Emily-Sue Ordway, the girl who'd started Jane's whole foreclosure story, lying dead on the grass outside her family's foreclosed house. Jake, standing on the front porch of Kenilworth Street. Saying exactly nothing.

Giving up on sleep, Jane had fed a demanding Coda, added a pat and a hug and a promise of more, and left the calico snarfing down the world's stinkiest cat food as she hustled to the newsroom. The morning paper, printed version, offered only an inside brief on the Kenilworth Street situation. "Family spokesman asks for privacy," it said. Jane had given the desk that nothing tidbit, though she hadn't used the word "family."

Anyway, that meant the overnight crew hadn't been able to get any more info. Or confirm the victim's name. Or that she was the bank president's daughter. *Why hadn't Liz mentioned that? She'd talked about her mother.* Anyway, that meant when it came to breaking the story, Jane was still in the hunt. Somehow she felt responsible for finding out what happened to Liz, making sure she was properly remembered. Calling her clients might help. And the boyfriend, as soon as she could dig up his name.

She spun a pencil on her desk, watching the yellow blur, speculating about why it was even part of journalism culture to call people for reactions to the deaths of others. Obituaries were history, exactly like news stories. They had to be properly written, with care and respect. That's what Jane would do for Liz McDivitt. Tell her story.

Jane stopped the pencil. Got up from her desk, clicked the monitor closed, and scrabbled in her tote bag for dollar bills pristinely flat enough to satisfy the basement's finicky vending machines. Sugar and caffeine would help. Twizzlers and Diet Coke.

When she got back from vending city it'd be eight-thirty. That was a civilized time to call strangers. She'd tell them she was doing a story on bank customer service, because that's what she'd promised Liz. Just the littlest white lie. If the reality were revealed, well, she'd handle that when the time came.

Too impatient to wait for the reliably unreliable elevator, Jane yanked open the battered metal door leading to the stairwell. By ten, she'd have to dash to the Sandoval arraignment, which promised to be a hell of a story. The prosecution was required to tell the judge what the DA's office knew about the case, elaborate on what evidence they had, and why they wanted Sandoval to be held in jail—without bail—awaiting trial. Peter Hardesty would argue to let him out. Since the DA's office generally got what it wanted, she expected Elliot Sandoval would be behind bars for a while. Poor Elliot. Poor MaryLou. All this because they'd hit some rough economic seas and lost their house. And the dominoes crashed on their heads.

Foreclosure claims another victim.

* * *

Footsteps on the *Register* stairs, someone a few floors above them clattering their way downstairs as Jake walked back up, stashing the fresh copies of news clippings he'd just been given into his folder. He rounded the landing of the newspaper's back stairwell, keeping his head down, all business. The guy in Archives had warned him about the elevator, and he didn't have time to wait for it, anyway. Already dressed for court, Jake had enough time to get back to police HQ, read the newspaper stories, and make it to the Supe's strategy session.

According to the leather-bound volumes of yellowing newsprint Jake had examined, the *Register* had gone all out on Lilac Sunday coverage. And, jackpot, the reporter had interviewed witnesses, well, not witnesses, but people who'd come to the Arboretum soon after Carley Marie Schaefer's body was found. Their names were not familiar, though, and not in his grandfather's files or the police records. Why hadn't the cops interviewed them? Some of them must still be around.

The reporter—Jake recognized the byline Chrystal Peralta, knew she still worked here at the *Register*—had even interviewed his grandfather. Those articles hadn't been in Grandpa's files, either. But maybe that was Grandpa being modest. Not keeping clips about himself, only about the crime itself. Jake had pulled the Thorley parole stories, too. Everything about Gordon Thorley.

The footsteps got closer. Sounded like a woman walking quickly, not clacking in high heels. He looked up.

Jane.

"Oh!" Jane stopped, two steps above him, one hand on the railing, the other holding a few dollar bills. She took a step backward, up and away from him, her eyes wide. "Ah. Jake."

His face must have looked as surprised as hers. And

she was probably trying to figure out what to say, too, same as he was.

"Can I help you with something?" She didn't take the next step down toward him, held her ground.

"I'm fine." Jake hesitated, knowing it was his turn to talk, but unable to come up with anything. What could he say about Hardesty? That didn't sound—weak?

"Something I should know?" Jane tilted her head, looking at him, quizzing.

He loved her hair that way, tucked behind one ear, the other side falling over her face. No jeans today, he noticed, black pants and a black T-shirt, and even her "go to court" pearls, he knew she called them. Headed for the Sandoval arraignment. That would be cozy.

"Sorry about last night," he began. "What happened was—"

"Oh, we're past that, don't you think?" Jane said. Her smile seemed off, maybe, and he didn't blame her. Last they'd really been together was on her couch the other night, when he'd had to tell her their vacation was blown, and he was assigned for a few days to Washington. Since then, he hadn't had a chance to explain what happened. Now she didn't seem open to hear anything he had to say. But she'd been at another guy's house, that made it *her* turn to explain.

"Jane, I—we—" Jake paused, considering. What was the most important thing? His responsibility to his job? Or to this woman, who he—*damn it*. This was not the time for a life discussion. One day soon, they'd have to face it all. Decide on their truth.

More footsteps on the stairs, a few floors up. Their private moment on the landing was about to end. Would their last conversation be in a gloomy back stairwell of a struggling newspaper?

"Listen," he said. "Jane. We should talk."

* * *

"Talk?" Jane put up a palm, trying to stop him. Her other hand clutched the banister, trying for equilibrium.

Here was the last person she expected to see, and the only one she wished for. And yet—what kind of relationship did they have, that he could be in town and not even tell her? When he could show up at the very building where she worked and she had no idea?

"We're talking now, right?" She lowered her voice. "Although clearly you were trying to avoid it. Avoid *me*. I mean—here you are, a detective, the morning after a murder, coming from the basement of the—oh."

Only one place Jake could have been. The *Register*'s archives. Happily, whatever he'd found, she could find, too. Archive Gus was an old pal, and would be all too eager to give Jane the scoop on whatever articles the cops requested. She'd have thought Jake would realize that. But then, he hadn't expected she'd even know he'd been there. *So it goes, buddy,* she thought. Cops don't have all the power, all the time.

Jake was silent. She should shut up, too, but she couldn't resist.

"So. How'd you get along with Archive Gus?" The balance was usually so in his favor, and now, the tiniest of bits, it was in hers. She touched her pearls, wondering if she'd see him later at the Sandoval arraignment. That'd be cozy. "He give you what you came for?"

She could tell Jake was unhappy. His eyes were soft, and only he stood that way, that wide stance, she could almost feel his arms around her. She was frustrated with herself for acting so cranky. But he'd left *her*, right? Instead of going to Bermuda, he'd made up something about Washington, D.C. Then he showed up in Boston. And then brushed her off at the scene of a heart-breaking murder.

Such things did not make for the most successful of relationships.

"Jane?" Jake was talking again, and Jane simply did not know how to unscramble her feelings. This was not the time to try.

"I'm late," she said.

She heard the bitterness in her own voice, regretted it, couldn't help it. Hurt was difficult, and life was complicated, and Liz McDivitt was dead and she still felt—yes, ridiculously—that somehow it was her fault. Jake knew what had happened to Liz, but he wasn't telling. Fine. Jane could find out on her own, and make sure whoever killed her got what was coming to them.

"I'm late," she said again. Looked at her watch, maybe with a little more drama than necessary. "I bet you have someplace to be, too. Perhaps Washington again?"

"I do," Jake said. He moved aside as someone else trotted down the stairs, carrying a stack of newspapers, coffee sloshing out of an open paper cup. "Have someplace to be. And you know exactly where."

His voice had quieted, softened, and Jane felt tears beginning to well. They had shared so much, and now—she was tired, that was it. Seeing Jake like this had caught her off guard. And now he was smiling at her, a look she knew from couches and cars and across rooms where no other person realized they were looking at each other. *Don't do this,* her brain instructed. *Tell him. Just say— I love you, this is crazy, I'm sorry, I'm confused, I'm sad, I'm tired, you're amazing, let's just—*

"So maybe see you in—," Jake continued.

"Court?" Jane said. "Maybe." She raced past him, down the stairs, not looking back, *not looking back,* down to the basement for sugar and caffeine, leaving him silent behind her.

51

"All rise, court will be in recess." A bespectacled court clerk, one tattooed angel wing peeking out from under the short sleeve of her starched navy blue uniform, stood in front of the shiny new woodwork of Suffolk Superior Courtroom 6. Jane entered the nearly empty room, seeing the black folds of Judge Rockland's silk robe disappear behind an opening tucked into the wall behind the bench. The door leveled into the woodwork as it closed. "Court will resume at ten fifteen."

A potload of taxpayer dollars had gone to revamp the moldy insulation and the moth-eaten carpeting in the old courthouse. Jane had investigated the whole debacle when she worked at Channel 11. Now some courthouse workers complained the place smelled "too new," pointing to the chemicals in the synthetic wall-to-wall that Jane discovered were provided by some state senator's half-brother's wholesale house. It was Massachusetts, after all, home of Whitey Bulger and James Michael Curley and the Boston Strangler. What was a little more graft and manipulation at the public trough? Pols wouldn't know how to handle anything if it were by the book. In this state, political insiders hardly knew what "the book" was.

Would Elliot Sandoval be ordered back to jail? Jane

spotted Peter Hardesty, alone, intently turning pages in a manila folder, a red accordion file open beside it. The Commonwealth's table, where the assistant district attorneys would make their case, was still empty.

Jane slid into the polished wooden bench in the spectator area, knowing the first row behind the defendant's side was always reserved for the press. A harried-looking stringer from the *Daily*, pencil stuck through the spiral of a battered reporter's notebook, had wedged himself into a corner seat. He swung his running shoes back on the floor, standing for a moment as the judge left the room. He was on Facebook, Jane saw.

No other reporters. And no TV cameras set up in the empty jury box. Local TV stations could take turns being *pool* for sessions like this, a day in court that could turn into nothing, so they sometimes hedged their news bets with a shared pool cam, knowing the video would most often be erased at day's end. On a slow day they'd show up on the off chance some crazed spectator would lunge at the defendant, or be led out by burly court officers, shrieking bleep-worthy expletives about unfairness and justice. Apparently today's docket didn't interest TV. According to Marcotte, the Sandoval arraignment would only be a news brief, unless something unexpectedly blockbuster happened.

Jane flipped through her notes from this morning's phone calls to Liz's customers. The Iantosca call had gone to voice mail, and Jane couldn't quite figure out how to say what she needed in a message. But the Gantry, Rutherford, and Detwyler calls were productive, telling her they'd be happy to talk about their experiences at the bank. She'd arranged to meet each couple after lunch so she could cover the arraignment, call in the results to the city desk, then get the bank customers' info.

A chair scraped. Jane looked up, following the sound.

Peter Hardesty had turned, scanning the audience, and eventually locked eyes with Jane.

She tilted her head, acknowledging, and he did the same. Suit and tie, khaki and stripes, looking very lawyerly with his stack of yellow pads and a line of sharpened pencils in front of him. The chair next to him was still empty. She pointed at the chair, raised an eyebrow, questioning. *Where's Elliot?*

Peter pointed to the closed door along one wall.

Ah. Still in holding.

She made a gesture like—*I got your call. You okay?*

He shrugged, then waggled a palm, *more or less.* He pointed to his watch, grimaced, pantomiming being sorry.

Jane waved him off. *No worries.*

The prosecution side, the mirror image of Peter's wooden table and two chairs, reserved for the DA, was still empty. Strange. Jane'd never been to an arraignment where the prosecution wasn't the first to arrive, files at the ready and gunning for the defendant. This whole thing was off, somehow.

Someone must have given the signal.

A door hidden in the wood paneling opened, and Elliot Sandoval appeared. A sound, someone arriving though the public door, made the defendant turn to the audience. Jane saw MaryLou Sandoval enter, eyes red, and hugely pregnant. She inched her way into a back row. Probably too awkward to get closer.

At the same time, a door opened on the other side of the courtroom. A parade of briefcases: Assistant DA Cardell Grainger, sixty-something, dapper in pinstripes and a red tie, glasses balanced on his forehead. A chignoned brunette, Jane didn't recognize her, the requisite white shirt, pencil skirt, and extravagantly sleek patent heels.

Behind her, Jake, looking at the floor as he walked.

Then that young uniformed cop Jane had seen at the Kenilworth Street house. The two police officers sat in the front row as the lawyers, in tandem, clicked open their blocky leather evidence cases on the table and unpacked them, pulling out yellow pads and brandishing pencils.

Jane willed Jake to look at her, turn around, notice her. He did. She looked away, pretending she hadn't seen him. When she sneaked a look back, ashamed at her high school tactics, he was leaning forward, talking with the DA. Jane closed her eyes, regretting. This was silly. They had to talk.

"Commonwealth case 0014-657, *Commonwealth versus Sandoval*," the court clerk intoned. "All rise for Judge Mavis Rockland."

With a murmur, everyone stood in a clatter and rustle of adjusting papers and laptops, then sat as the judge waved them down. This would be fascinating. And instructive. The assistant DA would give probable cause for why Sandoval should be held—that was standard procedure—and as a result, Jane would hear the key parts of their evidence.

Peter would argue for bail, of course. But murder defendants never got bail. Not bail they could pay, at least.

Jane flipped open her notebook. Sandoval would not get to go home today, she predicted. And who knew, he might be guilty. Either way, if all went as she expected, she was about to hear exactly why the state thought Elliot Sandoval was a murderer.

"And how do you plead, sir?"

Peter had warned his client that today was about lowered expectations. Get through it, he'd instructed. Stand, look straight at the judge, say "not guilty," sit down.

"Not guilty." Sandoval's voice, sand and gravel, was the only sound in the courtroom.

Until Peter heard someone gasp, poor MaryLou, probably, as Sandoval faced the judge, the back of his neck reddening, both fists clenched, luckily hidden behind their defense table. Peter had coached him: "Be calm, be low-key, don't react no matter what the state says or how the DA tries to goad you." Today's focus was bail. Unlikely as that was.

"Good," Peter whispered, touching the arm of his client's bedraggled suit coat as they took their seats again. "You're doing great."

"I have both your recommendations here," the judge said. "Mr. Hardesty is asking for no bail and a release on Mr., ah"—she checked her file—"Sandoval's own recognizance. I'll hear brief arguments now, if there's anything you'd like to add."

Judge Rockland wasn't looking at him, a bad sign. Peter'd never argued before her. Newly seated, and no one in the defense bar had a read on how she'd rule. She'd been an assistant DA herself, out in western Mass. Peter believed those ex-DA types never thought anyone who'd been arrested was truly innocent. Must-have-done-something syndrome.

"Nothing to add, your honor." Cardell Grainger stood, fingertips touching the table, his Harvard-crimson tie hitting the blocky leather evidence case in front of him. "You have our brief, as you said."

"Defense?" the judge said.

Peter swallowed, surprised. He'd been steeled to hear a damning litany of the case against his client, two-by-fours, DNA, fingerprints, real estate connections, and an unpaid mortgage. God knew what else the state had up its investigative sleeve. But the DA's office was leaving it at the paperwork? Did they think it was such a slam dunk they didn't even need to argue? Did they have this judge in their pocket, so brazenly and obviously that they didn't even continue a charade?

Peter stood, disappointed in the crappy system and the all-powerful cabal of judges and prosecutors who professed to show off their law-and-order creds when they were actually *preventing* justice.

He'd stand for justice. And fairness. And mercy. Someone had to.

"Peter Hardesty for Mr. Sandoval, your honor," Peter began. "Mr. Sandoval has no prior record, not even a traffic ticket. He's spent all his adult life as a contractor, and married to his wife, MaryLou, who is with him today."

Peter paused, watching MaryLou stand as he'd instructed, allowing the judge to see how pregnant she was. A guilty person could have a pregnant wife, of course, but it never hurt to pull out all the stops. "Mr. Sandoval, as you might imagine, is not a flight risk."

Peter laid out his prepared argument, knowing in the pit of his stomach it was a loser. The state needed to nail someone for the Shandra Newbury murder. *What the hell.* Might as well go for it. Plan B.

"And finally, your honor, last night Boston police discovered another body in an empty foreclosed house, similar to where Shandra Newbury was found. As you are well aware, my client was in police custody at that time. One might argue, your honor, that whoever killed Shandra Newbury—and you heard my client plead not guilty to that charge—also killed last night's victim."

Peter felt Elliot shift in the chair beside him, heard a low muttering from the spectator section. He looked at the prosecution team, but they were all busy with their paperwork, probably so certain of the outcome they barely listened.

"In closing, Your Honor, we would ask that my client, Elliot Sandoval, be released on his own recognizance. He is financially unable to provide bail. By law, bail amounts are not designed to prevent the defendant from release, but only to ensure their return. He is eager to show his good intentions, and offers to reassure the court by wearing a GPS device."

Peter cleared his throat, stalling, making sure he hadn't forgotten anything. Not that it would matter. He was sorry, but Elliot Sandoval was about to go back into custody. His first child would be born with a father in jail. Peter had done his best. That was all he could do.

"Thank you, your honor." Peter sat, trying to look confident, gave Elliot a pat on the back. Poor guy actually looked hopeful, which made Peter feel even worse.

The judge closed her files, adjusted the frothy white ruffle at her throat. She smoothed her already smooth hair away from her forehead, shifted in her chair.

"Motion granted, Mr. Hardesty," she said. "Own recognizance, with a twice-daily check with parole. That is all."

"Your honor!" The DA leaped to his feet, followed by his assistant. "We would strongly—"

"That is *all*, Mr. Grainger." The judge stood, signaling the clerk. "You made your bed. Mr. Hardesty, your client is free to go."

52

Holy shit. **Jane** almost said it out loud, stopped herself just in time. The judge was letting Sandoval out?

The court emptied again as the judge disappeared behind the quickly closing door panel. Sandoval hugged Peter, rumpling his jacket in the enthusiasm of his embrace, as MaryLou rushed to the bar, one hand on her stomach, sobbing full bore.

The district attorney's table packed up its briefcases and scuttled out the side door before Jane could even try to get a statement. Jake, too, and the cop, gone in an instant. All probably huddled somewhere, speculating about why the rug had been pulled out from under their prosecution. The *Daily* reporter was texting madly, Jane saw. No more Facebook. This was news.

Jane hustled toward the defense table, notebook out, needing to call this in to the desk, wishing just this once she was back on TV, or at least had TJ with her. What a moment this was, Sandoval and his wife embracing, both crying, Peter looking happy. And baffled. Small comfort that the TV stations had missed all this, though they'd certainly try to interview the newly released—Jane couldn't believe it—Sandoval at his home.

And of course, as she had to keep reminding herself, it didn't mean Sandoval was innocent. But he was out of jail, a big step. That had to mean the evidence was flimsy, charges teetering on dismissal.

"Peter?" Jane waved at him to get his attention as the court officer led Sandoval away. She approached the low mahogany bar, the thigh-high wooden barrier that kept spectators on one side, lawyers on the other. "What do you think? Were you surprised? Why do you think the judge released him?

"MaryLou?" Jane turned to the young woman. Mary-Lou was still in full sob, wiping away tears with both palms. "Were you surprised?"

"Jane? Hang on a sec, okay?" Peter interrupted, tucking a manila file under one arm and opening the bar's low swinging door. "MaryLou, Elliot will be out in an hour or so. I'm sorry, the processing will take a while. Want to meet me in the coffee shop? I need to talk to Jane, then I'll be right there. You all right?"

"I'm okay, yes," MaryLou said. "I don't know how to . . ."

"We'll talk," Peter told her. "See you in a few."

They watched MaryLou walk away, touching her hand to each of the pews as she waddled back to the heavy courtroom door. The court officer smiled as he held it open for her.

"She must be so relieved," Jane finally said. "What an amazing job you did, Peter. I can't believe the judge—"

"It wasn't me," Peter said.

Jane was surprised to see him frowning.

"Aren't you happy?" she asked. "I'd have thought you'd be—"

"Oh, I'm happy," Peter interrupted. "But something is up. Big time."

"Like what?" Jane tried to understand where he was going.

"She didn't even hear my arguments, you know? Wasn't listening. And the DA not even presenting? Shit.

Sorry. I mean—hell. She'd made her decision before we even came into session. I have no idea why."

"Your Kenilworth Street argument, don't you think?" Jane had been wondering about the same thing, even before Peter brought it up in court. "Reasonable doubt?"

Peter didn't answer. He loaded his paperwork, a file at a time, into the accordion folder, carefully tucking pencils into individual leather loops on the inner walls of his briefcase.

"Maybe they have someone, a suspect, for that?" Jane persisted. Maybe that's why Jake had been so protective. So annoyingly silent. Maybe they'd solved the Liz McDivitt murder, and Shandra Newbury's, and even Treesa Caramona's. Maybe they were all connected by some bad guy still out there. "Because they were all in empty houses. But Elliot was in custody, couldn't be involved. Exactly as you argued."

Peter clamped his briefcase closed. Turned to her. His tie twisted to one side, probably the result of Elliot's awkward bear hugs. He raked a hand through his hair.

"Wish I knew. If I did? Maybe I could get this whole thing dismissed." Peter shrugged. "Anyway, Jane. I'm so sorry about what happened. I still owe you that dinner. How about tonight, now that my client is out? Unless that new victim is actually connected to him somehow. Then we're in trouble."

Jane stared at him, looking past him, seeing into the past and the future and into the possibilities of how these puzzle pieces might all fit together. She had an hour before her meeting with Liz McDivitt's clients. Liz. Sandoval. Newbury. Caramona.

Was poor Liz's death the reason Elliot Sandoval was freed? Because as Peter told the judge, whoever killed Shandra Newbury might also have killed the victim on Kenilworth Street. But because the name hadn't been made public yet, Peter didn't know it was Liz McDivitt, bank president's daughter, a person who handled those high-risk mortgages and imminent foreclosures.

Should she tell Peter what she knew was the truth?

As a reporter she couldn't reveal Liz's identity to the public, but telling a lawyer, that wasn't exactly public. And if Peter promised not to tell, she knew he was reliable. Lawyer-client privilege, after all. Though she wasn't his client, they were working on the Sandoval case together. Kind of together. Plus, the cops would release her name any minute now. Had to.

"Jane?" Peter had touched her arm, and she jumped back, startled. "You still with us here?"

"Peter?" she said. "Can you keep a secret?"

Aaron Gianelli stood on the sidewalk, corner of Batterymarch and Liberty. Freaking out. Watching each vehicle in the lunchtime traffic, scouting for undercover cars or blue-lighted cruisers. Expecting a cop to nab him, handcuffs and sirens, any second. A bafflingly ugly statue of refugees from some faraway place centered the traffic circle, all marble and pigeon poop. Girls in sleeveless dresses sat on the statue's pedestal, drinking Diet Cokes and unwrapping gyros from the Greek place on the corner. Pigeons battled for the crumbs, some fluttering on the refugees' arms and dive-bombing for leftovers as the sandal-and-sunglasses crowd tossed their waxed paper in the mesh trash bins and headed back to their offices. Like normal people. Not like him. Not anymore.

Aaron checked his phone. Quarter after. Twenty after. Ackerman was late. He'd wanted to meet in the office, where there was at least air conditioning and privacy, but Ackerman wasn't happy with the prospect of being seen together. So here he was, sweating it in the absurd heat. Truthfully, he'd be sweating it wherever he was. Lizzie McDivitt was dead. The "body found on Kenilworth

Street" was all over TV last night, the noon news on the radio finally revealing her identity twenty minutes ago. No doubt in hell he was about to be questioned by the cops.

He and Ack had to get their stories straight. And fast.

All Jake could do now was wait. When it came to Sandoval at least. The guy had to check in twice a day with a parole officer, or they could yank him back into custody in a flash. Jake predicted that's exactly what would happen. Guy was guilty as hell. This whole bail thing was about as big a risk as he'd ever seen in law enforcement. But that's why the Supe got the big bucks. Jake had put in his two cents, though when the Supe spoke, Jake's two cents weren't worth—well, two cents. Now it was all about keeping the lid on.

At least he could focus on Gordon Thorley. The tick-tick-tick to Lilac Sunday haunted him, though it was a deadline of Jake's own making. He felt so close to a solution. If only he could make his case.

He parked in a loading zone, slammed his cruiser door, and headed for the glass and chrome front door of Atlantic & Anchor Bank. On TV, detectives like him were always in shootouts, car chases, saving the damsels in distress at the last minute from the marauding bad guy. Jake was about to look at pieces of paper. But justice for a long-dead teenager's family might depend on those pieces of paper.

Officer Vierra in Records had discovered that a home deeded to a Gordon Thorley, someplace down the Cape, had been in the final stages of foreclosure. But, she told him, it seemed like now the foreclosure had been halted. Someone here at the bank would know why, and Jake now had the warrant requiring A&A to tell him all about it.

He whooshed through the revolving door, out of the

heat and into the marble chill of the bank's lobby. Up the elevator to five, where he'd requested the bank's public relations guy, a Colin Ackerman, help him get the documents he needed. Bank president Hardin McDivitt, Jake had been informed by the Supe, was unavailable. He wasn't needed at this point, anyway.

It was risky to come here, but Jake was in plain clothes. And if buzz started that the cops were around, maybe not such a bad thing. Liz McDivitt's identity had just been made public, the Supe's call on the timing. It'd be interesting if anyone here brought up her name. Jake sure wasn't going to.

"I'm afraid you came all this way for nothing, Detective." Colin Ackerman, right out of *Banker's Monthly Magazine,* if there was such a thing, greeted him at the elevator, no doubt alerted by the hyper-vigilant security guard at the lobby desk.

Inside his office, Ackerman handed Jake a manila envelope. "Here's all we have." He shook his head. "The mortgage was brought up to date, as you saw from the public documents, but with these money orders, bought at the post office. Someone paid cash, as you can see from the copies, and there's no way, as you are well aware, to trace those."

Jake took the envelope by one corner, wondering if that were true. Slid it into his briefcase. There could be surveillance video at a post office. Another item for the to-do list.

"Which post office?" Jake asked.

Ackerman looked at the ceiling. Then back at Jake. "I'm afraid I have no idea. If there's anything else?"

"There is," Jake said. "When did the payments start?"

Liz McDivitt's clients—three of them!—were telling Jane the identical story.

And Jane had no idea what that story meant.

Sitting on a plaid sofa in Cole Gantry's living room, interview number three of the afternoon, Jane pushed a snuffling cocker spaniel away from her knee, seeing with dismay a trail of drool he'd deposited on her black pants. The Gantry house, sparse and prefab, seemed held together with plastic tape and rubber bands, duct tape repairing the upholstery of a wing chair. Even the TV remote control had a rubber band holding it together.

The cops had released Liz McDivitt's name for the noon newscasts, leaving the *Register*, newsasaurus, to catch up with its online edition. She'd arrived at the Gantrys', same as the Rutherford and the Detwyler houses, to elicit a simple sympathetic reaction, figured it would be more respectful if she came in person instead of broaching such a sensitive topic over the phone. Apparently Liz hadn't contacted them prior to Jane's call—but with Liz gone, Jane felt better about approaching them. The couples hadn't even questioned how Jane knew about them, whew, and gave her the "we're so sorry" quotes she requested for an obituary-type story.

But seemed as if grief had made them talkative. And as they reminisced, they revealed more about their discussions with Liz McDivitt. Now Cole Gantry—fading jeans and a Patriots T-shirt—was relating, pretty much word for word, the same experience as the Rutherfords. And the Detwylers.

First, that they'd been on the verge of losing their home to foreclosure.

Liz McDivitt had called them to A&A Bank. They'd expected bad news.

Then Liz revealed the bank had made some kind of error. An error that meant they'd paid too much on their mortgage in the past, and as a result, were up to date. They would not lose their homes.

"That's it," Gantry said. "I don't really get it, but I don't care. It was good news."

"So no more foreclosure?" Jane tried to understand. The bank had made a mistake? It was interesting when she'd heard it from the Rutherfords. Intriguing when she'd heard the same thing from the Detwylers. Now, in the Gantrys' living room, it was downright bizarre. Of course, the families didn't know she'd heard the same story from anyone else. "A bank mistake?"

"I know, right? Ms. McDivitt wasn't really clear how the mistake happened but hell, we dodged that bullet." Cole Gantry took a sip of water from a red Solo cup, replaced it on the coffee table. Then he picked it up, wiped the wet ring with one finger, and set it on a do-it-yourself magazine. " 'Bout time we had some luck."

Jane waited, not wanting push him, hoping he'd reveal more without her asking. If this was true? A huge scandal. The bank making mistakes on mortgage payments? One, maybe. Two, even. But all three customers Jane picked—at random—from Lizzie's client list?

She thought of another possibility. Was Liz working on a massive cover-up? Had she been assigned to handle the bank's mistakes? By her father the bank president? Maybe? And been told to make it work?

Was she killed because of that?

Cole Gantry got to his feet, took a step or two toward the door. "Anything else, Miss—?"

"Ryland." Jane stood, brain in overdrive, pulled a business card from her wallet. Liz's death—murder—had taken a complicated turn. Could Liz's own father be involved? Had Liz gotten in over her head? Had she even known what was going on? Whatever it was. Empty foreclosed houses. Mistakes on mortgages. Liz McDivitt's murder, and Shandra Newbury's, too, were all about the bank, Jane was sure. But what about homeless Treesa Caramona?

She needed evidence. But bank records, people's personal finances, were beyond confidential. "Did she give you any paperwork about the mistake?"

"Uh, no, actually. The bills simply stopped coming." The floppy cocker spaniel followed Gantry to the front door. "But Ms. Ryland, now the wife and I are worried. You know? Can you find out for us? With Miss McDivitt gone, will we lose our home?"

53

"Tell me again?" What Ackerman was saying had to be the last thing Aaron Gianelli expected. Ack arrived at their meeting place in the park with tuna melts in brown bags, oozing oil through their paper wrappings. Aaron couldn't face food, not now, not in the heat and the fear and the uncertainty. He put his soggy packet on the heat-baked top of a red plastic news box. His ruined lunch would be the least of his worries. His ruined *life* was more like it. But now he was hearing Ackerman insisting he had no involvement in Lizzie's death.

"That's bull, Ackerman. Don't try to weasel out of this. You're in it, up to your frigging neck."

"I'm serious." Ackerman took a swig of some energy drink, tossed the can into an overflowing trash bin. "I'm as relieved as you are to hear she was out of the picture. But there you have it. Not us."

"But I thought—you said—we'd—" Aaron kept his voice down, watching every person, every movement, expecting at any minute the cops and humiliation and the end of life as he knew it. It was so goddamn hot, the sun searing his head, his shirt about to melt.

"I know, I hear you." Ackerman sat on the wooden park bench, avoiding a white glob of bird shit. Crossed his legs, yanked down his tie. "But then—last minute thing, I guess—they didn't do it. Decided to deal with her later. Another day, another way. But then—"

"So what the hell happened to her?" Aaron would be suspect number one, no doubt about that. Someone'd seen them at the Ritz. At the bank. Who knows who she'd told. That secretary Stephanie sure knew he'd been around.

His tie was strangling him. Why'd they have to be out in this heat? Why'd he ever agree to be involved in this? How much money did anyone actually need?

He flopped onto the bench, as far away as he could get from Ackerman, head in hands. "Shit. Shit. This is gonna be on me, I know it."

"Aaron. Chill. Listen. Look at me. You're out of control. You're not hearing me." Ackerman stood, facing him, hands on hips. "Don't you see?"

Aaron looked up. Ackerman, in silhouette, Liberty Street behind him, people rushing around with brown bags. People who weren't about to get nailed by the frigging cops.

"See what?"

"Christ. You are such a—it's good. It's a good thing. It gets us off the hook, we're not even connected. I mean, thing is, it's actually true. No one knows she was gonna meet you. Right? Right?"

Aaron nodded, stalling, calculating. He heard Ackerman's words, but still wasn't sure what they meant.

"This is great for us." Ackerman's voice was almost a whisper. He sat on the bench again, his leg almost touching Aaron's, arm across the back, face so close Aaron could smell the starch in his shirt, see the glint of the gel in his hair. "We'll keep the rentals on the down-low, back off for a while, keep it status quo. But about everything else? Just tell the truth—except the part about you setting it up to meet her there. We clear?"

"But who killed her?"

"Gianelli, for chrissake, who the hell *knows*?" Acker-man moved away, gesturing his dismissal. "Who the hell *cares*? Some crackhead, or homeless guy, some squatter in that house. The gods are smiling on us, right? What we needed to happen happened. And we didn't even have to get it done."

"I suppose," Aaron said.

"Frigging right. Sit tight. And hey, the cops were at the bank. Some detective, asking about—someone com-pletely different. Didn't even bring up the Liz thing."

"The cops?" Aaron's fleeting moment of reassurance vanished. *Cops.* Exactly what he worried about. "At the bank?"

"Are you deaf? That's my point. The cop didn't even mention her. Listen. Erase the whole thing from your memory. It never happened. It. Never. Happened. At best, you're the grieving boyfriend. Maybe her father will take you under his wing. Pretty nice wing, right? Now get back to work, bro."

Pretty nice wing. Aaron stayed on the bench, thought about this, calculating, as Ackerman walked away.

Maybe he was worrying for nothing?

Maybe.

A pigeon landed at his feet, pecking. Aaron watched the gray feathers, how they separated around the bird's pudgy neck, how his pointy bill kept pecking pecking pecking. Aaron couldn't even see any crumbs on the sidewalk. Bird was delusional. Maybe he was, too.

Because.

Because maybe Ackerman was lying to him. Maybe Ackerman was about to—Aaron leaned back on the bench, his shoulder blades hitting the hard wooden slats. Of freaking course. How could he be such a moron?

His head was about to explode, the people on the side-walk blurred as his brain focused, holy crap, on the trap he'd almost fallen into. He stood, pacing, crossed the street, leaned against the narrow concrete edging outside a men's store window, registering the foulard ties and Italian suit jackets but mostly his future, passing before his eyes.

How Ackerman, the asshole—*from the beginning an asshole, right?*—had once again steered him into a bad decision. The incredible jerk. Probably going back now, crowing that he'd duped old Aaron again, no one'd have to worry about him, all we had to do was wait.

Didn't know who killed Liz McDivitt? Who was he trying to fool? He planned to throw him, Aaron, right under a moving train. And right now was setting him up for the fall.

Aaron straightened, feeling the sun on his face, feeling his head clear, seeing the future unfolding in a new way. Smiling for the first time in he didn't know how long.

Aaron Gianelli was not about to be fooled. Aaron Gianelli was not the fall guy.

Tell the truth, Ackerman had instructed.

Exactly.

The freaking 100 percent truth. That's exactly what he would tell.

"I'm so sorry for your loss," Jane said. Stephanie, Liz McDivitt's secretary, knew Jane from yesterday's interview, so now they were old pals. "You must have worried when Miss McDivitt didn't come in this morning."

Stephanie shook her head. "Not really, you know? She'd been late before, we really didn't have a system." She glanced over her shoulder at the closed door to Liz's office. "She was new, you know. Her poor father."

"I know," Jane said. "Is he . . . ?"

"New York," Stephanie told her. "I hear."

"Must have been wonderful for her, working with her father." Jane could hardly ask whether they were involved in some kind of scheme. Time to simply fish and see what she caught. She was a reporter, after all. She'd report. She'd already sent TJ out on a little reconnaissance mission of his own. Might be a goose chase, might not.

Stephanie blinked. "I guess," she said. "He called her, I know, sometimes. But . . ."

Jane had a thought. "Have the police been here? Checked her office or anything?"

"Not that I know of." Stephanie seemed to be considering this. "Maybe they came before I got here this morning, though."

"Have you talked to her boyfriend?" Jane was happy to ask questions as long as this woman would answer. Maybe she could get her to tell the guy's name. "He must be devastated. Poor . . ."

"Yeah. Poor Aaron," Stephanie said. "They worked together on the REO stuff. He manages the empty houses, you know?"

Aaron. "Great guy, seemed like," Jane said, as if she knew it all along. She pulled out her notebook, studiously looking at a blank page. REOs, the properties the bank owned, the ones they'd foreclosed on. Jane knew all that from her foreclosure research. That's what Liz had told her, too, though it hadn't seemed significant at the time. "Aaron. I'm not sure I got the last name right."

"Gianelli? With a G?"

"Right." Bingo. Aaron Gianelli. *Got you.* Maybe he knew what Liz had been up to. Not that Jane would ask him directly. But the "mistakes" she'd heard about from Liz's clients—maybe Gianelli was involved in it, too. Whatever "it" was. Maybe Liz had told him about the bank's mistakes? Or maybe Aaron had told *her.* Did her father know?

"I'd love to talk with Aaron," Jane said. "About poor Liz. Is he here today?"

"He is, I think. Want me to bring you to—?" Stephanie

stood, lifting a pink cardigan from the back of her chair and wrapping it across her shoulders. Then she sat down again, the chair squeaking in protest. "I need to call him first. But it should be okay. Because it's Liz, after all."

Right, Jane didn't say. Because it's Liz.

Jane watched her punch buttons on the phone, waited as she navigated through explanations and inquiries.

"Okay, Mandy, I'll let her know he's out and that you'll give him the message. Like I said, Jane Ryland. From the *Register.* Her number is . . . ?" Stephanie looked up, eyebrows raised.

Jane gave her the cell number, instead of the *Register,* to make sure she didn't miss the call.

This Aaron Gianelli was about to be her new ally—or perhaps her new enemy. She needed to find out which.

Should he stop at Liz McDivitt's office before he left the bank? Just for show? Jake pushed the elevator button for floor 3. The cops were looking for a killer, after all, and it was reasonable there'd be evidence, clues, of some kind there. Maybe he should send in Crime Scene with a roll of yellow tape to seal the place.

But whatever was in Liz's office was already taken care of, the Supe's strategy session had assigned someone else to all that. Officer Canfield was also on the job, handling Liz's apartment. Even Bing Sherrey had an assignment. Jake's instructions would come soon, depending.

So while the McDivitt case progressed elsewhere, step by step, Jake was at the bank only to look into Gordon Thorley. He'd spent the last hour reading the mortgage records a harried PR flak, Colin Ackerman, finally agreed to provide—the same public paperwork available at the Registry of Deeds, Jake had insisted. He'd pulled out the old "I could get a warrant, but do you really want that?" routine.

Ackerman finally agreed, and all the better for Jake, even seemed in a big hurry to get out of the place. He'd left Jake in an opulent conference room, in the care of some prepped-out intern-looking kid who zoned out to whatever was on his earbuds the minute Jake tucked into the file. The documents had told the story. Part of it, at least.

Gordon Thorley's house in Sagamore was deeded to him and his sister, Doreen Thorley Rinker, the sister who'd hired the lawyer. It had tumbled into arrears, then foreclosure. But a few months ago, the checks started arriving, paid back in full and currently on time, and they'd bailed themselves out. Gordon Thorley's family had suddenly come into money. That was worth some investigation. Problem was, he couldn't question Gordon Thorley about it without alerting Peter Hardesty. *Lawyers*.

When the elevator doors opened on the third floor, he pushed the close button again. No need to scope out Liz McDivitt's office. But with an inch of space between the closing doors, he caught a glimpse of a desk in the hallway and a woman's back.

Jane. *Jane?*

The doors closed.

What was Jane doing at the bank? He stabbed the open button, almost without thinking, stabbed it again. But the elevator was already moving.

The doors opened, but at the bank's echoing lobby. Almost three thirty, a few tellers snapping rubber bands around wads of counted cash, one helping a white-haired woman who'd deposited three, no four, lumpy shopping bags on the tile floor and was shoveling rolls of paper-wrapped coins into a fabric pocketbook.

Jane was outside Liz McDivitt's office. Well, of course. She was covering this. They'd made McDivitt's name public a few hours ago.

Jake stood in the lobby, watching the customer lug her bags out the door, watching the tellers behind their cages, but thinking of Jane, and their crisscrossing lives. How they kept showing up at the same place, but never together. This time, if he waited, they could be together. There was only one row of elevators. Eventually Jane would have to appear. They could get everything out in the open.

He'd wait.

His pocket buzzed. A text. From Bing Sherrey. *SFSG*, it said. So far so good. Eager for his turn, Jake wondered how this would all unfold. If they could solve Liz McDivitt and Gordon Thorley? That'd be a good week's work. Big headlines about Lilac Sunday. The kind his grandfather never got to read.

He needed to dig into Grandpa's files again. He needed to read those articles he'd gotten from the newspaper archive guy. Where were the people Chrystal Peralta interviewed years ago? What might they know? He needed to track her down. He needed to call Peter Hardesty, insist on a meeting.

He sighed, watching the light go from red to green on the aluminum elevator doors, willing them to open. Willing Jane to step out, look at him, run to him.

They opened. Empty. They closed.

Too much to do. He couldn't wait.

"Bye, Jane," he whispered.

54

"**What does Detective** Brogan mean by this, Mr. Thorley?" It had taken Peter Hardesty an hour of the highest-level arm-twisting to arrange this jailhouse meeting. Now, after Brogan's phone call, Peter didn't feel like waiting for answers. "Your sister indicated you were both struggling financially. But bank documents show that the Sagamore house—the house you own jointly—is *not* in financial peril. In fact, someone recently bailed out the place."

Recently. As in, right before Thorley confessed. Peter's imagination did not have to try very hard to come up with explanations. But conjecture was a waste of time. He needed the truth.

Ignoring the question, Thorley swirled a white paper cup in front of him, the black coffee inside already staining the cheap low-bidder jailhouse paper cup. His skin had gone yellow-gray, even his hair looked drab, as if the swampy atmosphere of the jail cell had sucked all the color out of him. And the instinct to fight.

"You can listen to me or not," Peter said. "But I'm your lawyer. On your side. And my responsibility is—"

"Your damn responsibility is to do what I say." Thorley talked to the coffee cup. "So far you've sucked."

Thorley finally looked at Peter. Gave a hack of a cough, just one, cleared his throat. "All you've done is stall.

Opposite of what I want. I want to hurry the hell up, do my time, take the punishment. Get on with it. Maybe I should fire you."

"You can't fire me, because you didn't hire me, remember? And I talked to Doreen, only yesterday." Peter tried another tack, leaning forward across the table, extending his hands to bridge the gap. "Listen, Gordon? Did you get into your house by using the pansy pot key? I guess you remember your childhood, right? Doreen does, too. She almost cried when she thought of it. She's scared for you, Gordon. Your family wants you home. You know that, don't you? Do you really not love them back?"

Thorley took a sip of coffee, stared at the wall.

"All right. Let's try this, pure and simple." Peter crossed his arms across his chest. "The cops called me about those mortgage payments."

"So?"

"So this wasn't my discovery. It's theirs. You think the cops are going away?"

"So?"

"You can 'so' me all you like," Peter said, pointing at Thorley. "If you want to ignore me, your privilege. But the cops are not going away. Someone suddenly paid your mortgage, sir. You were in foreclosure. Now you're not."

"I don't live there," Thorley said. He knocked back the last of the coffee, crumpled the cup, looked for somewhere to throw it. No wastebaskets in the meeting rooms, Peter knew. Nothing an angry inmate could use as a weapon.

The crumpled cup stayed on the table. Thorley began to pick at its seam, peeling away a soggy layer of paper.

"I know you don't live there," Peter said. "But your family does."

"So?" Gordon sneered out the word. "You saw the place, right? You see she's not that desperate for cash, right? That big TV. She hired you, right? So Mr. Lawyer, why don't you—and the cops—ask *her* who paid the mortgage?"

"But—," Peter began. Doreen *had* seemed desperate. And she didn't seem to know about the rescued mortgage.

"Guard!" Thorley called out.

A face appeared at the door, the same cop who'd told Peter day before yesterday they called Thorley "the Confessor." "Yeah?"

"I'm done," Thorley said. "Get me outta here."

"They're all like this? The foreclosed houses?"

Jane stood, hands on hips, across the street from 310 Bentonville Street, pretending to be looking at the scenery with TJ. This split-level, with its two scrawny trees and sagging iron porch railing, was on the list of the foreclosed houses owned by Atlantic & Anchor bank, the REOs that she'd sent her photographer to scout.

If people were getting murdered in empty bank-owned homes, maybe there was something to be learned from the homes themselves. Who'd owned them, what they looked like inside, if there was some kind of connection. What if the bad guys—Aaron? Hardin McDivitt?—were renting out empty homes for use as, what, drug-dealing hideouts? Manufacturing meth? Prostitution? Jane's reporter brain could concoct a million ideas. What TJ had discovered wasn't any of those things.

What he discovered was—

"Yup, not empty," TJ said. "I didn't go up to the doors, but look. Cars, mail. Bikes. Curtains. People are living there. I got shots of all of the exteriors. Made a list. Like, ten of 'em. So far."

"You rock, Teege, thanks." Jane contemplated the house, the neighborhood, the puzzle. Pushing five in the afternoon, some kids played up the block, tossing a ball across the narrow street, playing Keep Away from a bounding black Newfie, their laughter and teasing half-comprehensible. A mom, or babysitter, maybe, sat on the porch steps watching, coffee mug in hand. Your typical neighborhood. Where people lived in houses that were supposed to be empty.

"On Waverly Road, where Shandra Newbury was found—just thinking out loud here," Jane said. "That house was empty. The deputies were cleaning it. And that first house, on Springvale Street, where Emily-Sue Ordway fell. Empty. Treesa Caramona, empty."

"Yeah," TJ said. "But Emily-Sue, that was an accident. The place was under renovation. Something broke."

"Yeah, okay. But Caramona. That wasn't an Atlantic & Anchor Bank house." Jane pursed her lips, calculating. "And where Liz McDivitt was—found. Not A&A either. But the ones I had you look up—"

"Are," TJ said.

"Are. So Emily-Sue and Shandra are connected. Maybe. And Liz and Caramona. Maybe."

"Maybe," TJ said. "Listen, is there anything else? If you're not going to solve three murders any time soon, I'm off at five."

"Oh, sorry Teege. I'm spacing," Jane said. "No, listen, go. Thanks. Download your video. I'll look at it when . . ." Her phone buzzed in her tote bag.

"Okay," TJ said. "See you back at the barn tomorrow."

She dug for her phone with one hand, waved TJ good-bye with the other. "Jane Ryland," she said.

"Miss Ryland? Colin Ackerman, from the bank?"

"Oh. Hi." What'd he want? Jane had given him her card, of course, but—

"You're looking for Aaron Gianelli? Might I ask why?"

Shoot. Naturally, the damn PR guy was gonna interfere.

"You know no one from the bank is allowed to speak

to the media"—Ackerman drew out the word—"without getting permission from me. You're aware of that, correct?"

"Well, sure. But in this case—" This was no biggie, she'd only wanted a reaction to Liz's death. Kind of. But that was her story now, and she was sticking to it. "You know he was friends with Elizabeth McDivitt," Jane went on.

"We are not commenting on that matter," Ackerman said. "The family has requested privacy. As you know."

"I only wanted a comment from him about—"

"As I said. Any comments come through me. Mr. Gianelli is not available. Anything else?"

Jane could picture Ackerman, that gelled hair and just-too-expensive tie. Weren't public relations people supposed to help the public relate? "There is, actually," Jane said. "Weirdest question of the day, I bet."

Jane took a last look at the house, headed for her car. Coda would be glad to see her, even though the cat always pretended Jane didn't exist. Peter had said he'd call about dinner. An intriguing prospect. Wonder what Jake was doing? She didn't care, if he didn't care what she was doing. And he didn't seem to.

"Weirdest? I doubt that," Ackerman said. "But try me."

Jane clicked open her car door, slid behind the wheel. "Okay. I'm wondering about the banks REOs," she said. She stared ahead, imagining she could see Ackerman's face.

Silence. Then, "What about them?"

"Do you ever rent them?"

"Do *I*—"

"You know what I mean. Does the *bank* ever rent them?"

"Why?"

Jane let the phone fall into her lap, annoyed. He didn't have to be so nasty about it. She picked it up again.

"We're looking into . . ." She paused, trying to figure out how to phrase it.

"No," he said. "We don't rent them."

Jane paused, calculating her next move. "So what would it mean if we've discovered—"

"We have a real estate agency, however, that does. Short term, of course. They do it for several banks. Why leave the homes empty? It's simply efficient business."

Jane's shoulders sagged. Not as exciting as drug-dealing meth-making prostitutes. But way more likely.

"Which agency?" Jane asked, because that's what a reporter would do. She saw her exciting exclusive evaporate in front of her. The agency was probably Mornay and Weldon, the company Shandra Newbury had worked for. Which is why she'd been at the house. *Bye-bye story.*

Silence.

"Mr. Ackerman?" It didn't matter, she guessed, but now she wanted to know.

"I can get that information for you in the morning, if you'll call me then," he finally said. "It's after five. We're closed."

And he hung up.

"Don't say a word." Ackerman's voice came through Aaron's cell phone. "Don't react, don't yell, don't freak out."

What the hell now? Aaron had spent at least half an hour walking the sweltering streets of Boston, finally winding up at the Pidge, a rathole of a bar down by the waterfront. A couple of construction workers, all canvas and sunburn, gave him the snake-eyed once-over—*outsider*—as he pulled up a bar stool. Some hockey game filled one big screen, and a black-and-white replay of a Celtics win on another.

He was three beers into it now, and had made and unmade his mind too many times to count. The beers weren't helping, and yet they were.

"I just talked to Jane Ryland," Ackerman went on. "You know who that is?"

"Queen a' Sheba?" Aaron said. The name sounded vaguely familiar, but he couldn't place it. Why was Ack making him guess? Say what he had to say.

"Where are you?" Ackerman's voice was a whisper.

"Can I guess again?" Aaron felt like laughing, for some reason.

"Shit. Listen. Gianelli. Jane Ryland is a reporter. She was calling you. *You*. And thank the bank employees' freaking handbook your Mindy or whatever her name is—"

"Mandy?" The assistant in his office. What was this about?

"Had the sense to call me instead of you. Listen up. Jane Ryland is a sneak and a liar. Like every reporter. She's at the *Register*. You know, Jane Ryland, the one who used to be on TV. She purported to be asking you about Liz McDivitt—bad enough, but that I could deal with. But then she asked about the REOs. Whether the bank rents them. How the hell did she—why is she asking about that?"

"How the frig do I know?" Aaron hunched over the bar now, one hand cupped over the phone, the other covering his face. The place stank of beer, and he probably did, too, and now—the bartender, a batter-faced bodybuilder with cheap tattoos and a once-white apron, swiped the bar in front of him with a striped towel and pointed, inquiringly, to Aaron's empty glass. "Sure," he said.

"Sure what?" Ackerman said.

"Not you," Aaron said. "What'd you tell her?"

"What d'you think I told her, asshole?" Ackerman said. "I'm the PR guy. I told her no comment. But it's not what I say that matters, it's what *you* say. Do not—I repeat—do not talk to her. Or to anyone else. Say it's bank policy, which has the added benefit of being the truth."

There was that truth thing again. Aaron smiled into his empty glass. Did Jane whoever really call? Or was Ackerman trying to prevent him from telling his side of the story? If Aaron didn't talk, it'd look like he was hiding something. Wouldn't it?

Aaron accepted the beer, his fourth? Fifth? Who cared. Toasted to his future. "My lips are frigging sealed," he said. Even though that was a lie.

"We'll take care of her," Ackerman said. "Reporting is a dangerous job. I'll call you when I know more."

And he was gone.

Aaron clicked off his dead phone, stared at the numerals on the keypad. This whole idea had seemed logical at the outset, easy to justify, the bank with so much money, him with so little. When Ackerman presented it, he'd made it feel reasonable, even brilliant. Certainly safe enough. But then, what happened to Lizzie—that was horrible. Like, horrible. And Ackerman was behind it. Waverly Road, too. And the other one. Now he was threatening some reporter? A little tinkering with bank finances, that was one thing.

But—his mind could hardly face the concept. Murder. And he was going to get blamed. Ackerman always talked about "we." Who the hell was *we*?

Him and Ack, he guessed. Some "we."

Aaron saw how the bartender's towel had streaked the bar, ran his finger through the residue, left a trail that disappeared.

It had gone too far. It had. He'd already decided what to do.

Question was—right now? Or later?

Maybe later. After one more beer.

55

Jane turned off the shower, listening. Was that her door buzzer? She paused, hair dripping, yanked back the map of the world shower curtain, listened again. Coda, balanced on the bathroom sink, was passionately licking the condensing water off the mirror. Cat was nuts. And, yes. The buzzer.

Someone at her front door at nine at night? Not Peter. He'd called, saying something had come up—seemed to be a pattern, but who was she to judge. And truth be told, she was looking forward to a night at home. A little TV, a little nuked baked potato and broccoli, a glass of wine. Tomorrow, she'd follow up on the not-empty house situation. And Sandoval.

She grabbed her fluffy terry-cloth robe, slipped on her black flip-flops, and flapped down the hall. Maybe it was Margot from downstairs, bringing her restaurant's leftovers? Or Neena, her building manager, with some condo news. If it was some kind of salesperson, she'd—whatever.

She buzzed the intercom.

"Yes?"

"It's me," the voice said.

Jake.

"Is everything okay?" she said. Silly question, but she

was so surprised it was him. Last person she'd expected. Funny to think so, after all they'd—

"Sure," his voice bristled over the intercom. "Janey? Can I come up? Can we talk? Okay?"

And of course it was okay, this was their lives, the push-pull of responsibility and desire, like two poles of a magnet, repelling and attracting, but physically unable to undo what nature, or something, had designed.

Wine for two. Pretzels and reasonable cheese, Jake on the wing chair. Jane on the couch. Small talk, small talk. She yanked the belt of her robe tighter as she tucked herself into the corner.

"Thing is." Jake took a sip of wine, then put his glass on the coffee table. Picked it up, swiped away the ring, replaced it on a napkin.

"Sorry," he said.

"No problem," Jane said.

Silence.

She laughed. "We're really communicating, huh?"

"I'm tired of it," Jake said.

Jane closed her robe tighter, even though it couldn't go tighter. Was this the end of their—whatever it was? Was this why he'd canceled Bermuda? Now he was telling her the truth? Saying good-bye? "Tired? Of what?"

"Pretending. Calling you 'Miss Ryland.' Ignoring you in court this morning. At Sandoval."

"Why'd you—?" Jane began.

"Let me finish, or I won't, okay?" Jake interrupted, smiling.

"Okay," she said. Felt weird to be in a bathrobe, towel over her shoulders. Hair wet. Vulnerable, kind of, with Jake all dressed still in his sport coat and oxford shirt. He'd left his court tie on—the one she'd given him, blue like the Bermuda sky, she'd told him—though he'd yanked it open at the neck. He needed a shave, and maybe a haircut, but it was all she could do not to get up and—but she wouldn't. Not now.

He leaned forward in the chair, elbows on his knees, hands clasped in front of him. "I'm tired of having to be so careful. I mean, what if we admitted it? Told the Supe, told your boss? Victoria?"

"Marcotte." What he proposed—was *proposing,* she almost laughed when the word came to mind—was impossible. Wasn't it? She took a sip of wine, the last sip in her glass. Two glasses, she could handle that. Even though she was starving. She sliced off some cheese, balanced it on a cracker. Took a bite. Stalling.

"Marcotte." Jake reached over, poured more wine. "Just consider it. Would they really fire you?"

Jane held the remnant of cheese on her cracker, one tiny crumb falling onto the couch. How was she supposed to answer that? It wasn't really about whether she'd be fired, it was about the reality of this conversation. Their truth.

Stalling. She took a sip of wine, the soft red wrapping itself around her food-deprived brain.

A noise. *What?* The door buzzer.

Jake stood, smoothing down his jacket. He eyed her robe, her hair, her bare feet. "Expecting someone?" he said.

She stood, making sure of the terry-cloth belt. Now what? "Grand Central," she said. "And—no."

He gestured toward the intercom. "Better check."

She pushed the button, baffled. "Yes?"

"It's me," the voice said. "Peter."

That's why Jane had been so nervous. Jake watched her at the apartment door, finger on the intercom. "Peter?" *Peter Hardesty?* That's why she kept looking at the mantel clock. Drinking her wine so quickly. Fussing with her robe. At least she wasn't wearing a *towel*. She'd been waiting for Peter Hardesty. Which explained why she'd refused to look at him at the Sandoval hearing. Which proved Jake had been right the first time.

"Ah, Peter?" She put one hand on the doorjamb, leaning toward the intercom. Jake couldn't see her face.

Pretending she hadn't expected him? Jake slugged down the last of his Cabernet, clattered it back on the table. No matter how tonight's ridiculous encounter ended, there was no way for him to leave without Hardesty seeing him. Unless he hid in the bedroom. He snorted, laughing. Like some TV sitcom. On TV, interloper Hardesty would discover the hiding Jake, the laugh track increasing, when the guy carried Jane to her bedroom. Dumb cop, ha-ha, finally going for it, getting the guffaws when the fancy lawyer shows up.

But this was real life, and the personal shit was about to hit the fan. Jake's own fault, really. For stopping by. For assuming Jane would be alone, and available, while he'd gone to D.C. Seemed like Jane had quickly found alternative plans.

"It's not a good time," Jane was saying. She turned to Jake, eyes wide, put up a palm. *Hang on.* "I'm in my—in for the night."

"My apologies," the voice said. "Just took a chance."

Peter Hardesty, no question. It appeared all three of them had secrets.

Jake took a deep breath. Was he overreacting? Jane had every right to see whoever she wanted, he was just surprised, and well, disappointed, that she'd—but now she seemed to be sending the guy away.

"We'll talk tomorrow, then, Jane," Hardesty's voice was all business, Jake had to admit, not like a disappointed suitor. "I'll leave a package by the mailboxes, okay?"

"Package?" Jane said. She looked at Jake, shrugging. *No idea.*

"No big deal," Hardesty said. "Talk to you tomorrow. Thanks."

"Thanks."

Jane turned back to Jake, leaned against the door as the intercom went silent. She clasped her hands under her chin, wincing. "Well," she said. "That was awkward."

What on earth was Peter doing? Why had the irony gods instructed him to show up right when Jake was saying—whatever he was saying?

"Don't you want to get the package?" Jake hadn't sat in the chair again, clearly he was on the verge of leaving. Which she didn't, *didn't* want to happen.

"I'm sure it's nothing. It's probably about the Sandoval case we're working to—" She paused, trying to assess whether she'd said too much.

"I saw you in court today," Jake said. Still standing. "Why wouldn't you look at me?"

"Why wouldn't you look at *me*?" Jane said. She sat on the couch again. Maybe if she went back to status quo, he'd take the cue.

"Jake?"

He sat, but all the way at the other end of the couch. Arms crossed. "The Sandoval case is confidential. Sorry."

"So what else is new, right?" Jane had to keep him talking, find out what was wrong. "We're all about confidential, right? But if we can't trust each other, who can we trust?"

Jake gave a half-shrug. "Maybe Peter Hardesty?"

"Yeah, interesting, huh?" At least he was changing the subject, had picked up his wine. *Good.* "How about that Gordon Thorley? He pulls out a *knife,* I go to the cop shop with—"

"Peter Hardesty," Jake said. "Imagine. You two seem to have quite the late-night thing."

Jane frowned. Felt her shoulders slump. Thing? Where was Jake going with this? "Well, he's the lawyer for Gordon Thorley, sure. And also the lawyer for Elliot Sandoval. So it makes sense that—hey. What do you mean, 'late night'?"

She watched Jake finish his wine, consider it, pour another glass. His third, if she was counting, and she was of course, which is how she knew she'd only had two glasses herself. Or so. Why was he suddenly interested in Peter Hardesty?

"Late night? Jake? Come on, you don't really think—"

Jake raised an eyebrow. "I leave town. For the job. I miss you. I call you. You're not here. And where are you? In the middle of the night? At Hardesty's house. And one of you is wearing a towel."

Jane stood, hands on hips. Mouth open. "Jacob Dellacort Brogan, you are such a big—" She scratched her head, trying to decide what he was. "I can't decide whether to be bullshit angry, or, or—"

She shook her head, sat down right next to him. "You're jealous. You are so cute when you're jealous. Come on, Jake. We were about to jet off into the sunset, and you think I'd—"

"Well . . ."

"Ha. You're blushing. I love it." Jane poked him in the arm. So that's what this all was about. She held up three fingers, girl scout. "It's all business," she said. "Like your oh-so-whirlwind 'trip to D.C.' was all business, right?"

"It *was,* if you'd let me—"

"So why didn't you—"

"The Sandoval arrest."

Oh. Jane thought this through. Maybe *she* was the jealous one?

"Okay. Okay," she said. "Truce? No more D.C. cracks,

but no more ridiculous Peter Hardesty stuff. It's completely business."

Jake raised his glass. *Deal.*

"Deal," Jane continued. "Now, Mr. Jealous, shall we start over? I'm still packed, you know."

"Maybe try on that bathing suit?" Jake was finally smiling. "Now?"

"You wish, buddy," Jane said. "So. Speaking of your trip to Washington." Something in her brain was working hard, and she struggled to let it complete its task. "You were supposedly researching false confessions."

"I *was*," Jake interrupted. "And you said—"

"Okay, okay, I couldn't resist. But so was Peter Hardesty," Jane went on. "Did Elliot Sandoval confess to someth—no. Not Sandoval. So Gordon Thorley? Confessed? To what?"

"Jane?" Jake studied the red of his wine, then turned to her. "What you said about trust. Let me ask you something. Can you keep a secret?"

56

It felt great to tell her. Jake hadn't discussed the possibilities with anyone. Not the Supe, not DeLuca, not even his grandmother, because they had stakes in it, and what if he was missing something or on the wrong track? But he was close. He was sure of it. Jane had promised the Peter thing was all in his imagination. Someone you—*love*—you have to trust. Even if it was complicated.

And Jane was the perfect sounding board. Her reporter instincts were on the money, almost coplike. He thought about those airport lilacs, wilting in the backseat of his car. Wished he had thought to bring her new ones.

"You have the Lilac Sunday killer?" Jane's eyes went wide, she'd moved to the edge of the couch, crossed her bare legs, carefully closing that thick white robe over them. "I wasn't in Boston when it happened, but Chrystal Peralta was just talking about it. And your grandfather was in charge? That I didn't know."

Jake watched her process the whole thing, the cold case, his grandfather, the girl's family, the looming anniversary, the confession. The parole board's controversial decision to let Thorley out after serving most of his robbery sentence. The murder of Treesa Caramona, which might prove Thorley was guilty. Or not.

"Now, his mortgage payments at A&A are up to date," Jake said. "He owns a home in Sagamore, with his sister, and it was almost in foreclosure. Now it isn't. Hey. You were working on that foreclosure story. Anything I haven't considered?"

Jane stared at him, her body still except for one foot, snapping the bottom of her black flip-flop.

"A&A Bank," Jane said.

"Yeah."

The flip-flop snapped again.

"You know Liz McDivitt," Jane finally said.

"Yeah," Jake said. Risky ground here. "I know of her."

"Well, listen. I may know what happened. And the change in Gordon Thorley's mortgage may be connected to her. I didn't see his name listed, but—"

Jake couldn't read her expression now, except to see her brain going a mile a minute. He stood, came to the couch, sat down next to her, one cushion away. He could still smell her grapefruit shampoo and something like peppermint and lemons and summer.

"*Listed?* Gordon Thorley connected to Liz McDivitt?" Jake said. "Jane? How?"

Jane was shaking her head, droplets of water from her wet hair sprinkling the navy leather of her couch. She swiped them off with a corner of the towel, one by one.

"Now I have to ask *you*." Jane draped the towel around her neck again, and looked him square in the eyes. "Now that we're confessing to each other. Now that we're trusting each other. Now that we're trying out our new—relationship."

She eyed her empty glass. Put it down.

"Ask me what?" Jake said.

"Can *you* keep a secret?"

* * *

Jane told him as much as she knew, the Gantrys, the Detwylers, and the Rutherfords. And now—Gordon Thorley, too?

"If the bank made 'mistakes' on the mortgages, they'll have the Banking Commission and the Justice Department and the Comptroller of the Currency and the Attorney General fighting to see who could nail them first. It'll be at least a major-league scandal, possibly the end of Atlantic & Anchor. End of Hardin McDivitt, that's for sure. Liz's father. So then maybe, somehow—ah . . ."

She shrugged.

"Liz McDivitt," Jake said.

"Yeah."

"Did those people, Miss McDivitt's customers, mention anyone else's names?" Jake asked.

Such a cop. Here it was almost midnight, the wine gone, the street sounds fading, Jane still starving, the cheese and crackers down to crumbs and crumbles.

"Nope," she said. "But—"

Jake was thumbing something into his phone, *such a cop*—and Jane knew a line had been crossed, they'd crossed it together, sharing things they shouldn't. But clearly they both had information about the same stories, and clearly there were threads that connected them. It was frustrating not to know how, or which ones, or who would know.

Chrystal Peralta, Jane thought. She might have a whole list of clients. Maybe other notes she hadn't given Jane, or that Jane couldn't decipher. Chrystal seemed knowledgeable about Lilac Sunday, too. She paused, tucking that away.

What if Jake caught the Lilac Sunday killer?

"Honey?" Jake had put away his cell and moved closer to her on the couch, now touching her still-damp hair, moving it away from her neck. He traced the edge of her ear with one finger. "Can we stop talking business now?"

"Hmm?" With his touch, somehow, the long-ago cases and the search for headlines, the swirl of possibilities and the potential bad guys and the stakes of being a reporter and—whatever—it all fell away. They couldn't figure out the answers tonight. There was only Jake, and her, and midnight, and they were alone.

She turned to him, agreeing, accepting, wanting—the terry cloth opened, and the belt seemed to loosen, who was doing that? Someone's wineglass tipped, rolled on to the carpet, it didn't matter, there was only—

Jake's phone buzzed. Buzzed again.

"Never mind, never mind," she said. "You were saying . . ."

Jake stopped. She could feel the difference in his muscles, in his skin, in the sound of his breath. She closed her eyes, letting go.

"It's okay. Answer it," she said. She'd have done the same thing. She had answered her front door, two hours ago, when Peter buzzed.

Jake kept his arm around her shoulders, she didn't try to move it, and she leaned with him as he took the cell from his jacket pocket. He turned the screen so she couldn't see it.

She felt his arm slip away as he stood.

"Jane. Honey." He held the BlackBerry in one hand, the other he held out to her. "I have to go."

"Why? Did something—"

He shook his head, the picture of regret, but she didn't care, it would never change. "I can't say."

Jane rewrapped her robe, tied the belt in the tightest knot she could. She smiled, had to, what else was there to do about reality?

"You want to live this way?" she said.

"What other way is there?" Jake said. "I'm sorry, Janey. I have to go."

And he was up, and over, and out, and gone.

A minute later, less, thirty seconds, the downstairs buzzer rang.

"It's Jake." His voice came over the speaker.

A wash of relief, of desire, of joy, she felt it to the back of her neck and in her suddenly tightening heart. He was back. She buzzed, not saying a word, heard the opening of the outside door, heard his footsteps on the landing, on the way to her.

He appeared, her Jake, and there were—flowers?

"Your 'package,' I assume." Jake said. "From Peter Hardesty."

He handed her the bouquet of white roses, wrapped in pink tissue paper, tied at the bottom with a trailing lavender ribbon.

"Business," he said. "I see. Have a nice life, Jane."

He turned, and was gone again.

57

Open season, **Jane** thought. New day. Square one. *Have a nice life?*

She yanked her Audi into third and powered up the Mass Pike, top down, hair blowing and caution to the winds. In about fifteen minutes this morning, semi-hangover notwithstanding, she'd finished the silly bank customer service story on her home computer (leaving out Liz McDivitt, sadly, but including quotes from the officious Colin Ackerman) and zapped it off to the news desk, making her Friday deadline and checking that dumb assignment off her list. Maybe she should put *Jake* in her rearview.

And why had Peter brought her flowers, anyway? The card said "thank you," whatever that meant. Maybe an apology for almost getting her killed. Or missing their not-date. Which was either adorable or ridiculous. She'd have to deal with that. And with her whole life. Somehow.

By the time she got to the Pike's Cambridge exit, she'd considered and discarded the idea of going blond. Through the toll booth, considered and discarded the idea of leaving town, maybe moving to D.C.? Hang out with her friend Amy. Or even going home to Oak Park and starting over.

Starting over. A person could do that, right? Passing the Prudential exit, she made her final decision. No. Her life was in Boston, and here she'd stay. She'd make the best of it. Make it work.

She punched up her phone. Time to start making it work.

"Hey, Chrystal?" Rats. Impossible to hear with the top down. "It's Jane Ryland. But hang on a sec, okay?"

Jane swerved to the South Station exit, spotted a parking spot outside the Federal Reserve. Banged into reverse, did the parallel park in one try. "One more second." She aimed her voice at the speaker.

She wouldn't be here long enough to have to feed the meter. She hit the UP button for the top, decided for the hundredth time that it should say DOWN, and waited, briefly, as the black canvas descended, with a whump, over her. Finally, quiet enough to hear.

"I'm sorry to disturb you," Jane began again. "I know you're sick."

"No problem." Chrystal's voice came over the speaker, then another sneeze.

"*So* sorry. I know this is rude. But I finished the bank story, so that's all set, okay?"

"You hear about Liz McDivitt?" Chrystal asked. "Incredibly disturbing."

"I know," Jane said. "It's awful. I kind of feel—but no, nothing new. Anyway, quick question. You know that list of bank customers you had? In your notebook? I couldn't read them all, and was wondering, does the name Gordon Thorley sound familiar? Or anyone Thorley? Was it on your list?"

Jane heard only silence.

"I know a Gordon Thorley," Chrystal finally said. "I covered his parole hearing, a million years ago. He was one of the last cons to get paroled, remember? Before the new law-and-order regime? Oh, right, you weren't here.

But anyway, yeah. Armed robbery, he was in for. It was a big deal—" She sneezed again. "When he got out. They fired the parole board chairman."

Jane tried to envision a calendar, tried to make a time-line. A car pulled up next to her, window down, seemed to be inquiring about the parking spot. Jane waved him off, *sorry, not leaving.*

"Was Thorley in prison on Lilac Sunday?" Jane asked. "When that girl was killed?"

"No, the armed robbery was after that." Chrystal's voice had changed. "What're you really asking, Jane?"

"Huh? I'm losing you," Jane made some scratching noises on the phone, hoping they didn't sound too fake, moved away from the speaker. She didn't want to share with Chrystal. She needed Chrystal to share with *her.*

"About Liz's customer list," Jane said. "It was a little difficult to read. You have quite the handwriting, you know? Anyway, was Gordon Thorley's name on it?"

"No," Chrystal said. "It wasn't. But listen, if you've got something on Thorley, you should let me know. I covered that."

"I will," Jane lied. Better nip this in the bud. "Hope you're feeling better soon, Chrystal. Thanks so much."

She clicked off, hands on the steering wheel, looking out the windshield. Into the oncoming traffic, and into possibilities. What if Gordon Thorley had killed Carley Marie Schaefer, then gone to prison for something else? No wonder they couldn't find the bad guy. He'd gotten paroled, and then, a few years later, confessed. The cops had let him go—because of Peter? And then, according to Jake, he'd confessed to killing Treesa Caramona.

The Lilac Sunday killer had walked into the police station, confessed, and the cops had freed him to kill again. Is that why Peter showed up at her door? Had the legal system and the cops combined to release a murderer? No wonder Jake was distracted.

She cranked the ignition.

If Jake was blowing her off, *have a nice life?* Did that release her from their "I won't tell if you won't" deal? Talk about starting over. Did the truth ever trump off-the-record? This was the story of the century.

He had two hours, Jake calculated as he turned off the Pike at Exit 17, before the next session at the police station. The Supe was playing it close to the vest, but clearly there'd been a break. That was the phone call that had taken him from Jane last night. Not what they'd expected, not at all, but certainly good enough. The guy they had in the Superintendent's side office meant the Liz McDivitt case was about to blow wide open. But nothing Jake could do, right now, to make it happen any faster. He turned right, sneaking through the yellow light, wished DeLuca was back in town. He'd love this. Now Jake could use this time to work on the Thorley case.

He rolled down the cruiser window, assessing the tiny brick one-story on a side street in Newtonville. The street's centerline was painted green, white, and red instead of yellow, a testament to the passionate Italian heritage of this neighborhood, called the Lake.

Tramping up the front walk to Chrystal Peralta's house, he realized he could have simply called her, but he wanted to show her the articles in person. The Peraltas were a big name in the Lake, another of those random facts in Jake's head. A ceramic doorplate, green vines and purple grapes, promised BENVENUTO. The paper'd told him she was out sick, so fifty-fifty she was at home.

"Who is it?" A voice came through the dark green front door, female.

"Chrystal Peralta? Jake Brogan. Boston Police." He felt

like a salesman, trapped on the front stoop. A salesman holding out a badge wallet.

She pulled open the door, one hand on the doorjamb, didn't invite him in. Gave him an up-and-down, frowning. She didn't look that sick, except for that wild hair and faded orange tracksuit.

"Yeah, I see who you are, Detective. Is something wrong?"

"No, no, nothing," Jake said. "Don't mean to upset you, and I know you're—"

Peralta sneezed, and Jake took a step back. Maybe he didn't want to go in, after all.

"Bless you," he said. "Anyway, if you have a minute? I'd like to ask you about these articles from the *Register*." He flapped open his leather portfolio, showed her the top copy, one of her Carley Marie Schaefer stories. "For instance, in this story—"

"Are you kidding me?" she said. "That was twenty years ago."

"I know. But we're following up now." Jake pointed to the names as he talked. "I'm looking for these people, this one, and this one, all the ones you interviewed at the scene. The ones who were there when the body was found. I can't track them down, not any of them. Do you—and I know it's a long shot—possibly still have their contact information?"

Chrystal's laughter stopped only when she had a coughing fit, doubling over, somewhat over-dramatically, Jake decided. She straightened, wiping her red-rimmed eyes. Her hair had gotten even crazier.

"I'm so sorry," she said. She clamped a be-ringed hand to her chest. "Best laugh I've had all day. That was twenty—freakin'—sorry, officer, darn." She rolled her eyes, apparently making sure Jake understood she was being sarcastic. "Twenty years ago. Even if I wanted to help you—which, I must say in the interest of journalism, I don't, since I don't really appreciate being questioned by a cop. Forgive me, *police detective*. But even if I wanted to help you, no way I have those notes. Now can I go back to my VapoRub?"

Jake waited. Let the sarcasm fade. "We're investigating a death," he said.

She took a deep breath, shook her head. "Poor Carley Marie. Okay?" she said. "Now if you'll excuse me—"

"I saw you wrote the Gordon Thorley parole stories, too," he said.

She eyed him again, up and down. He held his ground, hoping she didn't sneeze again. She took a step closer.

"Carley Marie. Lilac Sunday. Hey. Two and two together, you're saying you like Gordon Thorley for Lilac Sunday?" she said. "There's a lot of that going around, Detective. If you wanna talk about *that,* well, come on in. *Benvenuto.*"

Jake stayed where he was. Of course she'd ask, but time to call a halt to this line of questioning. "Miss Peralta? We've arrested Thorley for Treesa Caramona, as you know."

"Oh, right." Her head tilted. "Detective? What's going on?"

"You wrote about Gary Lee Smith." Jake flipped the pages of the articles, ignoring her question. "The parole officer? Who testified at Thorley's hearing?"

Chrystal moved her hand to the knob and began closing the door. "I see now. *Cops.* All alike. If you'll excuse me? We're done here."

Jake put his foot in the door.

"I can get a warrant," he lied. Whatever Chrystal thought he was asking, she knew something she wasn't telling. Something she was unhappy about. He'd been a cop long enough to read that, and take advantage of it. "But look. As you like to say. Off the record. Between us."

He paused. "And I'll owe you."

Chrystal chewed her bottom lip, holding the door tight against his foot. "I cannot believe you'd ask me about this, about Gary Smith," she said. "You're telling me you never had a 'relationship' with a source?"

Did she know? Jane would never—even if she'd dumped him for Hardesty?—this woman had to be fishing. He called her bluff, ignored the question. Waited.

"Okay, we had an aff—well, a thing," Chrystal finally said. "I spent forever covering those damn parole hearings, we got to know each other. What can I say? He was a pal of Eddie Walsh, and I used to get some juicy stuff from him. We all have sources, right? Some closer than others?"

"And?" Bluffing. *Chrystal and Smith.* Another puzzle piece. Edward Walsh was the parole board chairman, the one some said was scapegoated in the criticism over Thorley's parole.

"And nothing. Gary's dead. Car accident. I last saw him—a couple of months ago, maybe six? And yes, he'd kept up with Gordon Thorley, that what you're asking? They'd, I don't know, their lives were connected. Eddie'd got the axe over Thorley, but remember, Gary had argued to let him out. Kinda like Gary and Thorley were a team. They'd bonded over the release, and sports, baseball, something like that. Thorley'd been out for a while, when—well, it was a shock. The cancer diagnosis. We used to talk about it—before Gary, well. Died."

"Gordon Thorley? Has cancer?" That was the headline from this. As Jane would say.

"Bad," Chrystal said. "Sucks, doesn't it? You get a reprieve from the parole board, then a couple of years later, you get a death sentence from mother nature. And you still owe me, Detective. Don't think I'll forget."

She shut the door, the click of the lock closing the case. *And there it was.*

Thorley is gravely ill.

He confesses to a cold case murder.

His family's mortgage is suddenly paid.

A reason for a false confession Jake never considered. A reason he hadn't read in any of Nate Frasca's files.

A bribed one. Had Liz McDivitt—or her father—made that happen? Why?

Jake slid into the driver's seat, plugging possible candidates into the bad guy role as the real Lilac Sunday killer. Gary Lee Smith? That could be.

Or maybe Liz McDivitt's father? Someone else at the bank? Someone had strong-armed Gordon Thorley. Someone who had the inside track on Thorley's family finances. Question was who.

Was that person waiting, right now, in the Superintendent's office?

58

The phone. **Jane** was so immersed in the articles Archive Gus gave her—the exact ones Jake had requested, thank you so much—she'd lost track of everything. Two in the afternoon. Starving.

Even though she was mad at him, Jake had sworn her to secrecy about Lilac Sunday. Even though he was obviously pissed at her, and as a result she wasn't the happiest person herself, there was no way she could break that promise.

However.

"Off the record" didn't stop Jane from doing some research on her own, and what if she came to the same conclusion? Trying to finagle a way to get the Thorley story without involving Jake, she'd pitched Marcotte a Lilac Sunday update, a retrospective. She would follow up on Chrystal's original reporting, she'd told Marcotte, find some of the witnesses she'd talked to back then. And Marcotte was all for it.

Jane had to give Chrystal credit—she'd done a great job on the coverage, all those exclusive interviews. Jane knew the Carley Marie murder was a big deal, but hadn't realized how big. Jake's grandfather, the commissioner, seemed like a sincerely devoted guy.

The phone rang again. *Starving.*

"Jane Ryland." She opened her desk drawer, searched for her stash of crackers.

"Miss Ryland? This is Brian Turiello."

Jane racked her mental Rolodex. Brian Turi—who? *No idea.*

"Brian—?" Ah. Wheat Thins. But she needed two hands to open the box.

"Turiello," he said. "Colin Ackerman from the bank asked me to call you. I'm with Mornay and Weldon, the real estate company that handles the REO rentals for the bank. He said you had a question?"

Mornay and Weldon. Mornay and Weldon. Why did that sound familiar? Jane put down the cracker box, willed her brain to retrieve the reason. Oh. Shandra Newbury. Shandra Newbury, found dead in a foreclosed house. She'd worked for Mornay and Weldon, the agency that rented it. Did that matter?

"Oh, yes, thank you so much," Jane stalled. She'd asked Ackerman about that in passing. But now that she had this real estate guy on the phone, might there be a story here? Maybe about the Sandoval case?

"I'm so sorry for your loss of Shandra Newbury," Jane began. "You worked with her?"

Turyellow—was that right? she should have written it down—didn't answer. Oops. Maybe she shouldn't have brought up his murdered colleague.

"I'm sorry," she went on, regretting she'd upset him. She put down the Wheat Thins, focusing. "How do you spell your name?"

Where was her notebook? She wrote "Turiello" on her desk calendar as he spelled it.

"We continue to mourn the loss of Miss Newbury," Turiello said. "But back to the foreclosed homes. If you're interested in that, as a story, it's really quite fascinating. A win-win, you know? People who need homes can live in them until they're sold. As a result, they're maintained, and property values are not affected. Happy to chat with you about it in person, if you're interested."

Not so win-win for the foreclosed people, Jane didn't say.

"Do you deal with Aaron Gianelli at the bank?" Jane went on. Actually, this was all fitting together nicely. Maybe she could still get a quote from Aaron, maybe she could meet him through this—she checked her note—Turiello.

"Ah," Turiello seemed to be pondering her question. "I see you're researching this."

Might as well try to impress him. "Yes, we have a list of all the bank's REOs. We're looking now to see how many of them have been rented, and who lives there, and how that all works. For a possible story."

She'd made it up on the fly, but now she'd convinced herself. Not a bad idea. "So yes, Mr. Turiello, I've love to come interview you about this. When is convenient?"

She could hear murmuring on his end of the line, papers rustling.

"Surprising about Elliot Sandoval," Jane said, thinking of foreclosures. "Being released."

"Indeed."

Everything Jane brought up, this guy sounded annoyed. Should she apologize?

"I was only—," she began.

"Maybe we could meet. Perhaps at one of our available empty homes, Miss Ryland," Turiello interrupted. "We could show you around, let you get the whole picture."

Jane almost burst out laughing. Not a chance on the planet. After what happened to Shandra Newbury, and Liz McDivitt? Going into an empty foreclosed house? No matter who was escorting her, that was so not going to happen.

"Thanks," Jane said. "But I don't want to inconvenience you. And certainly, if the story progresses, maybe then?"

She had another thought. One which might make it safe. Safer. "When the time comes, I could bring my photographer."

A reporter's best weapon, the photographer. The one with the camera. If it looks like someone's coming to haul off and hit me, Jane had always instructed, make sure you're rolling. And lies on video were preserved forever.

Turiello was conferring with someone else again. "Miss Ryland?" he said. "What if you simply came to our office this evening? No photographer. What time is good for you?"

Peter arrived at the jail in record time. Jake Brogan had called, saying they had to talk about Gordon Thorley.

"Had to talk" was often police shorthand for "make a deal." Maybe Brogan had been assigned to feel him out.

Ironic that Peter's career success, and Jake Brogan's career success, depended on exactly the same question: was Gordon Thorley telling the truth about Lilac Sunday? There was only one truth. Both their jobs required they find it.

It took half a frustrating hour to battle through security to sign in, and an uncomfortable stint in a hotbox of a waiting room before he got to see his client.

Gordon Thorley sat like a handcuffed shadow in his metal chair, two empty coffee cups and a can of ginger ale in front of him and a scowl on his face. Could he have gotten even thinner? His dank hair plastered to his narrow skull, his cheekbones even more hollow than Peter'd remembered. If he were here much longer, Peter would get him sent to the infirmary. Petition the court if he had to. Thorley was not thriving in lockup. Who would?

Elliot Sandoval had told him he'd taken a two-hour shower, trying to wash off the memories. Now he and MaryLou's lives were on hold. But at least they were on hold on the outside.

"Thank you for coming on such short notice," Jake Brogan said. He gestured Peter to a folding chair. "Mr. Thorley, with your permission, I'm going to lay out some things."

"I'd prefer you and I did this alone, prior to including my client," Peter began. He could not let Thorley respond to whatever Brogan was about to say. What's more, he'd feel a hell of a lot more comfortable if he knew what it was before this cop sprang it on his client.

"Trust me on this, Hardesty, okay?" the detective said. "I know it's against your nature."

"I reserve the right to stop you at any moment." Peter put his briefcase, a brown canvas barrier, between them. "Mr. Thorley, I instruct you not to say a word. Detective? We clear?"

Brogan nodded.

"You have the floor," Peter said.

I could just head for the frigging hills, Aaron thought. He'd been waiting in this office for hours now. Way too long. He eyed the door. Closed. Was he a guest? Or a prisoner? What if he tried to leave? He rose from the leather armchair, briefly wondering who'd sat there before, and what'd happened to them.

Someone had recently vacuumed, he could tell from the stripes on the tan wall-to-wall. He went to the window, pulled back the heavy curtains, seeing the still-sunny day. People winding through the parking lot. People who knew where they were going. Unlike him.

He'd made the first move. He'd taken control. Now he had to see what'd happen next.

First to talk, first to walk. At least that's what they said on the cop shows.

He held his cell phone, his lifeline, turned it over and over in his hand. They let him keep it, admonishing him not to call or text anyone, not to answer it, to let calls go to voice mail until they got back. They were "checking on things," they said. Checking his story most likely. They probably had the room bugged, on closed circuit, were probably watching him this very minute. Seeing if he'd call anyone. He turned, did a three-sixty, scanning the curved molding that edged the ceiling, looking for little cameras. Let them watch. He'd do as they said. He was here to play ball.

He paced to the door, ten steps, then back to the chair. Ten steps. What was their deal? Letting him sit here, freaking out? Not even a newspaper, or water, alone with his own racing brain and his own fraying nerves.

His phone rang, and he reached for it. Maybe they had—but no. He closed his eyes, clenched his teeth, ignored it, as instructed. The caller ID read *Ackerman*.

It rang again. He dropped into the chair, legs stretched in front of him, head against the padded upholstery, letting go. It rang again. Aaron Gianelli would win this one.

The call went to voice mail. And the room went silent.

59

"Let's start with the money," Jake said. "Mr. Thorley—"

"Don't say a word, Gordon," Hardesty interrupted. "Brogan, I'm warning you."

"No need," Jake said. "Hear me out. Mr. Thorley, we know about the mortgage payments. I assume your lawyer told you that."

Thorley sat, motionless, in the BPD interrogation room. Blinked once, that was it.

"I told him," Hardesty said.

"And, sir? We know how sick you are."

Hardesty stood, his metal chair screeching as it slid on the linoleum floor, almost tipped over. "How *sick*?"

"I see," Jake said. "Yeah. Mr. Hardesty, we have it confirmed, by the Department of Correction. I know this is difficult, Mr. Thorley, and I'm sorry—your client's been diagnosed with a particularly unfortunate type of lung cancer. Diagnosed a little more than a year ago. When I talked to your new parole officer, he called Mr. Thorley 'poor guy.' That's what he meant, I suppose."

Hardesty looked at Thorley. "True?"

Thorley shrugged, *got me*. In that one defeated motion, a dismissal of Jake, and Hardesty, and the world.

Hardesty turned away, scratching the back of his head. Paused, then turned back to Jake.

"I'm not clear where you're going with this, Brogan. This whole discussion is—irregular. I'm on the verge of cutting it off. Since my client did not divulge any illness, and since medical records are confidential, there was no way for me to find out. Only individual parole officers have access to the records, only they know the status of their parolees' health, and they're not allowed to discuss it."

He yanked the chair back into place. "Fine time for Arsenault to play by the book."

Jake nodded. Arsenault, Thorley's current parole officer. Worth noting that Hardesty was in the dark about this. Thorley had actively kept it secret, which meant it was important. Jake would propose his theory, and see if anyone bit.

"Cutting to the chase, Mr. Thorley. I'm unclear on how much your attorney knows about whatever is going on, but I urge you to tell us the truth. If someone paid your family's mortgage to convince you to confess to a murder you didn't commit—well, let's put it this way. That's not going to fly. Because I can find out. And I will. And it won't work."

Jake waited, his words dissolving into silence. Gordon Thorley was clearly not the Lilac Sunday killer. But he certainly knew who was. If he decided to tell, Jake's next risky tactic—asking a question he didn't know the answer to—would pay off. Big time.

Thorley seemed fascinated by the pitted metal of the interrogation room table.

"Hardesty?" Jake said. "You know about any of this?"

Rubbing his forehead with his fingertips, Hardesty was silent. Finally looked at Jake. "News to me," he said.

"So let me ask you, specifically, Mr. Thorley," Jake persisted. "Who killed Carley Marie Schaefer?"

"Don't answer," Hardesty put out both palms, stopping him. "Brogan, you know that's crossing the line."

"I did," Thorley said. "I killed her."

* * *

Six o'clock was just over three hours from now. That gave Jane plenty of time to dig into the Lilac Sunday story. Mornay and Weldon offices were open until eight, but Turiello told her business slacked off early evening until the after-dinner browsers of homes took over. So, around six, he said, they could have a bit of "alone time" together.

Meanwhile, Thorley. Had Jane actually been attacked by the Lilac Sunday killer? Had Peter *known* that? Good thing Thorley was in custody now. Not that it happened in time to help his latest victim, Treesa Caramona. The nightside reporter on the story said Caramona was a street person, no address, no family, no obvious connections. Why'd Thorley kill *her*?

The whole story was full of dead ends. Not one of the original witnesses Chrystal Peralta had interviewed was findable. Not a trace of them. Frustrated, Jane had called Chrystal again, but her call had gone to voice mail.

Back to the archived articles. Was there anyone else she could contact? Jane read about Thorley's armed robbery arrest, and his subsequent parole years later. The testimony, the controversy. Some stuff that appeared to be the sports pages. Maybe they'd been copied wrong? A big article on Sheriff Edward Walsh, made head of the parole board. Maybe he'd have some insight into the guy? But parole records were all confidential, except for the hearings themselves, and they were recorded on minicassette tapes that took weeks to obtain. Probably no one even had a machine to play them anymore. Talk about dead ends.

Still, if Thorley was arrested for Treesa Caramona, that'd be a good news peg. Jane could find Edward Walsh, and ask him about—*wait*.

If Thorley was guilty, that meant four years ago or so,

Parole Board Chairman Edward Walsh had released the Lilac Sunday killer.

A killer Jake's grandfather had been unable to track down. A killer the source of Jake's preoccupation.

A killer now in custody for murdering someone else.

Hell of a story. How could she confirm it?

Jane finally attacked the innards of the Wheat Thins' unopenable packaging with her teeth, ripping the plastic and spilling the crackers down her front, leaving a trail of salt on her black T-shirt. Annoyed, she moved her chair and heard a crunch under the wheels. The cleaning people would love her.

Her phone rang again. *Jake?* But of course it wouldn't be. He was probably convinced she was seeing Peter Hardesty. Ridiculous. But she had to stop thinking about Jake. *"Have a nice life"?* She stood up, brushed off the crumbs. A couple of the crackers had fallen on her desk, leaving greasy patches on her calendar and note pad.

"Hello? I mean." She shook her head, swallowed. She was so focused on Jake she'd forgotten how to answer the phone. "Jane Ryland."

"Jane? It's Elliot Sandoval."

"Oh, hey, hello, how're you doing?" Certainly doing better than while he was in custody. She leaned forward in her chair, hearing more crackers get pulverized under the wheels.

"Fine," he said. "Calling to ask—have you talked to Peter Hardesty? Did he mention interviewing me?"

Peter. Last night flooded back. Peter's arrival. Jake. The roses. They hadn't talked at all. Peter hadn't called this morning, no surprise. She hadn't called him, either, not exactly knowing how to handle the flowers.

"No, Mr. Sandoval," she said. "I think Mr. Hardesty tried to get in touch with me, but—well, what's up? You okay?"

"Sure," Sandoval said. "Here's the thing. Peter and I,

we—well, we're so glad for what you've done for me, and MaryLou, and it looks like we've found a house, you know? He suggests you'd like to see it with us, this afternoon, maybe? Make it a part of our story. Life goes on, all that. You've played such a big role in this."

Aww. That was simply—nice. Reporters hardly ever got credit for anything, except making trouble, and here was this guy sincerely grateful for what she'd done. Not that she'd really done anything, but maybe it felt that way to him. He was out of jail, after all. What a terrific element for her story. Talk about exclusive.

"Sounds great. With you, and MaryLou? And Mr. Hardesty?" *Awk*ward. She'd have to figure out what to say to him. "I've got an appointment at six, but it's only—" She checked her computer monitor. "Two forty-five."

"We're on the way there now, if that's convenient," Elliot said. "It's forty-fifteen Rawson Avenue."

Where was her notebook? Jane jotted down the address on her desk blotter, calculating. "Can I bring my photographer?"

Sandoval seemed to be thinking. "Well, I didn't ask Peter about that. Can we—like, talk about it when you get here?"

"Sure," Jane said. She could roll some video on her cell phone if need be. It wasn't like she was on TV anymore. "See you in thirty or so. And Mr. Sandoval? Thanks."

"Don't thank me," he said. "This is all you."

60

"You did not," Jake said. "You did not kill Carley Marie Schaefer, Mr. Thorley. You could not have done it."

Jake unzipped his briefcase, pulled out an accordion file envelope, untied the dark red string, flapped open the cover. He drew out his grandfather's file, opened it. Had he found the truth in those pages from the past? Time had no guideposts in the BPD interrogation room, no clock, no computer, no window; no reckoning except the timelines of the stories that unfolded here.

"Could not have—how do you know that?" Hardesty said. "*Brady* rule, Detective. If you've got exculpatory evidence, you're required by law to provide it."

Thorley picked up his ginger ale can, sloshed it back and forth, maybe checking how much was left. Put it down.

"You'll have it, Hardesty," Jake said. "Mr. Thorley, let me ask you. Did you know my grandfather was the police commissioner? Back when Carley Marie Schaefer was killed?"

"So?"

Jake saw Hardesty roll his eyes. Guy must be a pain to represent. Sullen, unresponsive. Insisting he was guilty.

"So this. Commissioner Brogan kept an extensive file

of the investigation of the Carley Marie Schaefer murder. The commissioner vowed to find her killer, but—"

"And now he has," Thorley said.

"Gordon, I'm not kidding," Hardesty said.

"You could be right," Jake said. "He has."

"What?" Hardesty stood again.

Jake flipped through the paperwork, pulled out a page of tiny square photos, the junior class of Attleboro high school, class of 1995. He pointed. "Second from the right, second row down. Junior class. You see? Read the names at the bottom."

He held out the photo, Hardesty took it from him.

"Carley Marie," the lawyer said.

"Exactly. So, Mr. Thorley, early on you told us you 'had a thing' with her. She was in high school. But you were 'older.' "

Jake pulled out another folder, drew out another page of pictures. "And look, here you are. G Thorley, in your baseball jersey, on a page of the *senior* class. 'Older.' Yes, you were. And a baseball star. Before you took to armed robbery, I guess."

"See? Everything I said was true. This proves it."

"Well, here's the thing. On the night of the murder, Lilac Sunday, the Attleboro Eagles had a big game. Which you—varsity pitcher, in the rotation that night—would not have missed. And didn't."

Jake pulled out a photo, black-and-white, a blurry image of an extended leg, an arm with leather glove on one hand, and umpire making the unmistakable "out" sign.

"You probably don't have to read the caption," Jake said. "You made the big out. Go Bombardiers."

Hardesty was shaking his head, dismissive. "All very dramatic, Brogan," he said. "But Carley Marie was probably killed overnight, we all know that. Some baseball game, historic as it apparently was, would have long been over."

"True," Jake said. "Except for—well, Mr. Thorley? You want to tell us? Or shall I show your attorney your get-out-of-jail card?"

"My—?"

"Or shall I say, your 'I was in jail' card. All you crazy kids got plastered after that game, trashed the locker room and the coach's car, and spent the night in the Attleboro lockup. Here's the police report. Here the story from the paper the next day. No names in it, you were juveniles, but this morning I called a retired Attleboro cop. He remembered the whole deal."

"Let me see that," Hardesty said.

"It's easier to tell a lie if part of it's true. There's not so much to remember, right?" Jake said. "You and Carley Marie were in high school together. That was true. But maybe that was all. Question was, who else would have known that? Who told you what to do and what to say? If you don't answer me—it doesn't matter. Because I already know."

Peter held the police report in one hand, the blurry copy of the news story in the other. Dated 1994, a stilted but unmistakable account of the "rambunctious in victory" varsity baseball team who'd stolen a case of Pabst Blue Ribbon from someone's parents' house and "caroused" through the school and the parking lot. "Authorities report the students' parents insisted they should be taught a lesson, and were kept in the city lockup overnight. School officials are considering whether graduation should . . ."

"Hardesty? Your client's lie won't work," Brogan was saying. "I'll give you the benefit of the doubt here, that you didn't know. If he gives up the real story, right now, it'll make things much easier. I'm sure you can explain that to him."

There was a first. He agreed with a cop. He and Jake Brogan—who'd been acting like he had some kind of chip on his shoulder—were now in this together, on the same side. And now, flipping their usual roles, it was the cop who apparently had evidence his client was not guilty.

"Mr. Thorley," Peter began. "Detective Brogan is right."

Peter paused, letting that sink in. He was sure Brogan's face registered the irony for an instant. "If you're doing this for your family—whatever it is you're doing, whoever it is you're covering for—they'd rather have you home. They'd rather have you be the good guy. You helped them keep their house, maybe. But however you think you're working that, whatever someone promised you, your sister will be haunted forever, thinking that the Lilac Sunday killer is her brother. You're trying to help them by branding yourself as a murderer? Is that what you want?"

Brogan had taken out the photo of Carley Marie again. Showed it to him, then to his client. "And what about Carley Marie's family?" Brogan said. "You can be the hero, Thorley. The hero. Not the villain."

Jake's cell phone vibrated against his jacket pocket.

Damn. He hit OFF. Focused on Thorley. An icicle of sweat had started, down the side of the suspect's cheek. He'd swiped it away with the back of one hand. Thorley's orange jump suit, county issue, wilted on his narrow shoulders.

Jake had one more card—at least—to play.

"We're not done, Thorley," Jake said. He checked with Hardesty, his unlikely new ally. Got a nod, *go ahead.*

"The only one who'd pay an innocent person to

confess to a crime is the person who actually did it," Jake said.

"So we need to know—," Hardesty began.

"Hang on," Jake interrupted. He pulled up a chair, as close to Thorley as he could get. Opened his grandfather's files. *Grandpa's notes.* And they'd led Jake to the answers. Commissioner Brogan helped solve this case after all. Jake would tell Gramma later, when Lilac Sunday was finally closed.

"Mr. Thorley," Jake continued. "Showing you this photo of the baseball game again."

"So?" Thorley didn't look up. "I've seen it."

"Who threw you that ball?"

"How do I know?"

"Let me refresh your recollection, then," Jake said. His phone buzzed again.

Dammit. He punched it off. "It appears my grandfather had talked to some students at Attleboro High. Here's a list of their names, and I found every one of them in the yearbook. The principal's there, his name is crossed off, apparently he must have had a good alibi, too. There's also this name." Jake put the paper down. Pointed.

Hardesty stood, leaned over the table.

"Gary Lee Smith?" Hardesty said.

"Ring a bell?" Jake said. "Who was Gary Lee Smith, Mr. Thorley?"

"Parole officer. You know that." Thorley mumbled the words, aimed them at the floor.

"Correct. Went off to play minor league ball, got cut, became a parole officer. Your first parole officer, specifically, the one who argued for your release at the parole board. The one who died in the car accident. The one who—well, let's let your lawyer see for himself." He handed Hardesty the yearbook photo.

"The—," Hardesty began.

"Catcher," Jake said. "The guy who threw you that

ball. But he was in jail with you, too, the night of the murder. Couldn't have killed Carley Marie, either. Maybe he knew her? But the Commissioner crossed him off his list, because Smith was in jail, too. With you. He couldn't have known how you'd be connected with him again, all those years later."

Thorley didn't speak. He sat so still Jake checked, briefly, to see if his sunken chest was moving. Finally one of Thorley's hands, flat on the gray metal table, curled slowly into a fist. Then, just as slowly, uncurled.

"Gary Lee Smith argued for your release," Jake said. "And his boss, parole board chairman Edward Walsh, agreed. Lost his job over it. But eventually, as your parole officer, and your pal, Smith found out you were dying. Was that what made you the perfect fall guy? You'd confess, you'd get your family's house back, you'd die. Who came to you with that deal?"

Jake leaned in close to Thorley, tried not to breathe the scent of bleach and cigarettes and fear.

"Who killed Carley Marie?" Jake kept his voice still, still as the room.

"You *know* this." Hardesty's voice, almost reverent.

"It's over," Jake said. "Just tell us. Who killed her?"

"I don't know," Thorley said. "I. Don't. Know."

He looked up, his eyes widening at the reality.

He'd confessed.

61

Tucked at the end of a cul-de-sac, the house seemed nice enough, though Jane could tell it was definitely a fixer-upper. Crumbling front steps. All the windows, even on the garage door, boarded up with plywood. Yet with some carpentry and construction, this place could be renovated. And of course, construction and renovation were Elliot's specialties.

Jane sat in the front seat of her car, waiting for the Sandovals to meet her there. Just past three fifteen, but everyone was late in Boston's Friday afternoon traffic. With the baby so close, it must be such a relief that Elliot was released. Bummer, though, that the DA hadn't given evidence. Would have been interesting to know what they had on him. If anything.

Jane checked her messages. Nothing from the Sandovals. Nothing from Chrystal, either, on the Lilac Sunday witness names. Nothing from Jake. Nothing from Peter, though she'd see him with the Sandovals, at least, in a minute. Where was everyone?

A light went on inside the house. Didn't it? Hard to tell, with the glare of the sun. Yes, there. Movement behind an upstairs curtain. Were they already there? Maybe their car was in the garage? She was an idiot. *She* was the one who was late. *Dummy.*

She grabbed her bag, crossed the street, trotted up the broken flagstone path. The justice system had worked for the Sandovals, Jane thought. And she was about to share the results.

Three steps, two and a half, to the front door. A doorbell hung, dead, from two blue wires.

She knocked. Waited. Knocked again.

What the hell was taking so fricking long? Aaron had paced this office in police HQ so many times, he knew it was ten steps from the window to the door. The closed but not locked door. He'd opened it long enough to see the uniform in the hallway, a stubby guy who scowled at him, hand hovering over his weapon, as he quickly closed the door again.

Aaron had made his first move, calling police headquarters, almost at midnight. Arrived this morning, well, afternoon actually, after he slept off the night before. A cop named Sherrey had taken his statement. Aaron told Sherrey he knew who'd killed Liz McDivitt. And would give them the name if they made a deal.

Above my pay grade, the cop had said. But I'll check with the boss.

That was freaking hours ago.

Christ. You'd think they'd send in the freaking cavalry. Didn't they want to solve this? His ace in the hole, the insurance for the soon-to-be-deal, was the threat Ackerman had made about that reporter.

Better hope nothing happened to her in the time they'd kept him waiting. Wouldn't be his fault if—

The door opened. A big guy, obviously the boss, came into the room first, striding like a drill sergeant. An old drill sergeant. Aaron recognized him from TV, Francis Rivera, the ex-Marine police superintendent. Sherrey, the chubby weasel who'd taken his statement. A woman in cop uniform, then a preppy guy in a sport coat and jeans.

"I'm Jake Brogan," the preppy one said. "Detective Jake Brogan. Sorry we kept you waiting, sir, I was dealing with an—incident."

Aaron tried to gauge how to play this. What "incident" would be more important than solving a murder? But fine. Whatever.

"I know who killed Lizzie McDivitt," Aaron said.

"So you said. Detective Sherrey has filled me in," the detective said. "Sit down, Mr. Gianelli. Just to clarify? Tell me from the beginning."

This was the moment, Aaron knew, when the deal went down. He'd tell them all about Ackerman, but only after he got immunity in the rental scam. He'd go over what he'd already said, fine. But he wouldn't sit down. They were standing, he'd stand. He'd stand tall.

"I know who killed Lizzie McDivitt. The person as much as told me they were gonna do it. In fact, at one point, I was potentially, *unwillingly*"—he'd already revealed this, so guess no harm in saying it again—"semi-involved."

"Like I told you, Brogan. With the chocolate stuff," Sherrey said.

"Exactly," Aaron said. At least they were listening. "That's what brought me here. I *know* what's gonna happen. That person is going to blame *me*, and hell if I'm gonna let that go down. There's a bunch of other stuff, too. I'm sure you know the Waverly Road murder? The one in the empty house? I know about that, too. All connected."

Brogan looked at Sherrey. Sherrey looked at the superintendent. The superintendent looked at Brogan.

How about that, big guys? Aaron hadn't told them that part before. Now they had to play ball.

Brogan took out his cell phone—a BlackBerry, what was this, 1990? Checked the screen. Clicked it off.

"Mr. Gianelli?" the detective said. "Look. We're not dumb TV cops, Aaron. We know the only way you could know for sure who killed Liz McDivitt is if you killed her yourself. What's more, and it's corroborated by forensic tests on Miss McDivitt, we found rohypnol in her system. As well as traces of chocolate chip."

Brogan nodded to Sherrey, who started fussing with something on his belt, then came toward him.

"Aaron Gianelli," Brogan was saying. "You are now under arrest for—"

What was going on here? This was not going according to his script. And the chief was obviously trying not to smile, which was ridiculous. Asshole.

"—the murder of Elizabeth McDivitt. And for the murder of Shandra Newbury. You have the right to remain silent . . ."

Aaron's head exploded, totally. He barely heard the words coming out of that cop's mouth, barely felt the handcuffs click around his wrist. Holy freaking—he'd come there to tell them the truth, that he knew—he guessed he knew—Ackerman had killed Shandra Newbury, somehow, *and* that teenager in the Springvale Street house, the one the idiot cops decided was an accident.

Now they thought *he*—killed—?

"No way, no way," he said. He wrestled himself away from Sherrey, would have punched the guy, but his hands were—*cuffed?* "I don't wanna be silent! Kidding me? I trusted you! I came here to tell *you*—"

"Do you know how many times this kind of thing happens?" The big guy, Superintendent whoever, was talking, all patronizing. Leaning against the desk, like he owned the place. "Moke like you comes in here, guilty as hell, tries to throw another poor slob under the bus. They think we'll let 'em off their pissant drug charge, something like that, if they rat out a pal. Suckers."

"Thing is, Mr. Gianelli," Brogan said. "It has to be *true*."

"You can't just make shit up." Sherrey leaned toward him, one hand on his arm, whispering.

"It's not made up, that's—that's—" Aaron looked at the ceiling, looked at the floor, looked at the ceiling. And now he had nothing, no leverage, if he told, he'd have nothing to trade. "That's crap."

And suddenly, the answer. The freaking fabulous answer, the reason the cops were idiots and the reason Aaron was about to leave and walk free and if that reporter got killed, who cared, it was their fault for being idiots.

"I couldn't have killed Shandra Newbury," he said. He mustered all the venom he could, imagined himself winning a big fat lawsuit, maybe, for false arrest and whatever else there was, screw 'em. "I have an alibi. A big honking alibi. I was with someone that night. I was—"

And then, all the air went out of him, and the room almost went black, he swore it did, the shapes of the cops faded, along with his future. He sank into the chair, his cuffs hitting the padded upholstery behind him.

"Alibi?"

Brogan was actually smiling now, not trying to hide it. What a complete jerk.

"Yeah. Crap. I was with Lizzie McDivitt the night Shandra Newbury was killed."

Brogan shook his head. "That sucks."

"Sucks," Sherrey said.

"Sucks," the chief said.

"Listen, listen," Aaron said. He had to make this work. "It's Colin Ackerman, okay? You know? The guy from the bank. It's him, all him, and I don't know, someone he works with, all I know is Brian. Brian something, he'd never tell me. It was all about the rentals, the damn rentals." Aaron was talking as fast as he could, the words tumbling out, one track of his brain wondering about calling a lawyer, the other track panicking, having to tell, having to get away. He was trapped and about to be nailed for a murder. *Two murders!* That he hadn't done.

"The rentals." The Superintendent was scratching his bald head, all dramatic, like he didn't understand the word.

"We were *renting* bank *properties,* you know?" Aaron couldn't stop talking, needed to make them understand. "Ackerman's deal, totally, I was only a—so what, you know? But then Emily-Sue showed up, that girl, and found out, she was in the Springvale Street house when the construction guy was there, and—Ackerman told me they took care of it. I don't know. I don't know what they did, I don't know what that means, I'm only a—and Shandra, too, she found out—"

"We know," Brogan said.

"Yeah," Sherrey said.

"Okay then fine, fine, so find Ackerman, ask him, I'll testify, I'll do anything, I'll find out who Brian is, I'll wear a wire. I didn't kill Shandra Newbury, couldn't have, because I was with Lizzie McDivitt, and now she can't tell you it's true because she's frigging dead."

"Or not," Lizzie said.

62

Jane waited, knocked on the door again. Heard nothing. Shrugging, she tried the door knob. It turned.

Was anyone actually inside? She'd seen a light, but that could have been on a timer or something. Now she was making up reasons, but—

Her phone rang. "Jane Ryland."

"It's Elliot," the voice said. "I have you on speaker."

Jane craned her neck. Saw a shadow at the window.

"We thought we heard knocking. We're ripping off wallpaper, right in the midst of it, and it's hard to stop the steam machine."

More movement. Maybe it was the steam thing. Her neck hurt from looking up.

"That's a tough job," she said. "Do you want me to—"

"The door's open, right? Come on in. We're upstairs."

"Okay, Thorley, it's you and me now." Peter Hardesty sat toe-to-toe across from his client—his not-guilty client. Brogan had gotten some kind of crisis call, left them alone. A cadet had brought Thorley another can of ginger ale, Peter had a cup of bad coffee. He'd turned their metal chairs so their backs were to the mirrored window, just in case. It was lawyer-client now. Private. Time for the truth.

"I need answers," Peter said. "Legally, you've recanted your confession, so that whole charade is over. The mortgage payments, the house, that whole thing—done. But you could go to jail anyway. You're still guilty of obstruction of justice, providing false testimony, and no doubt a litany of other illegalities. You want to see daylight again before you die? See your family? Your house? You need to tell us who convinced you to confess to a murder you didn't commit."

The fluorescent lights buzzed, and one, with a snap, flashed, and popped to black.

"Walsh." Thorley stared him down for a moment, defiant.

"The parole board chairman. The one who set you free." Peter tried to make the pieces fit. The parole board chairman had power, but an entire board had to vote to release a prisoner. "But it couldn't have been a quid pro quo—a deal."

"Uh-uh. No." Thorley was shaking his head, looked authentically dismayed. "My release was all on the up and up. Fair and square. God knows I'd worked for it. Deserved it. Turned out Walsh kept a watch on all the parolees' health records. Guess he had access to them all," Thorley said. "Seemed like he'd shopped for a—I don't know."

"Shopped for a sick person? A dying person? Someone who had nothing to lose?"

Thorley shrugged. "I was released back in 2010. Then last December? They called me, told me they knew my family was in trouble. I was told to confess, that there wouldn't be any evidence to prove it wasn't me. I was dying anyway. If I did what they said? The Cape house mortgage would be paid for, the back payments, and every month on time till it was all paid off. If I didn't—my family would never get to keep the house. They'd make sure."

"How did they—?"

"If I didn't play ball?" Thorley put up a palm, stopping Peter's question, "They'd revoke my parole. Put me back in. Said it wouldn't be hard to do."

"Gary Lee Smith told you." A guess, but based on what Jake Brogan had uncovered, it made sense. "The parole officer. Your friend. The catcher. Talk about playing ball."

"Yeah." Thorley coughed, wiped his mouth with the back of his hand. "What did I have to lose? I was out, but long enough to see I'd never fit in. Long enough to see the Cape house again. Long enough to finally do something good for my family."

"How'd you know what to say? The details of the crime? Didn't you figure—this must be the person who did it? Or know who did?" That gave Peter an idea. A very intriguing idea. He'd wait, though.

"I always wondered if it was Walsh, you know?" Thorley made a breathy half-sound, almost a laugh. "He was a county sheriff back then, big shot, maybe knew Carley Marie's family, maybe knew her. But hell, he was never arrested, so maybe it wasn't him. He got rich being a 'consultant,' whatever that means. Guess it means money."

"Was Walsh the one who locked you all up that night? As kids? Did he even know about that?"

"Nope, that was the Attleboro cops. And they'd sealed our case, Gary and I knew that. But Sheriff Walsh—he was fired as parole commissioner, you know? At least he didn't get a death sentence. Like I did."

"Did Walsh ever tell you he did it? Killed Carley Marie?"

"Nope. But he had that Treesa Caramona killed. She was another of Walsh's parolees, had like, Hep C. Bad. That I *do* know. Guess that was so I could confess again, prove it was me. So now what?" Thorley said. "You need me to testify, better hurry the hell up, right? I don't have long."

"You'll have to go back into lockup," Peter said. "Let me see what I can do."

"Like it matters," Thorley said.

"It matters," Peter said.

Jake almost started laughing. The look on this moron's face was beyond priceless. The woman standing at the office door provided the proof that Aaron Gianelli, dupe extraordinaire, was not involved in Liz McDivitt's death. He'd truly believed she was dead.

Jake knew she wasn't.

So did the others on the Supe's hastily organized task force. It had been the Supe's idea to pretend Liz had met her fate and see who came out of the woodwork afterward. The *real* bad guy would know Liz was not dead, because he—or she—had not shown up that night to kill her. What came out of the woodwork was a rat.

"Hey, Aaron," Liz said.

"But—you—they—" Aaron stood, slowly. Closed his eyes tight, then opened them again.

"Yeah," she said. "I'm really here."

"Where to start?" said Jake pleasantly. "Ms. McDivitt came to us, terrified. She brought a chocolate pastry she'd taken, suspected it was drugged—you gave her those, right?—and the paperwork proving that you and your colleagues were covertly renting bank property and keeping the money. Why was she afraid? She'd heard you talk about Waverly Road, my friend. She worried she was next."

Some smart lawyer in the DA's office would have to assess how many laws this all broke. Jake hoped it was a shitload, including bank robbery, fraud, and larceny. Conspiracy. And accessory to murder.

They'd nailed most of their case. With Liz safely in hiding and Jake holding off the press after Officer Canfield revealed the Supe's plans to him that night on the Kenilworth porch, Sherrey had done a blast-canvas of the homes on the list Liz had provided, found those college students, pulled the leases. Canfield followed the money.

What they didn't have—was the brains behind it. And behind the murder of Shandra Newbury. And the set-up of Liz McDivitt.

"But you'd agreed to meet me on Kenilworth Street." Aaron's voice had thinned, as if he was not quite sure he was talking to a real person.

"Nice," Liz said. "So you *knew* they were coming to kill me? After you got me to go there alone?"

Jake couldn't imagine how the guy would get out of that one.

"Got to admit, that's a tough question," Jake said.

"Toughie," Sherrey said.

"Lizzie, I—" Aaron sank into the chair.

"Lucky I had the cops there with me. But Aaron. *Why* didn't the killer show up?" she asked. "Whoever it was? You told them I would be there, you got me there. Why didn't they show up to kill me?"

"I don't know!" Aaron's voice went up an octave, then went silent.

Jake smiled. The Supe smiled. Even Sherrey smiled.

Aaron Gianelli had just confessed.

"Good boy." The Superintendent raised his bulk from the desk, lumbered to the door. "Miss McDivitt, my gratitude. You're a brave woman. Want to come with me now? I'm off to make a phone call to your father. Officer Canfield, you, too—Miss McDivitt has certainly gotten used to your company these last twenty hours. Detective Brogan? You know what to do."

* * *

What to do? *What to do?* What the hell were they gonna do? Aaron's arms were hurting, the cuffs pulling them back, and he was going to throw up, this was incredibly— Lizzie was alive?

How could that even be? But she'd been all smiley, standing by that cop, like she just came from a meeting or something, instead of from—where the hell had she been?

How could that be?

Was this a good thing, or a bad thing, or—the whole world was so screwed up, he didn't even know what was real. They'd put all over the news that she was dead. How could they put something on TV that wasn't true?

"Mr. Gianelli." Brogan was talking again. Aaron couldn't stand it. He was an idiot to have come here. To have trusted them. To have thought he could make a deal.

He felt a prickling along his scalp, the simmerings of an idea. He could feel the sweat soaking the back of his shirt, under his collar. One last idea. One last way he could close a deal.

He'd given them Ackerman, he'd given them Brian, whoever that was. But he knew one more thing.

"I'm ready to make a deal." He cleared his throat, tried to find his voice, tried to get the old Aaron back. "A deal. One time only, one chance."

"I'm afraid you've lost your deal-making ability, Mr. Gianelli," Brogan said. "But what the hey. Try me."

"You give me immunity, I give you Ackerman's next victim."

Sherrey yanked him to his feet, put his face so close he could see the veins in his eyes, the cords on his neck. "I'll give *you*—"

"Hey!" Aaron pulled away, didn't get far. These guys were such *jerks*. "You can't do that!"

"Thank you, Detective," Brogan said.

The guy let go. Aaron shook out his shoulders. "So. Deal?"

"Gianelli," Brogan said. "Let me put it to you once. And only once. If you know who Ackerman's next victim is, tell me now. Right effing now. This is your chance. Or, and trust me on this. You will never see the light of day again."

In the movies, someone would arrive to save him, bursting through the door, or there'd be an earthquake, or aliens. An explosion, or a meteor. Aaron hoped, yearned, with his very soul that any of those, or all of those, would happen right here. He had no way out. No way, except to offer this one piece of information. His lifeline.

"It's some reporter. It's, uh—" *Damn.* Aaron needed to remember her name, but his brain was fried. He'd stall, thinking of it. "They were asking about the empty houses, asking abou—wait. Ackerman called me. I bet it's on voice mail. My phone is—"

Sherrey was patting him down, all hands, grabbed Aaron's cell phone. "Tell me the code. Do it. Now."

Aaron told him, and in seconds, a voice buzzed through the speaker.

"I got a call from Turiello," the phone voice whispered. Clatter and noise in the background.

"Ackerman," Aaron mouthed the name.

Brogan took a step closer, narrowing his eyes, leaning in to hear.

"That reporter?" Ackerman's voice said. "He called her. She knows, Gianelli. She knows. She asked about you, and the houses, and Shandra Newbury, she even asked about fricking Sandoval! How the hell did she know what he did? Where are you, anyway? Call me. I am not kid—do not say a word to anyone. She calls you? You call me. Instantly. She's done."

"Shit," Aaron said. Brogan was frowning. How could

Aaron predict what was on the message? "How was I supposed to know he wouldn't say the reporter's name?"

"You *asshole*." Brogan turned away, ignored him, frantically typing into his BlackBerry.

"Hey! I'm not an—" Aaron didn't have to stand for—

"Hell yes, you are." Brogan yanked open the door. "He didn't need to say her name, you *asshole*. I already know it."

And he was gone.

63

The door swung open into an empty living room, its motion causing dust balls and random empty-house flotsam to puff up into the air and down again. Jane paused, hand on the knob, looking around, hearing what must be the wallpaper steamer upstairs. Someone was playing the radio, too. So perfect, that Elliot and MaryLou got to be together for now. Maybe, if Peter was successful, they could start a new life.

The light in the room was strange, the windows in the front boarded, dark, but the last of the afternoon sunlight still beaming through what would be the dining room windows. No furniture, but stacks of wood and construction stuff, boxes and nails and coiled electrical cords. The power must be on, Jane figured, since they were using the machine upstairs.

"Hel-lo?" she called out. She left the door open behind her, took a few steps inside. Peered up the stairs, took another step across a tiled entryway. "Anyone?"

They probably couldn't hear her over the steamer.

Footsteps. MaryLou, in a billowy gray tank top, baggy jeans, and sneakers, held on to the banister as she waddled toward her.

"Hey, Jane," she said. "How d'you like it?" She waved a palm toward the living room.

"Nice," Jane said. "Sorry I'm late, but—"

"Well, tiny snag in the interview plans," MaryLou said. She puffed out a breath, held a palm against her stomach. "I'm feeling pretty—awful, you know? From the steam, I guess. Now Elliot wants me to go home. I mean, back to my sister's. He was going to take me, but then he got a call from—" She stopped.

"Me, huh?" Jane said. That was wrong, though. Elliot had called *her*.

"I told him I was fine," MaryLou was saying, "but—"

From outside, a car horn honked. Through the open door, Jane saw a silver car pulling up to the curb.

"My sister," MaryLou said. "Can you talk to Elliot without me? He'll be done in a few minutes. Once you start that job, you can't stop, you know?" She paused, flinched, held her stomach again.

"Are you okay?" In a flash, Jane pictured EMTs, ambulances, the baby born in an empty—

"Fine," MaryLou said. "No worries."

"I'll walk out with you," Jane said. She dropped her tote bag on the floor of the house, it was safe here, no need to lug it outside with her. Elliot could wait. And she still had time before the Turiello meeting. Lady with a baby came first.

"Find me Elliot Sandoval," Jake said to Sherrey as they ran toward the BPD parking garage. "Call his sister-in-law. Get the damn parole office, right now. Find out where his last call-in was from. Where he is now, if freaking parole even knows. The judge was *supposed* to put him on a bracelet. That was the *deal*. *Damn* it."

How would the bad guys get Jane? Where? Who? He'd called her, instantly, to warn her. But she hadn't answered her phone. "Be careful of Elliot Sandoval," he'd left the terse message. "Come to the police station. Call me. The second you get this."

As for "Brian"? Jake knew exactly who that was. Brian Turiello, Shandra Newbury's boss. Where was *he* now?

There was too much to do, and impossible to do it all at the same time. Parole, Turiello, Sandoval, Jane. *Frigging Aaron Gianelli.* Jane, Sandoval, Parole, Turiello. The order he chose, and the way the answers came in, might decide Jane's life.

He yanked open the driver's side, cranked the ignition, pulled out before Sherrey, huffing, closed his door.

"Hey! I'm not even—give me a—"

They jounced up the steep grade of the parking garage exit ramp. The miserably slow door creaked open, one ancient section at a time.

Jake pounded the flat of his hand on the steering wheel. "Crap. Anything on Sandoval?"

"No answer," Sherrey said. "No voice mail. Parole's looking it up, calling me back. It's Friday afternoon, they said. Everyone's gone."

"Turiello," Jake said. "Think he'd show up in person? Or who's he sending to get her? Where? Where the hell are they?"

He handed Sherrey his cell. *Jane.* First focus on Jane.

"Look in personal contacts. Find Jane Ryland at the *Register.*" Maybe she was in the newsroom. Getting Twizzlers. Safe.

"She's in your phone?" Sherrey was fussing with the screen. "Interesting."

The garage door had three hinged segments to go. One more, and Jake could time it to scoot under before the door was all the way up.

"Call it," Jake said. The car powered into the alley, Jake stomping the gas. He had to decide where to go. Turiello was the key—had to be—but where was he? At home? The real estate office? If Jake picked the wrong place—

"No answer at her desk phone," Sherrey was saying. "Where're we going?"

"Call the main number at the paper. Ask for Victoria Marcotte," Jake said. "Tell 'em who you are. Police. Emergency. Whole nine yards."

By the time Marcotte came to the phone, Jake was on 93 South, lights and siren, praying he'd made the right decision. Sherrey handed him the phone.

"Ms. Marcotte? We're looking for Jane Ryland. Yes, I know she's not there. Listen, no time to explain, but go to Jane's desk—you on a cell? Crap. Sorry. Okay, go to her desk and—" Jake veered into the fast lane. Three exits to go. He tried to keep his voice calm. He didn't have time to say anything twice. "Look for anything that might indicate where she is. Detective Sherrey will make sure you have my number. Then call me. Right back. Either way."

"Why?" Marcotte asked.

"No time. Just call me. If she comes in, keep her there." He handed the phone to Sherrey, steering with one hand through the choking jam of cars and trucks and motorcycles and assholes. Southeast Expressway on a Friday afternoon. Might as well be frigging walking. He wished his car had a louder siren, not that anyone around here would pay attention. "Give Marcotte my cell number."

"What is it?" Sherrey asked.

"What *is* it?" What was his own phone number? The green highway signs flashed by, Jake's brain accelerating even faster. Every second of delay meant—he remembered the damn number. Told him.

No call from Parole. No call from Jane.

Two exits to go. If he'd made the right decision.

* * *

"Careful!" Jane grabbed MaryLou Sandoval's arm, barely catching her as she tripped, flailing, both arms in the air, on a loose flagstone. "Stand here a second, rest a minute. You okay?"

"Sure," MaryLou said. She waved at the car, held up one finger. "Who knew being pregnant would be so—I burst into tears at the slightest thing, you know? Hormones. I keep thinking about Elliot, and jail, and you know, when they found the—well, thank God Brian is going to pay our legal bills, all I can say."

"Brian?" Jane was still distracted by the imminent likelihood this poor woman was about to have a baby right here in the front yard. What would she *do*?

"Yeah. The real estate guy. He's the one who hired El to work on the Springvale house, until—" MaryLou stopped. "Never mind."

"Oh, yeah, okay," Jane said. MaryLou turned to head for the car—but Jane still held her arm. Hold on. *Hold the hell on.* The Springvale? "To work on the Springvale house, you said. What Springvale house?"

"Nothing," MaryLou said.

"Brian Turiello." Jane took a chance.

MaryLou stood there. The sound of the steamer, a high-pitched whine, continued from inside, floated out an open window.

"Hired your husband to do construction work on forty-five Springvale," Jane said. Not in the form of a question. As if she knew. And—maybe—she did. "The house where Emily-Sue Ordway fell from the window. Poor little Emily-Sue. Someone's daughter. Was he there when she fell?"

"My baby." She touched a palm to her stomach, her face going white. "It was an accident. It *was*."

Her sister honked, and the side window rolled down. "You coming?"

"Was your husband at Waverly Road, too? Was Brian?"

Jane persisted. Brian Turiello was Shandra Newbury's boss. "With Shandra?"

"MaryLou!" Elliot Sandoval appeared in the second-floor window, leaned out, some kind of tool in one hand.

"I have to go," MaryLou said.

"Sandoval's not there." Sherrey gave Jake a thumbs-down. He'd been working the phones and the radio so Jake could drive. Not doing a bad job, Jake had to say, even though he was a blowhard and a pain in the ass. Jake had left his phone open for when Marcotte called back. Or Jane.

"Squad car out front at the sister's house, but no one's home," Sherrey reported. "Not even the sister."

Jake veered into the right lane, ready to take the final exit. "Okay, at least we know something. Turiello?"

"Not at his office. Supposed to be there 'soon,' according to the secretary. Whatever 'soon' is."

Sandoval not there. Turiello not there. Were they somewhere together? Waiting for Jane? Where? Jake banged onto the exit, took the curve too fast, Sherrey grabbing the strap as Jake steered the cruiser straight. Slammed through the red light, siren screaming, took the left. His phone rang. Finally. He punched it on speaker, keeping his eyes on the road.

"Brogan." The siren made him strain to hear.

"This is Victoria Marcotte."

"Go," Jake said.

"I don't know," she said.

"*Fu*—I mean . . ." Jake tried to calm his voice. Wouldn't get anywhere by scaring her. "Okay. Tell me what you found."

"A notation on her desk calendar," Marcotte said. "It says—well, it's hard to read, it's right on a grease spot. I'll spell it—T, U, I think—"

"Turiello?" Jake interrupted.

"Could be," Marcotte said.

Jake turned to Sherrey, lips pressed together, nodding. "Anything else? An address, maybe? Colgate Street?" Where Turiello's real estate office was. Where Jake was headed right now.

"No," Marcotte said. "It doesn't look like that at all. It could be—Rawson?"

Damn. At least Rawson Avenue was on this side of town. But was that where Jane was going? "Bing. The dash computer. Get me Brian Turiello's vehicle info from it. Car make, license plate. Home address. Everything. Do it."

"Huh?" Marcotte's voice came through the speaker. Jake hit the brake, banged a U-turn, headed back for the highway. Again, a risk. But what was he supposed to do, sit there? He had four blocks before he had to commit.

"Turiello has a Lexus," Sherrey read from the monitor. "Black."

A black Lexus? Where had he just—the car at the Waverly Road house? He'd asked Vitucci for that info. But no one had—*dammit*. Turiello had been where Shandra was killed? The damn deputies had cleaned everything out of that place. Maybe he'd been there to make sure of that. *If* that was him. It might not be.

"Detective?" Marcotte's voice. "Are you—?"

"Ready for the house number," Jake said. "And on the way."

64

What was she supposed to do now? Hell if she was going inside that empty house again—empty except for Elliot Sandoval, who she was pretty sure—not totally sure—had actually killed Shandra Newbury. And maybe Emily-Sue Ordway. With Brian Turiello?

Jane paused, watching MaryLou—she knew what had happened, she *must*—drive away with her sister. Was she truly sick? Or arranging to leave Jane alone with her husband? Was he the only one inside?

She looked at the house, deciding what to do. Elliot Sandoval knew she was there. Had seen her from the window. So what? She'd hop right into her car and—she stopped, mid-thought, regrouping. Her tote bag, with her cell phone and her car keys, was on the living room floor.

She had to go in to get it, or she couldn't leave.

Go to a neighbor? Knock on the door and say—what? My purse is in the living room next door but I don't want to get it because—she tilted her head back and forth, considering how ridiculous it would sound. If the neighbor recognized her, though, it might work. She could call Jake. Maybe.

She checked the window. It was still open, a curtain fluttering out in the afternoon breeze. The steamer had started again.

She could dart in, get the bag, run out. She took a step toward the door. Stopped. Saw the curtain flutter, a shadow pass by.

If only she hadn't left her bag. If only she hadn't helped MaryLou, who was probably up to her neck in this. If only she'd hadn't locked—wait. She *hadn't* locked her car?

She turned, ran, thankfully no cars were coming, dashed across the street, hoping she was right. Had she left her car open? The valet key was in the glove compartment. Should be, at least. She'd get away, drive somewhere, call Jake, or the cops or someone, it didn't matter, she'd be gone.

She almost slipped in the strip of soggy dirt between the curb and sidewalk. Her fingers curled around the car door handle, hot from the sun.

She pulled.

It opened.

Was the key there? She flapped open the glove box. She'd thrown it in there the last time, almost hearing her mother's voice, "if you put something away every time, it'll be there when you need it." She pulled out the Audi owner's manual, a CD from an audio book, a stash of napkins—it was just a *key*! A loose key, and where the hell was it?

Had Sandoval noticed she was leaving? She raised a glance at the window. Saw Elliot Sandoval, some kind of tool—hammer? wrench?—in his hand. Running down the shitty flagstone walk. Headed for her.

The key, the key. Forks, a paperback book, expired coupons from the—*damn*. He was almost across the street and she—"Jane, you moron!" She said it out, loud, slammed the doors locked. If she couldn't find the key, she'd be trapped in the car, she could blow the horn like crazy, if anyone was around, that's all she could do, but it would be better if she found the key.

And there it was.

And he was on her, at the car, it was a hammer, he had a stupid hammer, and he was running to the driver's side, raising his arms at the—he was right in front of—

She stabbed the key in to the ignition, cranked it.

"Get away!" she yelled and she gunned it, shifted, banged the accelerator, but then he was in front of her, daring her, *and forget about it!*

She heard a sound, a thud, he'd fallen into the dirt, she didn't care, she peeled away, eyes welling and terror clenching her chest, but she had to drive.

She looked in the rearview, praying. Had she hurt him? He'd *called* her there, lured her, to kill her. She couldn't believe she cared about his life, but—

He'd fallen into the dirt, rolled, and now he was running after her. He was alive.

And she was, too.

And she was gone.

"This the place?" Jake eyed the house, a beat-up two story on Rawson Avenue, as he pulled to the curb across the street. He'd killed his lights and siren when they were a few blocks away. Sometimes silent running was better, element of surprise.

"According to what Marcotte told us," Sherrey said. "Door's closed, don't see any cars, you know?"

"Jane has a black Audi," Jake said. He touched the weapon under his arm, unclipped the safety strap. If Jane was inside with that asshole Sandoval—damn it. "Who knows. There's a garage. You set? We'll have to play it by ear. If Jane's in there—"

"Right behind you," Sherrey said. "We'll take him now, ask questions later."

Jake scoped the place as they went up the front path, no cars in the driveways on either side, no one out in the neighborhood. Several of the houses appeared empty, from what he could tell. All of 'em shabby. Hard times around here.

Two teetering concrete steps up to the front porch. A weird sound from inside, a whine or a . . . some kind of machine.

"Knock?" Sherrey asked.

"Nah," Jake said. "Exigent. Big time."

He put his hand on the doorknob, waited a beat. Pushed. It opened.

"Hey, Detective Brogan." Elliot Sandoval. Red-faced, sweatshirt, one leg of his jeans filthy. Amiable, smiling, as if he and Sherrey had arrived for a beer and baseball. Except for the hammer in his hand. Place was a mess, though, construction stuff everywhere.

Where was Jane? Were they wrong? Had Jake picked wrong? Was Jane with Turiello, somewhere? Somewhere he'd never find until it was too late? Sandoval had to know. Wherever she was, he had to know. This was the address on Jane's notepad. She was coming here. Wasn't she? Where was she now?

"Got some bad news for you," Jake said. They walked in, leaving the door open behind them. "You didn't call your parole officer, Mr. Sandoval."

" 'Fraid that's a violation, Mister Sandoval." Sherrey picked up on the pretense Jake had concocted on the fly.

"So you're done, Elliot," Jake said. "We have a warrant for your arrest."

"That's bullshit," Sandoval said. "I called."

"Not what Parole told us." Sherrey had yanked the handcuffs from his belt, moved closer to Sandoval. "I'll take that hammer. Sir."

"You're also under arrest for the murder of Shandra Newbury." Jake was proud of Sherrey. Not a flicker at this impromptu charade.

"You know I didn't kill her," Sandoval said. "The judge let me out."

"Because we *asked* her to let you out," Jake said. "To see where you'd lead us. See who'd come out of the woodwork. Sadly, there's a rat in your nest. And he, sir, has ratted you all out. Brian Turiello? Your 'employer'? Emily-Sue Ordway? Ring a bell? We know that wasn't an accident. What happened, she surprise you? And you bashed Shandra Newbury with that two-by-four because you were batshit over losing your house. Dumb of you to leave the two-by-four there. Turiello even showed up to make sure the place was clean. Too bad he couldn't get inside in time to retrieve it."

"Too bad," Sherrey said.

"So, *Mr.* Sandoval," Jake went on. "That's the problem with mixing steroids and payoffs. Makes you overreact. Like right now. Sherrey? Cuff him."

Sandoval took a step back. Then stopped. Smiled. "Do what you will, Officers. But cuff me? You take me in? You'll never know what happened to Jane Ryland. Your call."

"You're full of shit," Jake said.

"Try me," Sandoval said.

"Prove it," Jake said.

Sandoval cocked his head toward a pile of two-by-fours. "See that bag?"

Jake edged toward the bag, never taking his eyes off Sandoval and Sherrey. Saw Sherrey adjust for his weapon. Saw Sandoval's fist tighten over the hammer.

Jake grabbed the black leather bag, didn't need to look inside, he'd seen it a million times. *Jane's.* He yanked it open. Her phone, right on top. She hadn't answered his message. Because she'd been separated from her phone. She'd been here, absolutely. So where the hell was she now?

"If she's in this house . . . ," Jake began.

"Well, there's a thought," Sandoval said.

Sherrey hovered by him, waiting for Jake's signal.

"Her car's not here." Jake's brain raced to figure out where this was going. Was Jane upstairs? Was she okay? What was that noise? He glanced at Bing, then upstairs.

"Good idea," Sandoval said. "Why don't you go look up there? Meanwhile, I'm outta here."

"Not a chance, you incredible jerk," Jake said. "Sherrey. Stay here. Cuff him."

"I wouldn't do that," Sandoval said. "No cuffs, or no Jane. There might be something you need to know. Something she might have—eaten. And you'd want me to tell you."

The chocolate? Like they'd given Liz McDivitt? Jane had no reason not to trust Sandoval. If they'd drugged her, he'd need to know what it was.

"Do not move," Jake said. Did he have a choice? Sandoval had the cards. He had Jane. How could Jake risk calling his bluff? Jane had to come first. Any victim had to come first. "I'm checking upstairs. Do not move."

He drew his weapon as he headed up the stairway. That infernal noise, whatever it was. Halfway up. "You okay, Sherrey?" He called out.

"Ten four. Got the cuffs."

Jake took the rest of the steps, two at a time. Followed the noise. An orange Rent-All wallpaper steamer chugged and bubbled, that was the noise. No Jane. Opened the closet, nothing. Next room, nothing. Closet, nothing. Bathroom, nothing. Attic? No attic he could see.

"Nothing, nothing," he called out over the steamer sound as he raced back down the stairs. "Sandoval, there's no one—"

He stopped, one hand on the banister. The other holding his Glock.

Sandoval had Sherrey in the cuffs. Was standing over

him, hammer in one hand. Bing's police-issue Glock in the other.

"Bummer about your partner," Sandoval said. "Shoulda frisked me. Isn't that cop 101?"

"Asshole," Sherrey said. "Sorry, Jake."

"Let. Him. Up," Jake said.

"Not. A. Chance," Sandoval said. "Well, actually, there is a chance. You let me go, I'll let him go. That seems fair."

"Where's Jane?" Jake aimed at Sandoval's center mass, but the man had his weapon right at Sherrey's head.

"Well now, that's where the deal goes out of whack, doesn't it?" Sandoval said. He twisted his lip, sniffed like he smelled something bad. "You get two things, and I get one? I don't think so. You want me to let your partner go? Or you want to know where Jane is? You get to choose one."

65

Peter felt the weight of it under his coat, his small-caliber gift from Dianna, the one he'd argued, all those years ago, he'd never need.

He sat in the font seat of his Jeep, parked across the street from the stone-facade two-story on a side street in Jamaica Plain. No McMansions for Eddie Walsh, man of the people, only a modest mid-century suburban split-level. Walsh's Cape house, however—an ostentatious Corinthian-columned boondoggle in Osterville Peter found online—that was a different story. Two sides to the man. Two sides to his real estate.

Peter wouldn't need the gun now, most likely. He was a lawyer. He thought for a living, he didn't shoot people. But if former Parole Board chairman and well-connected big shot Edward Walsh was monstrous enough to kill Carley Marie Schaefer twenty years ago, then bribe a dying man to take the fall, Peter might need more than words to come out on top.

He hoped not. He was not here to be the aggressor. He was here only to find the truth.

Tonight the Jamaica Plain house was dark, the carefully trimmed hedges surrounding lush grass and meticulous landscaping. No lights in the windows.

That meant their confrontation, well, conversation,

Peter should call it, would have to wait a while. Exactly like poor Gordon Thorley, waiting in a jail cell. Waiting for the truth. Sick and dying and trying to do one last good thing.

Peter would wait, too. Long as it took.

"Father?" Liz McDivitt saw his silhouette first, framed in the open door of the Superintendent's office.

He exploded through the doorway, came right for her. "Honey—Lizzie—at first I thought you were—"

Liz felt her father's arms around her, she couldn't remember the last time that happened, and she couldn't let go. She peered over her father's tweedy shoulder, saw Rivera watching them.

"Again, I'm so sorry, Mr. McDivitt," Rivera said. "There was no way we could bring you into this right away. Question was—"

"What if I were involved. I understand." Her father had ended the hug, but kept one arm around her. Liz could feel the weight of it on her shoulder, feel the weight of the years and the arguments, the years of misunderstandings and distance. "And?"

"Let's put it this way." Rivera sank into a massive black vinyl chair, his muscular bulk filling the space, his head almost reaching the brass floor lamp beside him. "Your Mr. Gianelli and Mr. Ackerman are downstairs, right now, in separate rooms. My detectives are now waiting to see which one will tell the whole story first. I'm sure whole teams of lawyers will arrive soon. Then we'll know. But at this point no one has mentioned your name."

A tightness in her chest. She stepped away from her father. Had he been involved in Aaron's scheme? She tried to calculate what that might mean. "Father, are you—?"

"Of course not," he said.

"Sorry about the protective custody," Rivera was

saying. "And positioning our plainclothes cadet at your house to hold off the press. But if your daughter was targeted, you might have been next on the list. Even when Liz was safe, we had to wonder—was it you who'd called them off? So far, nothing links you to any of it."

"And it won't," her father said.

"But then, what really happened, Superintendent?" Liz asked. "Was someone really coming to kill me? Who?"

"That's still under investigation," Rivera said. "And exactly what I'm about to go check on. I'll leave you two alone."

Liz watched the door close behind him, leaving her alone with her father for the first time in forever.

"So. You're okay?" He assessed her, up and down. "Are you sure? You're very brave, honey. If those people had—"

"They didn't." Lizzie sat on the arm of a big chair, balancing, one toe touching the carpet. "It's over. I didn't know what to do, or who at the bank might be involved. So I went to the police. Told them everything I knew, or suspected. The drugs found in that chocolate thing proved I was right. So that night, officers were waiting there with me, hiding. When whoever it was didn't show—they decided to go ahead as if he had. See what happened. I'm sorry you had to think I was—"

Her father stood, walked to the window. She'd never seen his shoulders sag before. She'd always thought of him as a bear, a big stocky lumbering bear in pinstripes. Now he seemed diminished.

He turned, outlined in the last dusky glow of Friday's sunlight. "I'll have to resign," he said. "The idea that those two—and whoever else—could be stealing from us, right under my nose." He shook his head. "Did I know about it? Of course not. But not knowing, that's equally as damning."

"We'll see." Funny, or not so, how he was thinking about himself. Not about how his only daughter had been targeted for murder. Still, Liz wanted to comfort him, because he was right. The scandal would change their lives.

And there was her own dilemma. Her father still didn't know the whole story, not at all. Not what she'd done, too, right under his nose. This was the moment, she knew. The moment she should tell the truth.

"Father," she began. She stood, touching the chair with the fingertips of one hand. Not trusting her knees quite yet.

"Your mother would be so proud of you," her father interrupted. "She always was, you know. She was never very good at saying it. Neither of us was."

Liz felt tears welling, all the pressure and the fear, and the deception. And now this, what she least expected, compassion. She'd made some terrible decisions, like with Aaron. Would she make the right one now?

What *was* the right one?

"Can we weather this one together?" Her father came toward her, smiling. Stretched out both arms to her. "I know I've ignored you, I know I've focused on the damn bank. But we could come through this, you know. We could."

Could they? If Liz revealed what she had done, those families would lose their homes. Her father would face even more humiliation and disgrace—his own daughter, manipulating bank records. She could imagine the headlines: "Bank Prez Daughter Is Robin Hood."

She held out her hands, as her father came closer. There'd only been, what, six families she'd "helped"? And though Aaron and Colin Ackerman had ripped off the bank to get money, she was in it only to do good. How could that be wrong?

She'd stop. She'd watch the numbers, and make sure no one ever discovered it. And if someone found out—well, she'd cross that bridge then.

"You're my father," she said. They linked fingers for a moment. Looked into each other's eyes. "I would never do anything to hurt you."

She hoped that was true.

66

Choose?

Jake could feel his face go white. His fingers clenched around the handle of the Glock, and with all his heart he longed to blast this guy into the stone age. But if he did, he'd never know what happened to Jane. He couldn't risk that.

Choose?

And this jerk Sandoval. Smirking. Enjoying it. The ridiculous clanking and hissing of that damn machine upstairs, he should have unplugged it, the steam now heating up the entire place. This was hell.

"Last chance," Sandoval hissed out the words. "You want me to let your partner go? Or you want to know where Jane is? You get to choose one."

The sound of the gun behind him.

Sandoval, with one crazed expression of bewilderment, seemed to rise, pause mid-air, then crash to the floor, his gun skittering away. Not another motion. Except for the rapidly growing pool of red on the hardwood floor.

Sherrey rolled, three times, hit the wall, struggled to his feet. Kicked the gun down the hall.

Jake whirled, saw the open doorway. Saw who stood there.

Jane.

And Paul DeLuca, holding his own Glock.

"Darn," Jane said. "I wanted to hear who you'd choose."

67

"I kept wondering, where was Peter?" Jane watched out the windshield of Jake's cruiser, relieved to be a pretend-cop in the front seat, now that she was safe. And Jake was safe. "Sandoval had told me Peter would be there, but he wasn't. I knew there was something off. And then—MaryLou. She's the one who clinched it for me. Brian? Paying the legal bills? Why? She knew, huh? That her husband had killed Shandra?"

Jake stopped at the light, no emergency now, and she tried to read his expression. Relief? Surprise? Affection? Maybe all of those.

She reached over and took his hand. "Hope there's no surveillance cam in your cruiser," she said.

She felt him squeeze her hand, let go to adjust the rear-view mirror. "We've got a guy out here now, at the sister's," Jake said. "But I suspect MaryLou knew something. About Emily-Sue Ordway, too. Apparently that wasn't an accident. We'll find out. Turiello must have been in on that cover-up, too. Makes it easy if you're also the one hiring the cleanup guys."

"She's pregnant," Jane said. She clutched her tote bag, none the worse for its adventure. Still, might be time to retire the thing. Those memories she could do without.

They made the turn onto Mass Ave., heading back to

retrieve her car at the cop shop. She'd broken every speed limit on the planet to get there, ecstatic to see DeLuca back on the job. He'd let her explain on the way. Now he was back handling the mess at the Rawson house with the rest of the cops who'd swarmed in to help.

Jake shook his head. "We'll do the best we can for her."

"Yeah. Whatever that is. Peter will—" *Peter*. Sandoval was his client. He had no idea of this. They'd promised to work on this story together, though it hadn't turned out the way either of them predicted. Still, justice had been done. Or was on the way to being done. She had to call him.

She dug into the tote bag, trying to ignore where it had just been. Found her phone, checked the messages.

"You called me?" she asked Jake.

"Yeah, to warn you to stay away from Sandoval. For what good that did."

"He couldn't have killed Liz McDivitt, though, you know?" Jane said, as she punched in numbers on the cell. "Because he was in custody when Liz was killed."

What was that look on Jake's face?

"What?"

"Jane?" Jake said. He paused. "You should know that—"

Jane put up a palm, listening to the phone ring. "Hang on."

"What?" Peter clenched his phone, listening to Jane, kept his eyes on the front porch of the Walsh house. Nothing. Wondered if Walsh maybe wasn't coming home. This was Friday night, after all. Wondered if that was the universe telling him to go home, too. Leave this stuff to the police. He was the justice end of it, not the enforcer. He couldn't believe what Jane just told him. "Sandoval?"

"I know. Shot in the shoulder, apparently. Looked worse than it was. They're taking him to the hospital now." Jane's voice came over the speaker, sounded like she was in a car, too. "He'd told me you'd be there, too, and when you weren't—well, I didn't call you to check, and then later—I couldn't. Since . . ."

"Yeah," Peter imagined it, Sandoval, shot by the cops as he threatened Brogan and his partner. "But why did— huh?"

Jane told him to hang on, clearly talking to someone else, muffled, like she was covering the phone.

"Peter?" Her voice crackled over the speaker. "I'm with Jake Brogan. And he says to ask you—did your guy say anything more? Whatever that means? And he says, where are you?"

"Can he hear me?" Peter said.

Jake pulled his cruiser behind Peter's jeep. The Walsh house was freshly landscaped, hedges trimmed judiciously so a burglar couldn't hide. Probably had motion-detector lighting, meaning he'd be blasted with light the instant he approached. Front windows were dark, garage door closed. Impossible to tell if anyone was home.

He opened the car door, put a foot onto the curb. Turned to Jane. "I'll be back," he said.

"But I want to—," Jane began.

Headlights. A high-beam glow swept around the corner, hesitated as it hit the two cars, then a black Lincoln pulled into the driveway. The automatic lights popped on, spotting the front door, the garage, a stand of hedge to the right. The left side of the two-car garage slowly began to move, the Lincoln idling as the door lifted.

"Police business," Jake said. "Stay here, Jane."

"Be careful," she said.

He closed the car door, leaving her inside.

Hardesty was getting out of his Jeep. Two steps, and he'd stopped him, too. "No," Jake said. "My job."

"You're talking to him alone?"

"I'm a cop," Jake said. He patted his chest, where he kept the Glock. "I'm never alone." He paused, couldn't believe he was about to say this to Hardesty. "Go get Jane, okay? Take care of her?"

Jake ignored the front walk, got to the driver's side door as the Lincoln began to pull into the garage. He walked alongside the car, flapped open his badge wallet, held it to the closed car window.

"Edward Walsh?" Jake knew that doughy face, all chin and jowls, seen him at hearings, and on TV. Ex-sheriff, Jake remembered. As Parole Board chairman, he'd held prisoners' lives in his hands. He'd let Gordon Thorley out—then, years later, strong-armed him to cover up his own crime. "I'm Detective Jake Brogan, Boston PD."

The car stopped. The ignition went off. The garage door stayed open.

"May I speak to you for a moment?" Conjecture was not a standard-issue weapon in police work, but sometimes a good bluff was. This might be the time to try it.

Edward Walsh, brown plaid sport jacket, narrow brown tie, thinning hair, saluted Jake as he got out, stood in the pool of light on the driveway.

"Welcome," he said. "Brogan, huh? Related to the commissioner, no doubt."

"My grandfather," Jake said.

"Knew him well," Walsh said. "So, Detective, how can I help you? Surprised you didn't call first. Must be important."

"Can we go inside?" Jake scouted the neighborhood as they walked, houses two driveways apart from each other, most homes with exterior lights. Out here was no place to confront Walsh about his past.

Walsh seemed to consider. "Do I need a lawyer?"

"Do you want a lawyer?" Jake kept his voice even.

"Come in," Walsh said. "We'll talk."

"So Thorley's *not* the Lilac Sunday killer?" Jane sat in the front seat of Peter's Jeep, Jake's suggestion apparently. So *that* chapter must be over. She'd thanked Peter for the flowers, finally, and he'd explained he'd brought them to thank her for being so "brave" with Thorley. What, did he think she would have freaked out? Cried? But it was a sweet gesture. He was a good guy. And would make someone very happy, someday. Someone. Not her.

She told Peter, again, the story of Sandoval, what she knew of it at least. Then Peter told *her*—off the record, naturally—about how he and Jake had joined forces to interrogate Thorley. Absurdly, Jane's first reaction was relief. What if she'd broken her word to Jake, and pitched the "Thorley as Lilac Sunday" story to Marcotte?

Now there was a better story, if she ever got to tell it. For a reporter, she sure was finding out a lot of stuff that wasn't getting in the paper. In the past five days all she'd written was a feature on bank customer service. But there was still time.

"And Gary Lee Smith wasn't Lilac Sunday, either," Peter said. "He was in jail at the time, too."

"So Walsh? The Parole Board chairman? Thorley told you that? For his mortgage money?" Jane paused, thinking it through. "Huh. I'd actually wondered if his mortgage was paid because—"

She stopped, the rest of her sentence hanging between them. She'd promised Jake she wouldn't reveal the bombshell he'd just dropped about Liz McDivitt, though he'd said it would be public soon. It stunk that her newspaper had been used to disseminate lies, though this wasn't the moment to discuss journalism ethics. Or the undertakings of the very alive Liz McDivitt. Liz. *Alive.* Amazing.

"Look." Jane pointed, changing the subject. "The door."

The carved wooden door had closed behind the two men, Walsh first unlocking it, Jake following him inside. Exterior lights clicked on, the trees making flutters of leafy shadows on the driveway and grass.

"They're in. I'd kill to be there to hear what they say." Jane thought back over Chrystal's articles. "From what I read, this Walsh was never linked to Lilac Sunday."

Peter shook his head. "He was a county sheriff, though, and according to Thorley, knew Carley Marie. Maybe they—maybe Brogan can find out. But whoever's guilty, it's not Gordon Thorley. He was only trying to save his family's home."

"Maybe Elliot Sandoval was, too. In some irrational way. That's how the whole thing started, for me at least." Jane looked out the window at the house, wondering who was saying what inside. "TJ and I went to that foreclosure on Waverly Road. We thought it'd be an empty house. Turned out to be a can of worms."

68

"I know everything." Jake had refused the chair Walsh offered, a buckskin leather throne dotted with brass grommets. They'd seen no one else in the house, Walsh hadn't called out to anyone, or announced his return. Jake hadn't planned on this, and didn't love being here alone, but he couldn't allow Peter inside. Now he was in a potential battle, and without a strategy. On the way to Walsh's overstuffed study Jake had considered and rejected several approaches—the truth, a lie, indirect—and decided on the big bluff.

"You know everything? There's an intriguing opening statement." Walsh swiveled in his desk chair, arms on the rests, one leg crossed over his knee. A black ribbed sock showed above his shiny loafer. The desk, glass-topped and glossy, held a stationery-store display of matching leather gizmos—holders, files, pads, and containers of pens. "Can I interest you in a drink? I seem to remember your grandfather liked his whiskey."

"No, sir," Jake said. Walsh was trying to defuse the attack. Jake's tactics were exactly the opposite. "You and Gordon Thorley. The mortgage."

"Who?" Walsh swiveled, once, twice, wrinkled that forehead, three lines creasing even deeper.

"The man you lost your job over, sir," Jake said.

"Ah," Walsh said.

"We know you were paying his mortgage." Jake kept talking, watching Walsh, looking for the soft spot. The flinch, the tell. Nothing.

"Cashier's checks," Jake went on. "Back in your day, they weren't traceable. Now? They are. Not to mention the security video from the post office. It may take a while to put it together, sir, but there's no doubt."

Still not a word from Walsh.

"You knew Carley Marie Schaefer, you knew her parents. What, did she have a crush on you? Or you on her? You drive her all the way to Boston? To the Arboretum? And then—"

"I think I'll have that drink." Walsh rose, his chair swiveling in a circle as he shoved away. Opened an elaborate wood sideboard, inside lined with crystal decanters. "You sure I can't offer—"

"Sir?" Jake said. He'd go for the whole nine yards now, some yards of which Jake wasn't quite sure of. Whatever wasn't true they could sort out later. "We know about Thorley. He's confessed. We can trace the checks, follow the money. We know about Gary Lee Smith. We know Treesa Caramona was another of your parolees. She trusted you, that how you got to her? That why she let you in to kill her? It's done. You're done. We know everything."

He watched Walsh choose a glass, rummage in a drawer. Jake took a step back, wary.

"Not quite, Jake. What you don't know, *Jake*," Walsh said. He turned, smiling, perfect host, napkin in one hand, glass in the other. "If I killed Carley Marie Schaefer, why isn't there one bit of evidence that leads to me? Not a shred? Have you examined the police files? I'm sure your grandfather made copies. And yet, no matter how hard he tried . . ."

Walsh paused, poured something brown from a decanter into his glass, wrapped it with the napkin, slugged the whole thing. Shook his head, as if in sorrow.

"And yet no matter how hard he tried, he could not catch that bad guy. Used to talk about it all the time. Like I said, *Jake*. I knew him. In fact, when the case was new? Yours truly Sheriff Walsh was one of the first to get a look at all the evidence. Thanks to my friendship with your dear grandfather. He thought we could solve that heinous"—he stumbled over the word—"crime together."

Walsh poured another glass. Drank it. "That, however, was not my true objective." Put the glass down, but missed. The glass fell onto the thick pile carpeting, rolled under the desk. He watched it, seemingly fascinated. "Not after dear Carley Marie told me she wanted to stop—'seeing' me. I knew what her medical records would show. I'd planned her visit to the—doctor. But sadly, she wasn't happy with that plan. Sadly, your grandfather's cops neglected to notice the medical files weren't exactly the same after I examined them."

"You took—you changed—?" Jake began. He felt the back of his neck tighten, thought of his grandfather, his sorrow and defeat; his grandmother, who'd watched failure eat away at her husband. Walsh—a law enforcement officer—had access to the evidence, knew exactly what to alter, and how to do it. Back then he'd tried to erase the history of his guilt.

Now it was Jake's turn to play with the truth.

"*Times* change, Walsh. These days tests are better. And they're already underway. Even if Thorley had convinced us, we'd still have found you." Jake was semi-bluffing, since they probably had no samples of Walsh's DNA on file. He had to rely on Walsh's fear. "We have the rope, remember? You ever heard of 'handler DNA'?"

"Ah. Progress." Walsh almost smiled. "Your grandfather, devoted as he was, simply didn't have the tools. Died a bit, over the Carley Marie case, I always thought. So sad. And now, after all this time, here's another Brogan, come to solve the Lilac Sunday case. After twenty damn anniversaries, twenty damn years of frigging DNA and forensic tests and God knows what else. Twenty damn anniversaries waiting for some cop to show up here with a warrant for a cheek swab. Now here you are. And a Brogan to boot."

Jake thought about what Nate Frasca had told him: how crime preyed on the mind, how relentless fear could fester and destroy, could become a man's personal poison.

Walsh reached into the drawer. Took out a gun.

"Walsh!" Jake pulled his weapon, aimed it.

"No need, my boy," Walsh said. "Happy anniversary. Good luck to you."

Walsh aimed at his own head. And fired.

69

Nothing better than a front-page story.

Jane leaned against the doorjamb of the city editor's office, her eyes still on the gorgeous Saturday morning paper. "Internet or no," she said. "You can't beat real paper with real words printed on it."

"Former Parole Chief Cons Con," the page-one headline said. "Lilac Sunday Plot Foiled, Murder Solved." Not exactly *The New York Times*. Victoria Marcotte, of course, had composed the headers.

"Looks great." Marcotte sat at her desk, eyes on her monitor, clicking through the online edition. She nodded with every click, approving.

Jane had stayed up all night, banging out the stories on her newsroom computer, fueled by coffee and passion. Truth be told, she thought. She'd finally gotten her exclusive. Two of them. As far as she was concerned, today should be Jane Ryland day at the *Register*.

On the front page, a huge spread on Lilac Sunday. Edward Walsh, the altered evidence, Gordon Thorley, Treesa Caramona, the mortgage payments, all of it. After a late-night flurry of promises, concessions, and court orders, Gordon Thorley was released, able to spend his last weeks with his family at their Sagamore home.

Which would stay their home. What Jane couldn't

reveal yet, Peter Hardesty had told her—off the record, *of course*—he was negotiating with the cops to give Thorley, now a hero, the reward money for turning in the Lilac Sunday killer. Pretty funny, if it turned out Thorley's deal with Edward Walsh would *legally* provide his mortgage payments. There'd be plenty to pay the whole thing off, in full.

Jane's bank story, just as blockbuster, splashed across the front page of Metro. The whole juicy thing, complete with the police pretense about Liz McDivitt that uncovered the bank employees' rental scheme and the stories behind the two empty-house deaths, culminating with the arrests of Brian Turiello, Colin Ackerman, and little fish Aaron Gianelli. It featured Jane's own cell phone photo of Turiello—Lexus guy—at the scene of Shandra Newbury's murder.

Elliot Sandoval himself, arm and shoulder bandaged, confessed what happened to Emily-Sue Ordway: "It was an accident," the re-arrested Sandoval had insisted from his hospital bed. As for Shandra Newbury, he'd publicly confessed his role in that, too. Jane was at police headquarters when the cops perp-walked him to the transport van. "'Turiello made me do it, she found out about the rental thing,' Sandoval yelled as he was led away. 'Said he'd frame me for Emily-Sue if I didn't . . .' And then he'd disappeared into custody."

Peter had refused the legal fees once he learned the funds came from Turiello—he was now representing Sandoval pro bono. "A client is a client, and plenty of them have lied to me," he'd told Jane. "Innocent or guilty. The system has to work."

MaryLou was in hiding. Soon as the cops found her, she'd need a lawyer of her own.

Jane also quoted Superintendent Rivera in her article: "Apparently Miss Newbury had discovered the rental scheme and threatened to blow the whistle."

Another Rivera quote was boxed in the sidebar, in bold. "We didn't lie to the public about Elizabeth McDivitt. We did what we had to do."

Civil rights groups were up in arms over the deception, social media going crazy. "Trampling our rights is just plain wrong," one Tweet began. Jane had to admit the cops duping the press did feel wrong, 100 percent wrong. Jake insisted sometimes you had to lie to get to the truth. That conversation was far from over.

"This whole cop thing is so buzzable," Marcotte was saying. Her silver bracelets jangled as she propped an elbow on her desk. "Sorry about your deal with Peter Hardesty."

"*Our* deal," Jane said. "Besides, I was never too hot on—"

"And we'll skip your Lilac Sunday retrospective," Marcotte continued, ignoring her. "Handle Walsh as breaking news."

"I suppose." Jane reluctantly closed the gorgeous paper, planning to snag a few extra copies. She'd send one to her dad, proof she'd redeemed herself. But one part of the story still bugged her.

"About that retrospective," Jane said. "I simply could not find those people Chrystal interviewed back then, you know? It would have been such a great follow-up if I—"

"Jane." Marcotte flipped her monitor to black. "Good job on that. Have a seat, okay?"

"Good job on what?" Jane hated that couch. Stayed standing.

"I should tell you—I've been using you to fact check."

"Fact check what? Or, who?"

"Chrystal Peralta," Marcotte said. "We determined— and I know I can trust you to keep it quiet—she's been creating quotes. Inventing interviews. For years. Not all the time. Only, we found, when it was—convenient. We suspected her draft of the bank story was fabricated. Now you've discovered she apparently created the 'supposed' bystanders at the Lilac Sunday murder."

"*Supposed* bystanders?" Jane sank into the couch. She didn't care how low it was. She remembered, a few days ago, Chrystal had suggested she "just make it up." Jane had dismissed it, an obvious joke.

"Her stories are lies?" Jane tried to grasp the consequences, the damage. "How are we going to address that? We need to make the public aware—"

"We most certainly do not," Marcotte cut her off. "From what we found, it was nothing critical. Or legally actionable. Chrystal is certainly not going to open her mouth about it. What's more, she actually admitted having an affair with a source. Talk about unacceptable—well. She's history. No longer with the paper. Circulation is up, finally. What the readers don't know won't hurt them."

Jane stood, shaking her head. So much for the tell-Victoria-the-truth-about-Jake idea. But Chrystal Peralta was fabricating news stories? And Marcotte ignoring it? No. No way.

"We're in the business of history," Jane said. "Readers rely on us. What we write—*becomes* the truth. Especially after what the police did. We can't allow this."

"Of course we can," Marcotte said. "No one will ever know, right? Now, go. Write your story."

Lizzie stared at the front page of this morning's *Register*. She'd read Jane Ryland's story, over and over. All in black and white, the words "murder" and "conspiracy" and "fraudulent rentals." Her own name, again and again, accompanied by "courageous" and "insider" and "bait." But in reality, nothing was black and white. Nothing.

She was back at her desk at the bank, open as usual

on Saturday morning, her father back upstairs in his executive suite. How long would they stay there? The A&A board of directors would meet this afternoon. His future hung in the balance.

Hers? That was in question, too.

She was alive, at least. She soaked up the normal for as long as she could, gazing through her open office door, out past Stephanie's desk to the familiar hallway, and finally to the elevator door. Which would never again open to reveal Aaron Gianelli. She shook her head, seeing the empty spot on her desk where his photo used to be. She'd tossed it into a wastebasket. Done. *History.*

Superintendent Rivera told her they were charging Aaron and Colin Ackerman and Brian Turiello with attempted murder and conspiracy to murder. Brian hadn't known his pawn, Elliot Sandoval, was in custody. No way he could have gotten to that empty house to kill her.

Turned out, if Lizzie hadn't gone to the police, she'd have been safe that night. But what about the night after that? She'd gone to the police, told the truth. And it had saved her life.

Now Aaron was blaming Turiello, Rivera had told her. He'd insisted his own life was being threatened. If Aaron didn't plead guilty, Lizzie would have to testify at his trial.

Again, she'd tell the truth.

She clicked open her computer, pulled up the mortgage files. Smiled.

As much as she could.

Jake's warrant gave him the legal right to search, examine, read, and confiscate whatever he wanted in Edward Walsh's now vacant house. Three more desk drawers to open, but Jake had already found what he needed.

Crime Scene was finished here, and the cleanup crew

as well. The study reeked of disinfectant, crackling strips of brown paper protected the still-damp oriental rug. A white drop cloth covered Walsh's leather chair. He'd died here, by his own hand, died out of panic and fear. Died when the truth caught up with him.

Walsh couldn't have predicted this Lilac Sunday would be his last. Couldn't have predicted he'd need to hide anything. Like the letter.

Unfolding it with his gloved fingers, Jake slipped the cheap lined paper into a glassine evidence bag. The crabbed signature showed though the transparent plastic, answering the final question. Treesa Caramona.

In painfully drawn letters and determined underlines, a chaotic mix of capitals and lower case, Caramona's threat was clear.

"I will NOT say *I* did it," her letter said. "But I WILL tell the COPS I know that YOU did. Unless you give me . . ."

Caramona had been paroled on Walsh's watch, like Thorley. And she was dying. Hep C. Thorley had told Jake.

What if Caramona refused Walsh's "offer" before Thorley accepted it—then mistakenly hoped she could call his bluff by using some blackmail leverage of her own? Maybe Walsh had lured her to Moulten Street with the promise of a payoff.

That's where Edward Walsh tried again to extinguish the truth. And failed.

Edward Walsh. Murderer and manipulator. The final victim of Lilac Sunday.

70

After all these years, we're so grateful to the Boston Police . . ."

Jane watched the woman at the stand of microphones touch frail fingers to her throat, glance at her husband beside her. For the past fifteen minutes, answering questions from the gathered reporters, the couple stood shoulder to shoulder, centered in a grove at the Boston Arboretum, pillars of gray and sorrow. Behind them, a froth of lilac blossoms, lavender and white, ruffled with green leaves, surrounded them with color in the mid-morning sunlight.

Gerald and Maureen Schaefer, in Boston for Lilac Sunday, as they'd been every year since their daughter Carley Marie was found murdered twenty years ago. Carley Marie, forever seventeen. Now they knew who'd killed her, and how he'd gotten away with it for so long.

Jane, with Jake beside her, stood next to an ancient maple, needing to hear the final moments of the drama played out.

Gerald Schaefer stepped to the mic stand, looked left, and then right. Took a deep breath. "If you have no more questions? Thank you so much. We'll come back next year, of course. To say good-bye, once again, to our Carley Marie. We love our daughter. And we miss her still."

Maureen Schafer cradled a framed photo of Carley Marie, the same one Jane had seen in the newspaper archives, pink sweater and pearls. Maureen wore pearls today, too. Jane wondered if they were the same ones.

"Thank you," the woman whispered.

Carley Marie's mother clutched the frame to her chest as the couple turned their backs, linked hands, and walked across the grass, down a lilac-lined slope and away from the reporters. The group of journalists, for once, not shouting questions or calling out for answers, not chasing after them for one last quote. There was a moment of silence, then with murmur of thank-yous and a rustle of notebooks, the crews walked quietly to dismantle their equipment.

Case closed, Jane thought.

"Case closed," Jake said. He reached for her hand, held it briefly, let go.

The sounds of laughing commotion, children and families, floated across the lush expanse, picnics and celebrations underway, as they were very year, under the fragrant branches of the Arboretum's famed lilacs. Every year, on Lilac Sunday, somehow at their peak.

"Every year, on Lilac Sunday," Jake said, "my grandparents used to come see the Schaefers, out of respect. Grandpa said it was his duty, even though it reminded him, every time, of his failure. Wish he had known it wasn't his fault. When I told the Schaefers about Walsh, they both cried. I almost did, too."

"It's over now," Jane said. "Because of you. And your grandfather knows. He knows."

They stood on the soft grass, in silence, Jane allowing Jake his own "closure," even though she knew he hated that word. Come to think of it, she needed a bit of closure of her own.

"Jake?" She took a deep breath, unsure of her timing, but unable to resist. "Those flowers from Peter were an apology for the Thorley-and-the-knife episode. Nothing more." She took one step away, so she could look him in the eye. "But Jake? 'Have a nice life'? That was—"

"I know. I'm a jerk." Jake took her hand again, not letting go this time. Drawing her back. "Listen. Jane? What if your 'nice life'—is with me?"

Footsteps behind them.

Jane turned, dropped her hand, saw two women approaching. One chic and fashionable, all cheekbones and linen, the other maybe thirty years older. The older one, walking with a shiny cane, raised a hand in greeting.

"Gramma Brogan," Jake whispered. "And Mother. I can't believe—"

Jake's mother? Jane patted her hair, considered her black pants and white shirt, almost exactly what Jake's mother—*Jake's mother!*—was wearing, minus the jewelry and expensive flats. And Jake's Gramma Brogan. The commissioner's wife. Here again, on Lilac Sunday. Jane's eyes misted. *Strange,* somehow, here in this fragrant garden, the past and the future were meeting.

"We're here for Lilac Sunday, dear." Jake's grandmother had tucked her arm through his. She was no taller than his shoulder, Jane saw, her lacy white cardigan next to Jake's pale blue shirt. A brace of lilacs framed the two, the lavender and green coloring the portrait of springtime and family. "I suppose it will be the last time. Your grandfather would be—"

She paused, looking up at Jake, her cheeks a soft pink, and her eyes welling with tears. "Good job, dear."

"We'll come next year, too, Gramma." Jake patted her hand, quickly kissed the top of her head. "Time to make our own history."

"Where are your manners, Jake?" his mother said. She turned to Jane, one hand outstretched. "I'm Priscilla Brogan. This is Jake's grandmother, Evelyn."

"So lovely to meet you," Jane said. "I'm—"

"Jane Ryland. Of course. Your story in this morning's paper was quite the tale," Priscilla Brogan continued. "You must have reliable sources in the police department. Wonder who—?"

A little girl wearing a white dress and shiny black shoes ran past them, waving a branch of dark purple lilacs, squealing with laughter, as a little boy in a Boston Strong T-shirt chased after her.

"Mother," Jake interrupted. "Jane and I are simply—"

"—colleagues," Jane said. Even though she wasn't quite sure what she would do, now that the *Register* apparently planned to hide the truth instead of tell it. *Have a nice life?* Did she have a different future to contemplate? "Jake and I are simply colleagues."

The little girl's laughter faded into the afternoon.

Evelyn Brogan, her face creased with a smile, still held her grandson's arm. She briefly pointed the rubber tip of her silver walking stick at Jane.

"Oh, my silly dears," Jake's grandmother said. "Truth be told? I don't think that's the whole story."

ACKNOWLEDGMENTS

Unending gratitude to:

Kristin Sevick, my brilliant, hilarious, and gracious editor. Thank you. The remarkable team at Forge Books: the incomparable Linda Quinton, indefatigable Alexis Saarela, and copy editor Julie Gutin, who noticed everything, thank you. (Sometimes, I repeat words. Imagine.) Talia Sherer, hilarious empress of libraries, I am so grateful. Bess Cozby and Desirae Friesen, you are terrific. Seth Lerner and Vanessa Paolantonio, thank you for turning words into pictures with another incredible cover. Brian Heller, my champion. The inspirational Tom Doherty. What a terrifically smart and unfailingly supportive team. I am so thrilled to be part of it. Thank you.

Lisa Gallagher, a wow of an agent, a true goddess, who changed my life and continues to do so.

Francesca Coltrera, the astonishingly skilled independent editor, who lets me believe all the good ideas are mine. Editor Chris Roerden, whose care and skill and commitment made such a difference. Ramona DeFelice Long—your insights are incomparable. You all are incredibly talented. I am lucky to know you—and even luckier to work with you.

The artistry and savvy of Madeira James, Charlie

Anctil, Mary Zanor, and Jen Forbus. To Linda Miele and Chris Wayland and Ed Ansin and Bob Leider, who understood.

The inspiration of Linda Fairstein, John Lescroart, Mary Jane Clark, Tess Gerritsen, Suzanne Brockmann, Lisa Unger, William Landay, Nancy Pickard, Michael Palmer, and Robert B. Parker.

Sue Grafton. Mary Higgins Clark. And Lisa Scottoline. And Lee Child. Words fail me. (I know, a first.)

My dear posse at Sisters in Crime. Thank you. And at Mystery Writers of America—Reed Farrel Coleman, Jessie Lourey, Dan Hale, and Margery Flax.

My amazing blog sisters. At Jungle Red Writers: Julia Spencer-Fleming, Hallie Ephron, Rosemary Harris, Roberta Isleib/Lucy Burdette, Susan Elia MacNeal, Jan Brogan, Deborah Crombie, and Rhys Bowen. At Femmes Fatales: Charlaine Harris, Dana Cameron, Kris Neri, Mary Saums, Toni Kelner, Elaine Viets, Donna Andrews, and Catriona McPherson. At the old Lipstick Chronicles: Nancy Martin and Harley Jane Kozak, who brought us all together.

Financial insiders who, yes, will remain nameless, thanks for the scoop.

My dear friends Amy Isaac, Mary Schwager, and Katherine Hall Page, and my darling sister Nancy Landman.

Dad—who loves every moment of this. And Mom. Missing you.

And Jonathan, of course, who never complains about all the takeout dinners.

Do you see your name in this book? Some very generous souls allowed their names to be used in return for an auction donation to charity. To retain the magic, I will let you find yourselves.

Sharp-eyed readers might notice I have tweaked

Massachusetts geography a bit. It is only to protect the innocent. And I adore it when people read the acknowledgments.

Keep in touch, okay?

http://www.hankphillippiryan.com
http://www.jungleredwriters.com
http://www.femmesfatales.typepad.com

Turn the page for a preview of

WHAT
YOU SEE

HANK PHILLIPPI RYAN

*Available from Tom Doherty Associates
in October 2015*

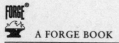

A FORGE BOOK

1

"Somebody saw something. And most of them took pictures of it." Detective Jake Brogan watched the uniforms try to corral the chaos of tourists and brown-bag-toting Bostonians while two crime scene units unspooled parallel rolls of their yellow plastic tape. Sirens wailed, three EMTs leaped from a red-and-white ambulance, the beeping Walk signal ordered clustering pedestrians to cross Congress Street, and angry drivers honked disapproval as police cadets in orange bandoliers signaled all cars to stop.

Jake had heard screams through the plate-glass window of the Bell in Hand, abandoned his carry-out roast beef sub on the restaurant counter, ran half a block. Found this. Radioed his partner. Lunch hour, now put on hold by murder.

"Wall-to-wall spectators, the good news and the bad news." Paul DeLuca shaded his eyes with one hand. The two detectives had split up to grab lunch, D opting for the corner Dunkin's. DeLuca still held his iced coffee, third of the day. "Who called nine-one-one? Anybody run away?"

"That's what we're about to find out," Jake said. "Most cases, nobody saw anything. Here's the opposite. Too many witnesses. That's a new one."

In the center of the circular redbrick plaza, in the noontime shadow of the burnished bronze knee of the Mayor Curley statue, some poor soul in a once-white shirt lay facedown, his running shoes splayed, a navy blue Sox cap teetering on the concrete, the hilt of a knife protruding absurdly between his shoulder blades. Jake had immediately radioed the medical examiner, who was now only minutes away. They'd need to dispatch the cleanup team, too. With the Fourth of July a month from now, the mayor would go ballistic over the growing puddle of red staining this concrete pathway along the visitor-magnet Freedom Trail. So much for the beginning of tourist season.

Across the street, in the teeming marketplace behind Faneuil Hall, persistent vendors offered Sam Adams tricorns, BOSTON STRONG T-shirts, and plastic lobster souvenirs. Visitors unlucky enough to witness this noontime stabbing had already received a souvenir they'd likely want to forget. But not until Jake picked their brains. And cell phone histories.

"I want names. I want addresses," he told DeLuca. "I want their phones and I want their cameras."

From moment one, Jake knew this would be a mess. Some of these people would lie, some would make stuff up, some would see things that never existed, some would have something to hide. Some would run. Complicating it all, he and DeLuca technically needed individual warrants to seize property. If any onlooker knew the law and gave them grief about it, it'd be even more of a shit show.

He pointed his partner toward the cadets. "The supe sent the new kids to 'help.' *All* we need. Tell them not to let any witness leave without giving contact information."

"Where're we gonna put 'em all, though?" DeLuca sucked a hit of coffee through a clear straw. "The Garden? Maybe they can watch *Disney On Ice* while we get their deets."

DeLuca had a point. Even the bleachers of the nearby Boston Garden sports arena were no solution. How could Jake keep fifty or so witnesses, from little kids to one guy in a wheelchair, in semi-custody while a group of cadets practiced collecting personal information and asking for photos?

"If we'd gone to Santarpio's like I wanted, we'd be all the way in Eastie," Jake said. "Dispatch might have sent someone else to handle this mess."

"There is no someone else," DeLuca pointed out. "Vacation time, budget cuts, short staffing. We get the short straw."

"We get all the straws," Jake said.

A lanky blue-uniformed EMT wearing lavender latex gloves, black running shoes, and a pencil stabbed through her graying ponytail trotted up to the two of them. She gestured toward the two medics kneeling over the victim.

"Not a whole lot to tell, Detectives. White male, approximately forty-five years old, deceased. Stab wound to the back. Just the one. Happened, I'd say, pretty much instantly," she said. "We got here at twelve-oh-four. Called it at twelve-oh-five. Knife's still in, wouldn't have mattered. Thought the ME should see it as is. We'll let her look for ID."

"She's on the way. Thanks, Doc," Jake said. EMT Deborah Kratky wasn't actually a doctor, but she'd been on the job long enough to know as much as any medic. She'd even been there to see a rookie Jake handle his first homicide. It was up in the Blue Hills, a disturbingly arranged female corpse, turned out the victim of a Boston Strangler copycat. Ten years later, Jake no longer felt like throwing up at crime scenes. Not necessarily a good thing. Cops get bored, cops make mistakes. Jake never wanted to get used to murder.

"Anybody know anything?" he asked. "See anything? Say anything?"

"Not to me." Doc looked back at the crime scene, hands on hips, one eyebrow raised. "Crap. Would *you* stand there? With your little kid? Rubbernecking a dead person? Blood on the sidewalk? I sure wouldn't, if it wasn't my job."

A dusty yellow city bus, emblazoned GO BSO, wheezed up to the stop across from the bank. One of the cadets waved both arms at the driver, signaling him to move on. Faces peered from each square window, a puff of exhaust pluming to the curb as the bus pulled away.

"Whoever did it's gotta be big, lot of muscle. One blow like that?" Jake scanned the crowd for anyone who fit the bill. Would the killer be dumb or strange or crazy enough to hang around? Cadets were taking names, writing on clipboards. Couple of people tried to leave, didn't succeed. Most were texting, calling, taking photos. *Better not be erasing anything.* Evidence these days was ephemeral. One click of a button, it got zapped into nothing.

"Big? Maybe. Or maybe angry. Or full of adrenaline. Or drugged up. And spattered with blood," Doc Kratky said. "Maybe. Unless he—or she—has already dropped their clothing somewhere."

"In which case we're screwed," D said.

"One step at a time," Jake said. "Look at all those phones. Each one's got a possible photo."

Might as well try to stay positive. Maybe the days of relying on tiny specks of evidence in glassine bags, untrustworthy eyewitnesses, and fabricated alibis would fade into law enforcement history, as antiquated as a posse on horseback, wiped out by night-scope lenses and twenty-four-hour videos and satellite pings. They'd nailed the Marathon bombers using video from department store surveillance. All they needed to catch this bad guy was someone who'd clicked a cell phone camera at exactly the right time.

"Makes you understand how movie stars feel, right? Paparazzi?" Doc said. "Guess that's good for you guys, though. Reporters will be here soon, no doubt, trolling for tourist cam photos."

Ordinarily, Jake would be wondering whether "reporters" might mean Jane. This time he knew it wouldn't.

"What you see is what you get," DeLuca said. "Cameras don't lie."

"Witnesses do," Jake said.

Still, whatever was caught on camera could be their ace in the hole. Some of the bars that lined one side of Congress Street, not to mention the monolith City Hall itself on the other side, must have security systems. Those videos they could instantly seize.

"So we won't transport till the ME—" Jake heard two quick beeps of a horn, Kat's signal she was arriving. Jake knew she hated the siren. *No rush for me to get there,* she always said. *No need to announce another death.* "Speak of the devil."

The gawkers turned, each camera and cell phone now pointed toward North Street and the blocky white van, stenciled in black letters MEDICAL EXAMINER. The right-side wheels jumped the curb onto the sidewalk. The driver's-side door clanged open, slammed closed. Jane always referred to Dr. Katharine McMahon as one of those Russian dolls in a doll, all dark hair and red lips and curves. Jane and Kat had taken a month or so to reach feminine détente, but they were okay now. Under her white medical jacket, Jake saw that Kat's hot pink T-shirt said LOVE IT LOCAL.

"See that?" DeLuca whispered. "You bet I will."

"Have some respect," Jake said.

"Why start now?" DeLuca said.

"So why'd you leave the *Register*?"

The very question, word for word, that Jane Ryland feared most. And the very question, word for word, that Jane had no idea how to answer.

Channel 2's news director, Marshall Tyson, all smiles and pinstripes, office strategically landscaped with award statues and celebrity photos and one duPont gold baton, had sprung it on her, but only after an excruciating half hour of niceties and journalism chitchat, followed by a play-by-play commentary on the A-block of the noon *Eyewitness News,* the broadcast still under way from the newsroom anchor desk outside his corner office.

"Well, it's complicated," Jane began.

Complicated wasn't even the word. It was a mess, from moment one, a mess.

Jane had walked the gauntlet of speculation, escorted by a chatty assignment desk intern, weaving through the newsroom's warren of cluttered desks and flickering computer monitors toward Tyson's office. Jane would be recognized, of course, from back when she was an on-air competitor. In the news business, which "talent" was "crossing the street" to a rival station was the most delicious topic of gossip, even better than who got fired for stealing promotional swag from the mail room, which reporters were getting sued, and why the noon anchor kept so many extra clothes in her office. No outsiders knew the scoop on what happened to Jane at the *Boston Register* last month. And how could she explain it?

In the midst of triumphant headlines at the *Register,* her investigation had uncovered a problem close to home. Jane proved a longtime reporter there had been fabricating stories. *For years.* Bad enough, but the clincher was worse. The newspaper decided to cover it up. Ignore it.

For Jane, that left only two choices.

She could be complicit. Or she could quit.

If she ratted out the paper for using fabricated stories, she'd argued, didn't it also put articles by *all* the reporters in question? If the public suspected some were partly fiction, would readers ever believe anything?

So here she was, once again a victim of her own damn ethics. Here she was, at the TV station that used to be her biggest competitor, discussing her third reporting job in five years. Not the most reliable-sounding résumé for a thirty-four-year-old, even in the nomadic climb-the-ladder world of journalism.

The intercom buzzed, and Tyson's cell phone *ping*ed with a text.

"Sorry, Jane." The news director tapped on his keyboard with one hand, used the other to grab his phone, tucking it under his chin. "Gotta take this."

At least this time she wasn't a supplicant. Marshall Tyson had called *her*, using a "heard you're no longer with the paper" opening ploy in his voice mail, followed by "come chat if you're interested in getting back on the air, if you're not too busy."

Busy? Jane had rolled her eyes as she listened to his message. Oh, she was busy. Busy being unemployed again. Busy facing her younger sister's wedding this coming weekend. Busy entertaining bride-to-be Lissa, arriving in Boston this afternoon. Busy prepping to meet her sister's fiancé, "Dan the man of mystery," Jane privately called him, who'd arrive whenever Daniel Fasullo's corporate jet landed from whatever exotic overseas location. Busy preparing for a trip home to the Chicago suburbs to play maid of honor.

The good news: Jake had promised to come with her to Chicago. This weekend.

Now that she was unemployed, and therefore no longer encumbered by the reporter/source prohibition against dating, she and Jake had been experimenting with going public with their . . . whatever it was. Relationship. Still being careful. But not always hiding.

Tyson was still deep in his phone conversation, looking out into the newsroom as he spoke. Jane followed his gaze, saw three young women at the assignment desk with two phones each plastered to their ears. Something was going on.

"When?" Tyson glanced at her, rolling his eyes in apology. She waved him off. She understood news came first. Anyway, it gave her time to think.

If Channel 2 offered her a job, did she want to go back to TV? Her bank account could certainly use the paycheck. And if the good guys quit, who'd be left? Maybe she could make a deal with Tyson to do only in-depth stories, groundbreaking investigative stuff.

Yes or no? Saying yes would mean she and Jake would have to return to the shadows. Right now, in this news director's office, she had to decide: Love or money? Seemed like she was doomed not to have both.

But wait.

She could simply say maybe. Consider it, talk to Jake. If Channel 2 wanted her, they would wait. She mentally acknowledged her own wisdom, patted herself on the emotional back. She had control of her life. She needed to remember that.

Tyson raised a palm to her, pantomiming *sorry, one moment,* as he stood. His door opened. The newcomer, horn-rims and oxford shirt, clipboard, looked at Jane, assessing.

"Sorry to interrupt, Marsh, but—"

"We got anyone who can go over there?" the news

director asked. He'd hung up the phone without saying good-bye. "Jane, this is Derek Estabrooks, our assignment guy. Derek? Anyone?"

"Negative, that's the thing. Hey, Jane." He acknowledged her with a quick up and down. "We got the morning crews doing outta-town live shots for the noon, and the next shift is the two thirty people, so we're kinda screw—"

"You ever do freelance, Jane?" The news director, interrupting, pointed a forefinger at her. "We've got a big story we can send you on. Right now. You up for it? But we gotta have an answer. Right now. Yes or no?"